Vindictive

RYAN LAWRENCE

Vindictive

Copyright © 2021 by Ryan Lawrence

All rights reserved. No part of this publication may be reproduced, distributed, or transmitted in any form or by any means, including photocopying, recording, or other electronic or mechanical methods, without the prior written permission of the author, except in the case of brief quotations embodied in critical reviews and certain other non-commercial uses permitted by copyright law.

Tellwell Talent
www.tellwell.ca

ISBN
978-0-2288-6474-5 (Hardcover)
978-0-2288-6473-8 (Paperback)
978-0-2288-6475-2 (eBook)

For my husband Todd. I would gladly
travel the path of revenge for you.

PROLOGUE

"Jules, h-help me! I c-can't h-hold on."

Due to unseasonably warm temperatures, the lake's coating of winter ice was dangerously unstable. Eight-year-old Jules knew she would fall straight through into the frigid waters below if she walked upon it to save her friend. She understood the potential hazards; a deadly outcome was a near certainty should the water be unsoundly frozen.

Though it meant going around the lake to get back to the chalet from the woods, using the lake as a shortcut was forbidden. So was skating.

Jules had obeyed the rules set by the adults. Ethan had not.

Ethan was three years older than Jules, but that had not stopped them from becoming friends. Their relationship fostered a remarkable closeness that each child desperately desired. Ethan was rugged, fearless, and risk-taking, while Jules was petite, cautious, and pragmatic.

The glaring differences between them should have been enough for the children to despise each other. Their youth should have equated a nebulous degree of maturity, preventing them from being able to fathom or tolerate the nature of such an illogical, disruptive counterpart to themselves.

Remarkably, Jules and Ethan saw past the superficial contrariety of their unique personalities. They felt a bond, an affinity that connected them on a much deeper level than either child understood intellectually. Still young and innocent, their bond was strictly platonic but exceedingly profound.

Jules's parents, along with Ethan's, were part of a small consortium of wealthy professionals that formed a tight-knit group of friends.

Ethan's family, the Falsworths, originally hailed from Great Britain. They had relocated to Ottawa when Ethan's father, Maurice, was tasked with overseeing their family's business interests in Canada. The Falsworths were, without question, the wealthiest, most revered of the group; their lineage boasted lords and war heroes.

The consortium congregated at the Falsworth chalet, located in British Columbia's Okanagan Valley, near Big White Resort, every winter. The chalet, as well as its surrounding property, was massive. It was a blessed escape from their professional lives. The worlds of politics, high finance, medicine, and law.

The children found pleasure in spending quality time with their parents. Family time together was a luxury rarely afforded to most of the children due to the nature of their parents' monetary success. Only Ethan's family had "old money" to bolster them; all the others had to work long hours for their riches.

During their first encounter, Jules and Ethan, the youngest of the children, had been encouraged to play nice and get along. The adults naturally feared the youngsters would be at odds; after all, Ethan was restless and mischievous, while Jules was exceptionally sophisticated for her age. A book always in her face, Jules absorbed information like a sponge; conversely, outdoorsy Ethan was rough around the edges.

The au pairs had been put on notice to watch for signs of discord and control rambunctiousness. To everyone's shock and subsequent glee, the two opposites coalesced seamlessly without incident.

The link that bridged the gap between them was their identification of each other's deep-rooted, though immediately recognizable, loneliness. Jules and Ethan saw their isolation reflected in the eyes of their counterpart, and their mutual need for comfort and friendship burned away the layers of difference. Each desired companionship outside of their loving yet constantly preoccupied parents.

When they were not together at the chalet or other sporadic social engagements throughout the year, Ethan and Jules remained in constant contact through email and phone calls.

This February weekend, Jules's family had arrived at the chalet ahead of everyone but the Falsworths. They had come down earlier that Saturday morning. The adults had immediately sought recreation in town without the children in tow.

Unfortunately, the Falsworth's au pair had debilitating stomach flu. Jules and Ethan had to be baby-sat by William, Ethan's not so fun older brother.

At fourteen, William Falsworth was unnervingly cold and guarded. However, he held a soft spot for his brother, loving him unconditionally. Despite this affection, William rarely emerged from his shell of misanthropy and self-absorption to engage with Ethan. That said, his unabashedly protective and suspicious nature surfaced whenever anyone attempted to gain his brother's favour.

Not surprisingly, William disliked Jules.

She had not done anything purposely to slight him; it was because William genuinely found Jules to be, like most people he met, a bore and a nuisance. For starters, she was too young for him to associate with, but what was unforgivable was that she was a girl. William considered females to be irritatingly weak physically, emotionally erratic, and downright unpredictable.

Unpredictability frightened and unnerved Wiliam. He hated the unknown—the uncontrollable. He planned everything down to the minutiae of detail, and this provided him comfort and stability.

William's predilection towards misogyny and sexism was apparent to others. Most of the people who interacted with him found his behaviour offensive and gave him a wide berth. They quickly learned that any attempt to educate and enlighten him fell on deaf ears. William was unquestionably a brooding, angry young man.

As the day progressed, Ethan tried to entice his brother to entertain them, but to no avail. Forbidden to go outside unless

William accompanied them, Ethan and Jules grew increasingly bored stuck inside.

Ethan eventually convinced a hesitant Jules to sneak out and venture into the woods nestled behind the chalet. Their favourite spot to play was among a large body of evergreens across the lake. Ethan figured his brother, preoccupied with his video game, would not notice them leave.

He was right; William was none the wiser when the two children made their escape.

The journey towards the evergreens was arduous, so Ethan wanted to take the shortcut across the lake. He figured their outside playtime had a time limit due to William's eventual detection of their absence. So, ignoring his parents' rules and without waiting for Jules, he boldly stepped out onto the seemingly frozen water.

Jules's mounting dread counterbalanced Ethan's total lack of fear. She never moved one centimetre from the edge of the lake, knowing her friend had made a terrible error in judgment. Jules's parents had warned them that much of the lake was still liquid beneath the deceptively frozen surface.

As the harrowing feeling grew inside her belly, Jules fervently beckoned her impetuous friend to come back.

Ethan ignored her at first. Eventually, having walked some distance, he turned around, pointed at Jules and screamed, "Chicken!"

It was at that moment when Jules heard the ominous, nearly imperceptible crackling noise. The noise quickly grew louder and bolder until the dire sound escalated into a thunderous explosion of water colliding against ice.

Jules looked on helplessly as Ethan fell through the ice, consumed by the dark waters below.

Though he had only gone about six meters out from her, it seemed like an ocean of distance to Jules. Eventually, she saw minor splashing around the newly formed hole. In response, she took a few small steps out onto the lake towards it. That was all she managed to do before promptly backing up and returning to the safety of the solid, frozen earth.

As quick as lightning, Ethan's hands furiously shot out of the water and grasped onto the slippery edges of the icy opening. He tried maniacally, yet without much success, to pull himself out of the strength-sapping waters.

Ethan started crying. Much of the liquid from his torrent of tears froze almost instantly upon contact with his chilled skin. Through chattering teeth and bluish lips, his words broken and strained, Ethan clamoured for Jules's help. He begged her; he was terrified; he did not want to die.

But what could she do?

Thinking fast, Jules considered spreading her body out onto the ice and inching forward on her belly. She understood it had something to do with dispersing her weight so she would not fall through the ice or risk making the aperture larger by walking. Perhaps she would be able to reach out to Ethan.

But then what? Jules doubted she had the necessary strength to pull his larger, heavier form out of the frigid water, and she was pretty sure he would not offer her much help. He would probably pull her in!

To reach her desperate friend, Jules considered looking for a tree branch to use. Despite her best intentions, however, and overwhelmed by anxiety and powerlessness, Jules remained motionless. Who was she kidding? There was no time to find a tool to aid her, and she did not possess the muscle to pull Ethan out of the water if she did have one.

"William," she whispered. But he was far away. Jules hated to admit it, but she did not believe she had the time to get William and bring him back to help before Ethan drowned. It was all up to her.

Time was her enemy, Jules got that, but there was something that gave her pause. All the myriad possibilities of rescue that filled her head inevitably included one terrifying, essential element for success; she had to go out onto that fractured lake. This equated to personal risk and dangerous uncertainty. She could die.

They would both die.

Jules came to the heartbreaking conclusion that she would inevitably fail at any feeble attempt to rescue her best friend. Even more frightening, more unacceptable, was that Ethan would drag her down with him into a watery grave. Unintentionally and without malice, but he would do it just the same. All her hopes and dreams, the promise her parents saw in her, all of it would be over.

With a deep breath and a steel resolve uncommon for a girl her age, Jules chose her safety and survival over that of Ethan's. She would not allow the bad choices of another, regardless of who they were and despite how much she loved them, to destroy her.

"I'm s-slipping! Help me, J-Jules, please g-grab my hand! Please!"

"I'm sorry, Ethan!"

"Please, Jules. I d-don't wanna d-die!"

"I'm sorry, but—no."

Jules's last word was a breath, barely audible.

Ethan's eyes widened, and his face contorted into a ghastly grimace; he had heard Jules's whisper of refusal. Even in his terrified state, he understood the shocking reality of what his best friend had just said to him; she had condemned him to certain death.

Ethan screamed and screamed—and then he stopped, exhausted, beaten by the cold. For a few minutes, he bobbed up and down from the water to the surface, flailing about futilely for something stable and solid to anchor himself.

Then, semi-conscious, barely keeping his head above water, Ethan watched in horror as his best friend deliberately turned away from him.

Jules knew that Ethan, in his final moments, would not understand, his thoughts too filled with fear and anger toward her cowardice. She accepted this but took no pleasure in her decision; in fact, she hated it immensely. Jules did not want Ethan to die, but he was the one who had put them in this no-win situation.

Jules loved Ethan too much to watch him suffer. She could not bear to watch her best friend die right before her eyes, especially knowing he would never understand why she could do nothing to avert it. Her hated limitations! Jules wondered if, at any point, Ethan honestly thought that she really could have saved him.

Eventually, Ethan, his strength and willpower sapped, slowly, and with little pomp or ceremony, succumbed to the cold and slid under the water for the final time. A deafening silence quickly fell over everything.

At the very moment of Ethan's death, something sacred inside Jules perished alongside her friend: her innocence.

Jules recognized that she had just made her first real adult life and death decision, and her perception of the world around her had changed irrevocably. Life was cruel and threatening when it had once been gentle and fascinating. Now that she knew her life, or the life of someone she loved, could be snatched away without warning or provocation, Jules would never feel completely safe or secure.

Even though she knew they were far away from her, Jules cried out for her parents. She cried for Ethan and for the bright-eyed girl she could no longer be. Jules wanted to run away from this place of death. She also wanted to run away from her selfish choice to ensure her survival, her future. Jules wished all of it had never happened. But it did happen, and she would have to live with it for the rest of her life.

"Ethan! No! Ethan!"

Startled, Jules quickly turned and looked in the direction of the shrieking bellow. It was William, tearing down the woods, screaming his brother's name over and over again.

Having discovered his charges missing from the house, William had reluctantly gone about searching for them outside. Sadly, it was not soon enough to intervene and prevent the devastating incident.

When William finally reached the clearing, he stopped at the edge of the lake and looked out upon the scene of broken ice and still water. With clenched fists, he fell to his knees and screamed in anguish. His brother was dead and gone, swallowed whole by the cold, murky depths.

Angrily turning towards Jules, William showered upon her a rage so pure, so palpable it might as well have been a physical smack across her face. His glare was full of hate. And so were his words.

"Why didn't you help him, you fucking bitch?! You did nothing! You let him drown!"

Jules stood as immobile as a stone and ate her emotions, swallowing all her sadness, guilt, and self-reproach. She owned the choice she had made. The only one possible. The correct choice. She understood William's pain, but she was well aware of his vile nature.

Jules had her suspicions of what might diffuse her attacker: using his own words—his ignorance and prejudice—against him. Maybe then he would leave her alone. She had only done what was necessary. All she could do.

And who was he to blame her anyway? Was he there when it happened? No! He had been too busy playing video games to look after them, too busy to save his brother, too busy to have prevented all of this in the first place.

Be mean, Jules silently told herself. *Act like a grown-up.*

With unwavering resolve, staring William down with cold, hard eyes, Jules scoffed, "What the hell could I have done? I'm just a girl. Right?"

I

Inside the bedroom she shared with her husband, amid the dim morning light trickling through the partially closed curtains, Jules admired herself in the ornate Baroque mirror. The one mounted on the wall above her vanity table.

At twenty-eight, Jules was a striking woman. She was crowned with flowing blond locks that cascaded down her perfectly formed shoulder blades. She disliked the rebellious nature of her mane and ritualistically straightened it daily. It was a symbolic representation of the type of control she demanded of herself and enacted over her environment.

Her soft yet finely edged face bore two orbs of dazzling sapphire blue; they were practically preternatural in their sparkle and clarity. Her nose, small and elegant, was aligned exquisitely with her high cheekbones and sculpted chin.

Dermatologically speaking, her skin was flawless and creamy. Her body? The physique of a fitness model. Slim, yet athletic. Taught, yet effortlessly feminine.

Jules had never gone under the knife. She emphatically told anyone brave or stupid enough to inquire about the validity of her natural perfection this fact. She always gave the questioner a slow withering once over, stating that, unlike some people, she did not need the assistance of cosmetic surgery. Jules was one shady bitch if provoked.

However, it was not her physical beauty she currently focused on in her ostentatious vanity mirror. It was her clandestine cunning and indomitable resolve. Jules gazed into herself, past the flesh. She went beyond the sapphire blue orbs to hone and enhance, through sheer force of will, the power that percolated behind them.

Jules remembered and held dear the strategies learned by studying Rasputin's ideology and the teachings of Niccolo Machiavelli and Sun Zhu. She took inspiration and knowledge from the disciplines of ancient warrior women like Artemisia, Boudicca and Fu Hao.

Jules drew from many sources, ancient and modern, in her constant quest to gain power over others—friend and adversary, alike. Recently, and for very personal reasons, she had taken quite a shine to Thane Rosenbaum's Payback: The Case for Revenge.

At puberty, Jules had been taught a valuable lesson by her parents about physical beauty and sexuality. They had their uses, and there should never be any shame attached to them, but they were the typical weapons for a woman to utilize and exploit. Too obvious and far too limiting. A brilliant mind could conquer any adversary regardless of gender, age or wealth.

According to her parents, intelligence, cunning, and preparation equated to power and success. Jules had always believed them and followed their direction. To her, only weak, imperceptible women like Marie Bergé, a woman Jules openly despised, relied solely on their looks.

Jules understood that physical beauty, the kind Western culture extolled, faded away much faster than wisdom and smarts. She liked having the best of both worlds, but she planned for her inevitable future of lost youth in a youth-obsessed culture. No one was going to put her out to pasture against her will. Her looks were intact; her mind was razor-sharp.

Now more than ever, Jules needed her wits about her, her mind to perform at peak efficiency. Her ongoing vengeance upon the family she had married into needed uncompromising strategy and nerve. Jules visualized the successful completion of her endgame. It was fast approaching, she was ready, and she would feel justifiable elation once the Cartells finally got their much-deserved comeuppance.

Jules just needed to be patient a little longer.

Like many times before, Jules looked up at the old photograph pinned between the frame lip and the glass of her mirror. The photo of her with her dad, Jason, taken of them at her eighth birthday party, generally induced a feeling of great sadness within her whenever she looked at it. It also fed her strength, nourished her willpower, and gifted her with directed rage. The photo validated her need for revenge.

Jules especially desired the destruction of the man she once professed to love, truthfully, but now despised, utterly and openly.

Her husband.

Phillip Cartell was still asleep. His muscular and seasonally tanned body was spread out on their bed, provocatively exposed. His right leg and groin were barely covered by the silk sheets that, for the most part, rested on the carpeted floor below.

At thirty-two, Phillip was physically imposing and painfully handsome. He had tousled but not unruly blond hair a few shades darker than Jules's own. His eyes were the palest of blue. His body was toned and muscled in all the right places. The Nordic fairness of his configuration balanced his intimidating masculinity, softening him.

In a loud, distinctly passive-aggressive manner, Jules cleared her throat. She walked over to the bed, stopping just short of where her husband slumbered and began methodically rapping her manicured nails along the dark espresso headboard. Impatient, Jules waited for her emphatic bark and deliberately annoying noise-making to rouse her husband.

Languidly opening his eyes, Phillip looked upward into the lovely yet stern face of his wife. He beamed a welcoming smile towards her, wilfully enlivened his body, and threw the remaining fabric still covering his naked form away from him. With prurient intent, he exposed his Herculean physique and his large, semi-erect penis.

Rising seductively, Phillip clasped Jules by the shoulders, intending to plant a sensuous kiss on her supple pink lips. However, the forceful separation of his hands from her body abruptly arrested the forward trajectory of his hungry mouth.

"Really?" Jules questioned acerbically. She looked less than impressed. "Don't be ridiculous! Get your lazy ass moving!"

Indifferent to her husband's nakedness, Jules opened the bedroom door and marched out into the hallway.

Phillip's smile faded swiftly, as did his erection.

Now alone, Phillip turned towards the vanity mirror across the room and stared at his image. Sadly, the only thing he saw reflected back in the glass was a defeated, dejected man overwhelmed with disappointment and heartache.

Phillip had come to believe this abject image of himself to be his shameful truth. He felt like a failure as a husband and as a man in the eyes of his wife. Nothing he did interested, satisfied, or enticed her anymore. Not in the boardroom. Not in the bedroom.

Phillip regarded the beautiful, powerful male form the mirror held as naught but a superficial husk. Nothing but an illusion for the benefit of the masses created by regular visits to the gym, good genes, and various expensive grooming products. And this display of physical perfection did nothing anymore to entice the one person who mattered the most to him: his wife. All it ever seemed to do was repulse her.

For some time, all of Phillip's attempts at seduction and affection had been met with nothing short of hostility and contempt for reasons unexplained to him. Why did he still try? Why did he still care? He felt like the fool his wife believed him to be. Without a doubt, he was at his breaking point.

Despite the early hour, Phillip craved a vodka tonic.

At Château Bergé, in the kitchen of his family's suite, Jacques Bergé waited patiently for his absent wife, Marie.

Awakening just after dawn, Jacques had immediately noticed his wife's absence which was not an unusual occurrence. Marie often slipped away before dawn for reasons Jacques was not privy to. Still, he trusted his wife implicitly, never suspecting her of anything extramarital. He believed Marie was too timid a creature to invite such risk into their relationship, too pure of heart to hold the thought of betrayal within her.

Jacques suspected that something inside his wife, some traumatic experience unknown to him, frightened her terribly, and she was desperately trying to escape the memory of it. Or fight against it? He knew nothing concrete as Marie routinely refused to talk about it.

Resignedly, Jacques waited for Marie to return to him. And when she did return, he intended to comfort and console her, like the supportive husband he was. He also planned on questioning her again about her mysterious disappearances, whether she liked it or not.

Without warning, a stray thought of Jules entered Jacques's mind. His skin heated, his breath quickened, and his cock hardened. The sexual image was aggressive in its visceral depiction of his body entangled with hers. Jacques took a deep intake of breath, steadied himself, shook the ill-timed sexual musing off, and went back to fixing his wife's breakfast.

Attempting to distract himself from his covert desire, Jacques thought about the daily business ahead. His duties concerning Château Bergé's unrelenting upkeep invariably helped focus his mental faculties. Work always helped take his mind off both Marie's absences and the deep-rooted mysteries surrounding her mental instability. Still, it did little to divert his subconscious from thinking about Jules's perfect breasts.

In the early part of the twentieth century, under Jacques's great grandfather, Henri's supervision, the idea of Château Bergé became a reality.

Historically, the wealthy Bergé family originated in Lyon, France. They had remained there until sometime around the early nineteenth century when a fire destroyed much of their ancestral home. A public scandal related to the mysterious origins of the fire had forced the family to flee to the colonies in Lower Canada. The Bergés initially settled in what eventually became the southern part of modern Québec.

To this day, Jacques had no clue as to the origin of the fire or the nature of the scandal that had forced his powerful family to leave not only a country but an entire continent.

Bergé family history was a commodity traded in secret only between the older, male generations and worth more than gold to all. After Jacques's grandfather Bertrand's death, his son Ambroise, Jacques's father, became the sole guardian of the secret family history.

Jacques had always believed his father would eventually share that knowledge with him, but Ambroise's untimely death had prevented that. Jacques's parents died during a New Year's Eve gathering on their yacht when the boat's engines caught fire and exploded while travelling down the Ottawa River. It had been officially ruled a tragic accident due to improper upkeep.

As expected, Jacques had inherited everything, but Ambroise's will left no note or clue regarding their family's mysterious past.

Over a hundred years ago, several of the Bergés, led by Henri, left Québec and moved to Fairporte, Ontario, a town along the Ottawa River. At the time, Fairporte was no major player in anything except, perhaps, scenery. The land was gorgeous, serenely still, and populated with family-owned farms near majestic maple and ash forests.

Henri lusted after this beauty, and over several years aggressively purchased nearly all the local family-owned farms to possess and transform the land into the ideal spot to build his legacy: a replica of the Bergé ancestral home. Space and milieu needed to be optimal and vast.

Henri spent close to a decade and nearly every cent he had excavating the land and building his Château. It was the first large-scale country estate built in Canada since the erection of the Château Laurier.

No expense was spared. Henri selected and secured the best in timber, marble, and stained glass himself. He hired the most renowned European architects, stonemasons, and craftsmen money could buy to carry out his orders and bring his ideas to life. Henri and his son Bertrand, both brilliant visionaries, had had ridiculously privileged upbringings. Neither possessed any labour skills.

Every manner of luxury, including the furniture and artwork, had come from France and Italy. Nothing had been acquired locally. Henri always believed "the rustics," his colourful reference to both Franco and Anglophone Canadians, would never equal the calibre of taste as their European counterparts. Hiring locals, or worse, vulgar Americans, to design, foster, and create culture was an unconscionable act.

Throughout his life, Henri often postulated that it was his duty to elucidate "the rustics" on all things European, especially French—sophistication, taste, and affluence. Château Bergé was his gift to the uncouth Canadian land and its boorish people. That he had been born in Canada, like most of his living kin, was something dismissed outright.

For centuries, the Canadian Bergés considered the blood flowing through their veins to be undeniably European. It was a deeply rooted belief that fostered aggressive elitism. In modern times, Jacques was one of the few who openly defied the family's bigoted conviction that, culturally or otherwise, they were not Canadian. He took pride in being a canuck.

The building of Château Bergé had attracted many opinionated detractors. Henri was sick of the constant comparisons to Charles Melville Hays and Château Laurier. Halfway through construction, Henri decided to alter the original design. He felt the intended replica of their ancestral home needed more size and pomp to overshadow the grandeur of its rivals.

Henri added extra floors, one hundred more rooms, additional turrets, an Olympic-size swimming pool, and an 18-hole golf course.

The changes inevitably extended the construction time frame, and more land was needed. Henri nearly bankrupted his family in the process.

Despite the modifications, the overall design of Château Bergé remained loyal to the French Renaissance style. The builders utilized the traditional copper roof and used granite blocks as the structure's base, with Italian marble throughout the design. There were multiple corbelled corner turrets on the building outside, and bronze gargoyles, watching over the guests from their high perches, peppered the vista.

Château Bergé's immense imperial staircase was built much larger than the original and ascended the first three floors. It was constructed out of the finest Italian Carrara marble and was the focal point of the main entrance.

The opulent chandeliers, which hung regally around the interior, were made from the finest French crystal. Spanish carpets, Rococo sculpture, and nineteenth-century impressionist paintings appeared over time, enhancing the grandeur.

Upon completion of the project, Henri officially christened his citadel Château Bergé. To this day, it is second only to Québec's Château Frontenac in size and grandeur, boasting five hundred rooms and twelve floors.

Henri, a slight man, had been hindered by poor health throughout his entire life. Many said erecting the Château had destroyed him, both physically and mentally. Just as many said, he had always been crazy. Sadly, Henri Bergé died a frail, broken man.

When Jacques became the legal owner of Château Bergé, he dared to introduce contemporary and twentieth-century Canadian and non-European influences to the historically rigid design palate. Anatolian rugs, artwork from the Group of Seven, and furniture supplied by Klaus turned up on several floors.

The changes, though subtle, initially caused controversy among his extended family and some long-standing clientele. Many questioned Jacques's loyalty to his patriarchal ancestors' traditions, but Jacques cared little for what his detractors had to say. He was his own man and held fast to his vision.

Jacques and Marie, along with their twin sons Henri and Etienne, were the only Bergés still residing at the Château.

While Cartell Worldwide currently drove Fairporte's business and economic prosperity, it was the Bergés who had been the original power behind the now booming economy. Ambroise Bergé, in particular, truly modernized Fairporte. Using money from his many business ventures, plus the allure of Château Bergé's grandeur, he took Fairporte from a small town to an emerging city and travel destination in less than ten years.

Ambroise was known for his charisma and business savvy, which attracted both commercial and private businesses, foreign and domestic, to Fairporte. Unlike his staunchly old-world, conservative father Bertrand, Ambroise loved entrepreneurs and new money. He understood the concept of marketing Château Bergé to private and public sectors, the elite and the working class.

Château Bergé was regarded internationally as a place for company retreats, business meetings, and conferences. Many Fortune 500 companies were built, improved upon or destroyed within its walls. The occasional political intrigue changed the international landscape for the better and, just as often, for the worse. It attracted Hollywood royalty, A-List recording stars, and political heads of state.

Needing a temporary respite from her troubled marriage to Arthur Miller, Marilyn Monroe once sequestered herself in the ostentatious *Marie Antoinette* room.

The tales of the many sexual trysts and clandestine romances that supposedly went on under the roof of Château Bergé were varied and provocative. They were also always unsubstantiated. Much to the annoyance of the press, the Bergés never sold a story, broke confidence, or betrayed a trust. All their employees signed NDAs.

Phillip's father, the late Joseph Cartell, had been a frequent guest of Château Bergé, both for business and pleasure. Sometimes publicly—sometimes not. He had also been a longtime friend and business associate of Ambroise.

Jules had fallen under Château Bergé's spell after just one visit.

Business savvy, Jules had recognized Fairporte's untapped potential for economic growth on an international scale. She saw the possibilities of a city very much like Montréal, but one drenched in its unique blend of French and English culture. It was a small city, for sure, but one that felt alive and fresh.

Jules appreciated how Fairporte appeared somewhat isolated on the map but was actually well situated, having easy and direct access to Toronto, Montréal, and Ottawa.

Immediately after Joseph's death, Jules convinced Cartell Worldwide's Board of Directors to transfer the main branch from Toronto to Fairporte. Vocal about her desire to create and control a national business hub, Jules believed the unconventional move would spawn international buzz. A new playground for the rich and enterprising.

And it absolutely did.

As far as convincing the board went, they really had no choice in the matter. Jules, aided by her father, Charles, had done things after Joseph's death to ensure she controlled all voting outcomes, always in her favour.

Though raised in Montréal from the age of five, in conjunction with boarding school in Switzerland, Joseph had been born in Fairporte and kept ties with the city throughout his adult life. His friendship with Ambroise and his infatuation with Château Bergé played pivotal roles in his ongoing relationship with the city.

The fact that Fairporte was Joseph's birthplace had been completely inconsequential to Jules during her decision-making process. To her, it was merely a "fun fact" in the company's biographical portfolio, nothing more.

To mark her arrival in Fairporte and represent her ongoing presence in the city, Jules had a new, modernized headquarters built in the centre of town. It was a beaming citadel overlooking her new domain.

Cartell Worldwide Tower stood one hundred and twenty meters tall, a mixed concrete skyscraper, the first of its kind in the area. It towered over all its neighbouring structures. Compared to the Vancouver tower, which was just under two hundred meters in height, and the Toronto tower, which was over two hundred meters, the Fairporte structure was distinctly moderate. For the area, it was impressive, nonetheless.

And most important, it was Jules's baby, untouched by Joseph's influence.

Representatives of the award-winning architectural firm hired to design the tower claimed the project would take three years to construct. In response to that declaration, Jules boldly informed them that she wanted the project done in less than two years. Money was no object, and if they could not guarantee that time frame, she had no qualms about firing them and finding someone else.

Jules got her tower in eighteen months.

Jules considered her building the "head" of the city, a powerful symbol of Cartell Worldwide's leadership in Fairporte's thriving economy. She wanted her version of the company to outshine their competition, stand out among the money-making drones that predictably set up shop in Toronto, Montréal, and Vancouver. Jules intended to set the trend—not follow it.

Château Bergé was considered by everyone, including Jules, to be the "heart" of Fairporte, a constant reminder of its rich past and history.

Jacques had paid little attention to Cartell Worldwide's relocation to Fairporte. He had been grossly preoccupied with a legal battle against his paternal aunt, Patrice, and other extended family members over his late father's estate at the time.

Despite Ambroise's iron-clad will, Jacques's costly legal battle ran on and on and had city officials worried. Had their founding family and decades-long benefactors finally stretched themselves too thin? Were they falling apart at the seams from in-fighting?

The trial was not good timing for Jacques. The city council had begun renegotiating their contracts with Ambroise directly before his death. This untimely distraction ultimately proved disastrous. Jacques unwittingly allowed his family's contracts with the city to lapse.

Jules took advantage of the situation, swooped in, and bought out most of the contracts the Bergés had with the city.

During the trial, Jacques discovered that his father had sold a considerable amount of real estate in the city without his knowledge to purchase additional land around Château Bergé. Jules contacted every owner who purchased city land and properties from the Bergés, offering them twice what they paid if they immediately sold to her.

And they did—every last one of them.

When the smoke finally cleared, Jacques had won his legal battle, retaining ownership of Château Bergé and the private airport. He lost his family's monopoly on the city, however. In response, he dismantled his father's company, the Bergé Holdings Corporation.

Secretly, Jacques was relieved and thankful to Jules for unburdening him from unwanted responsibility. A graduate of CMH Paris – Centre of International Hospitality Management, he only ever wanted to be the best owner and manager of Château Bergé he could be.

Unlike his forefathers, Jacques never held any interest in corporate business or city politics. He truly believed Jules was the best thing for Fairporte's future. Publicly and privately, there were no hard feelings between them.

Jules did not suffer fools. Respected by her peers, she was a shrewd, intimidating businesswoman who stopped at nothing to make her ventures successful. She understood there were generals and cannon fodder in big business; Jules knew which category she fell into.

Adopted at birth, Jules did not know who her biological mother and father were. It was a closed adoption. Growing up, Jules never asked questions. In her view, she had the best possible parents, and that was the end of it. Her adoptive fathers never pushed any further inquiry into the matter.

Charles Dunning, a corporate attorney, and Jason Bainbridge, a highly respected physician, cared deeply about the happiness and health of the beautiful child they had brought into their lives. At the time, they resided in Rosedale, a wealthy area of Toronto.

Charles named Jules after his much-revered, deceased grandfather. The name meant strength, reason, and graciousness to Charles. These were traits he wanted his child to understand and possess. Jason agreed, adding his own father's gender-neutral name Shawn to their child's intended sobriquet.

Jules Shawn Dunning-Bainbridge entered the world immediately loved and privileged. Charles became her father or "Pops," while Jason was always dad or daddy. Despite having both her parents' last names, Jules had been legally adopted by Charles alone as a single parent. When Ontario law evolved to allow for same-sex couple adoptions, Jason quietly adopted Jules as well.

Tragically, Jason died on Jules's fifteenth birthday. A transport truck collided with the back of his car, forcing him off the road and into a tree; the impact drove his head into the steering wheel. Sadly, both his seat belt and the airbag delivery system had malfunctioned.

Charles, emotionally distraught, unable to accept the abrupt death of his husband, spiralled into a state of severe, crippling depression and isolated himself from the world. Without the strength and attention of her father, Jules mourned the loss of her dad alone.

Though Jules loved her father without restraint or callous judgment, his inconsolable nature at the time inevitably proved an unflinching obstacle to her future plans and desires. She needed to move away from sadness with or without him.

Right after she turned sixteen, Jules had herself legally emancipated. As expounded in Jason's will, the sole beneficiary of his insurance policy was Jules, making her financially solvent. She remained at Branksome Hall, a leading International Baccalaureate School for girls, living in residence.

Charles continued to be a ghost in her life.

After completing high school at an accelerated rate, Jules moved to downtown Toronto, purchased a loft on the Lakeshore, and enrolled at the University of Toronto. In three years, she graduated with Honours in both Business and Economics. Immediately transitioning to York University to attend Osgoode Hall Law School, Jules earned her law degree by twenty-two, graduating top in her class.

Highly sought after by Canada's top law firms, Jules ultimately chose her father's law practice. Despite Charles's hiatus, Castle Dunning and Briggs remained a highly respected and profitable firm; still, it was a controversial decision no one saw coming.

Jules felt she had something to prove; she also wanted her father back in her life and back at his firm.

Now that she had completed her transformation from an ambitious girl to an accomplished woman, Jules devoted herself to the rescue of her father from his prison of self-pity. She was done with conveniently ignoring her father's never-ending melancholia, thus enabling his refusal to accept and deal with the loss of his husband.

Jules was confident that her adult framework possessed the necessary strength, reason, and graciousness needed to make a miracle happen. She intended to show her father that she had undeniably mastered the traits he had always wanted her to embody.

With her indomitable will, Jules forced a change in her father, specifically his mood and ability to reason. Candid, emotional conversations between father and daughter about working side by side evoked images of future achievements. Jules roused her father's fighting spirit by enumerating his many business triumphs and landmark legal wins.

Jules even went so far as to shame him for his self-indulgent sequestration. She admonished him for quitting on her and despoiling the memory of his husband and the selfless work he had done in life.

After a month under his daughter's care, Charles mostly returned to the man he was before Jason's fatal accident, and Jules flourished under the mentoring of her newly resurrected father.

Not long after Jules finished working on her father's reclamation, Gregson Castle, the founder of their firm, died of colon cancer. His death occurred within Jules's inaugural year with the firm. Her aggressive determination and hard work had not gone unnoticed by him, however. Jules had known Gregson forever. He was one of the few family friends who had continued to watch over her after Jason's death, and he had grown extremely fond of her.

A childless widower, Gregson willed his interest in the firm to Jules, which gave her a valued seat at the table. With Charles's blessing and support, Gregson had made her a name partner mere days before his death, much to the annoyance of the associates who argued nepotism behind Jules's back.

Colton Briggs, the third partner, had voted against the naming, certain their competitors would viciously mock them.

Never one to miss an opportunity to expostulate his opinion anytime someone did something to displease him, Colton loudly voiced his concern that Jules was too young and too inexperienced for such a position. He argued that this move diluted the power and the prestige of the whole process to make a first-year associate a name partner.

But it was a done deal, and no one dared to go any further with their astonishment or displeasure. Gregson was gone, but the far more fearsome Charles had very much returned and was now managing partner. Eventually, Colton backed down, begrudgingly accepting the new status quo.

For unexplained reasons, Jules chose not to add her hyphenated last name to the firm's moniker.

After settling into her new position, Jules proved all of her detractors in the firm wrong when she brought in their biggest client yet: Cartell Worldwide.

Years back, Joseph had been in the early stages of hiring the firm; after Jason's death, Charles dropped out of sight. Eventually, without his friend to facilitate the deal, Joseph lost interest and backed out.

Once he felt fully acclimated to being the managing partner, a newly empowered Charles aggressively rekindled his friendship with Joseph. In turn, Joseph quickly arranged for Jules to meet his son. Six months after meeting Phillip, Jules got the Cartell Worldwide account. Another six months after that? She and Phillip married.

It was then, unbeknownst to all, that the newly crowned Jules Cartell began her secret takeover of Joseph's company from the inside. At the time, her desire for power and position was purely for capitalist reasons; after Joseph's death, it became something far more personal.

Jules's hunger for power transformed into a burning need for revenge.

The Cartell Worldwide executives seated at the conference table anxiously awaited the arrival of their leader. The air was afire with chatter; questions, complaints, and speculative whispers abounded.

As expected, the clicking of expensive heels was finally heard by all. As the sound got closer to the room, agitation set in. A morning meeting with Jules meant knots in the stomach. Everyone in attendance had to be on top of their game, or she would eat them alive.

Phillip opened the boardroom's door, instinctively holding it for his wife to enter. Jules walked on through without thanking or acknowledging him and took her place at the head of the congregation. Ignominiously ignored and forgotten about by everyone present, Phillip quietly took his seat at the opposite end of the table.

Jules glared watchfully at the remaining whisperers. This made her CTO, Miles Chen, who sat directly to her right, smile smugly.

A first-generation Chinese-Canadian, Miles had been handpicked by Jules from the many in-house applicants to be not just another vice-president of some long-titled aspect of her company, but her self-appointed protégé. Many had sought this enviable, coveted position, but Miles had been the one to catch Jules's scrutinizing eye.

Miles was often underestimated and discounted by his co-workers due to his narrow frame, compact stature and quiet countenance.

Jules, however, saw past the illusion and knew this caricature to be a crafted facade used by Miles to keep his rivals off-balance and vulnerable to attack. His eyes and ears were always open. He knew when to take centre stage and when to remain hidden in the background. He was a spy when it was prudent and an assassin when it was necessary.

Certainly, Miles possessed the necessary qualifications for the position. He was well educated, having an Honours undergraduate degree from Western and an MBA from Ivey. His work for the company? Exemplary and above reproach. Still, it was not his sharp mind, practical dress code, work ethic or eagerness that had impressed Jules enough to take him under her wing.

In her estimation, Miles was her—after a fashion. Jules recognized the traits and gifts that had served her well during her climb to the top: calculating, cunning, and determined. Miles was an erudite chameleon, adapting to survive in any situation. Survive and thrive! His natural tenacity and adaptability inevitably won Jules over in the end.

Miles hung on Jules's every word, revelling in the personal power his intimate association with her allotted him within the company. If Miles gave a command, it was assumed, without question, that it had originated from Jules's lips.

"Quiet!" Miles snapped.

The senior staff members glared at their chastiser. They not so secretly despised Miles yet were powerless to contradict or negate his command. Jules had created the position of Chief Technology Officer specifically for him, and his office had clout.

They settled down, almost instantly knowing Jules's eyes were also upon them, empowering Miles's decree.

"Have all the children finally settled down?" Jules hissed dramatically. "Yes? Good. Today we begin our meeting with my proposed acquisition of Château Bergé."

II

"The room looks magnificent!" Jacques exclaimed with no small amount of pride. He was pleased with the efficiency and calibre of his team's work in preparing the ballroom for the Cartell Worldwide party, an event he understood was going to be less a jocund celebration and more a theatrical business meeting.

The uniqueness and grandeur of Château Bergé's ballroom was an expense Jules was always willing to pay for to impress. Jacques had successfully transformed the space into an elegant version of a conference room, which he knew would please his favourite client.

Per Jules's request, seasonally appropriate fresh flowers elegantly peppered the ballroom, filling the space with their individual yet harmonious scented bouquets. The room and table decor were minimal yet tasteful, and the colour scheme was grey and white with just a splash of navy blue. Jacques's choices for linens, china, and silver in the adjacent dining room were all properly laid out on a large, solid walnut Henri 11 table.

A professional string quartet would serenade guests during cocktails and dinner. The Château's house DJ was on tap to spin later in the evening when everyone re-entered the ballroom for drinking and dancing.

For the price she was paying, Jules demanded a flawless execution of her orders. Jacques understood it all had to be perfect.

Perfect, just like she thinks she is.

Despite the sarcasm that peppered his silent proclamation, Jacques's frequent thoughts on Jules's healthy ego were devoid of malicious intent. He often joked about her vanity, but he believed Jules was just about perfect. It was a feeling, a conviction, and one he did not share openly with his wife.

Fortuitously, due to his hyper libido, a stray carnal thought crept into his mind of Jules's perfect body laid out naked, wanton before him. Amid his thoughts where his wife was currently and more frequently absent, Jules enticed him into transgression. Jacques felt sexy, desired; his penis intractably hardened in his already body-hugging underwear in response.

Instinctively, Jacques worried his staff might glance over at and notice the outline of his large erection through his form-fitting dress pants. *Stop it, man, stop thinking about her. Focus on the damn job.* Once again, he endeavoured to use his work as a surrogate cold shower instead of his marital status.

"Jules is sure to be pleased," Jacques stated aloud as he deftly folded his hands in front of his groin. There was a strange breathy quality in his statement's cadence: hot and bothered.

"You have excellent taste, hon. I'm sure that bitch will approve."

Jacques whipped his head around at the sound of his wife's voice behind him.

Marie walked up to her husband and kissed him full on the mouth.

Shocked by her out-of-character aggressiveness, Jacques's footing faltered slightly. Once he caught himself, he moved into the kiss and reciprocated vigorously.

Trained to appear invisible, the staff tried not to stare but a few gasps, grins, and approving nods managed to escape their professionalism.

Eventually, Jacques separated his lips from his wife's eager aperture, backed up, and gazed down at her.

Marie wore a simple, elegant vintage Chanel dress; it loosely wrapped her body as it draped to the floor. Marie was rarely one to advertise the sensual nature of her physique. The strapless Versace mini-dress Jacques had bought for her, hoping she would be inspired to wear it to the party, remained in the back of her closet, still inside the garment bag. She had not even tried it on.

Jacques quietly wished his wife would have taken an epicurean risk for his sake, just this once, but as usual, her demure, prosaic self had won out. Marie looked lovely to him, of course, but predictably safe and sensible.

In her hair, Marie wore a small, pearl-encrusted comb. Jacques had had it custom made for her as a special gift when she had shorn her long mane of chestnut hair in the spring. A few simple, shiny sterling silver bracelets adorned her delicate wrists. Marie's one attempt at flamboyance was an expensive Tiffany pearl choker that she adored.

Though enamoured by his wife's quiet beauty, Jules's visceral, powerful sensuality had not totally left Jacques's thoughts. He hoped his wife assumed his ample erection, if she noticed it at all, was for her alone.

"Marie, you look—"

"Ravishing, I believe, is the word you're looking for," she teased impishly, finishing his sentence for him.

The two of them stood together and kissed once more before being interrupted by an employee.

"Jules Cartell has arrived, sir."

Jules and Phillip casually exited their limousine, aware that the car transporting the remainder of their family was nowhere in sight. Slightly annoyed by this, Phillip quickly realized that his wife had no intention of waiting for them.

Brazenly, Phillip took hold of Jules's hand, stopping her before she got too far ahead.

"Wait, Jules. This is a Cartell Worldwide function, and last time I checked, both mom and Denise were Cartells."

Jules glared at her husband and angrily yanked her hand free from his grasp. She despised being pawed, affectionately or otherwise. No one pressed themselves upon her, and no man, except her father, did she deign to embrace without making the first move herself. Jules knew Phillip's handhold was no romantic gesture. He wanted to control her actions, and that was unacceptable. His touch revolted her.

"You'd better be pleasant tonight, Phillip," Jules threatened. "So lighten up on the booze. How we look, act, and speak must be done with precision, style, and competency. Something you're shit at. Tonight will go off without a hitch as long as everyone obeys my—I mean, of course, follows my lead."

Phillip understood that his wife wholeheartedly meant "obeys." Her mocking grin supported that belief.

"I won't tolerate anything but your best tonight, Fido. Am I understood?"

Phillip screamed inside his head. *Fido! Like I'm her fucking lapdog?*

Infuriated, still smarting from Jules's rejection of his touch, Phillip suppressed a sudden urge to strike her. By nature, he was not a violent man. Never in his life had he raised a hand to a woman in anger. Unfortunately, Jules's toxic behaviour and dismissive attitude towards him often brought to the surface the darkest parts of his psyche.

Not wanting to give in to that darkness, Phillip contained his rage and controlled his desire to lash out physically.

"You're unfuckingbelievable! I want this just as much as you do, so ya, I'll act accordingly. I know what's good for *my* family's company!"

Phillip's emphasis on that one specific word was a calculated move to annoy his wife. He meant to remind her that she was not a Cartell by blood. It was a pretty bold move on his part as he rarely talked back to her.

As he stared into the pissed-off face of his wife, Phillip reflected upon the time before he was married to Jules. He thought about his first love, Genevieve, and how she had disappeared one day from his life, forever. Her inexplicable departure had nearly destroyed him. He reminisced about the day when Jules first entered his life—long before she controlled it.

Immediately after graduating from McGill University's Master's program in Business Management, Phillip had been sent to the newly erected Vancouver branch of Cartell Worldwide by his father. Joseph had wanted to verify his son's hunger for success and his competency in achieving it. Did Phillip have what it took to move beyond textbook scenarios and conventional internships to take on the cold, often brutal reality of the corporate arena?

And to do it all without his father watching out for him?

Phillip spent his time in Vancouver working, too busy to engage in social activities outside of the occasional charity fundraiser. In record time, he impressed his father by successfully stabilizing and promoting the Cartell Worldwide brand on the West Coast.

On Joseph's order, Phillip eventually returned to Toronto, the throne of Cartell Worldwide's power, swollen with pride that he had successfully matriculated his father's test. As was expected of him, Phillip moved back in with his family.

The Manor House, a grandiloquent title penned by his mother, was the family's palatial headquarters. Cementing the mansion's appellation was an ostentatious bronze sign built into the brick structuring and supporting the iron gate. The gate ran the full property line, which was substantial.

A former model, discovered at fourteen in Poland by Yves Saint-Laurent, himself, Stella, born Estella though she never went by it, was much more than just a pretty face. With minimal aid from a hired professional architect, she had designed the entire compound from scratch.

The Bridle Path, an upscale residential neighbourhood in the former city of North York that was now part of Toronto, was the location of the family estate. The area was characterized by large multi-million dollar mansions and two to four-acre lot sizes.

Upon returning to Toronto, Phillip worked slavishly as his father's right-hand man to appease him unequivocally. He firmly believed socializing with beautiful women was a distraction and a detriment to this objective. Phillip was not interested in anything beyond casual sex, anyway. His one experience with real love had proved a disaster; he had no plans to open himself up to that kind of pain again.

After being back in Toronto a few months, Phillip reluctantly agreed to a blind date with the daughter of one of his father's rich friends. Busy with work, he considered the outing a waste of his time, so much so that he never bothered to creep his date's social media presence.

One Saturday night, Phillip casually drove to the Lakeshore in his Jag to pick up his date. He planned on being the perfect gentleman. If she proved a bore, however, he intended on ending the evening early and returning to his office. The drive towards the waterfront was calming; the early summer air was warm and without humidity.

Phillip looked sharp in his John Varvatos polo and pants combo. He had chosen Gucci shoes and matched both his belt and his socks with them. His hair was cropped short at the sides and back, his blond curls only mildly unfurled on top.

Upon reaching his destination, Phillip walked up to the door of the ultramodern condo, announcing his presence with a sharp rap of his knuckles. Within moments, the door opened.
Phillip's breath caught in his throat as he gazed upon an extraordinarily beautiful, fit, and stylish woman.

But it was not only her beauty that enthralled him. Even at first glance, he reasoned she was a no-nonsense woman, as her manner and stance belied, prepared for a silver-tongued charmer, like himself.

What Phillip found most mesmerizing, though, were her eyes. They were a shade of blue he could not recall having ever seen before on another person. When she finally smiled at him, Phillip lost all pretence that the encounter would be a waste of his time.

"Hi, Phillip, I'm Jules. It's not short for Julie or anything, in case you were wondering, and please don't think up a cutesy nickname for me. I'll never understand why men think calling me a glittery rock is endearing. Anyway, it's a pleasure to finally meet my handsome and delightfully on-time date. I'm not the type of woman who waits around for a man."

Slowly, methodically, Jules gave Phillip the once-over. "You look nice."

Nice, huh? Phillip thought, amused. *Ya, I'll take it.* Jules did not immediately fawn over him, impressed by his fancy duds or his last name. Phillip liked that a lot; he gave her a huge grin.

Jules smiled back congenially. Then, gently taking Phillip's hand in hers, she leaned in and kissed him on the lips.

Initially caught off-guard by Jules's tenacity, Phillip quickly recovered, leaned into the kiss, and gave as good as he got.

The moment of intimacy was brief, ending when Jules pulled away first.

"Now, our first kiss is out of the way. We can continue with our night without either of us silently fretting throughout dinner over the whole cliché end-of-date kissing scenario. Your lips are surprisingly soft but firm. Nice. Alright, let's go."

Not wishing to appear antiquated regarding social modernity, Phillip quickly changed tactics when he realized Jules was no silly social butterfly expecting or desiring the man to take the lead. Instinctively ready to take Jules's arm and lead her to his car, Phillip immediately thought better of it and kept his hands to himself.

When they reached the car, Phillip, afraid Jules may not appreciate old-fashioned ideas of chivalry, tentatively asked if he could open the door for her. He stated that he knew she was quite capable of opening the door, but it would give him great pleasure to be at her service if she would allow it.

With a mischievous grin, Jules accepted. She got that Phillip was intimidated by her, and she liked that.

They drove to the Drake Hotel on Queen Street West.

During dinner, they talked about everything under the sun, from business to fashion trends. Jules even knew every minute detail about Phillip's Jaguar XK and the history of the company.

"It's quite a fascinating bit of history," Jules quipped in between sips of Rose port. "Jaguar was founded as the Swallow Sidecar Company in nineteen twenty-two, originally making motorcycle sidecars before developing passenger cars. After the

Second World War, the name was changed to Jaguar to avoid the unfavourable connotations of the SS initials and the Nazi Party. Of course, you probably know this already."

Phillip did not, and he suspected that his date had quickly determined that for herself thanks to his bizarrely timed cough and awkward smile.

Of course, Jules had, but she was gracious; she winked flirtatiously and moved on to another topic.

Phillip was thankful Jules let it go, but he reasoned her moving on was not because she was afraid of challenging his masculinity or embarrassing him. Phillip believed he knew Jules well enough, even at this early stage, to know she would never play the giggling, dumb bunny role to safeguard a man's pride and ego. Phillip got the impression that she did not press further simply because it was not that big of a deal in her mind.

As strong-willed as Jules was, Phillip suspected she confronted gender and sexist stereotypes daily. If she knew more about an automobile than he did, well, it was just a fact.

And he was correct in his thinking; it was a total non-issue for her.

Jules eventually got around to asking Phillip about his family and where he saw himself in ten years.

Phillip answered all questions as honestly and with as much energy as he could muster. He wanted to show Jules how much he loved their conversation, how engaged he was with it. Phillip liked how Jules made reciprocating easy. He asked her all the same questions, genuinely wanting to know everything about her.

Phillip pretty much fell in love with Jules that night. She had dexterously galvanized his passion and hunger for things outside of his work. Unknowingly, Jules had extinguished his need to brood and lament past personal losses, specifically, Genevieve. Jules's candidness, openness, and lust for life had awakened him, quickening his benumbed heart.

While the cerebral and emotional connection was amazing, Phillip was not afraid to admit to himself his desire to tear Jules's clothes off and fuck the hell out of her.

Only once during their time together that night did they quarrel. Phillip had roused Jules's ire when he brought up the topic of his parents' marriage and, specifically, his mother's pride in becoming a Cartell.

Jules was never a woman who shied away from controversial issues or automatically agreed with her paramour to prevent tension, social awkwardness or uncomfortable silences. She never bowed down and altered her opinion for a man simply because he was a man.

"Phillip, I don't understand this need women have, especially today's modern woman, to readily and willingly give up their last name to latch onto their husband's lineage and identity. Like it's some great prize. It's ridiculous and so disempowering."

"I think it's meant to be a romantic gesture, Jules."

"Romantic? How so? Please enlighten me."

Jules sat back in her chair, straightened her back as firmly as she could, and folded her hands together methodically on the table. Her mouth became a line devoid of emotion. Her eyes, however, conveyed deep contemplation and, perhaps, a seething fury that she attempted to mask with her quickly formed stoic persona.

Jules was only partially successful in the cover-up.

Phillip panicked, noticing the slight yet cogent change in his date's demeanour. He quickly attempted to explain himself, to lessen the disastrous impact his ill-considered, rushed statement had on Jules's formerly congenial disposition.

"Jules, well I—I—"

"I need a verb," she interjected sarcastically but without malice.

"Well, in keeping with tradition, the wife takes her husband's name, symbolizing her commitment to building a new family with her husband. It's a romantic gesture, sure, but it doesn't mean she innately gives up any of her sense of self—her independence. You see?"

"No, I don't see. If we wed, would you change your last name to mine? Phillip Dunning-Bainbridge. Yes, it has a nice ring to it, don't you think?" Jules's face remained frozen. Her tone? Crisp and controlled.

"What? No, I'm a Cartell! My father intends for me to take over one day from him. The Cartell name is important. Not that your name isn't, of course! I mean, it is important, but I have a responsibility to my family. Oh man, I'm blowing this, aren't I? Are you just playing with me?"

Phillip smiled awkwardly. He hoped that Jules was pretending to be mad and not questioning him. Or worse, testing him.

Jules waited a moment, took a deep breath, and then spoke calmly and frankly.

"Phillip, I don't accept society's assumption, a historically patriarchal society, that a woman, without question, should give up the last name bequeathed to her at birth to take on her husband's surname at the time of marriage.

"I find the assumption most appalling. It's not some universal law—it's a choice! And I'm only talking about male/female couples because of the gender-based power dynamic, socially and culturally speaking. If committed couples entering marriage mean to be equals, then it's paramount they agree upon their last name together. She takes his name, he takes hers or they keep the ones they have individually.

"Or they create a brand-new name for themselves. This idea is my favourite because women have only ever had their father's name to cling to before a husband's name is imposed upon them. To choose a name, emotionally and legally, to utilize that power is revolutionary!

"Sadly, society doesn't encourage couples to have a conversation about it in the first place. Men have always assumed women will follow history and take on the husband's family name. Disappointingly, most women believe this is just how it is and blindly follow an old, outdated custom they had no say in creating. If questioned, their reply is frustratingly trite. 'Oh, I don't really care about that.'

"Is that their truth? Certainly, it's the less-treasonous opinion that has been forced into their minds since birth by the patriarch and its constant social conditioning. This blind devotion to another time's sexist custom is insanity."

"But Jules," Phillip protested, "lots of women hyphenate their last name. That's keeping a part of their identity, isn't it? Their premarital individualism?"

"Oh, Phillip," Jules sighed. "These women are still met with ridicule. You know how the social order treats women who don't conform to society's rules and customs as agitators pushing a feminist agenda. Like those assholes even remotely understand what feminist ideology is.

"True equality between men and women isn't a reality. We still devalue and degrade the feminine in this culture. Women accept this choice of a surname as sufficient compromise, but they don't see that it's still giving into the patriarchal system. Why? Because no one questions it when their husbands don't reciprocate and hyphenate their last name.

"Like you just insinuated, Phillip—it's silly for a man to think that way. Men don't compromise on this issue. Who tells them they have to? Who pressures them? No one asks a man the question I just put to you, Phillip, and I found your response typical and, sadly, expected. You won't give away something of yourself that you take pride in, yet you readily expect a woman to do it.

"Upon reflection, I guess it doesn't matter in the end because a woman's last name is only ever another man's cognomen—her father's. A simple trade from one man to another. There, there, don't be upset, Jules. It's tradition, after all."

Realizing Jules was done talking, Phillip took a moment to process her words before speaking his mind. He knew he owed Jules patience and thoughtfulness; still, he considered this some real heavy shit for a first date conversation.

"Jules, I truly didn't mean to upset or offend you. This is a topic steeped in historical presupposition, and admittedly I've never really thought about it. You aren't wrong in what you're saying. I did assume my wife-to-be would take my name without making a fuss. It never even crossed my mind to have an actual discussion with her about the name change beforehand. I do see now that my expectation is condescending. Even subjugating."

Releasing the tension around her mouth, Jules smiled and unfolded her hands. Phillip had pleasantly surprised her. He truly listened to her and engaged in thoughtful discourse, even when it meant questioning his male ego.

Jules was suddenly very turned on and knew she wanted to see the man again. She felt the chemistry between them. There was something there she could foment to further her career and satisfy her libido.

And if she fell in love along the way? That would be fine. Jules was not averse to romance; the prospect of marriage was not unimaginable.

"I'm going to make you a deal, Phillip Cartell. If you and I ever end up marrying, I'll take your last name, no argument. Here's the thing, though, and it might sound crazy. I promise you, eventually, everyone we meet will believe Cartell was my last name from the get-go. I'll become synonymous with that name and all it entails. Power, wealth, strength—all the things I see in you.

"Not to mention your attractive brain. I love a man who can hold his own against me in intellectual combat. You're not just a pretty face with a great ass."

Both Jules and Phillip had understood the game that was afoot between them that night. Only later did Phillip realize to what extent Jules had controlled the game's landscape, defining the rules to suit her purpose.

All of Phillip's memories, both painful and wonderful, of his first encounter with a young Jules Dunning-Bainbridge, quickly faded as his wife punched his arm. Snapping her husband back to reality, Jules glared in his direction and scolded, "Stop daydreaming, idiot."

"Don't act so high and mighty, Jules," Phillip snarled back. "We both control this company, not just you."

"That knowledge haunts me, trust and believe," Jules replied, composed yet snarky. "Only, you've failed to realize something crucial though your poor, fragile ego might fracture more than it already has by this revelation. And you must know by now that I'd rather cut off my arm than cause you even an ounce of pain."

Jules's sardonic look washed over Phillip like a harsh slap to his face. To keep a modicum of restraint and professionalism amid resounding irritation, Jules lowered her voice to a whisper; still, it was one composed of indomitable will and strength of purpose. She wanted Phillip, and Phillip only, to hear her follow-up words.

"The thing is, Mr. Cartell—by blood, I'm the fucking power behind this company. In the eyes of everyone, I am Cartell Worldwide, the only fucking Cartell that ultimately matters. Just like I told you I would be, all those years ago, remember?"

That said, Jules turned and marched towards Château Bergé's main entrance. Brushing aside the doorman, she disappeared behind the ornamented oak and stained-glass doors.

Near tears, Phillip stood outside alone, comprehending how accurate his wife's proclamation was. She was the Cartell everyone talked about and wanted to engage with. She had overshadowed him ages ago.

Even though he had already knocked back a few brews at the mansion before leaving, Phillip was in desperate need of another drink to drown his sorrows in. Another—or four.

III

Marie grew more uncomfortable as the festivities moved along. Hobnobbing with the enemy, which was what she believed Jacques had forced her to do by hosting Jules's party, turned her stomach. Her hatred for Jules was palpable; it tasted like poison in her mouth.

At the edge of the room, cloaked in the anonymity she preferred, Marie watched Jules like a hawk. She saw that her enemy was about to be introduced to one of the many wealthy American businessmen who had recently come to stay at Château Bergé. Much to Marie's annoyance, Jacques had invited several such wealthy, self-important guests to the party to meet Jules. She furrowed her brow in disgust.

Unaware of Marie's hateful leer bearing down on his group, Miles made introductions.

"Mr. Chesterton, may I introduce Mrs—uh, Ms. Jules Cartell."

Miles was painfully aware of the faux pas he had just made using that hated sobriquet. Referencing Jules's marital status was a no-no. Her severe glare was proof enough that he would be taken to task for it later. Jules revelled in all that the Cartell name provided her but detested an epithet that might minimize her power. Miles could not reasonably affirm why he had faltered in a task that had become routine and boring in its methodical usage.

Peaked with curiosity at the sudden change in Jules's status, the Texan investigated further. "Divorced, darlin'?" he probed.

Without missing a beat, Jules smiled, tilted her head coyly, and answered with a sigh. "Sadly, no." That said, she sipped her champagne and acted as if the entire misunderstanding and subsequent dismissal of her marital status were thoroughly uninteresting to her.

Mr. Chesterton laughed heartily. He added a conspiratorial smirk suggesting he understood an insinuation that Jules could casually mix business with sexual pleasure despite her wedded state.

He was wrong, of course. Jules was more than prepared to chastise and punish anyone who overstepped the boundaries of professionalism and respect.

From her shrouded corner, Marie saw that Jacques had finished his cordial greetings. She smiled to herself, eagerly anticipating his expected advancement towards her. Marie imagined the two of them dancing across the ballroom floor. Two people so in love that the whole world would stop to watch them, whispering among themselves how lucky she was to have a husband who clearly adored her.

Marie could never take her eyes off her handsome husband.

Jacques was tall, like all the Bergé men, and towered over most others. His hair was black as night, lustrous, and full of sheen. He kept it clipped short on the sides but allowed for gradual, longer pieces on top, almost spiky. Marie loved running her fingers through his hair, even though she always met resistance from his minimal yet ever-present hair wax.

Jacques's patrician cheeks and Romanesque nose recalled the gods of ancient times. His slim, taught musculature brought on images of Olympic javelin throwers. Jacques was Marie's Roman god: graceful, strong, and commanding of presence.

Unlike the gods Marie envisioned, Jacques bore the skin tone of the Bergé bloodline, pale and delicate. He was nothing like Phillip, a bronze Adonis under the sun's beaming rays.

Jacques's eyes were far more piercing than the average person's. Caring, sagacious, and as penetrating as they were sapphire blue. They were the same hypnotic eyes Jules possessed, and this unnerved Marie deeply. She knew how attractive and compelling people who had such rare eyes could be to others who would stop at nothing to be in the presence of such radiance.

Marie waited for Jacques to come to her; however, all expectations shattered before her very eyes. She gasped, completely caught off guard by how quickly, yet purposefully her husband left the entryway and moved towards Jules to join in *her* conversation.

Several party-goers quickly retreated from their intimate communions. They moved en-masse like a swarm of locusts towards the ever-growing congregation now led by Jacques and her hated rival.

Jules Cartell and Jacques Bergé, unquestionably treated with large amounts of awe and reverence, were akin to royalty to the people of Fairporte.

Marie felt ignored, defeated.

Not once did Jacques look for her to check to see if she was having a good time or even determine if she was still in attendance before racing to Jules's side.

Begrudgingly, Marie understood Jacques was working, and his job tonight, which he excelled at, was to charm the habitue. It was not to constantly build up her confidence and protect her from her social anxiety.

This logical thinking was cold comfort. Marie felt her radiance—her spark—was significantly diminished in the presence of the whirling dervish that was Jules Cartell. She worried incessantly about competing with a woman as outwardly gregarious and strong-willed as Jules. A woman who made it all look so effortless compared to her, a woman who barely kept her nightmares at bay with medication.

Marie resigned herself to the fact that all she could do was watch and wait for her moment to get Jules alone, when she would not have all eyes on her, and confront her. When that time came, Marie hoped she would be able to muster the strength needed to openly oppose the harridan who had bewitched her husband and everyone around her.

Recalling the faces she had scanned during her surveillance of the room, Marie wondered if perhaps not everyone had been so favourably affected by Jules's spellbinding ways.

Phillip seemed just as disenchanted with his wife as she was.

Marie was keenly aware that Jacques and Phillip avoided each other. She wondered if Phillip recognized the chemistry between Jules and her husband, two souls so at ease in their skins, never shying away from social interactions or appearing uncomfortable or unprepared around societal obligations.

How much like Phillip she was, Marie noted. The both of them troubled and lamentably intimidated people eclipsed by the much larger shadows of their respective spouses.

Phillip had not left the bar since first entering the room; Marie wondered about the extent of his suffering. She took a moment to contemplate the misery and torment he certainly endured at the hands of his wife's terrible ego. So much suffering that it had forced him to scurry from Jules's presence as soon as he entered the room to acquire liquid courage.

How strangely connected Marie felt to Phillip. She thought about her medicine cabinet filled with pills, taken daily to augment her weak stability and precarious nerve.

Marie's thoughts stayed on Phillip until she saw Jules move towards the ladies' room.

Now you're mine, bitch!

"Wh're th' hell 're they?"

Phillip's question was a slurred muttering, not an exasperated, query. Not surprisingly, no one answered his near unintelligible question. Those closest to him at the bar quickly moved away, uncomfortable with his intoxicated behaviour.

Calling over the bartender, Phillip ordered another Dry Manhattan. He silently speculated on the cause of his family's ridiculous tardiness to their event. Denise had not responded to a single one of his texts. While it was common for his sister to be less than punctual, he knew his mother considered such a thing unforgivable rudeness.

Phillip had explained vociferously to his family how much he needed their support tonight. A united front to show the world that the Cartells were not represented solely by Jules.

Lingering at the bar, unwilling to engage with his guests without reinforcements, Phillip remained alone in the background, a quiet observer, watching his wife work the room expertly.

Like a shark hunting its prey, Jules moved fearlessly among the wealthy guests, both the local sycophantic nouveaux riches and Old Money sects of Fairporte high society. All were glued to her ear as if every word she spoke was a magical incantation that compelled them to find her utterly fascinating.

Phillip winced, sickened by the mob's flattery of Jules, the expected and altogether tiresome compliments on her beauty and style. They were all just as eager to bend her ear towards the talk of business. Jules was always the best informed, whether it was local, national or international business. She knew how to make money, and everyone wanted to know her secrets to success.

The Parisians and their international textile business was Cartell Worldwide's current priority and the reason for this particular event. Jules, however, never wasted an opportunity for new investment; that was why she had asked Jacques to invite so many of his contacts to the party. Them, and any guests of the Château Bergé who seemed interesting. Phillip wondered if Jacques would have been so accommodating had he been the one to ask for this favour instead of his beautiful wife.

He highly doubted it.

Phillip appreciated Jules's brilliance in business, but the hard truth was she had become an unsupportive wife and business partner, treating him like a low-level employee. She had turned most everyone at the company against him. Hardly anyone had any confidence in his ability to lead anymore. Phillip realized this but had done nothing about it. He was utterly ashamed that he had allowed his wife to supplant him as head of his family's company.

Someone Jules never treated as a lackey or condescended to was Jacques, and Phillip was very aware of this, hating the more than casual flirtation between the two of them. Unfortunately, he had no idea if Jules had ever been unfaithful to him with Jacques. Phillip only knew one thing for sure, and that was that he had not been intimate with his wife in a long time despite his desire for her affection.

Phillip's one attempt at hiring a private investigator to follow Jules and determine her fidelity had been a complete disaster thanks to his father-in-law's interference.

As managing partner of Castle Dunning and Briggs, Charles was the head of Cartell Worldwide's legal representation. He was also the company's current CFO. A well-connected, influential man, Charles had easily discovered his son-in-law's dalliance with private investigation. As the target of Phillip's investigation was Jules, Charles had terminated the operation with vehemence.

Charles's legal knowledge and vindictive determination drove the investigative firm out of business soon after.

Phillip was further humiliated when his mother admonished him for his failed scheme. Stella believed if he could not do things as clandestinely as his father had, he should not even try.

Infuriated by the impertinence of Charles's interference in his marriage, Phillip intended to somehow get even.

Knowing Phillip picked the wrong battle to fight, Stella intervened before her angry son went and made an enemy of his late father's closest friend and business associate. In a long-winded and pretentious speech, Stella explained the importance of knowing when to act and when not to.

Her lecture went as follows: *My darling son, think of business as a dance with an ever-changing line-up of partners. Some partners will give freely of themselves for the mutual benefit of both participants. These are the principal dancers that one must engage with for as long as possible until they have nothing left to give. Only then should they be gently discarded.*

Others will come with good intentions and occasionally produce favourable results but are generally bumbling clods stepping on your toes. Therefore, they leave you with no choice but to cast them aside. But always separate from them without malice. Remember, they tried their best, meant well, and may one day improve, becoming useful. Best not to burn any bridges if you want to exploit them in the future.

Now, the most fickle dancer is one with both technique and passion. Charles is this type. The most dangerous. This dancer, with all their proficiency and skill, can bring the world to your feet. However, you must learn that with great passion comes even greater unpredictability. The fickle partner may abruptly leave you to your own devices. Flummoxed by their behaviour, you falter, questioning your power position.

Just as viable a possibility, for reasons all their own, you might be dropped to the ground by them, hard, on purpose. They will continue without you while you remain behind, bruised and bleeding—vulnerable! This partnership is forever spoiled. The trust is gone. And as mysterious, maddeningly inconvenient, and ultimately disastrous as all this is, you cannot predict its occurrence to avoid it. There is nothing to foreshadow their erratic unpredictability or treasonous behaviour.

You must promenade with the fickle dancer cautiously to bolster good feelings and produce great work. Cross them, and you may lose not only your partner but, potentially, the entire competition. Do you understand me? Do you get my meaning? Charles is privy to much of the same sensitive information your father possessed. Public and private. Let it go!

Stella's final statements, layered with secret meaning, had infuriated her son. Phillip understood the damaging subtext and how it weakened his position. Unlike him, Charles knew countless dirty little secrets his father had amassed during his reign. Phillip suspected that Charles, being his father's lawyer and best friend, had hidden many of them personally.

The fact that he had no idea what secrets could be used against his family distressed Phillip greatly.

Phillip respected Charles, albeit begrudgingly, for the loyalty shown towards his family. Still, he was insanely jealous of the close relationship Charles had shared with his father.

In the end, Phillip had listened to his mother, held his tongue, and immediately stopped spying on Jules.

Sadly, Phillip wasted countless hours fixating on the exact moment when his life with Jules altered irrevocably. Over and over again, he deconstructed the events of the day when his seemingly perfect, happy marriage completely shattered apart.

Jules's demeanour towards Phillip and his family had changed dramatically on the heels of Joseph's funeral; she became cold, mean, and distant towards them.

Towards her husband, especially, Jules grew increasingly hostile and dismissive. Initially, she acted erratic and viciously aggressive but eventually, her emotions cooled to a simmering hatred despite Phillip's best attempts at loving her. Trying to understand his wife's dramatic change in temperament had caused him nothing but frustration and misery.

In his Last Will and Testament, Joseph had given clear instructions that both his son and daughter-in-law were to legally share the titles of CEO and Chairperson of the Board, as well as his entire Cartell Worldwide stock portfolio. Jules effectively became more powerful, more influential regarding the company's future direction than Joseph's daughters.

Phillip, madly in love with his wife, took no issue with these unexpected stipulations to his inheritance. It had truly meant nothing to him. He would have given Jules everything he owned.

Due to an iron-clad prenuptial agreement, Stella had signed away her right to inherit controlling interest in the company upon Joseph's death. She had willingly done so, confident her children would naturally succeed their father. Financially, she was solid, and much of the family properties, including the Manor House, remained in her possession.

More unexpected than the direction of Joseph's will had been Jule's unexplained metamorphosis. Without warning, she had abandoned her generally affectionate and attentive—though still bossy—role as a supportive wife and egalitarian business partner. In place of that, a woman who openly despised her husband and his family emerged.

And she wanted nothing but absolute control over the entire Cartell Worldwide empire.

Four days after Joseph's funeral, in a dynamic Donna Karen suit, Jules had marched into a board of directors meeting and unequivocally declared herself the absolute sovereign of the company.

Phillip, unprepared for this startling shift in his wife's attitude and presentation, floundered, unsure how to respond; over time, he became increasingly and openly deferential to Jules.

With the notable exception of Stella, outraged at her daughter-in-law's audacity, not one Boardmember contested Jules's proclamation. They all knew her worth and value; her significant contribution to the company's financial success was unquestionable. Also, several members had something to lose if they caused trouble for Jules by defying her and backing Stella and Phillip.

The day before Jules made her bold and dictatorial announcement, Charles had discreetly met with select long-standing, influential, and potentially problematic board members. In a not-so-subtle manner, he warned them that if they resisted Jules's leadership in deference to Phillip, he would make them very sorry.

Generally, Charles's reputation and clout usually swayed or intimidated anyone to his way of thinking. This time, however, he had ammunition to strengthen his position. Revealing to each person he spoke with a single, specific, devastating secret of theirs, Charles promised to make it public knowledge if they did not cooperate.

Taking a page from Joseph's book, Charles knew this was how he had kept people under his thumb, staving off any potential insurgency. Many of the rich and influential who travelled in the elite world of the Cartells often engaged in provocative activities and questionable legal transactions. They certainly did not want these things brought to light.

Stella acted too slowly to stop her daughter-in-law's rise to power. Much to her dismay, Phillip had refused her pleas to work with her against his wife. Denise had sold her shares in the company and had nothing to offer. Despite her seat on the board and access to Sonja's voting power, Stella had lost, unable to prevent the inevitable; Phillip was pushed into the background.

Her staunch unwillingness to accept Jules's new station eventually proved Stella's downfall at the company.

Well prepared for an attack on her leadership, Jules saw her enemy coming a mile away.

Her surprise proposal to the board of directors to vote Stella out and offer her seat to someone with actual credentials and business experience had been an overwhelming success. Stella was ousted under the more palatable guise of retirement. In her vacated seat, Jules wanted a more appropriate corporate representative than some former fashion model; in her eyes, her father was the obvious choice.

Barring the removal of his mother, in which he had been thoroughly out-voted, Phillip continued to support Jules in nearly every decision she made. It was all in the hope that the woman he married would see his faith in her, his love, and come back to him.

He was still waiting for that to happen.

"Please excuse me," Jules announced. "I'm sure Jacques will entertain all of you with stories of his savage youth abroad until I return."

Jules liked how Jacques appeared amused by her playful words. Leaving his side, Jules moved graciously towards the powder room to touch up her make-up. She tried not to notice her mollified husband at the bar drinking himself into a coma.

Walking in her hour-glass-shaped Versace gown, Jules turned many heads; Phillip was no exception. Jules enjoyed seeing how he beheld her with both lustful and angry glances, for they betrayed his insane jealousy. Jealous of her power, naturally, and jealous of her social intimacy with Jacques. If it hurt Phillip to know that she was desired by others, all the better. His torment was ecstasy to her.

Jules's designer dress was amber in colour with lace brocade sewn into the silk-cotton blend. Exquisite lace, tastefully woven down the body of the gown in a mosaic of floral stitching. The dress had a frontal slit that started just above the knee, which allowed her shapely calves to feature prominently. Her exposed neck, shoulders, and arms were fluid and graceful in their movement.

Jules politely acknowledged two older, high society women as they exited the powder room and passed her. They nodded back and smiled as best they could through their Botox and fillers.

Sauntering regally into the clean space, Jules positioned herself in front of the wide vanity for some lipstick touch-up. She smoothed out her hair, which had been back-combed into a perfect updo and secured by two antique pearl clasps that matched the diamond and pearl choker around her neck.

Earlier that evening, Jules had informed her stylists that she wanted to embody the elegant yet playful refinement of Kim Novak, an icon she revered.

The last thing I want to embody is the dull as dishwater look Marie sports so often. Jules quietly giggled, imagining the ridiculous comparison between the two of them.

"Do you find something funny, Jules? Or are you just laughing at the fool you're making of yourself? Flirting with everything in that room with a penis!"

"Oh, Marie, such a comedienne," Jules scoffed. "And look at you! I—love—what you're wearing tonight?" The fact that Jules's acerbic statement sounded like a question was absolutely intentional. So was the drawn-out hesitancy in her sentence. "I simply must know the designer. Wait, don't tell me. It's homemade! You do have so much free time, after all, being a homemaker—with a staff of hundreds. Good on you for keeping busy. Kudos."

Marie scowled. "It's vintage Chanel," she responded meekly. "You just love to belittle me."

"Well, you do make it easy for me, Marie," Jules snickered. "Still, the dick joke was a bold attempt at verbal repartee. I didn't think you had a churlish bone in your body. You do know what 'churlish' means, don't you? It's a big word, I know. I do forget you were home-schooled. Or was that just a rumour I started?"

Jules laughed loudly, unfettered by the thought that people could hear her and possibly judge her blatant skewering of a less than capable adversary as mean-spirited. She was very confident in her impunity. By getting Marie, a woman many people considered a hopeless bore, hot under the collar, Jules believed she was doing the bitch a favour. She wanted to quicken Marie's pulse, fan her fire, get a reaction.

"There's no one here but you and me, Jules, so you can stop the performance. No one is present who finds you the least bit charming. I'm onto you. Stay away from my husband. Jacques has a kind, generous heart, and you're mistaking that for some personal interest in you. It's not!

"I may seem meek and mild to you, but I'm far from stupid. You want Château Bergé, like Joseph did, and you'll stoop to any level, manipulate anyone in your attempt to get it. We stopped him, and we'll stop you. It will be over my dead body—"

"Temper, temper, dear," Jules interrupted, "you'll get wrinkles. Wait, never mind, I see it's already much too late for that. I know a wonderful dermatologist who can fill in those unseemly lines with Restylane. He's practically a magician. I better get you his number—and fast by the look of things."

"Why, you hateful cow, I—"

"Sweetie," Jules interrupted again, turning back towards the mirror, "save your threats for someone who might be intimidated by a person, such as yourself, who is as menacing as a circus poodle. You have absolutely no power, personal or professional, to alter or arrest anything I may or may not have set in motion. But please, hit me with your best shot. I never shy away from a good scrap. Meow."

Marie realized that she had been utterly dismissed by Jules, pitied, reduced to nothing more than a pathetic, mewling nuisance by a woman who possessed a quick, cutting tongue. Marie hated to admit that Jules was, by far, her superior on the battlefield of threats and condemnations.

Marie suddenly felt a fire growing inside her and a voice booming to be set free. It was a voice she had heard before. Once again, it called out to her to let go and allow the fire to burn hotly. It wanted to immolate her enemies with flame and fury. The voice screamed from deep inside her: *Let me out!*

Instead, Marie subjugated the powerful voice, hung her head down, and cried.

After finishing her final touch-ups, Jules placed her cosmetics back into her Gucci clutch and turned to leave the lavatory. However, she was unable to "live and let live" when it came to Marie. Jules detested weakness in women, and the sight of Marie's tears disgusted her. Where was the woman's fighting spirit? Something needed to be said.

"Look at yourself, Marie," Jules seethed. "Pathetic. You disgust me, always have. You and your pitiful tears. You're exactly the kind of woman I despise. Weak. Hesitant. You hide your feminine power behind a curtain of mousiness and uncertainty, constantly looking for the approval and protection of your husband. You whimper and cower instead of fighting back, hoping, no doubt, that Jacques will hear your sobbing and come rushing to defend your misery and feebleness.

"I've heard all the excuses. Your past hurt, your 'issues.' Should I show you empathy, take pity on you? Fuck that! You're pitiful and damaged all right, but that changes nothing in my eyes.

"You think I don't know things about you? The medications you're on and your unexplained disappearances. I just don't care. It might be interesting if I thought you did anything even remotely provocative during your absences.

"Now, there's something I have to know. Tonight, at any point, did you notice the pearl clasps in my hair or my strapless Versace gown? Does this ring any bells, honey? I told Jacques you wouldn't wear that dress—and look, I was right! Here you are all covered up. Safe, unalluring, and absolutely overshadowed by me.

"You're so outclassed, outgunned, and all-around outsmarted by me, Marie, that it's downright embarrassing. If I wanted your husband or Château Bergé, both would be mine easily. Now, I suggest you leave my function, go to your bedroom, and continue your little pity party away from my sight. And if you come for me again, well, I just wouldn't. Eviscerating you a second time would be downright boring. I hate repeating myself."

Jules chuckled and waited for a retort, a response, anything to come out of Marie's mouth, but all she got was silence and more tears.

Sighing, Jules resigned herself to the fact that she could not ignite any kind of fire in her opponent. There would be some backlash from this incident, words, at the very least, between her and Jacques, but she could handle him.

Not wanting to waste any more of the evening in the bathroom, Jules pushed Marie aside and marched out of the lavatory, nearly knocking over Denise in the process. Denise cursed at Jules, who naturally ignored her. This snub inflamed Denise.

"Cunt! Sorry, Marie, I didn't mean to be so crude, but that bitch does my head in. Is everything alright? You're crying! What did Jules say to you?"

Unable to articulate her feelings, Marie stormed out of the restroom, waving her hands erratically in front of her tear-stained face.

This left a stunned yet curious Denise alone to speculate with great interest on the events that had just transpired before her arrival.

IV

Having ordered Denise and Christophe to enter before her, Stella waited a moment to make a fashionably late entrance. She had not planned on being intentionally late, but it was what it was. She figured she would make the best of it by making a statement.

With as much flourish as she felt appropriate—awe-inspiring, yet respectably demure—Stella entered the ballroom.

The various ephemera gave their full attention to the former model, exclusively and without hesitation; Stella, in her mid-fifties, cut an imposing figure. She was well known in rarefied circles as the top socialite in the region; paying respect to her was expected.

Stella was a coveted ally in social and political realms. She was well-connected thanks to her marriage to Joseph and, to a smaller extent, affairs with influential men during her modelling days. Despite her neutered influence at Cartell Worldwide, she was the only person Jules considered a valid threat and potential obstacle to her.

And Stella was gleefully aware of this.

Resentfully, Phillip turned away from his imbibing to see what the commotion at the door was. He quickly lost interest when he realized his mother had entered the ballroom. She carried herself like an old Hollywood movie star walking the red carpet at her premiere. He watched as her wide smile and open arms dazzled, enticing the crowd to fawn over her.

Phillip loved his mother, but he had observed this dog and pony show too often to be taken in by it.

He understood what others never grasped; his mother was a spider spinning a thick web of manipulation and control. She needed to dominate every situation, every environment, every moment by orchestrating the perfect smoke and mirrors routine. She had a need to make people believe she was an important enough person to warrant absolute reverence.

Phillip accepted his father had conveyed a god-like control and authority over people through secrecy, information, and threats. He had been quite duplicitous in his machinations. His mother, in comparison, was more straightforward, predictable, and always had been. If you stayed on her good side, she was a powerful friend and ally. If you crossed her? She became your worst nightmare!

Bored by his mother's same old song and dance number, Phillip turned back to the bar. As he was about to order another drink, he heard his sister's voice in the crowd.

Spinning around, Phillip saw Denise waving to him from across the room. The blessed arrival of his sister made his eyes light up for the first time that evening. Phillip loved both his sisters but secretly favoured Denise. She did not share the vain, superficial comportment of their mother as Sonja did.

Phillip was not happy with Sonja these days. Overseas for quite some time, Sonja had been wasting, in her brother's opinion, her education and family money on vapid European suitors and countless random yacht parties in the hope of landing herself an actual Prince. Phillip loved that Denise was more like him, more business-minded like their father had been.

Denise owned and operated a successful fashion boutique, SIMPLY DENISE, located in the newly modernized downtown core of Fairporte. She had big plans to create a chain of boutiques across Canada. Construction had already begun on the Toronto and Vancouver stores.

Denise possessed a natural talent for spotting trends and knowing just when to pounce on a great idea or business opportunity, no matter how risky it seemed to others.

The only one of her siblings to attend university on the west coast, Denise had graduated with a Masters in Business Management from the University of British Columbia.

Growing up, it had been her dream to turn her love of fashion into a profitable business. She desperately wanted to distance herself from the all-encompassing machine that was her family's company. More specifically? Her father's long shadow. She wanted to be her own woman, like Stella McCartney, and not so much like Stella Cartell.

Denise had always known Phillip was to be their father's natural successor at Cartell Worldwide. She wanted to prove she could be independent and successful without relying on her father or family name. Denise believed it was too easy for a woman to accept living under the shadow of a powerful man; it was unacceptable to her.

Joseph, impressed by his daughter's tenacity, had agreed to never interfere in her business endeavours or attempt at any time to bully or entice her back into the family metier.

Stella, however, repeatedly refused to be ousted from her daughter's professional life. Occasionally, and rarely with her daughter's blessing or knowledge, Stella assisted Denise with her business.

As a former fashion icon, Stella had countless years of experience in the industry and possessed an extensive portfolio of contacts. Whenever Denise discovered her mother secretly helping her, she would first be angry, then quietly acquiesce to the assistance. After all, her mother had acquired her connections before she became a Cartell.

Regarding her family genetics, Denise was not the physical embodiment of Joseph's Nordic heredity. Not like Phillip and Sonja were. While fair-skinned, Denise was unabashedly crowned with a mane of dark, chestnut brown hair, almost black, and possessed deep hazel eyes. Stella, who had dark eyes but wore blue-coloured contacts, often compared Denise to her half Polish/half Italian great-grandmother.

This glaring difference was not something Denise liked about herself, and she secretly wished she looked more like her siblings. It was her one admittedly irrational and self-effacing insecurity. Denise was grateful for Phillip's uncanny ability to tan beautifully despite his fair skin. It allowed the belief there was some Italian or Eastern European ethnicity in effect. Denise wished she had a photograph of her maternal great-grandmother in her possession for reference, but none had survived the ages. At least, according to her mother.

"I'm going to check on my brother," Denise announced.

In response, Christophe used all his natural charm to persuade her to avoid her drunk-ass brother and go out on the dance floor with him. Denise, however, loudly declined his invitation, brusquely entreating his departure from her presence. She wanted to speak with Phillip alone.

Seeing that nothing was going to distract her from that endeavour, Christophe rolled his eyes and took off in search of Jacques to hang with.

Denise walked over to Phillip and hugged him with great affection. When she pulled away, she was instantly taken aback by the massive scowl on his face. She was also very concerned by the turmoil she saw locked tight behind his tired eyes. That, and the strong smell of liquor on his breath.

"What's wrong, bro? This is a party, not a funeral. Not having fun? Or maybe a little too much fun?" Denise looked discerningly at his half-empty glass.

A gruff Phillip took another gulp of his drink and blurted out a nearly incoherent response to his sister. "Thoshhe damn Frenchmen haven't arrived yet, and itshh nearly eight-thirty. Thishh whole shhtupid function washh shhupposed to be for their shhtupid benefit and they can't even be on fuckin' time. Why were you late? I told you guyshh how—how important thishh washh to me."

Phillip turned in closer towards his now very concerned sister. Nuzzling into the crook of her neck, he whispered conspiratorially, "If anything goessh wrong t'night, Jules will have m' ballshh."

Sighing loudly, Denise held her slurring, barely coherent brother up as he suddenly became physically awkward and began to slump. Instinctively, she looked out towards the ballroom in Jules's direction to divine if her sister-in-law had any concern whatsoever for her husband's whereabouts or condition.

Just as Denise expected, Jules, with Jacques by her side, was oblivious to Phillip's declining state. She laughed, caroused, and consorted with a variety of bigwigs and venture capitalists. Denise suspected Jules was less blind and more indifferent regarding her husband's current state of being, more interested in Marie's husband than her own.

Thinking about the confrontation in the powder room between Jules and Marie that she had regrettably not witnessed, Denise was infuriated by Jules's continual lack of respect and consideration for others. Seeing the need to manage the situation, Denise motioned at the bartender to remove her brother's drink. Then she nodded at the chilled water jug.

The experienced mixologist understood her meaning. He poured Phillip a large glass of ice water after discreetly removing his alcoholic beverage.

"Drink this," Denise commanded, pushing the glass into Phillip's hand.

Phillip did as he was told.

"We need to get food in you. Bro, you've got to get your shit together. Christophe, Mom, and I are here now to support you. I'm sorry we weren't here earlier. It's Christophe's fault we were late, much to Mom's displeasure, you can imagine. Don't worry about the Parisians. They'll be here. Besides, Jules doesn't seem too concerned by the fact that her guests of honour are absent."

Phillip quickly ate the half dozen hors d'oeuvres Denise set in front of him and gulped down two more full glasses of water. After shaking his head a few times, he cleared his throat and said,

"Nothin' ever seems to faze her. F'only I had that ability I might be more of a match for her. Maybe."

Denise was happy that her brother had, for the most part, stopped slurring his words. It was a good sign, but he still looked like a hot mess.

"Keep it together, and I want you to understand something, Phillip. Look at me! You're a winner. You're a Cartell, and no one messes with us. Jules isn't infallible. She's not impervious. There are cracks in her foundation and chinks in her armour. You just need the willpower and the patience to find and exploit them. I'll always help you. Guaranteed."

Clasping Phillip's hands, Denise looked pointedly into her brother's eyes, willing him as much confidence and positive energy as she could. Sadly, Denise still saw that damnable flicker of love in Phillip's eyes for his shrew of a wife. Nevertheless, that inconceivable love had yet to stop her or her mother's crusade against Jules.

"Ya know, Denise, you're my favourite. Don't—don't tell Sonja, though, as it'll hurt her feelings."

Denise smiled, and she encouraged her brother to eat a few more of the fancy hors d'oeuvres to help soak up the alcohol in his system.

When Phillip realized that he had been slurring his words, he was embarrassed. He hated that he had portrayed such a lamentable figure to his baby sister. He knew he had to get a grip and man up, at least for the sake of Denise, because her opinion of him meant everything.

"You know, Sis, the water and food have helped. I'm already feeling better and—yes, finally! The Parisians are here!

Stella watched the ballroom's large Tiffany clock like a predatory bird eyeing its prey. Since the moment she entered Château Bergé, she had been waiting for the perfect time and opportunity to quietly disappear. Everything had been planned; they would meet tonight.

It was time for answers.

Stella had believed, justifiably, that cruel fate had separated them forever. Days ago, however, she answered her cellphone, heard his voice, and nearly fainted.

Using the boisterous arrival of the Parisians as a means of distraction, Stella quietly extricated herself from the ballroom. She quickly advanced towards the south side of the Château using an indirect route she was very familiar with. In case she was being followed, it provided her with the appropriate amount of misdirection. She could have used a more direct, less awkward route, but secrecy was paramount in her mission.

When she finally arrived at her desired location, a disused hallway, Stella unlocked a door to a room that, to her knowledge, had been unoccupied for years. Scurrying inside, she was instantly startled by a deep, husky voice that hung in the air amid the darkness. Startled, yes, but very delighted. Not that she let on that she was; Stella's demeanour remained icy.

"I was wondering when you'd finally show up, my love," the deep male voice said.

Suddenly, a small table lamp switched on, and as the darkness receded, a lone male figure appeared. A bearded gentleman, older than Stella and dressed in a tailored black Kiton suit, sat stiffly in an authentic, exquisitely preserved Louis XV vanity chair. Uncrossing his legs, he licked his lips and grinned lustfully at his newly arrived guest.

Stella rolled her eyes in response to the bearded man's bold display of lewd, carnal behaviour. She wanted to appear disinterested and calm to maintain her position of strength, though what she ached to do was run into his arms and cry.

He was standing right there in front of her! Alive!

But first, there was business to complete and answers to get.

"I don't have time for chit-chat," Stella barked, closing the door, "or any base desire you're contemplating. The others will soon notice I'm gone. Let's get down to business."

The bearded, ruggedly attractive man shook his head, grinning at the boldness of this woman, a woman he found utterly desirable and utterly fascinating. Their relationship went back a lifetime; they knew nearly everything there was to know about one another.

Despite Stella's show of steely nerves and cut-throat attitude, the bearded man read between the lines. He knew she wanted him to tear the expensive gown off her body, throw her on the four-poster bed, and fuck her silly. They were both on the same wavelength regarding one major thing: not even his supposed death had diminished their connection.

Stella, however, was angry. Why had he stayed away from her for so long? Why keep the fact that he had never died in the first place a secret from her?

The bearded man rose from his seat and moved towards the woman he loved. "Stella, honey, it's been a long time since our last encounter, eh! Can't you spare even a single kiss? A hug? T'es beau comme un p'tit coeur! *You are beautiful, like a little heart.*"

"Pretty words sprung from the mouth of a snake and a liar. Oh, very well!"

Though irritated out of her mind, Stella enjoyed the verbal foreplay. Sensually, she conveyed her still firm body over to the bearded man and opened her mouth to accept his offering—his tribute—to her beauty. As their lips met, the two elders once again felt the spark that had first ignited during their younger years, during their first sexual encounter.

Yes, the fire was still there, and it burned hotly.

As she continued to give in to desire, pressing further into his body, Stella began to doubt her resolve. She worried that if this intimacy between them continued unchecked, her will and strength would eventually give way to unbridled lust. It had to stop, now, or it never would. She had to stop it; he certainly would not; his hands were already squeezing her ass.

Reluctantly, Stella forced her body to separate from the man she loved and still craved. It was not the right time to reacquaint their bodies with one another. It would happen; he would demand it; tonight was just not the appropriate juncture.

Stella accessed her long practiced, often used ability to close herself off from inconvenient emotions. She brought to the surface the cold-hearted, adamantine Cartell matriarch persona that put fear in others.

"Stella, Stella, ever the pragmatist. Business first, pleasure later, eh?"

"Patience, darling. I'm worth the wait."

Tepidly, Stella removed a zip drive from inside one of the white lace Hermes wedding gloves she wore. She had thoughtfully repurposed the gloves for use with the sublime Vivienne Westwood white taffeta gown she had selected to wear that evening.

Stored inside the device was Jules's plan for Cartell Worldwide's proposed acquisition of Château Bergé, along with some other deals on the table. Stella had no idea why her paramour wanted this information or what he planned to do with it. Frankly, she could not have cared less. As long as he held up his end of their agreement, his promise to her, she would ask no questions.

As always, Stella preferred to remain ignorant of his business deals. The shady ones, at least. He was a dangerous man, and though Stella found that sexy and exciting, his world outside of the one he shared with her often led to bloodshed and violence. She preferred to remain safely on the periphery of that world.

Stella believed wholeheartedly in his love for her, and she had no fear of him, utterly convinced he would never do her harm. Still, Stella was not stupid or a lovesick fool. She was shrewd and had always managed to avoid getting caught in the crossfires of his less than reputable side enterprises.

Stella casually tossed the small piece of technology onto the bed's duvet. The device's supposed value held little interest for her.

"It was difficult getting past Jules's security, but I have my ways. I still have allies at the company. Others can be bought. The cost of securing that information isn't coming out of my pocket, however. Now, no empty promises. Tell me what happened to you! Where have you been? How could you not tell me you were alive?"

The bearded man smiled wickedly, mentally lauding both Stella's success in gaining the information and her boldness in demanding anything from him. Whether loved and admired or hated, he was a man people respected and feared intensely.

His reputation for getting whatever he wanted was legendary. The inevitable pockets of dissent and rebellious defiance that prevented, however rarely, any intended procurement was swiftly and harshly dealt with. Insolence was punished brutally and served as a warning to others who thought to stand in his way.

And despite what the world at large believed, he was not dead, and he continued his work in secret, unencumbered by the inconvenience of laws and ethics.

"I'll tell you everything soon, my love, I promise."

Rolling her eyes, Stella sneered, "Yes, you will, or you can go straight to hell!" She was one of only a handful of individuals who could speak to him as an equal, question him, curse him, make demands, and continue breathing.

The bearded man walked back to his work area. Opening a desk drawer, he removed several well-stuffed plastic bags full of money and gingerly handed them to Stella.

"It's all there," the bearded man asserted. "Fifty thousand dollars. There's a Gucci bag over by the bed you can use to transport it. I know how you love Gucci. I don't know why I couldn't just transfer it into a bank account. This seems so archaic, so old-fashioned, like a Bogart film, eh? You always wanted to be a silver screen movie star."

Without missing a beat, Stella slapped the man hard across his bearded face. With wrathful intent, she threw the sealed bags onto the floor.

"I don't find any of this amusing! Do you think I give a damn about the money or the theatrics of this situation? I'm doing this to get that damn woman out of our lives forever!"

Shocked yet oddly aroused by Stella's sudden violence towards him, the bearded man rubbed his cheek and turned away so that she would not see him smirking. He felt his manhood hardening, and his sex drive, his need to fuck, was amplified by Stella's animus towards him. It was twisted and kinky, and he loved it.

Any other time, he would have beaten or killed anyone who dared to strike him. His darling Stella, however, was universally exempt from his wrath. Right now, he understood her fury.

Hastily turning back to Stella, the bearded man apologized for his flippant tone. Looking into her eyes, he verbally castigated himself for not understanding how hard it must have been for her to have mourned him for so long. And now she had to deal with his resurrection and subsequent demands for secretive, conspiratorial aid. He promised that the next time they were alone together, he would tell her everything—and then make passionate love to her.

Stella returned to her stone-like countenance but still managed to muster enough feeling to reprimand him one last time before leaving him to his shadows and clandestine activities.

Bending down, the bearded man quietly collected the money, placing all of it into the expensive bag. He promised to have it sent to her limo for safekeeping.

"Just keep your promise," Stella snarled. "It's the least you can do after putting me through all this."

"And if Phillip gets in the way?"

"I'll handle Phillip."

The bearded man grinned mischievously. "Like you handled Charles?"

"What's that supposed to mean?" Stella snapped back.

"Stop fearing his knowledge, my love. He can't make most of it public to injure you without implicating the company. He knows Jules won't stand for that. The company is her life. Don't fret about it. I'll deal with Charles soon enough. Denise looked lovely tonight. Is she well? Happy?"

"Leave her be," Stella commanded. "She has her problems right now, and, yes, I'm handling it. You don't need to get involved."

Satisfied she had made her point, Stella turned towards the door to leave; however, she was stopped in her tracks by the bearded man's closing statement to her. It was a most welcome overture of affection. It was a declaration, a promise, that put a cruel, delighted smile on her formerly frozen countenance.

"My love, per our agreement, Jules will be dead by tomorrow night."

Denise scanned the busy room, frenetic with loud conversation, looking for her mother. The chaos created by the Parisians' arrival was thick, crafting visual confusion. There was no trace of her anywhere.

Denise stared at her brother as he stood quietly next to Jules like a handsome somnambulist. She scoffed at how Phillip, the legacy of the Cartell empire, the pride and joy of their dearly departed father, had been reduced to the role of Jules's arm-candy. He stood at his wife's side, bereft of intellectual substance, seemingly forbidden to join in the conversation.

Shaking her head angrily, Denise was disgusted at the impotent eunuch her brother had become. She loved Phillip immensely, but she was secretly ashamed of him for what he had let happen to himself. Denise could not comprehend the power Jules had over her brother. One that compelled him to remain in a sham marriage, claiming he still loved his utterly unlovable wife.

Denise took a moment to reflect on the promise she had made to herself months ago. *It has to end, no matter what. Jules has to go!*

Several minutes earlier, Denise had joylessly witnessed her downtrodden brother's feeble attempt to greet the Frenchmen. She had watched helplessly from the sidelines as Phillip was passed over in favour of his wife's loquacious salutations and forceful presence.

After abruptly leaving his sister's side, Phillip had trekked across the ballroom floor to welcome the guests of honour as his duty as co-CEO. Extending his hand outwardly in friendship towards the first of the three Frenchmen, Phillip had smiled widely before speaking, "Bonjour, mes amis. *Hello, my friends.*"

Right on the heels of her husband, Jules had pushed Phillip aside, exclaiming in a more forceful, captivating tone, "Bonsoir, messieurs. Il est tout simplement merveilleux de vous voir tous à nouveau! *Good evening sirs. It is just wonderful to see you all again!*"

Instantly charmed and impressed with Jules's more appropriate greeting, the Frenchmen completely ignored Phillip, brazenly brushed past him, and shook hands with his wife.

She hated to do it, but Denise had to admit that Jules's French accent and diction were flawless.

Denise was fluently bilingual like her father had been and like Stella was, but rarely spoke it outside her professional life.

Joseph had loved the language, speaking French conversationally as well as professionally. Phillip could converse in French, but he continuously mixed up his conjugations and tenses, often forgetting that European French and Québécois French had several distinct differences.

While Denise continued searching for her mother, Jules zealously waved down Jacques to invite him over to meet the Frenchmen. After a brief introduction, Jacques ushered the group into the dining room. Dinner was ready.

As the four men departed, Jules quickly pulled her husband aside to yell at him. She had no desire to be subtle or reticent; in fact, she planned on being loud enough for Denise to hear everything.

"Really, moron?" Jules hissed. "Formality means everything to them, and you go with 'Bonjour, mes amis?' They're not your friends, and they're from France, not Québéc. Your father spoke French as well as any Québécois, yet here you are tripping over words a child could master. All that time in Montréal, and you're still completely useless in these situations. I'll do the talking for the rest of the night. Just stay at my side, be silent, and look pretty."

With a pernicious grin, Jules motioned her husband towards the dining room.

From her vantage point, Denise lamented the hang-dog expression her brother now wore. She made a mental note to make sure Jules got what was coming to her.

Abruptly, Christophe snuck up beside Denise and nudged her out of her thoughts. He alerted her to her mother's sudden reappearance and suggested they join the other guests at the dinner table. Denise directed Christophe to go ahead of her, which he begrudgingly did; he was used to obeying her constant, bossy directions.

"What's with the disappearing act, Mom?" Denise boldly asked, blocking her mother from entering the dining room. "Jules is running roughshod over Phillip, and you decide—what? You're bored and wander off? It's bad enough we arrived too late to curtail his drinking, but now she's got him acting like a hired escort! He's one step away from carrying her fucking purse around! I needed your help! Where were you?"

Stella waved away her daughter's questions and condemnations. She had no intention of explaining her clandestine actions to anyone. Instead, she brushed Denise off and suggested she stop being rude and vulgar. Stella insisted that there would be time to talk about Phillip and Jules later.

Denise knew better than to continue to assault her mother with more questions. She stifled her interrogation, took her mom's arm, and walked with her towards the dinner that was already underway. The two Cartell women made their gracious apologies to everyone for their tardiness and took their assigned seats.

Jules and Phillip were seated opposite each other at the two ends of the table, but Jules had made sure the focus was on her section. She had deliberately placed Jacques, Miles, and the Frenchmen close to her. Marie's assigned seat, directly to the left of Jacques, remained empty.

Despite the irritation Jules knew percolated behind Jacques's handsome face, hidden by exquisite French charm and manners, she felt completely indifferent towards the empty chair.

Just moments before the Parisians' arrival, Marie had sent Jacques a text explaining her unplanned but necessary absence.

She had returned to the suite to relieve the nanny, and she was going to bed. The text also included the words *headache*, *hate*, and *that bitch*.

Not pleased, Jacques had furtively whispered in Jules's ear a warning about the coming discussion he planned on having with her about whatever went down between the two women that evening. Jules had simply sighed and smiled devilishly.

As the waiters poured the wine, Phillip, depressed and embarrassed by his drunkenness, declined his server's offering of Château Le Pin. He sipped his water, passively picking at his meal.

In a not-so-low whisper, Christophe made an off-colour joke about Phillip's uncharacteristic refusal of alcohol. He referenced it as a sign of the coming apocalypse. In response, Denise jammed the high-heel of one of her Manolo Blahniks into Christophe's leg and quietly, but firmly, told him to shut up.

Attempting to distract from Christophe's noticeable wincing, Miles complimented Jacques on the wine's vintage, aroma and fullness.

The Frenchmen commented on how they could taste the richness of the black cherry and currant infusions.

Jules exalted Jacques's taste level and accommodating nature. "Only the best of everything for the guests of Château Bergé."

The Parisians nodded to one another in agreement and toasted their hosts.

Jules sat back in her chair, extremely self-satisfied.

Having no interest in Jules's smugness, Stella moved on to other conversations with the dinner guests seated close to her and Phillip.

Denise was extremely puzzled by her placement so close to Jules. At this distance, she was forced to sit through her sister-in-law's shameless outpouring of admiration for Jacques, Château Bergé, and the Parisians' successful textile business.

After Jacques, who sat directly on Jules's left, and Marie's vacated seat, the only thing separating Christophe and her from Jules was Miles. This put her within earshot of anything Jules said, including the inevitable disparaging comments about Phillip. Denise wondered if that was the point of her assigned seat.

So why had her mother been spared?

Denise knew very little about Miles except that he was gay and consistently well-dressed. He seemed somewhat stuffy to her, a suit and tie guy, and basically boring. She doubted her sister-in-law kept him around for his conversational skills or social dynamism. Like Jules, he was all business; Denise figured he was likely excellent at following orders.

Even though Denise had never heard Miles speak a negative word towards or about Phillip, his loyalty to Jules automatically placed him on her "not to be trusted" list.

As the dinner rolled on, Denise watched in amusement as Miles expended a great deal of energy attempting to engage her boyfriend in conversation. Christophe, a model, was charming and devastatingly handsome even by industry standards, so it never surprised Denise when anyone flirted with him. Like Jacques, Christophe was prettier than her brother, less robust. He did share more of the athletic brawn of Phillip than the leanness of Jacques, though.

An intellectual, however, Christophe was not, at least in Denise's approximation. She was good with that because he was excellent arm candy at social events and great in bed. For now, that satisfied her needs.

Denise was unbothered by Miles's interest in her boyfriend. In their short time together, she had come across people who found themselves insanely attracted to Christophe. Denise was not the jealous type; at least, nothing had been overt enough to bring on that feeling of insecurity. She found the current situation humorous. And Miles? Completely harmless.

Giggling to herself, Denise leaned in towards Miles and disclosed her take on the situation. She thought for sure he would appreciate the candidness of her observations.

"Mr. Chen, if you want to flirt successfully with my boyfriend and gain his attention, you need to start talking about Christophe's weakness—expensive cars. Or talk about his career. Butter up his ego. Otherwise, I doubt he'll give you the time of day. Stop going on about business and finance. Trust me, it's going way over his gorgeous head."

Denise laughed hard, completely aware she had just mocked her now angry, red-faced boyfriend's intelligence to embarrass Miles in front of Jules.

Unamused by Denise's buffoonery, Miles sneered at her. Then, he proceeded to ignore the intrusion into his private conversation. However, he subtly turned the focus of his verbal exchange away from business towards his admiration for the well-tailored designer suit Christophe wore.

When she realized that Miles was not taking the bait, would not play with her, Denise resolved to move on and stick it to Jules.

"My hat's off to you, Jules. This is an amazing event you put together at the last minute. Bravo! It could have been a huge bust. I bet you wish you could have done more, but I'm sure you tried your best. At least there aren't any balloons. Joking, joking! But it's a shame you had such short notice about their arrival."

Denise punctuated her last statement by rudely pointing at the Parisians.

Confused, the Parisians looked at each other and mumbled to themselves.

Returning his attention to Jules, one of the French businessmen said, "Je ne comprends pas. *I don't understand.* You knew we were coming weeks ago."

Jules, perturbed, shot her sister-in-law a nasty look.

Denise shook her head, pretended to look mildly embarrassed, and continued her tall-tale.

"I'm sorry, gentlemen. Perhaps I shouldn't have said anything. You see, Jules is a wonderfully autocratic dictator at Cartell Worldwide, but she tends to spread herself a little thin. She has so much on her plate these days that she forgets things. To clear up space on her overbooked schedule, I'm sure Jules would gladly overlook her marriage to conduct meetings in her bedroom if it proved convenient."

All three sets of Parisian eyes grew big as they attempted to accept and process what they had just heard.

The other guests ended their intimate conversations to listen to Denise skewer Jules. Despite their reverence and admiration for Jules, these representatives of wealth enjoyed seeing one of their own knocked down a few pegs now and then. Just to keep things interesting.

Though linked to the joke, Phillip understood his sister's intent, and he loved her all the more for it. He joined in the uncomfortable yet welcome blitheness everyone felt at Jules's expense.

Unfortunately for Denise, Jules never backed down from a confrontation; she was a fighter, and her armoury was extensive. Words were weapons to her.

"Denise, my sweet sister-in-law, you certainly are jocose. I shouldn't have wasted money on live music when I had a clown right in my midst waiting to perform for free. What luck to be in the presence of a comedic master like yourself, one so naturally, so absolutely devoid of common sense, she makes a fool of herself for the direct purpose of our entertainment. Our very own personal court jester.

"Now, is the Sol the Clown hair and makeup all part of the unexpected comedy routine? Or were you just in too much of a hurry to get here for the free food to finish applying it properly?"

Unable to stifle their mirth, several of the guests chuckled out loud.

Christophe quietly mentioned to Miles that he loved watching old Sol the Clown clips on YOUTUBE as he had not been born yet when it was running on TVOntario. Miles replied, coolly, that he had no idea who this person was. He had not been allowed to watch television growing up or use the computer for anything unrelated to schoolwork.

"I guess there's no point in bringing up *Jeremy the Bear* then," Christophe sighed, rolling his eyes.

Ignoring the whispers around her, Jules quickly turned back to the confused Frenchmen. She explained in a low, conspiratorial tone the root of what they had just witnessed.

"Messieurs. Mes sincères excuses. *Gentlemen. My sincere apologies.* My sister-in-law is mentally unsound. Sadly, Denise is also a compulsive liar, and I'm afraid alcohol brings out the worst in her. What can you expect? Just look at her brother. Unfortunately, in this country, one cannot lock away disruptive family embarrassments in asylums like they used to. It's generally best to ignore the poor, pathetic soul as I do.

"Now, everyone, please finish your meal, and we'll continue with our night. Jacques and I have a wonderful evening planned — without any more banal interruptions."

Instinctively, Jacques came to Jules's defence. He promised the Frenchman that he had personally worked with her for two weeks to ensure their stay at Château Bergé was exceptional. This party for them had definitely been planned in advance and prioritized.

Jules winked at Jacques. Though she did not need a knight in shining armour to rescue her from vexatious situations, she still appreciated his support.

Placated by Jules's quick tongue and Jacques's professional decorum, the Frenchmen accepted the explanations and the apologies. The Parisians all turned and looked at Denise. With pity in their eyes, they shook their heads in unison.

This act of dismissal infuriated Denise, yet she remained oddly quiescent. She felt conquered by Jules's fierceness. Despite wanting to verbally retaliate, Denise realized that going further with her insulting quips, she would have to contend with Jules and her cogent thrall and supporter, Jacques. For now, she simmered, ceding the battle of words and wits to Jules.

Not long after dinner, Denise and Stella convinced Phillip to accompany them home. They knew that if he stayed without their watchful eyes on him, he would eventually succumb to the free bar again as well as Jules's unrelenting disdain. Phillip was only too glad to leave, but he made a mental note to visit the well-stocked liquor cabinet in his den before going to bed.

As for Jules, this en masse departure left her exactly where she wanted to be: with Jacques, free of her husband and his family, and the need to be constantly on guard.

V

Christophe's SRT Viper drove smoothly. The drive around town was just what he needed, giving him time alone to ponder and reflect. Denise found his fascination with fast sports cars childish, and she would have called this car a supercilious show of male ego. He was glad she was ignorant of its existence.

When Denise left the party, Christophe had gone with her, but it was not by choice. It was an expectation. His preferences were irrelevant; ultimately, where Denise went, so did he.

Christophe had been relieved when an invitation to spend the night was not issued. Frankly, he had had enough of the Cartells and their haughtiness for one evening, partaken enough of the bullshit drama, including his calculated charade. He needed his Oscar-worthy performance as the doting boyfriend to end—at least for the rest of the night.

It was only a matter of time before he could deep-six it all together.

When he finally had his fill of driving around, thinking about his life, Christophe turned back in the direction of his luxury condo. He owned the place, it was in his name, but someone else had paid for it. He kept this secret, like many others, close to his chest. It was a secret the one who had bought the place had asked him to keep.

Christophe had his own money. His career was very successful. One could often look in the pages of GQ or Numero Homme and find his handsome mug in a designer suit plastered across a photo spread. He was currently refocusing his brand towards high-end catalogues, fashion magazine spreads, and product endorsement rather than runway work. He had recently signed a million-dollar contract with a top men's cologne manufacturer.

Christophe's extravagant lifestyle, one to which he had not been born into but had grown very accustomed to, was gladly augmented by the love of his life. They had been together for years, but their relationship was a long-time secret. It was not his choice. Christophe had no idea when it would ever be made public, but he was in love and did what was asked of him whether he agreed with it or not.

Parking in his garage, waiting for the automatic door to close, Christophe looked at his iPhone. The device had beeped during his drive. He recognized the number instantly.

The text message was two words: **Come over.**

Christophe checked himself over in the rear-view mirror for sheer vanity. His seductive Scandinavian features looked back at him in the glass. "Damn, I'm hot!"

His straight blond hair, styled to the right of his scalp in the flirty, innocent way Christophe liked to wear it, remained in place thanks to his Paul Mitchell Finishing Spray. His high cheekbones cast a slight undershadow, and his piercing eyes betrayed the tiniest amount of redness due to the late hour. Overall, his comeliness eclipsed the signs of fatigue.

Christophe licked his naturally plump, pink lips, quickly applying lip balm when he noticed how dry they were.

Taking out a blue, half-empty bottle of cologne from his messy glove compartment, he spritzed himself a few times for good measure. He loved Jean Paul Gaultier's Le Male so much he once jokingly tweeted about filling up his bathtub and bathing in it.

In and out of different automobiles over the last few hours, Christophe's designer suit was somewhat wrinkled by the constant contorting of his body. *Oh well, it won't remain on too much longer for it to matter.*

Jules's eyes opened wide. Her toned muscles, conditioned by years of Muay Thai training, tensed as they revived and reacted to what her mind commanded of them: prepare to strike. Jules's instincts were sharp, and she always trusted them.

A noise, just loud enough to wake her, told her there was an intruder in her home.

Jules quickly scanned her bedroom, but the area was too thick with shadow, curtained by darkness her eyes could not penetrate. She thought about turning on the table lamp next to her but immediately dismissed the notion. She did not want to alert the invader to the fact that she was conscious and vigilant.

Instead, she turned towards her husband.

Phillip laid blissfully asleep beside her, utterly oblivious to the potential danger lurking nearby. The copious amounts of alcohol he had ingested earlier that evening had rendered him completely unconscious.

Jules doubted Phillip's senses were properly functioning; nevertheless, she attempted to secure his aide. If there was a trespasser in their home, it was his responsibility to deal with it as well.

"Phillip! Wake up! There's someone in the house. The party's over, and we're home, about to be violated, quite possibly murdered." She did not believe that, but it sounded good to her. "Wake up, idiot!"

Jules received no significant, animated response. She rolled her eyes, irritated, but not surprised by her husband's utter uselessness.

"Drunken piece of shit! Like everything else, I'll deal with this myself!"

Secure in her belief that silence meant safety, Jules got out of bed and walked across the room. Soundlessly, she eased her naked body into the Chanel robe that hung on the back of the en-suite bathroom door.

Jules occasionally slept naked next to Phillip in bed. Teasing him mercilessly with the frustratingly close yet just-out-of-reach presence of her bare flesh provided her with endless joy and satisfaction, especially knowing that it confounded him, driving Phillip mad with blue balls.

Jules enacted her tortures wherever and whenever she could.

Once her breasts were inside the robe and covered up, Jules wrapped the satin belt around her waist, tightly tying it. It was crap armour, but she had to make do.

Due to the lack of light, Jules carefully returned to her side of the room, sat on the edge of the bed, and positioned herself closely in front of the custom-made, thick cherry wood nightstand. The top drawer, always locked, contained only one object, and it was rarely opened due to the function of, and need for, this one specific item.

Jules removed a hidden key from the near-invisible, secret alcove clandestinely built into the back of the nightstand on her request. Hastily opening the drawer, she reached in and removed a loaded Beretta NANO 9mm semi-automatic pistol.

Despite her long-standing distaste for firearms, Jules eventually came to realize that the modern world was often brutal in its unpredictability; its lie of rational civilization in the face of constant violence precluded that she had to know her way around a gun. After careful research, including testing how it felt in her hand, Jules ultimately decided that the Beretta NANO was her gun of choice.

Until tonight, Jules had never removed the pistol from the drawer for any reason other than scheduled target practice. She planned on using it to wound—or kill if she had to. The thought of calling 911 or alerting the neighbourhood security patrol never crossed her mind. Even in a moment of potential peril, Jules believed she could handle things better than anyone.

Gripping the weapon securely, she exited her bedroom.

Motioning cat-like down the hallway, Jules listened carefully for unexpected movement in the mansion. Squinting, she peered into the obsidian darkness, searching for her enemy.

Suddenly wondering if she was overreacting, Jules considered the possibility that her home's current guests, both of whom had long overstayed their welcome, had made the startling noise. Not that they were ever welcome in the first place. At least not by her.

Immediately after Sonja departed for Europe, Stella had informed Phillip that the Toronto residence held too many memories of her life with Joseph to endure alone and planned to relocate, at least temporarily, to Fairporte, to be close to him.

Believing it to be the perfect solution to curtail his mother's loneliness and provide him with an ally against Jules's ever-increasing hostility towards him, Phillip had invited his mother to move into his home, a massive dwelling with many unoccupied rooms.

Phillip did not consult Jules. Feeling betrayed by his own company and forced into removing his mother from the Board of Directors, he would be damned if he let anyone tell him who could and could not live in his own house.

Blindsided by Phillip's unexpected resolve and refusal to back down, Jules pushed back hard; it got ugly.

The situation forced Charles to intervene. He was a calming influence. He told his daughter not to waste her valuable energy fighting Phillip on this, reminding her that she had already won the more significant fight in making Stella inconsequential to her family's business.

Jules eventually conceded—with one catch. Stella was set up on the opposite side of the mansion, as far away from her daughter-in-law as possible.

Unfortunately for Jules, Stella's "temporarily" had morphed into "semi-permanent" with no foreseeable plans to move back to Toronto.

And now Denise lived with them too.

After finishing her graduate work, Denise had moved to Fairporte instead of remaining in Vancouver or returning to Toronto and its famous Fashion District. She saw the same untapped potential for success in Fairporte that Jules did; it was one of their commonalities, of which there were few.

When Phillip opened his home to his family without Jules's permission a second time, the same quarrel had occurred between husband and wife, forcing Charles to step in again. He reiterated his stance that fighting this scenario was an unnecessary distraction. He reminded Jules that Denise was the least important of all the Cartells and presented no real threat to anyone. She was merely an annoyance.

Again, Jules reluctantly relented, but that was the last time she allowed Phillip to get the upper hand.

Currently, as she listened to the untrustworthy silence emanating from her mansion, Jules discounted the involvement of either woman in the creation of the circumstance she now found herself in. Stella and Denise were in their rooms on the other side of the mansion with no actual need to be in her immediate vicinity at this late hour; Jules was confident it was an intruder. How they got past the state-of-the-art security system was a mystery.

Unfortunately, Jules knew it could only mean one thing; they were well-trained professionals and not random thieves.

They?

Unsure of the number of intruders, Jules scolded herself for making assumptions. She was glad she had the gun and her martial arts training.

Suddenly, the clang of a bell rang out in the darkness.

Jules instantly scowled, recognizing the unwelcome sound as something from her past. Back then, it meant a training session was about to commence. Jules figured her instinctual recognition of the sound was what had forced her to consciousness earlier.

She now knew, without question, that the intruder was a single person.

But this was no ordinary intruder—this was an assassin.

Upon arriving at his destination, Christophe parked in the visitor section of the luxury condominium. Walking into the security-locked entrance, he buzzed the memorized number. When a long, loud mechanical hum unlocked the main door, Christophe entered and made his way to the sixth floor. When he got to room 612, he knocked twice and waited.

The strong fragrance of incense wafted out from under the door into the hallway. Christophe despised floral scents, but whatever. He planned on being invariably too occupied to obsess about it or be distracted by it. He only had one thing on his mind, and it sure as hell was not potpourri.

When the door finally opened, Miles stood in front of him, wearing nothing but a grin on his face.

"That was a pretty ballsy move seating us next to you," Christophe smirked.

Remaining composed, Miles asked, "Speaking of balls, Mr. Bennet, is this visit business or pleasure?"

"Shut up, Miles."

Aggressively, Christophe pushed his way inside. He slammed the door closed behind him with his long, muscular leg and hungrily crashed into Miles's mouth with his own.

Moving stealthily along the contours of the mansion's walls, Jules darted in and out of the darkness. The shadows embraced her, masking her advancing figure. She listened with skillfully trained ears for the slightest break in the silence—a creak from a floorboard, a displaced item of furniture, anything. Despite this action, Jules highly doubted she would hear her assailant, for she knew the assassin's skills to be unparalleled.

Without warning, a black shape dislodged itself from the darkness and lunged at her.

Jules was startled, but only for a second. Still, she was shocked by her unpreparedness.

Quickly silencing her mind, Jules gave herself over to instinct—the instinct to survive! She summoned up the abilities she had learned and mastered from her extensive training to aid her. *Be silent. Be sleek. Be quick.*

Jules positioned her gun directly in the path of the figure, prepared to fire. Unfortunately, the dark, human shape possessed speed Jules was unprepared for, and as a result, the figure disarmed her with a roundhouse kick that knocked the weapon to the floor.

"Slow and sloppy," the dark figure chided. "I trained you better than that."

Jules silently cursed the unwelcome and all too familiar female voice. Although she could not see her face, there was no doubt in Jules's mind about the identity of her attacker. If she wanted to match her opponent's ferocity and proficiency, she had to perform better. A lot better. Jules had one serious fight on her hands; it was a fight she was not sure she could win.

Now, out in the open, the assassin moved and stood in front of the large, first-floor windows. Bathed in bright moonlight, they became all the more perceptible to Jules.

Yes, it's her. Damn you, Amanda.

The assassin's lithe body, clad in a skin-tight, black catsuit with full head covering revealing only her eyes, struck a powerful fighting stance. Jules recognized it immediately: Doko Ichimonji no kamae—the angry tiger stance.

"Ninjitsu, eh," Jules whispered.

The assassin gave no response.

Jules quickly assessed her opponent. *No obvious weaponry on her uniform, no bladed weapons, and certainly no firearms. So, strictly hand-to-hand combat.* She was uncertain of the purpose of this melee, her assassin's objective, or the inevitable outcome.

Amanda Reid. Top in her field, a hit-woman extraordinaire, she was a killer known in secret circles as the Silver Dagger.

Despite how things had ended between them, Jules never thought Amanda would accept a contract, possibly taken out by Stella, to kill her, not with their history. Unfortunately, the proof was in the pudding, and Jules had to accept it. Amanda was here—in her home. The Silver Dagger, the blonde-haired purveyor of death, had come for her.

Regardless of how good her opponent was, Jules was determined to give her the fight of her life. She countered Amanda's pose with her defensive Shotokan position, figuring Amanda expected her to use a strictly Muay Thai leg and elbow attack. Jules thought her selection of Karate would surprise her assailant.

It did not.

"I'm aware of your training in Shotokan, Jules. I trained with Master Hiroki, as well, years back. We keep in touch."

Damn! Jules's thoughts raced. *Keep calm and breathe. Change strategy from defence to attack. Now!*

Jules leapt into the air, twisting her body into a forward kick motion. Pulling her left leg in tight, she focused all her momentum and strength into her extended right leg and directed it toward Amanda's head. Jules hoped her unexpected, aggressive strike was enough to place her opponent off-balance, allowing her devastating blow to connect.

Supple, like a blade of grass in the wind, Amanda effortlessly bent her head and upper torso back, away from the crushing blow; as a result, Jules's body flew right over her opponent, completely missing her.

Disgusted by her failure to connect her blow, Jules reverted to her Muay Thai training. She swiftly transformed the now crouched position of her body into a deadly elbow thrust that sprang upwards towards her adversary's nose.

Amanda deftly deflected this new attack with her strong right arm.

Now on the offensive, Amanda clasped her arms around Jules's outstretched limb, quickly set herself in the best position for balance and strength, and body-flipped her opponent onto her back.

As Jules gasped for breath, Amanda laughed, stepped over her, and walked away slowly, her back exposed, unprotected. She did not take advantage of her enemy's weakness at that moment. She should have brought her foot crashing down on Jules's trachea, crushing it, killing her, ending the melee. Amanda did not see a threat to her and wanted it to be known.

This action angered Jules terribly, which she figured was the point. *Not that I want to die, but to be so bloody disrespected!*

To get back into the fight, Jules quickly transfigured her body. She bent her arms, placed her palms down on the ground behind her head, brought her legs in toward her chest, and then jumped, rapidly swinging her legs forward. Once upright, her feet firmly on the ground, Jules raced towards Amanda.

Without hesitation, she jumped into consecutive forward flips, building up momentum as she went. The goal was to snap Amanda's spine with the built-up force of Jules's leg coming into contact with it.

Jules had attempted this move once before, with questionable success, during a practice session with Master Hiroki. She had no idea if this flashy move would work in reality, but she was desperate to try something Amanda would not expect.

Concentrating on keeping her balance and trajectory on-point, Jules did not see her opponent's counter-move coming, too caught up in the performance of her own complicated movements.

Amanda, calm and focused, turned in a perfect pirouette and jutted her leg out like a deadly naginata.

Unable to stop herself, Jules's solar plexus connected with the powerful limb, and the suddenness and potency of the strike was too much for her acrobatics to compensate for. Jules was, unequivocally, laid—out—flat.

"That was an excellent show of creativity and desperation, Jules. You do realize that I know you've always wanted to try and master that move from *A Nightmare on Elm Street*. The fourth movie, right? 'Welcome to Wonderland, Alice.' Trust me, moves like that take too much thinking to work. They're fun, I'll give you that, but they're highly inefficient movie magic fantasy. This isn't the Matrix, honey. Now, get up!"

Jules understood clearly that her opponent's moves were too well-choreographed, too exact, too powerful. Amanda was just too damn good! Jules had no idea how she could win this and survive.

With no other option but to keep going to her last breath, Jules got back on her feet and repositioned herself back into her

Shotokan defensive stance. She could not match Amanda's skill, but she refused to lay down and die.

Suddenly, a plan of action came to Jules. She realized that she needed to think logically. It was better for her if she remained on the defensive and wore her opponent down by consciously making an effort to deflect and repel, not attack outright. If she could keep that up long enough, she might eventually find a weak spot in Amanda's fighting technique to exploit.

For ten minutes, the two warrior women fought, their aggressive moves remarkably graceful, hushed. Jules's movements were almost all reactive, striking out only if she saw an opportunity to land a blow. Amanda's moves were all offensive, unrelenting.

Jules knew enough killing blows to understand Amanda was deliberately avoiding using them. *This bitch is holding back, sparring with me, testing me! She's not trying to kill me. Enough of this!*

Jules waited for the perfect moment to move out of her opponent's direct line of sight. As soon as Amanda took a second to change her stance, Jules knew now was the time to end this game. She had to act fast.

Running over to where her gun had landed, Jules swiftly picked it up and fired several shots through the windows. The glass shattered; the noise was deafening; that was the point. Jules wanted to rouse Phillip and bring others to her defence, like her gated neighbourhood's private security force.

Her gun had only one bullet left.

"Help will be here momentarily. Unless you plan to kill all of us, I suggest you leave, Silver Dagger."

Amanda bowed graciously. "I guess our time's up. This was fun, just like old times. You did—okay. Anyway, I'll be in touch. Soon. And Jules? Tonight I'm Amanda. This was a simple, playful visit. If Silver Dagger had come for you, you'd no longer be breathing."

Having got the last word, Amanda jumped out the damaged window, easily side-stepping the shattered remains of the glass with Olympic-level agility. Like a ghost, she disappeared into the night.

Out of the corner of her eye, Jules noticed lights on upstairs. Then, the sound of Phillip's loud, distressed voice called out to her. She figured the neighbourhood security detail was probably only moments away from her door, too. *If there was ever a time to think fast on your feet, woman, this is it.* Amanda's involvement in tonight's chaotic happenings had to remain a secret.

"Jules!" Phillip called out, his eyes still crusted with sleep. "I heard gunshots! Are you okay? What the hell's going on?"

Phillip's genuine concern for his wife, his instinct to protect his family took full command of his body. As he came into the living room, Phillip reached out for Jules, grabbed her aggressively, and wrapped her in his arms. He held her tight; he was almost in tears.

Jules's instinct was to knee Phillip in the groin and forcibly remove his grasping, lumberjack-like musculature from her aching body. But she stopped herself. No one could know that she had just engaged in actual physical combat. It was in her best interest to pass off Amanda's intrusion as an attempted robbery.

Against every fibre of her being that screamed for her to push her hated husband away, Jules allowed Phillip to comfort her. It sickened her to no end, but she did it, even placing her head on Phillip's heaving chest. It was a noteworthy performance, having never played a damsel in distress before, but Phillip needed to be distracted from noticing the bruises forming on her legs.

While Jules and Phillip remained in their quiet embrace, Denise entered the room alongside the mansion's live-in butler, Jackson. He had been in Stella's service for years. At the time of her relocation, she had brought him along. Jules thought he did good work, but she trusted him about as much as she trusted Stella.

"It had to be a burglar," Phillip explained to his sister.

Denise cast a strange glance at her brother and sister-in-law. As affection and concern were not the driving emotions of their relationship, she was shocked that Jules had allowed Phillip to be so close, so physically protective of her. Despite the unwelcome violence that had entered their home, Denise was glad it had rattled Jules's composure.

Calculating that enough time had passed to warrant her extraction from Phillip's embrace, Jules pushed against her husband's muscular arms, reminding him that she was still in possession of a loaded gun.

With a broad smile, Phillip released his wife. He then joined Jackson in intercepting the security team, who had been banging on the front door for some time. A few of them had already circled the outside of the house to survey the broken windows.

"Yes, a burglar," Phillip stated again. "No, he got away. Yes, you may come in, but my wife is very shaken up. You will give her a minute!"

Denise moved to ambush Jules. It was her ardent desire to test a theory.

"Jules, are you hurt? Do you need medical attention? Let me help."

Jules moved away from her sister-in-law and folded her arms. This pose placed the gun she held right into Denise's direct view. Jules had no interest in false concern. The look she rendered for her sister-in-law was threatening.

"I'm fine," Jules proclaimed coldly, storming out of the room to seek temporary refuge in the kitchen. She needed a minute to herself to collect her thoughts and concoct a story that everyone would believe. She knew it was not over between her and Amanda. Her past had come calling.

"I knew it," Denise whispered. *Jules isn't scared, and that ridiculous show of frailty in front of Phillip was a big fat lie. That bitch is hiding something. I have to find out what.*

VI

Stella sat regally at the head of Jules's custom teak dining table, enjoying her healthy, low-fat breakfast. Munching away on sugar-free marmalade drenched toast, she wondered about the events that had transpired mere hours ago. Sound asleep—thanks to a little blue pill—she had missed all the excitement. Having heard only staff gossip, Stella wanted facts. So far, only Phillip had spoken to her, and he had told her nothing of substance.

Earlier, on his way out the door to make an official police statement, Phillip had responded to his mother's request for answers by kissing her gently on the cheek, smiling widely, and telling her she had nothing to worry about.

This milquetoast response came as no surprise to Stella. Phillip lived in a perpetual state of chivalric regard towards his mother, constantly endeavouring to shield her from life's unpleasantries.

Stella understood this behaviour was a performance, a well-meaning facade of strength and certainty he put on for her, stemming from his deep feelings of guilt, shame, and remorse. Dark feelings brought to life the day he had been unable to prevent her ousting from Cartell Worldwide.

Stella meant no disrespect towards her son, but the truth of the matter was that Jules had psychologically and professionally castrated him. Phillip could not successfully lead or protect their family anymore. Of course, Stella had every intention of changing this fact with secretive and deadly help soon. Once Jules was permanently dealt with, the family fully expected Phillip to thrive again.

So, knowing all this about her son, Stella had played it coy, aped indifference, and allowed Phillip to act for her, prodding him no further to confirm the whispered gossip as fact.

Stella was not overly bothered by Phillip's predictably uncooperative demeanour; she was confident she would get the truth out of Denise once she emerged from her room.

Suddenly, Stella heard the sound of Jules's stern, shrill voice barking commands to her house staff; it sent shivers of irritation down her spine.

"Make sure all the glass and wood are swept up and removed before the contractors arrive," Jules ordered. "I want all traces of this incident erased today. Am I understood?"

Jules rarely ate breakfast at home, practically living off green tea Frappuccinos from Starbucks, so she was generally gone before anyone else was up. Today, however, she was running uncharacteristically late.

Jules's surprise appearance made Stella wickedly gleeful; the opportunity to sit down with her was one Stella was not going to let slip through her fingers. Believing this was probably the last time she would speak with Jules or see her breathing for that matter, Stella planned on interrogating her daughter-in-law for as long as possible. She wanted answers, and she planned on getting some now.

Annoying Jules in the process was simply a bonus.

Sitting up straight in her chair, Stella surveyed her imposing backdrop. It was how she liked it, not as it had been at the beginning of her residence in her son's home when she had been taken aback by the minimalist way the mansion was designed, furnished, and accented.

As a design theme, Stella appreciated modernity, but she felt Jules had taken contemporary flair and transmogrified it into cold, regulated dreck. Her daughter-in-law's penchant for starkness, clean lines, and muted colours was nothing short of a reflection of her icy, calculated, emotionally regimented personality.

Stella continually manipulated Phillip into allowing her to adjust the mansion's decor. Through the addition of warm, autumnal-coloured accents, dark espresso woods, and antique pieces, Stella incorporated as many personal touches as she could into her supposedly temporary home.

Combative towards the changes at first, Jules had quickly lost interest in fighting over trivial matters like furnishings and tchotchkes. She had bigger things on her plate to contend with than Stella's pathetically obvious manipulations of her son to gain herself material things.

Oddly enough, Charles liked the stylistic decor changes even though they had all come from Stella's meddling. Incidentally, as a testament to his conviction that Jules needed to embrace colour and texture, he had given her the vintage Baroque mirror she now used as part of her bedroom vanity.

Backed by Phillip's decree that all household employees were to follow his mother's commands to make her stay more pleasant, Stella had trained Jules's house staff to become as familiar with her habits and preferences as Jackson was.

Jules rarely acted like a diva towards her staff. She appreciated and lauded a hard work ethic, rewarding and chastising those in her employ based solely on their ability and attitude. It was never about being bitchy, dismissive or belittling for kicks; Jules did not subscribe to classism. She expected everyone in her employ to act professionally at all times and possess a high level of competency in their position.

Unfortunately, while her actual intent was always quickness, efficiency, and a recognizable set of boundaries between employer and employee, Jules's imperious behaviour perpetually came off as abrasive and unrelenting.

Stella worked this constant misunderstanding to her advantage, and she played the household staff against Jules by pretending to be their understanding, sympathetic ally.

As Jules spent less time at home and more time at her condo, the Cartell matriarch gradually stepped into the role of head of household, something she had wanted from the beginning. On paper, Jules's word was law, but the staff invariably followed Stella's direction. She was the most consistent presence in the home.

Stella was the person who despised the poor and working-class, not Jules, and she manipulated them whenever possible to get what she wanted. Her Polish parents had been working class, and she hated that she had grown up struggling and deprived. Her natural beauty and cunning ended up being her ticket out of mundanity. Modelling had given Stella the chance to escape, see the world, and she had never looked back.

Stella was a woman whom the universe had seemingly set up to be served by others, believing she was better than most, living her life as if she were royalty. And she felt she had put one over on her hated daughter-in-law.

Jules knew what was going on; she was no one's fool. She played her mother-in-law's games as well as the old bat herself. Better. Jules figured the higher Stella sat on her self-created throne, the farther and harder her inevitable fall would be.

When she eventually threw Stella out on her ass with just the clothes on her back, Jules planned to burn everything the old bitch had brought into the mansion, film the entire event, and upload the video to all her social media platforms.

To Jules, no form of revenge was petty; all revenge was reasonable.

Stella's habitual morning breakfast routine was a perfect example of her unwillingness to settle for anything but the best.

The Royal Doulton china and tea set, brought with her from Toronto, had been set out; the expensive dishes, plates, and tea service had the Royal Albert Moonlight Rose pattern on them. Jules's silver cutlery from Bed, Bath, and Beyond was gone, replaced with Stella's exquisitely beautiful and rather costly Reed and Barton Francis flatware. The crisp white table linens from Marks and Spencer were hand-embroidered in lace with her initials on them.

Gazing around the table at her fussy trappings, Stella was content.

"Jules, how unexpected to see you this morning," Stella prickly announced as her daughter-in-law came into view. "Please, sit down and partake of some refreshments. You look a little peaked, dear! Quite pale, almost sickly.

"You should have stayed in bed longer for extra beauty sleep. Sleep is important. I firmly believe it's one of the main reasons I'm so pretty. You should really get some more rest. All has not been copacetic with your day so far, I see. And to think—it's barely begun! The exhausting excitement from last night's frivolity coupled with this outrageous intrusion shows quite deeply—on your face."

Worry and anger concerning Amanda's unexpected visit had taken a toll on Jules. Sleep had not come easily, her mind racing throughout the rest of the night. It was true the strain did show across Jule's face, but it had not diminished her physical beauty one bit.

Though used to Stella being a cunty bitch, attempting to get a rise out of her, Jules never enjoyed showcasing any sign of weakness to her enemies. The punishment for her momentary loss of control over her routine was now having to contend with Stella's smug intrusiveness, her pathetic attempt to read her, and the unabashed display of elitism covering her dining room table.

"Stella, if anyone should be concerned about faces, it's you, considering you have two of them. I have to say this is quite the set-up here. Breakfast time with the royals, hmm? Frankly, I see more Mad Hatter than Elizabeth Windsor in front of me."

"Charming as ever, Jules. I'm going to ignore your indelicate taunt and pose a question. What exactly happened while I slept? I didn't hear a thing that occurred last night. This morning, I came down and saw that mess over there! What am I to think?"

Glaring down at Stella, Jules's thoughts were quick and angry. *Who the fuck cares what you think, you vile hag!*

Jules considered the older woman nothing more than an intrusive interloper who had the constant audacity to question her about things that were none of her damn business. Jules had no intention of revealing anything to her hated mother-in-law, and she had no plans to engage in a conversation with her that expanded beyond a few customary jabs.

While she wholeheartedly despised Phillip, Jules hated Stella nearly as much; both were complicit in the crime that had been perpetrated against her family many years ago. It mattered little to Jules that one was utterly unaware of the incident while the other knowingly helped cover it up. Jules had plans for all of those responsible for her pain to pay dearly. Stella's ousting from Cartell Worldwide had just been the first step.

Never doubting Stella's ability to be ruthless, Jules was thankful that the woman's only immediate recourse of vengeance was decisive verbal warfare and prying. Jules considered both weak attempts at retribution; neither had the power to derail her plans.

"It must kill you, Stella, to be so out of the loop, so inconsequential to everything that happens around here. I'm sure you've already grilled the staff to death using your trademark fake niceties in a pathetic attempt to glean information about last night.

"Let me give you some good, long-time-coming advice. Read your magazines, drink your tea, and don't think about anything other than your next Botox appointment. It's better for everyone if you just sink quietly into senility. No one owes you an explanation about what goes on in my home, not my staff, and certainly not me.

"I have much more important things to do, like run your dead husband's company and grind what's left of your worthless son's self-esteem into the ground."

Jules punctuated her last statement with both the physical movement of her foot, mashing her heel into the floor and a hearty, pernicious laugh. She eagerly bathed in the ire directed at her from Stella's newly harrowed countenance; the venomous rage nourished her, strengthening her resolve.

Stella briskly stood up from her seated position and slammed her fists down hard on the table. Violently disturbed by the force of her blow, several china plates careened off the wood surface and shattered to pieces on the floor. She quietly ignored the destruction of her beloved property, deciding instead to focus all her anger on her daughter-in-law and her vainglorious smirk.

Stella cocked her head and spat out a barrage of pointed curses.

"You arrogant, smug bitch! How dare you speak about my husband or my son in such a disrespectful manner! Enjoy your false sense of power and security, Jules, while you can. Cling to them like dying lovers while you still possess the luxury of ignorance. Sweetie, your days are numbered. Believe it!"

Jules kicked several pieces of broken china out of her way as she walked closer to the table and leaned in towards Stella. "Tough talk considering your weak position. Tell me, Stella, where are your allies and benefactors? Your cronies from the good old days? Looking at this pathetic makeshift surrogate of a boardroom, all I see around you is some overpriced dishware and empty seats.

"Sad, simple Stella. You're good at hosting parties and schlepping dresses down a runway, but without Joseph to back up your self-aggrandizing big mouth, you're nothing but an ineffectual fossil. Sticks and stones, bitch. My weapons are better, sharper, more precise. That's why I always win. And that's why I'm off to Cartell Worldwide, and you're staying here to wait for *Judge Judy* to come on.

"Now, as much as I always enjoy these little bonding moments with you, I need to be—well, anywhere else, really. Oh, one last thing before I go. As far as sleep helping you be pretty? Not by the hairs on your chinny-chin-chin."

With that last dig, and without wasting another breath, Jules ceremoniously dismissed her antagonist with another one of her baneful, condescending smiles. She categorically, and with much haste, turned her back on Stella, picked up her Dasein faux leather satchel bag from its resting place on top of the cherry-wood hallway desk and marched out the front door.

Stella moved away from the dining room table and hurriedly walked over to one of the smaller, undamaged windows in the living room. Scowling, she watched as Jules's limo drove away. Knowing the main obstacle to her family's happiness was on their way to inflict continued damage on her son's already fragile ego pained Stella greatly.

"I have to put a stop to this," she decreed.

Stella needed to find out more about the supposed break-in. If it was, as she suspected, the hired killer that was supposed to take Jules out, why did they fail?

"Jackson! Jackson!"

"How can I help you, Mum," Jackson inquired in his usual dutiful tone.

At the start of the volatile discussion between Jules and his employer, Jackson had hidden behind the main wall that separated the dining and living rooms to listen to the verbal duel, figuring the entertainment potential alone was incalculable.

No member of the family, including Jules, ever doubted Jackson's loyalty to the Cartells; they were never too concerned with what he heard or saw in the privacy of their home. He was the only member of the house-staff afforded this luxury of confidence. Jackson never assumed he possessed complete immunity regarding their ire and wrath, though. He was an employee, after all. He consciously made every effort to appear inconspicuous and non-threatening.

Like all the house staff, he had signed an NDA.

The truth was, Jackson was a hardened gossip who loved drama. He kept his eyes and ears open at all times. This attentive demeanour had garnered him the knowledge of a choice secret or two, and he guarded them closely.

Jackson liked his job well enough. Being a butler was in his blood as both his father and grandfather had been chief male valets in England, his country of birth. Still, he primarily loved the financial security his top-tiered household position provided him. Potentially losing that comfort due to a mistake or over-step on his part was not an option. To protect himself, he was not above blackmail if it ever came to that.

To complicate matters for himself, Jackson had fallen in love with his employer. Stella, of course, knew this and exploited that infatuation relentlessly. Long ago, Jackson had aided her in doing something very, very terrible.

"Jackson," Stella barked, "find Denise and tell her I need to see her immediately!"

After receiving Stella's command from a rather harried Jackson, Denise quickly prepared herself for an unpleasant conversation with her mother.

Standing on the landing at the top of the main stairs earlier, she had heard the angry, arguing female voices down in the dining room.

Getting into it with Jules was not for the weak of heart. Or the easily pissed-off. Denise regarded her sister-in-law as a master of verbal sparring who rarely lost her temper. On the rare occasions when she did lose her composure, Jules still managed to use her vexation and aggression to her advantage.

Denise felt Jules unfairly had both luck and skill on her side, and she suspected that her sister-in-law had gotten the better of her mother that morning. Much like she had done to her, Denise shamefully remembered during the dinner with the Parisians.

Gathering her courage, Denise walked down the stairs and went into the dining room.

"Good morning, Mom. Where's the fire?"

"Don't take that tone with me, Denise! I'm fit to be tied this morning! Why wasn't I informed immediately about this intruder last night? I had to hear it from Phillip as he left to go to the police station. Not that he said much of anything.

"What is this world coming to when a neighbourhood this exclusive isn't safe! And don't get me started on the lovely exchange I just had with Jules. How I hate that insufferable woman! What Phillip sees in her—what Joseph saw in her, I'll never understand."

"I think it's pretty obvious," Denise smirked. "Mom, I sometimes think that maybe you're just a tad jealous of her, no? Jules does tend to get the last word in."

Shocked, Stella looked at Denise sternly. She could not believe her daughter had just sassed her so outright. To think her own flesh and blood dared to suggest that Jules had something, possessed some traits or an ability she was lacking! It was an intolerable, absolutely ridiculous concept; Stella firmly believed Jules had nothing on her. Except for youth, of course, but she would pit life experience against that any day.

Stella decided right then and there that she had had enough of young people courting her ire with their ill-chosen words and indignant facial expressions. She was pissed, and someone was about to get an earful. *How dare my daughter speak to me this way! How dare she!*

"Wipe that smirk off your face," Stella roared. "How dare you suggest that Jules possesses anything I covet! What? Do you think because she has a quick, poisonous tongue, is unafraid to speak her mind, she possesses skills or traits that I once had but have seemingly lost? Do I look or sound feeble to you? Do you believe I've lost my touch?

"With age comes wisdom, dear daughter, and the savvy to know when to speak out or to hold one's tongue. When to strike and when to keep one's sword sheathed. I've already had this discussion with Phillip, but I now realize I've neglected your ongoing education for too long. Listen up, Missy.

"I've seen and done things in my life that people might call ruthless, brutal, self-serving. I'm not ashamed of my actions, and I would gladly do all of them again for the same results. I imagine these things I've done would shock and frighten someone like you. Born into privilege, protected, loved. You would be appalled, or at the very least disbelieve me, but make no mistake—it's all true! People like me will do whatever we have to and make no apologies.

"Denise, I love you with all of my heart, but if you *ever* sass me like that again, darling daughter, or suggest I desire Jules's youth, or lack Jules's vitality, I'll show you just how much of a spry, vengeful bitch I still am!"

Her mouth agape, Denise stood at the entrance to the dining room in disbelief. Her mother could be a bitch, but she had never spoken to her before in such a fashion. Not once had Stella threatened one of her children in such a Disney-villain way; not even conceited, self-centred Sonja, who often rebelled against her parents' strong imperatives.

Denise had to choose her following words carefully as they would determine her ultimate outcome: favourable or perilous. She figured it was probably unwise to further perturb her mother by standing up for herself and pushing back; Stella would only see it as further insolent back talk.

Denise decided it was safer to ignore everything her mother said after asking her initial question about the intruder. She would act like nothing vile had just happened to her.

"So—anyway." Denise paused for dramatic effect. "We assumed you had taken something to help you sleep. Since the gunfire and shattering glass hadn't woken you, I mean. We didn't want to force you awake and upset you in the middle of the night. Both Phillip and I decided to leave it until morning. The hidden safes are all intact. No personal items appear to have been stolen or even disturbed."

Stella poured herself another cup of tea and offered her daughter one as well.

Without lingering or showing annoyance on her face, Denise sat down at the table. With a silent nod, she accepted the offer. Denise watched her mother's languorous movements as she poured the hot brew: consummate control and poise.

"Denise, darling, I expect to be informed about everything concerning the family. Our well-being has always been my number one priority. If I'm kept in the dark or thought too infirm to handle negative news, I can't help anyone. I don't care how small or insignificant you think a morsel of knowledge is. I'll be the judge of its relevance and utilize it as best I see fit. Understood?"

"Loud and clear," Denise answered, devoid of sarcasm. She knew better.

"Good. Now, before I leave, is there anything else I should know?"

Thoughtfully, Denise pondered her mother's question. Yes, there was still one thing, but should she reveal her suspicions about Jules's strange behaviour earlier with Phillip?

Denise's rational mind could not write off those out-of-character actions as anything but dubious. The whole thing had come across like a ridiculous performance piece. The embrace, the show of weakness, allowing Phillip to enact a take-charge attitude regarding the aftermath of the incident—all of it!

It's all a ruse. It has to be. But to what purpose? What's she trying to hide?

Denise planned on investigating the matter further, but for now, she was not sharing. Not a scrap. Nothing. Not even juicy speculation about their shared enemy. Her mom did not deserve to know, not after the previous night's shenanigans. Denise sensed that her mother had something up her sleeve, her odd behaviour at the party suggested as much, and it bothered her that she was not in on it.

It bothered her a lot.

The only things Denise had been a part of lately were her mother's verbal abuse, her brother's drunken scenes, and Jules's disrespect. She was over the bullshit melodrama.

"No, mom, that's all I got. Now, if that's it, I have to get to the store."

Nodding approvingly, Stella watched her daughter leave the room with noted irritation. She knew Denise was angry with her, but she did not care about silly hurt feelings. Stella regarded the lesson she had just taught her daughter as understandably harsh but ultimately necessary, subscribing to the belief that, occasionally, one needed to be cruel to be kind.

VII

Leaning back in her chair, Jules slipped off her shoes and took a well-deserved rest. She had been going over contracts and other important documents all morning, checking to see if her legal team had potentially missed or omitted something. They were all very competent, top-notch performers, but they were not her. Nobody was.

Her father considered her a terrible micro-manager, but Jules was glad he respected her enough not to push the subject. It was not like anything he said would cause her to change her process, and they both knew it. She was an admitted control freak.

The breakfast meeting she had previously scheduled with Jacques had fallen through due to another of Marie's sudden disappearances.

Jacques spoke with Jules almost daily to talk about all kinds of things, but recently he had begun complaining to her a lot more about Marie's problems. With each conversation, Jules noticed Jacques's voice sounded less concerned and more annoyed. And this pleased her tremendously. Today, however, all she got from him was a short, apologetic text.

Rubbing her feet together under the desk, she quietly lamented the fact that she had not met up with him that morning. She had enjoyed being in his company at her party, and she selfishly wanted more of his time. She knew he wanted to be with her just as much.

Jules appreciated that Jacques never judged or condemned her for being a ruthless, determined woman, both personally and professionally. Even during the time of his family litigation issues, when she had taken advantage of his distraction and scooped up most of the city, he had not rebuked her. When the smoke cleared, they both knew that she had done him a favour.

Jules only wanted what was best for him, and Jacques never made her feel like she was a pushy, interfering bitch. They both freely gave each other advice and attention with no attitude.

Well, Jules *mostly* gave no attitude.

After the night she had just had, Jules needed something or someone to help ground her; Amanda's unexpected appearance in her home had seriously rattled her cage. As her father was away, Jacques was the only other person who could provide a calming effect. He almost always managed to ease her anxiousness by talking to her and kissing her doubts away.

Jules refused to sleep with Jacques as long as he was married, but kissing and other PG-13 forms of physical intimacy were not off-limits. Jacques acquiesced to all of it every time despite his so-called devotion to Marie. If he felt any guilt or shame, he never showed that suffering to Jules.

Some time had passed since Jules and Jacques first began confiding in one another. They shared their problems, empathized with each other's issues, and offered the best advice and direction they could. Since their very first meeting, their connection crackled with energy.

Jules's first visit to Château Bergé had been purely for business reasons, not for pleasure.

Six months into her marriage, Jules had transitioned from working exclusively as Cartell Worldwide's legal representation to a new position within the company: vice president of mergers and acquisitions.

At the time, Cartell Worldwide had been in the process of acquiring a new cutting-edge R&D company, a small, privately owned business that dealt primarily with biological research and experimentation.

Mode-Génétique Labs held various scientific patents at the forefront of innovation, but their funding was sporadic and unstable. Fearing stress and in-fighting precluded imminent bankruptcy, the owners realized they needed to be rescued by a company with deep pockets or face ruin. They were dreamers and scientists—not suits.

Unfortunately, much of the business community considered them a high-risk investment, publicly discounting their projected profitability and refusing to take a chance on them. They did not want to potentially compromise their financial solvency on what they feared was "questionable science."

Jules despised people who lacked vision, regarding those fools with contempt. To her, Mode-Génétique Labs would further diversify Cartell Worldwide's portfolio.

When she approached and offered the fledgling company a weighty proposal to acquire them, Jules guaranteed that Cartell Worldwide's resources and reputation would be at their fingertips to further their mutual goals and interests. Negotiations went smoothly until a business competitor from the United Kingdom threw their hat into the ring, attempting to undermine Jules's offer with something juicier. The building of a state-of-the-art facility for their exclusive use.

That rival company? Falsworth International.

Falsworth. A name that reminded Jules of two horrific moments in her life, moments she would rather forget.

With Joseph's approval, Jules and Phillip quickly set up a meeting with the heads of the R&D company at Château Bergé instead of Cartell Worldwide's Toronto headquarters. Joseph had been utilizing the Château for years to engage new business with a showy performance.

Jules believed in this young company's ingenuity and future success with every fibre of her being; incidentally, since Joseph believed totally in her, Jules was given the freedom and the finances to do whatever was necessary to win. That included using Joseph's connection to the famous Bergés.

At the last minute, however, an issue arose at the Vancouver branch. Joseph, too busy to go himself, sent Phillip to deal with it. Jules and a few of her brightest associates travelled to the meeting without the Cartell Worldwide heir in tow.

Instantly upon arrival, Jules's breath was taken away. She had never been to Château Bergé before, and though she had seen pictures of it, they did not do justice to the magnificence and elegance of the place. It was an absolute feast for the eyes, that is until Jules gazed upon Jacques Bergé for the first time. As he came into full view, a single word subconsciously escaped her lips.

"Dashing."

Jacques grinned. He had heard her; the word, barely a whisper, was audible nevertheless. He remained professional despite being flattered by the compliment; in fact, he was not even sure she realized she had spoken the word out loud.

Jacques jovially offered his hand to Jules; her welcoming smile lit up his face.

Jules noted his deep blue eyes appeared kind, as dazzling as her own. Jacques was dreamy and delicious, and her heart skipped a beat or two. Initially raising her hand to him weakly, Jules realized she was acting like a ridiculous schoolgirl, added more power to her limb and gave the man a solid handshake.

"Good morning, Mrs. Cartell. I'm Jacques Bergé. Welcome to Château Bergé."

Jules gazed at the man's striking form with piqued interest, a dash of desire, and absolute respect.

To Jules, Jacques was a man who had it all. Looks, manners, style, business aplomb. She admired the Diane von Furstenberg suit he wore. It was fashionable yet business-appropriate, and the fit was perfect. She pegged his silk, striped tie as Ermenegildo Zegna, and she knew he paid three hundred bucks for it. His shoes, dark brown with a high-grade sheen, were Ferragamo.

It took a moment before Jules realized that while she continuously shook his hand and inspected him from top to bottom, she had yet to respond to his greeting.

"Mrs. Cartell is my mother-in-law, M. Bergé," Jules stated directly. "Please, call me Jules or Ms. Cartell if you insist on formality. It's a pleasure to meet you. I have to say my breath was taken away—by your Château, I mean. What else could I have meant?" Jules laughed a little too heartily at that comment. "It's everything I imagined and more. You must be very proud."

Jules could not believe she was flirting with him. And so openly! She was not acting like herself, and it freaked her out. *You're married, and your husband is just as sexy. Get a grip. This is so not professional.*

"Yes, I am," Jacques admitted without a hint of arrogance or vanity. "My family has poured their life-blood into it, and I'm proud to be a part of its rich history and, hopefully, its continued prosperity. My family is honoured to host you and your guests this week. If there's ever anything I can do during your stay—personally—to assist you—and um—your associates, of course, please don't hesitate to call. Please, take my card."

Jules detected some flirting back. She thought Jacques's momentary verbal hiccup was endearing—and a total turn-on. He never once took his eyes off her as he spoke; it made her knees weak.

Taken aback by her impropriety, Jules remembered that she was not alone and turned in the direction of her nearly forgotten associates. They had all been watching her, smirking and whispering to one another.

Affronted, Jules promptly put an end to their nonsense by staring daggers at them. Her team quickly understood that their superior was not impressed by their smug, childish behaviour. Their animated activity stopped immediately.

Noting that Jacques seemed just as reluctant to let go of her, Jules pulled her hand free from his firm grip and placed her limb rigidly at her side.

Jacques removed a card from his jacket pocket, reached out towards Jules, and offered it.

"Yes, umm—well," Jacques rambled. And then he laughed.

His fumbled words and chortle were without condescension or malice. They were playful and honest. He was captivated by Jules but also intimidated by her powerful, alluring presence.

Jules read his feelings all over his blushing face. Thankfully, it made her own odd, out-of-character behaviour seem less unprofessional.

Jules and Jacques sensed a definite connection between them. A spark. An ease. An obvious powerful attraction. They enjoyed being in each other's presence, that much was obvious, and even though having just met, it felt to both of them like they had known each other for years.

They were also both married to other people.

Jules graciously accepted the card dangling in mid-air, held snugly between Jacques's fingers, and quickly regained control of the situation before any other unexpected feelings and thoughts took hold in her distracted mind.

It made Jules uncomfortable to know she had acted so uncharacteristically juvenile and silly. And all over a man who was being professionally amiable towards her. Perhaps overly friendly, sure, but genuinely harmless. A simple flirtation, nothing more. She was who she was; countless people found her attractive and desirable. Jules had learned long ago how to deal with lustful eyes, charming words, and the occasional grope.

Jacques Bergé, however, was the first person to make her think that love at first sight, not just lust, might be a real thing.

But Jules was married to Phillip, a good man, a handsome man, and she loved him. True, she had not felt the flutter of butterflies in her stomach during their first meeting like she did now with Jacques, but she had been intrigued by Phillip and grew to love him.

Enough of this! Jules forced herself to move beyond the base attraction she felt towards the man in front of her. She got back to reality and the reason she was there in the first place. No matter how damn much she wanted to stay in his eyes, it was time to leave.

"Thank you, M. Bergé. If I need anything, I'll be in touch. Now, could someone assist us with our luggage?"

"Of course. Allow me." Jacques lifted his arm in the air, snapping his fingers twice.

Two male hotel attendants came at once with luggage carts to shepherd them to their rooms.

"Thank you, M. Bergé, for your gracious hospitality and kindness."

Jacques thanked Jules again for her patronage and wished everyone well.

As she followed the attendants to the elevators, Jules fought the urge to look back, telling herself to remain professional and disciplined. She was certain Jacques was off and busy doing what he did best, like greet high-profile guests. She understood he was an important man here and had most certainly moved on from their fleeting flirtation towards thoughts of business and duty.

Despite that logic, Jules figured it could not hurt to look back once and casually, covertly, sneak one last peek at his gorgeous face. Nonchalantly, she craned her neck around and was pleasantly surprised by what she saw.

Jacques was still staring at her.

Truthfully, he had not ever stopped looking at her. He had followed her every movement towards the elevators and privately relished the sensuality of her form, the confidence she radiated. Jules was so different from his wife, and it was this delicious difference that had him bewitched.

With much puissant interest, Jacques winked at Jules. He bowed his head in pointed deference to her acknowledged eminence and smiled widely again.

Jules was confused by her unexpected feelings. There they were again—butterflies!

Much to her chagrin, Jacques eventually turned away from her; however, Jules promptly realized he did so only because he had heard his wife calling out to him.

Marie Bergé waved her husband down as she fast approached from the bottom of the lobby's massive staircase. Jules noted that his wife nearly ran over a bellhop in her haste to get to her husband and enfold him in her suffocating embrace. She had only seen Marie once before in a feature in OK! Canada magazine.

Then, she had appraised her as a woman of no consequence, dull as dishwater, and utterly forgettable.

With growing irritation, Jules watched the couple publicly hug. "Look at her," she quietly whispered to herself. "A parasite, the way she's latched on to him."

With a pernicious expression, Jules glared at Marie. Feeling a sudden hatred towards the woman, she wondered what someone as sophisticated, powerful, and stimulating as Jacques saw in such an insipid bore. Jules scrunched up her nose at the loathsome display of affection she despised yet watched like a car crash—horrified yet unable to look away.

Marie, wrapped in her husband's embrace, noticed Jules's nasty looks and stared her down with her own distrustful, invidious glance. Her anxious eyes relayed a clear message of ownership, of possession.

Jules felt hostile energy wash over her like a tidal wave; it was an invisible attack. In response, she returned Marie's malignant look with a not-so-subtle one of her own. A sinister grin that gradually turned into a contentious sneer. Jules curled up, ever so slightly, one side of her mouth and pushed her puckered lips forward. *Fuck you, you insecure bitch!*

Flipping her luscious blonde hair back once for good measure, Jules walked away but not before doing her customary trademark laugh. This specific laugh conveyed the explicit message that you had been measured up and dismissed as nothing more imposing than a leaf in a hurricane. Marie Bergé was no threat to Jules; there was no comparison between the two of them.

As she clung desperately to her husband in the lobby, poor Marie understood this silent declaration loud and clear.

For the rest of her stay, Jules remained focused on acquiring Mode-Génétique Labs and thwarting Falsworth International in their attempt to snatch them up. Jules's tenacity, prowess with words, grasp of the scientific method, and the promise of state-of-the-art equipment with funding inevitably proved to the owners of the small R&D company that she believed in them.

It did not hurt that the owners were more than a little reluctant to relocate their entire operation to England. Falsworth International no longer had a strong presence in Canada since the death of Ethan Falsworth, and their offer to buy the company was dependent on a complete relocation overseas.

Jules's guarantee that the scientists could utilize any of Cartell Worldwide's properties anywhere in Canada ultimately swayed the decision in their favour.

Jules was more than relieved that she had avoided dealing with any members of the Falsworth family or any of their company's envoys to claim her victory. She wanted nothing to do with them in any shape or form.

With one last goodbye to Jacques, Jules returned to Toronto before the ink was dry on the signed contracts.

Fate, however, was not finished with Jules and Jacques.

Joseph, extremely satisfied with Jules's triumph, routinely sent her back to Château Bergé on business more and more frequently, and Jacques was there to greet her personally, every time. Eventually, they struck up a quick, effortless friendship. Despite the clear attraction, their relationship remained thoroughly platonic.

As much as she desired Jacques, Jules loved Phillip, and she was painfully aware that Jacques loved his insipid wife despite her odd, annoying, whiny ways. Possibly even because of them. Jules took note of how ridiculously overprotective he was of her. She hated how Marie acted like a Victorian invalid—as if a soft breeze would kill her. If Jacques did not recognize it as manipulative behaviour, Jules certainly did.

Jacques and Jules were fundamentally star-crossed; still, they had their friendship, their closeness, and they trusted one another completely.

This trust and confidence in their connection came into its full potency when Jules learned the secret Joseph had long kept from her and Charles. The truth, in all its insidiousness, surrounding Phillip and his unforgivable crime. The despicable act Joseph and Stella had covered up so masterfully, so traitorously!

Right after the horrific revelation, the first person Jules had turned to for comfort, for solace, for strength was not her father—it was Jacques. Not only did he console her, but he had promised to help her in any way he could to enact vengeance upon Phillip, giving his solemn oath of loyalty to her forever.

That night, feeling vulnerable, lost and, deeply hurt, Jules had let unbridled passion overtake her and fell willingly into Jacques's loving, sensual embrace.

But it had never happened again; not as long as Jacques remained married; Jules refused to share a man, especially with someone as unremarkable as Marie.

Once Phillip was destroyed, Jules had plans for her and Jacques. He had a choice to make. Until then, they were allies, friends, confidants, and co-conspirators, but not lovers. Her need for vengeance was what mattered most to her, not some complicated romantic entanglement, and that need was all-consuming.

"No, dammit! I said I wanted them over by *that* wall."

"Sorry, Miss Cartell. I'll move them immediately."

Still upset over her mother's bitchy threats earlier, Denise was afire, and her timid, harried employee had taken the brunt of her irritability all morning.

"The window display looks amazing, Denise."

Violet Lougheed, a woman in her late forties with platinum hair and exemplary style, walked into the boutique with a wide smile. She had procured coffee and doughnuts from a nearby Tim Hortons for the staff to enjoy. Denise had not asked her to do that; that was just the kind of person Violet was.

Denise gave her boutique's manager a quick once-over, marvelling at how impeccably dressed she was from head to toe. Violet wore a sharp, tailored Alexander McQueen tartan button-up jacket, a trendy brown faux suede skirt with tights, black Chanel riding boots, and a Caroline Herrera wide-brimmed hat.

Denise greatly admired Violet's sense of style—the woman exuded fabulousness—but what truly fascinated her was how easily she engaged with their customers as if they had been friends for years. Violet could discuss brands and designers with a knowledge and understanding of fashion as deep as any Vogue Editor. Like Denise, Violet could articulate with great ardour the emotional, nigh spiritual connection people had with Fashion and Design.

The chic woman not only embodied the quintessential elements of the target client Denise coveted, but she also embodied the perfect type of person to sell successfully to that customer.

In her twenties, Violet had lived in New York, working for a major high-end department store.

Denise took a coffee from the tray Violet held and agreed with her about the display. "Yes. I think we've incorporated the on-trend colours for this upcoming season perfectly. It's just too bad the inside of the store looks like a hot mess. The new stock just came in, and I can't figure out where or how to showcase anything. I'm losing my mind."

"We'll figure it out together, Denise. We'll take our time and get it right!"

Whenever Denise became frustrated or irrational in front of customers or towards the staff, Violet took charge. The soothing Scottish lilt in her voice had a knack for creating calm and serenity. She had a talent for sorting out difficult people. Violet was not just a kindred spirit; she was Denise's saviour.

Denise used to be both owner and manager of the boutique, but it was not a good fit.

Despite her education and business experience, she tore through staff and alienated customers constantly. Her people skills were limited. Denise understood the business side of things. Buying garments, the inner workings of the fashion industry, that all made sense. Managing people, though? She was shit at that.

Denise talked fashion like it was her primary language, understanding numbers, data, money. She got the big picture, but she was a shitty retail salesperson. Calm delegation and customer service did not come naturally to her. As much as she hated the term "micro-manager," she was aware that she was one. Phillip once told Denise she was like Jules in that regard.

Violet went and put the coffee and treats in the back and then quickly returned. She eyed up the display Denise had been working on before judiciously giving her opinion.

"While I do think those gowns look perfect by that wall, Denise, I think we should be bold and shake things up a bit. Why not display those handbags by colour and size and not isolate them by designer or brand. It might be fun."

"Oh, I don't know about that, ladies," a male voice suddenly chimed in. "Mixing streetwear with, say, Fendi sounds risky."

Both women abruptly turned and faced their loud, unknown critic.

Miles, nonchalantly waving away the previously scolded sales associate, strutted right up to Denise and Violet.

"Mr. Chen." Denise muttered his name with mild aversion.

"Miles, please," he corrected, elated by Denise's obvious irritation. "Honestly, I wonder about your taste level and fashion aplomb."

"Well, sir, it was only a thought," Violet laughed. She smiled graciously before adding, "I guess it's back to the drawing board."

Miles grinned back devilishly. He had interpreted the older woman's quick reply and ebullience as unfettered appreciation for his comments; in fact, he was surprised that his deliberately snarky attitude with obvious intent to belittle had gone right over her head.

But Miles's appraisal of Violet was wrong.

Violet knew he had dismissed her as a silly Pollyanna. Or a woman blanched easily by intimidating customers. However, she was no shrinking violet, despite her birth name. She was no fool either; she had his number. Violet was familiar with the entitled bitches that frequented the store and misinterpreted her kindness and easy-going nature as a weakness.

No pushover, Violet knew how to play the retail game, especially regarding high-end merchandise and the arrogant, privileged clientele it often attracted. Her exceptional self-confidence protected her from feeling lessened, slighted or mocked. She had taken Miles's elitist attitude and criticism in stride; after all, she had years of experience dealing with snobs and pompous asses, and none had riled her yet.

Unfortunately, when it came to manoeuvring tactfully around opinions she had not asked for or agreed with, Denise possessed none of Violet's skill.

"That's odd! I don't recall asking you to come by my boutique to shit all over my display concepts. I never hired you to voice concerns or give ideas regarding my design aesthetic, either. You work for my bitch sister-in-law, and I doubt very much that you've come here to change your career path. Frankly, Chen, I'm shocked Jules let your leash stretch this far."

"Denise, you really should try and behave more like your affable boyfriend," Miles chided. "His ability to take constructive criticism has made him the man he is today. Successful, rich, an absolute sweetheart. Speaking of Christophe, he and I had a great talk last night. He must be starving for stimulating conversation and intelligent company for him to have spent so much time bending my ear.

Not sure how best to respond to her antagonist and his pernicious assessment of her, Denise remained quiet and stared Miles down. Also, she had come to see that they had attracted the attention of the boutique's customers. Much to her regret, Denise overheard her flustered sales associate making several quick apologies for the disquietude encroaching on their shopping experience.

Visibly chafed by all this, Denise realized her verbal duel with Miles had escalated further than it should have. Farther than she should have allowed it. It was not professional behaviour, certainly not on her part, and she cursed herself for letting Jules's lackey goad her into being bitchy and pugnacious.

Denise got the message loud and clear; Miles, like Jules, was a master at verbal sparring—quick and unrelenting. She did not want to become obnoxious and loud to counter him. Denise needed to think of a better way to get rid of Miles and fast, but an amazingly devastating rebuttal that would send him on his way was not coming to her.

Recognizing Denise's frustration, Violet took quick action on her employer's behalf. Remaining polite and even-tempered, she rather forcefully asked Miles to vacate the store if his only intention for being there was to act ungentlemanly and pick a fight with the proprietor.

"That's not my intent at all," Miles admitted apologetically. "Quite the contrary. I'm here to do Denise a favour. I apologize sincerely. Denise, I suggest we go somewhere more private to discuss business."

Denise openly sneered at Miles. "You must be fucking joking! I don't do business with Jules or her toadies, and I'm not the least bit interested in anything you have to say. Go play your stupid games somewhere else and get the hell out of my store!"

"Well, that's unfortunate," Miles snickered, cocking his head, "but not a completely unexpected response. Perhaps Stella will be more amenable to my offer. She certainly appreciated what I acquired for her just this past week, and I bet she'll pay substantially more for this info. More than you probably would—or could—and money talks. So later, bitch."

Be steel, be steel, be steel.

Since she did not have Jacques's aide currently to bolster her nerves, Jules had been relying on her mantra all morning to strengthen her resolve. Amanda would not get to her. And she would not let her concerns about the success or failure of her father's mission get the better of her, either. She had to relax, focus.

Charles had texted his daughter an hour ago; he was undeniably close to an answer for her. Jules was sure this was the ammunition she needed to finally punish Phillip and take the company away from his family. She needed to be patient a little longer.

As Jules slipped her shoes back on, she heard the sound of her assistant buzzing her. She pushed the flashing red light on her desk phone. "Yes, Nazneen, what is it?"

"I'm, ahh, sorry to disturb you, Ms. Cartell," the soft, slightly shaky female voice said, "but you have an unscheduled visitor that won't take no for an answer. She's refusing to leave until she sees you and, well, you see, ahh—"

"Spit it out already! I'm ageing by the second."

Jules had emphatically told her executive assistant she was unavailable to anyone except her father until further notice; still, she had never heard the woman so rattled before.

"I called security to escort her out of the building, Ms. Cartell, but she—well, she—well, she knocked him unconscious! She says if I don't let her in, she's going to beat me stupid with my stapler!"

Jules sat up straight in her chair. *She has the nerve to come here! She wouldn't dare to try anything here, would she? In the light of day?* The woman had just laid out one of her highly trained, former military security guards. *Fine, if she wants to see me so badly, I'm not going to hide from her.*

Of course, Jules knew there was no place on the entire planet to hide where Amanda could not find her. Hiding was a pointless endeavour, and cowering away in some corner like a scared rat was so not her style.

"Send her in. I'll be fine. Also, please make sure the guard gets medical attention. I'll deal with him later. And Nazneen, if you value your career here at Cartell, don't speak of this incident to anyone. Am I understood?"

"Yes, ma'am. Of course. I'll send her right in."

Jules bolstered her nerves, calmed herself, and watched apprehensively as the door to her office swung open.

Amanda.

As she stood in the doorway, Amanda haughtily placed her hands on her hips, craned her neck, and sauntered into the room like she owned the damn place.

VIII

Intentionally avoiding eye contact with Jules, Amanda strutted around the unfamiliar office hemming and hawing, mentally critiquing Jules's design choices.

Jules remained seated behind her desk, watching. With a begrudging admiration, she marvelled at her uninvited guest's appearance. She was no longer the masked, cat-suited assassin who had broken into her home hours earlier.

Amanda had on a body-hugging cream skirt that ended just above her knees. Her matching cream jacket, tailored perfectly, was accented with bronze lapels and cuffs. Jules had seen these exact pieces at the last Dior runway show in Paris. Amanda had accented her outfit with a pair of Christian Louboutin nude pumps.

Her naturally blonde hair was up in a tight, severe, modern bun, fixed and sprayed so that not one strand was out of place. Her soft, glowing face exemplified purity, the natural look. It was the application of expensive makeup meant to look like you were not wearing any.

Jules marked that Amanda was as beautiful now as the day she had first laid eyes on her. They looked so much alike they could easily be mistaken for sisters.

Despite the feminine softness, Amanda was a wolf in sheep's clothing. She was brutal, mercenary, and deadly; she enjoyed inflicting pain and punishment on others.

And she was very, very good at it.

Jules never doubted why this woman, or more specifically, The Silver Dagger, was considered one of the world's top assassins. Seeing Amanda use her deadly skills for the first time, up close and personal, had been the catalyst for Jules in deciding that these were skills and abilities she had to possess, herself.

Jules thought back to when Amanda first entered her life.

One evening, during her final year at U of T, Jules had left a computer lab uncharacteristically late, foolishly deciding to take a questionable shortcut back to the parking lot. She had refused her male lab partner's offer to walk with her to her car, explaining to him, haughtily, that she had years of self-defence training and was more than capable of taking care of herself. She did not need a man to protect her.

And so he had left her by herself.

Unfortunately, before Jules had even walked five meters down the long, winding path that connected the deserted park to the parking lot, she was set upon by six stinking drunk, brutish men.

The thugs taunted Jules menacingly, shouting lewd, sexually obscene comments. Through inebriated speech, they explained in grotesque detail what they planned on doing to her. They were the kind of scum that got their jollies off overpowering and hurting females, especially ones as young and pretty as Jules was. There was no chance for a woman to talk her way out of this situation.

Though trained to defend herself against multiple attackers, Jules thought six at once was more than she could handle. Panicked, she decided that flight, not fight, was her best course of action and made a desperate run for the safety of her car.

To her utter dismay, she did not get very far.

The sinewy arm of one of the savages connected brutally with her solar plexus, and she hit the ground hard.

Out of breath but still conscious, Jules rolled over and looked up at her assailants. They had all gathered in a circle around her, leering at her lecherously. They did not see her as a person, just a toy.

Although she realized they were about to do her considerable harm, Jules refused to beg them to let her go. She understood these sacks of shit were beyond reason and empathy, and she refused to give any of them the satisfaction of thinking they had intimidated her or destroyed her spirit.

Instead, Jules formulated several different plans of attack she hoped would save her by drawing public attention to her plight. She refused to go down easy.

Before Jules could let out a scream, a voice distracted her.

"Why don't you sick, ugly fucks come play with me."

It was a loud, female voice, but Jules was sure it had not come from her. She was hurt, yes, but not delusional.

From out of the shadows came a shape. Too dark, Jules could not make out the specifics of the face but figured this had to be the possessor of the voice she had heard. Taking note of the newcomer's size and stature, she realized that the woman was no bigger than her. Jules was utterly perplexed and worried.

Was this bitch crazy? Why not run for help? Why did she taunt them? Did she want to be beaten and raped?

Jules willed her body to move, to get up off the ground to aid the brave woman, but before she accomplished this feat, the woman yelled at her to stay down. She obeyed, and everything around her went crazy real fast.

Jules watched the mysterious woman systematically incapacitate all six men, using various martial arts moves. The woman kicked, jabbed, and punched with finesse and power Jules had only seen in movies. The spectacle was hypnotic. Jules was in awe, beyond impressed; her martial prowess paled in comparison to this woman's consummate skill, precision, and ferocity.

At breakneck speed, the brutish men went down like bowling pins, one after the other, unable to withstand the mystery woman's unrelenting attack. Every last one of them eventually collapsed into a pathetic heap upon the hard ground. Most of them puked. All were gasping for air.

Jules was sure she had heard bones snap. She hoped their injuries hurt like hell.

When the proverbial dust settled, Jules made out more of her mysterious saviour's visage. The woman was blonde, athletic, and about her age. She wore black and grey military fatigues and laced high combat boots. She looked damn tough despite being, ostensibly, damn beautiful. What she did not look, however, was familiar; Jules had never seen her before on or off-campus.

"Listen up, you fucks," the woman growled. "If any of you attempt this again, I'll find you and kill you. And just so you know that I'm speaking the absolute truth, I'm taking your IDs. I know who you are now. I know where you live. If any of you still don't think I'm serious, I have one more thing to say to you. Daniel fucking Johnson."

The men who could still walk picked up their battered and bruised friends and shuffled away as fast as their bloodied, broken bodies could move. As they left, they apologized profusely to both women for their heinous behaviour towards them. They were all utterly terrified.

Jules was confused. Even though the name sounded vaguely familiar, she had no idea who Daniel Johnson was; for that matter, she had no idea why mentioning his name would deter this scum from their criminal ways.

Besides, she damn well wanted to press charges against these assholes for attempted assault. Their contrite words were hollow and meaningless to her.

However, after a few moments of quiet reflection, Jules reconsidered her planned involvement with the authorities. Ultimately, those animals did not matter. Only she did—the mystery woman.

"Thank you so much," Jules gushed. "Who the hell is Daniel Johnson?"

The woman smirked and told Jules the moral tale of Daniel Johnson.

"Last year, at another University, he raped three women on campus grounds. Even though all three of his victims reported him to campus authorities and the University's President, nothing came of it. The powers that be quietly covered up the three incidents to avoid bad publicity. Apparently, rape reports and trials negatively affect enrolment. Imagine that!

"The victims' parents were ultimately silenced by threats of endless costly legal battles from Mr. Dan's rich as fuck, well-connected father. The prick even planned to use victim-blaming, saying he'd make sure his lawyers ripped their daughters to shreds on the witness stand. So the bastard got away with it.

"One of his victims eventually killed herself. She couldn't live with what he'd done to her, and that sick fuck blabbed openly about it like it was just some big fucking joke to him. Johnson believed he was untouchable.

"Well, he wasn't. He was found in his driveway hanging by the neck from a basketball hoop with a bloody, severed dick shoved in his mouth. I'm sure you can guess whose dick it was. They never caught who did it. Karma, eh?"

Jules finally remembered reading about this guy's death in the Toronto Sun. The woman had not exactly admitted to doing the deed, but Jules was sure she had killed him to give those women the justice denied them. And more than that—she had made an example out of him.

Jules surmised something else that was potentially troubling. She was told this story by the same person who had just very audibly threatened to murder people. She also used the murdered rapist in the story as verification that she carried out her death threats if not obeyed.

All this led Jules to believe that the woman was utterly unafraid of exposure or legal punishment regarding her vigilante activities. She found this supreme level of confidence astounding and a tad unsettling.

But Jules had no intention of ratting the woman out to the police. On the contrary, she needed her to be free and accessible; she wanted to learn how to be more like her. Jules had no intention of ever murdering anyone, but she downright coveted those fighting skills.

"Listen, if you're okay, I have to go."

"Wait!" Jules pleaded. "What's your name? I promise not to involve the cops."

Unconcerned by the authorities, the woman snorted at their mention. She winked at Jules and gave her a sly grin. "Sorry, no names. I've got a mystique to protect. Later, gorgeous."

With nothing else to say, the woman ran like a cheetah back through the esplanade, parkouring her way around all obstacles in her path. Eventually, the darkness swallowed her whole.

Within minutes of the woman's departure, Jules contrived a thorough, well-designed plan of action to track down, observe, and eventually convince the mystery woman to train her. She did not care what she had to do to persuade her. Nothing was off-limits. Nothing was too austere to try.

Factoring in the woman's military-like outfit, butch affectations, and penchant for kicking the crap out of male douchebags, Jules guessed the warrior woman was probably same-sex-oriented. Stereotyping aside, she had cogently picked up on the woman's blatantly erotic language regarding her.

Jules had yet to meet anyone she could not convince to do what she wanted. However, regardless of past victories, she was not confident that intellectual reasoning, scheming, or deal-making would work this time. Jules had never resorted to using sex as a weapon, but something in the recesses of her mind told her that seduction mixed with subtle manipulation was the stratagem that would work.

Believing that the way to gain access to this woman's power was through her heart—and other bodily parts, if necessary—Jules promptly studied lesbian sex, culture, and social politics.

Jules spent a month hunting her prey. Every free moment she had in between classes, social commitments, and physical training, she devoted herself to her search, staking out the park, the campus, and the downtown core. She went to LGBT clubs and underground, alternative queer hangouts putting feelers out regarding the woman's identity.

Frustratingly, no one claimed to know her. Disheartened, Jules eventually gave up, accepting the reality that this unfathomable creature did not want to be found by anyone.

Jules never considered the possibility that her mystery woman was secretly observing and investigating her, too. The woman was just as interested in this stunning mirror image of herself as Jules was with her. After an extensive background check, when she felt with absolute certainty that Jules was not a threat to her in any way, the woman revealed herself to her stalker-admirer.

Her name, she hesitantly revealed, was Amanda.

Right out of the box, Jules asked her, "Where did you learn to fight like that?"

"My father started my martial arts training when I was three," Amanda revealed. "And believe me, my age was no excuse to be sloppy or uncoordinated. Karate and gymnastics to start. Soon it was Taekwondo and Kendo. More disciplines as I got older, tougher.

"I was an army brat. My family travelled the globe. In every country we went to, I made it my business to learn and master anything I could from the local fighters, athletes, and mystics. Brazilian Jiu-Jitsu and Capoeira to Sudanese stick-fighting. Hand-to-hand combat is my passion. I love the power, energy, and control. Knowing that I can defend myself but also destroy my opponent.

"My father was hard on me. My brother, too. He wanted us both to be the best. Unbeatable. My dad was an excellent combatant. The bastard thought he was Frank fucking Dux, and he expected his kids to be just as good, just as relentless. He can't fight anymore. It doesn't matter."

Jules's interest piqued immensely at the mention of a brother. That morsel of information was a potential game-changer. A male sibling just as proficient at fighting would mean Jules would not need to manipulate Amanda. Not if she could get to the brother, ensnare him, and bend him to her will.

Men had always been easier targets for Jules to dupe and exploit—without the need to engage in coitus. Their anticipation of her body, the promise of it, had always been enough to get what she wanted.

"Is your brother as good as you?" Jules asked pointedly.

Amanda paused and looked skyward, appearing disturbed. "Anyway," she whispered, her voice strained.

Jules did not push the topic any further when it became apparent that Amanda had said all she planned to say about her brother.

"Go on," Jules pleaded coyly, "your life seems fascinating."

Amanda continued, revealing a cursory backstory. She lived in a partially renovated warehouse loft in Leslieville and was a recent graduate of the Royal Military College of Canada. Her father was a former high-ranking military officer in the Canadian Armed Forces. Sadly, her mother died of cancer when she was two years old.

After she finished her brief life story, Amanda informed Jules that she found her breathtakingly beautiful.

It was not much, Jules thought, but it was a start, and she was thrilled her instincts were right about Amanda's sexuality. Jules immediately began the process of deceiving and manipulating her by pretending to be interested in her sexually; later, as dictated by the level of involvement it took to get Amanda to open up, romance and emotional intimacy became a part of her strategy.

Used to being alone, depending on no one but herself, Amanda initially proved reluctant to share both the secrets of her life and her combat knowledge. Jules cared little about the one but was desperate for the other. Realizing a "friends with benefits" relationship was not getting her anywhere, Jules quickly moved beyond it, attacking Amanda's heart directly, managing to scheme and finesse her way into becoming nothing less than her "soul-mate."

It was a false, one-sided relationship, but Jules felt no remorse regarding her duplicitous behaviour. In no time at all, Amanda willingly trained Jules in whatever combat discipline she wanted to learn.

Their relationship, one-sided or not, had lasted for over a year.

During the early part of Jules's first winter semester at Osgoode, an incident at Lake Simcoe occurred that had destroyed things between them for good. Though not learning nearly as much as she had wanted, Jules ended the relationship because of what happened, outright refusing to speak to Amanda or see her anymore.

Confused and hurt by Jules's sudden dismissive behaviour, Amanda had eventually left Toronto feeling unsettled by how things had ended between them.

And very bitter.

"Miles, wait!"

Denise's heart pounded. Her head, now filled with even more perplexing questions than it had been earlier in the day, wanted to explode. What had her mother done now? And why was she talking to, let alone conspiring with Jules's lapdog? None of it made sense. Like it or not, Miles had the answers she sought, and she was not about to let him walk out the door before he answered them.

Denise saw an opportunity in front of her, but first, she had to get rid of her audience.

"Mrs. Lougheed, give us a minute." Denise followed her statement with a rather obvious, forceful head-snap to the right.

As Mrs. Lougheed departed, Denise motioned Miles towards her office, where privacy awaited. Once inside, she shut the door to prying eyes and listening ears. "Speak—and it better be worth my time."

"And your money," Miles chuckled. "I'm not providing this information for free out of the goodness of my heart."

"So, you're betraying Jules? See, I just don't buy it. Selling me information that could potentially hurt your mentor, your employer? I mean, come on!" Denise's voice trailed off, unable to find the words to express her disbelief. She shook her head back and forth, incapable of understanding Miles's objective.

"Denise, let me make this abundantly clear to you. I'm not Jules's puppet. I am what I've always been—an opportunist. I take whatever I can get from people. Money, education, employment, and yes, even sex if I want it.

"Jules is no stranger to this belief system. She knows not to trust anyone completely. She keeps an eye on me, sure, but I know how she thinks better than most. It's my ace in the hole. Jules is a rung on the ladder of success, necessary, but I owe her nothing. Well, gratitude and appreciation, I guess, but never fealty.

"She's no different than all the ones that have come before her, including my parents. I feel no shame or guilt around that. My methods are totally self-serving, so what? I use people for what I want and need. That's how I survive, flourish. People should want to be more like me. Fuck everyone else.

"When I first came to your mother, she immediately understood my intentions. Stella's no dummy. She's used and tossed away countless assets on her way up the social ladder. My lifestyle—my goals—don't come cheap, lady. It takes a lot of effort to be me. I hope now it's painfully obvious to you that I have no loyalty to anyone but myself. My services, my silence, can be bought. Cool?"

Denise pondered Miles's words carefully. To a degree, she comprehended his parasitical, megalomaniacal point of view, even appreciated it. It was the very essence of corporate thinking, after all. Very capitalist.

Denise was wary, but if her mother had believed Miles's greed and self-interested goals enough to, if not trust, exploit him as a viable resource against Jules, who was she to remain stoically dismissive?

If she refused to believe his intentions were purely motivated by money, she would lose this opportunity to get something to use against Jules. Besides, it was in Miles's own best interest for Jules not to find out about his duplicitous nature.

"One last thing before I bite. Why come here first and not go directly to my mother? She's already paid you once for information, so why not just go right back to her?"

"Why not?" Miles snorted.

"That's what I asked!"

"No, Denise. That's my answer. 'Why not?'"

"Huh?"

"All you Cartells have money, so why not try to cash in with as many of you as possible. Different information is desired and useful to different people. Besides, I wanted to ask you something personal that Stella probably wouldn't know."

"And what would that be?" Denise asked, her curiosity piqued.

"I want to know—how should I phrase this? What's Christophe like in the sack? Is he a good lay? I've seen him at the gym, so I know he's packing."

Denise recoiled, taken aback by Miles's crudeness. "You're disgusting. And you'll never know how good he is, how good *it* is, so you can fuck off with that absurd question and remain jealous as hell that I get to hit that whenever I want."

"Well, you can't blame a gay for trying. He's a fine piece of ass, but as you said, I'll never know how fine." Miles grinned, winking at Denise. Inside, his gut almost hurt from holding in his laughter. *If you only knew the truth, you dumb bitch.*

"The mouth on you! I doubt you get that bawdiness from dowager Stella. She'd wash your mouth out with soap. Okay, I get it. No more talk of Christophe.

"I have information concerning the Parisians and their deal with Jules. It relates to Phillip and how it's going to destroy his career. That's all I'm giving you for free. The ball is in your court now, honey. Do you pay and we play? Or does Phillip inevitably get fucked over because you don't like me?"

Denise watched Miles as he folded his arms, scrunched up his face, and shook his head. She knew, deep down, he expected her to walk away from this transaction. Too mistrustful. Too uncertain. Too scared.

Shallow and vain Sonja? She commanded respect and deference from others with greater ease and with far more occurrence. It made no sense to Denise, the only sibling brave enough to sell off their stake in the family business and go it alone. Sonja was the one who lived off the family name and the wealth and privilege she was born into. She had not worked a day in her life on anything except her tan.

Denise had confidence in herself; she believed in her success. Her father had told her before his death how proud he was of her. In his eyes, she had grown into a fine young woman, as competent, as shrewd a business owner as himself.

So why then was there still this childlike uncertainty that clung to her, weighing her down? Why did she often feel like she was swimming in a pool wearing concrete shoes? It was palpable to others, this bizarre weakness of spirit. She knew people talked about her behind her back.

It was this strange otherness about her, this unCartell-like fearfulness, that caused people to see her as forgettable, nondescript, bland, and generally ill-suited to be the legacy of such giants as Joseph and Stella.

Denise saw Phillip as a stronger, more assertive person than her. Despite his recent failings, he was still their mother's favourite child, the golden boy. Sonja, in her eyes, was prettier, more easygoing, and considerably more popular than her. When matched up against her siblings, Denise always felt she was of lesser quality.

And this was why she had freed herself from her father's one-time birthday gift of shares in the company. From the money made off their sale, she had moved into a venture of her own creation.

Denise had plans for a massive chain of stores and, one day, she intended to design and sell a signature line of luxury, high-end clothes. She wanted to eventually fall in love, marry a man of her choosing, take his last name, and cleave the burden of being a Cartell from her being, permanently.

During the initial stages of brand creation, Stella had wanted her daughter to use her full name for her business appellation and eventual fashion line. Deciding against that, Denise told Stella she was her own person, not just her father's daughter, her sibling's little sister, or her mother's pale imitation. She was simply Denise—and that was good enough.

It had to be. Denise secretly feared she had nothing else.

"Alright, Chen, I'm going to surprise you," Denise smirked. "I'll bite. What do you feel your information is worth to me? Or should I say, how much is it going to cost me?"

"I'm so glad you asked. Twenty-five thousand dollars seems a good number. I'll take a cheque."

"What do you want, Amanda?" Jules asked through gritted teeth.

There had been nothing but silence between the two women for several long minutes.

Turning towards Jules, Amanda halted her inspection of the office, admitting, "I really wouldn't have walloped her with a stapler."

Jules did not believe that for a second.

"I see you're still barking orders at people, threatening their livelihoods," Amanda stated, admonishing Jules. "So predictable. Always the controlling bitch. All that potent femaleness drenched in an ugly masculine ego. You haven't changed."

"That's rich coming from the lipstick lesbian psychopath who kills people for a living," Jules retorted.

"Touché," Amanda laughed. "I guess I deserved that. Though, I'm hardly a psychopath. My mental faculties are very acute and medically sound, thanks."

"Says you," Jules smirked.

Amanda rolled her eyes. "Okay, I get off on what I do, sure, but I don't kill for sport or at random. I'm a killer, yes, but not a murderer. There's a difference, Jules, and you know that. We've already gone over this. I'm much more retribution than revenge. I can't help it if I'm good at what I do and take satisfaction from it.

"These are bad people. I think of myself as Karma's agent, paid to make sure they get what they deserve. You wouldn't shed a tear over these monsters. So, I won't judge your profession if you don't judge mine, okay?"

Without answering, Jules motioned Amanda to take the seat across from her.

For what seemed like ages, the two women sat quietly, each scrutinizing the other's face. Eventually, the stare-off ended when Amanda surrendered to Jules's obstinate, unflinching gaze and sheepishly looked away. At that moment, Jules immediately grasped something crucial: Amanda was still in love with her.

The feeling was not mutual, of course; it never was.

Jules intended to use Amanda's emotions against her if she proved unwilling to take a hint and leave. Just to be rid of her, she would hurt the woman all over again.

"Amanda, I don't have a desire to judge you. I have no desire for you at all. Why are you even here? And I don't mean in Fairporte. If you're here on business, fine, but why involve me?"

"Admittedly, last night was a little unconventional, but can't an old friend drop by to say hello? Catch up?"

"We aren't friends," Jules coolly replied.

The statement, like the one about not being desired, stung, but Amanda refused to let it show.

"Speaking of business, you know I can't talk about the specifics of my work. It's a professional necessity if I want to stay active and in good standing. You're a lawyer, you know all about client confidentiality, and my clients are always satisfied. I clean up their messes, take care of their enemies, and remove their obstacles."

"I'm still not hearing a reason for this visit," Jules snapped. "And stop bragging, or selling yourself, if that's what you're doing. I'm not looking to hire you. You promised to leave me alone."

Since their breakup, the two women had crossed paths only a few times over the years.

Their last run-in had been during Milan Fashion Week, and brief as that reunion was, Jules still found the time to say countless hurtful things. Disgusted by the harsh, ugly confrontation,

Amanda had promised to stay away for good; not surprisingly, her backpedalling on that promise greatly concerned Jules.

While she never expected to see Amanda again after Milan, Jules never wanted to see Silver Dagger, either! She hoped this most unexpected encounter had nothing to do with the woman's profession.

Jules had known for some time that Amanda Reid was the assassin known as Silver Dagger. While reading Joseph's secret files, Jules had discovered Amanda's connection to him; she was not surprised that someone as rich and powerful as Joseph Cartell contracted the Silver Dagger to take out his most dangerous enemies.

Amanda's quest to rid the world of dangerous, heinous people only ended up connecting her to more of the same type of people. The absurdity of it all amused Jules.

Something Jules found shocking? One of Joseph's targeted enemies had been his lifelong friend, Ambroise Bergé. The Silver Dagger had rigged Ambroise's yacht to explode with him and many of his top men aboard.

To this day, Jules had no idea why Joseph wanted Ambroise dead. His reason why was not written down anywhere in the secret files. She assumed that at some point in their friendship Ambroise had done him very wrong.

Not wanting to be responsible for destroying the memory of the father he adored, Jules had decided not to tell Jacques the truth. And if she owed Amanda anything for the time they had shared, for the skills she had learned from her, she owed the woman her silence.

Not long after Ambroise's funeral, an intoxicated Jacques reluctantly revealed to Jules his deep concern over his late father's illegal operations, guiltily admitting his knowledge of some of the illicit activities but consciously choosing to look the other way. How could he betray his father?

Jules saw how heavily it all weighed on him, but she did not give advice or direction at the time, just comfort. His inebriated state played a role in her silent empathy.

Interestingly, on that auspicious night, Jacques ended up disclosing quite a few secrets to Jules. The most shocking being the one connected to his mother's death that no one outside of a few key members of the Bergé family knew: the lie that Clara had died with her husband in the explosion.

After reading all the "Silver Dagger" files, Jules knew something about Clara's part in the explosion was off. The issue was that there were no survivors, as the Silver Dagger intended, but Clara's name had not been on Joseph's hit list.

Jules had no problem assuming that the nine other men on the boat who had perished alongside Ambroise were ne'er-do-well associates of his, connected to the same unknown heinous crime against Joseph that warranted their deaths by a professional assassin.

After seeing how much Joseph paid Amanda for the job, Jules's eyes almost bugged out of her head. It was a staggering amount.

Jacques always referred to the men who had shadowed his father by the colourful, somewhat juvenile sobriquet "henchmen." Jules considered them something more mundane, less overwrought with a theatrical punch: Amanda's targets.

Clara, a henchman? No.

Jules believed Amanda never murdered innocent bystanders to complete a job. They had often talked about the limits and boundaries of personal morality during their relationship, and they both thought collateral damage was messy, sloppy, and unjustifiable. Jules was sure that Amanda had a conscience and kept a personal code of conduct.

The explosion on the Bergé yacht left no survivors, and that was problematic.

So how did Clara die? And why? The woman was an old-school Francophone, a devout Catholic, pious, painfully shy but kind. If she was innocent and ignorant of all atrocities her husband was responsible for, why was she dead?

Jules spent months picking away at Jacques's resolve, asking all the right questions, pointing out the holes in his story until one night, drunk and sad, he finally told her the truth.

Clara had not been anywhere near the boat when it blew up.

Upon learning of her husband's death, Clara was inconsolable. Unable to accept life without him, she overdosed on barbiturates. A long-time sufferer of debilitating migraines, Clara had used the very pills that eased her pain to end her life.

Her death, in that way, horrified her family.

As a Catholic, the fact that Clara committed suicide was an abomination in the eyes of those who did not follow a more forward-thinking path of understanding and compassion. While Jacques and Marie had left the Church behind ages ago, the rest of the family had not. The ones in the know were outraged. They ranted and raved, refusing to have such an ugly stain imprinted upon the Bergé name and legacy.

If the Church and the general population found out what she had done, that is.

A friendly, gentle soul, Clara had been well-liked, and no one truly wanted this tragically unfair ending for her, no matter how angry they were towards her self-serving actions. Everyone agreed to say that Clara was on the yacht when it exploded. The funeral home cremated the corpse posthaste, which staved off questions about its unblemished nature.

Jacques acquiesced to the plan without any trepidation. He could not besmirch the memory of his dear mother or allow the Church that she had loved to renounce her—not after all she had done for them during her lifetime. Jacques paid off all the people involved in making this lie a reality.

Neither Patrice nor the Québecois cousins dared to use the truth of his mother's death as leverage against him during their legal battle. Family secrets were sacred and never used as ammunition, never revealed in anger. To do so meant absolute expulsion from the family by the entirety of the clan—no exceptions.

Jules often forgot that Clara had not been on that boat, the lie was so pervasive, but she supposed that was for the best. She honestly believed that no matter his affection for her, Jacques would never forgive her if she slipped up and revealed the truth about his beloved mother's death to anyone.

Jacques had put Jules's troubled mind at ease; Amanda had not betrayed her convictions.

Now, unfortunately, in her office, staring into the woman's eyes, Jules had reason again to question Amanda's motives and boundaries.

"Jules, you're so impatient, so impertinent," Amanda sighed, exasperated.

"How's that?"

"Before you rudely interrupted me, I was about to reveal that even though I never talk specifics, I will say this. If a certain blowhard Texan, one I believe you conversed with last night, is found dead as a doornail this morning, pretend to be surprised by the news."

Jules immediately connected the dots. *Mr. Chesterton.*

"So, I have to ask," Jules queried, "since you've already broken your own rules for me, anyway."

"Bent, honey, not broken," Amanda piped up. "Never broken."

"Whatever. I'm curious about something. I'm assuming there was no physical confrontation, considering how portly the guy looked. Not someone worthy of your skills. So, knowing you and your methods of creativity, was it death by heat stroke or a fatal allergic reaction to an insect bite or sting?"

"Bee sting," Amanda declared proudly. "A lovely slow-acting venom I discovered in India. Rare and difficult to procure even on the black market. It mimics the symptoms and inevitable result of a severe bee sting allergic reaction. My client wanted a clean, quiet kill. Boring, I know, but I try to indulge in some theatricality even in this mundane of a job.

"My award-worthy performance? I played a gorgeous German model who had just finished filming a movie with blah blah blah, and I'm so drunk, tee-hee. I was the quintessential ditz with the most adorable broken English accent trying to impress the older man with money.

"And you can get that look off your face, Jules! I didn't crash your stupid party! I wasn't confident you wouldn't see through my disguise. I waited for him at the bar. Honestly, you're taking all the fucking fun out of this.

"The best part? My little trick ring with a retractable, razor-sharp tip. The perfect method of delivery for the poison. A little prick for the big prick." Amanda laughed, amused by her own joke. "You should have seen him trying to get me into bed! All sweaty, his beer belly popped out from underneath his alcohol-stained shirt.

"The eye rolls, again, Jules! He was a serial rapist. He got what he deserved! No, he deserved worse."

Jules would never give Amanda the satisfaction of knowing this, but she found her story entertaining. And it did partially answer her principle question. Mr. Chesterton's assassination did confirm that Amanda had actual, albeit unsavoury business here, in Fairporte. However, Jules was not satisfied; she had some questions and concerns still.

From the relaxed look on Amanda's face, she had fulfilled the contract requirements. So why was she still here?

More importantly, Jules wanted to know what Amanda thought she was doing breaking into her home in the dead of night. Why set up scenarios to make her recall their shared past? Why drop by Cartell Worldwide Tower in the light of day dressed to the nines? And all this after Amanda had promised to stay away from her!

Frustrated, Jules once again questioned whether insinuating herself into Amanda's life for purely self-interested reasons all those years ago had been a bad idea in the long run.

Believing her past with Amanda was put to rest, Jules had foolishly lulled herself into a false sense of comfort. She wondered if the woman ever planned to leave her alone. Had she done such a number on the bitch that she would not—or could not—let go and move on?

Initially, Jules had every confidence that she could use Amanda's infatuation to her advantage, but now she was afraid she had created a monster outside her control.

"I see no valid reason for you to stay in Fairporte any longer, Amanda, now that your business here is over. I'm sure a jet setter like yourself is dying to get back to Toronto or New York or wherever it is you spend your time.

"Since I'm still waiting for an answer to my question about why you're stalking me, a question you seem incapable of answering and quick to deflect, I'll accept your hesitation and silence as the only response I'm going to get. You don't have a reason to be here anymore, do you? No, that's not entirely true. There is one reason. You're obsessed with me.

"But enough already! Get over it! Move on! You're a smart lady. Read the writing on the wall—there's nothing here for you. There is no us! Leave. Permanently. Have a nice life. Sayonara! That's all, folks! Fuck off! Catch my drift?"

Amanda winced at the brash resoluteness of Jules's statements.

It was a subtle, barely perceptible recoil, but Jules detected it. She knew Amanda had been buying time with her banter, stalling because she did not have any reason to be around her former paramour other than a continued obsessive infatuation with her.

Jules was so over it. She had finished her performance as Amanda Reid's lover, girlfriend, and disciple years ago; consequently, when Jules bowed out of the production, it was with the understanding that there was never to be an encore performance. Enough was enough. Jules had too much going on in her life to allow herself to be distracted by Amanda's nonsense.

"So, there was never anything real between us?"

"Oh, for fuck's sake, Amanda! We've been down this road over and over, time and again! I'm not doing this. It's so tiresome, so boring, and you're making a fool of yourself. It's pathetic. No more niceties, just fucking leave!"

Amanda's right hand clenched and balled into a tight fist. Her eyes narrowed and bore down on Jules. Her face turned red with unfettered rage; a merciless heat born of anger, hatred, and desire mixed up together in an emotional melange radiated off her skin in feverish torrents.

Jules immediately felt threatened, unsafe, and wholly unprepared for the ferocity of Amanda's reaction to this unmitigated exorcism from her life. She had never seen her in a state like this before. Not ever. Not even during their last meeting in Milan when poisoned words and vitriolic condemnations had passed between them like thrown daggers.

Jules was afraid she had pushed Amanda too far this time and now faced a woman who had lost all logic and sense. Had she finally seen the true face of the Silver Dagger? Would it be the last thing she would ever see?

Panic-stricken, Jules reached for the security button built into the underside of her desk, hoping she would not have to push it. Her finger hovered around it as she waited to see what Amanda's next move was.

But Jules's paranoia and fear were all for naught. Amanda quickly unclenched her fist, relaxed her face muscles, breathed in heavily, and allowed herself a moment to find her centre. She smoothed out her skirt with both hands, checked to see that her hairstyle was still in place, and straightened out her posture.

Dispassionately, Amanda picked up her Louis Vuitton handbag. Her composure and demeanour had changed from hot, ardent emotion to cold, hard impassiveness.

This detachment, this frosty indifference, was something that appealed to both women; both understood its power. It protected them from emotional pain and prevented others from knowing what they thought, felt or intended to do.

"Goodbye, Jules," Amanda whispered in an almost robotic cadence. "I hope every time you use what I taught you, you remember what you did to me to learn those skills. I hope it was all worth it. I truly won't bother you again."

Amanda stormed out of Jules's office.

IX

Christophe reached for his complimentary white towel. He had just finished up a strenuous CrossFit workout at his gym, and the hot shower afterward had successfully relaxed him, soothing his sore muscles. He worked out five times a week; his hard body displayed the results of his rigorous efforts. Christophe's body fat percentage was currently at nine percent.

Lucky for most of his modelling career, Christophe considered himself at the top of his game. The harried work pace of his early twenties was gone, and despite his recent choice to limit his runway appearances, he continued to work steadily.

Based on his most recent million-dollar deal, he was right to think that.

Though yet to reach "David Gandy" status, Christophe was still very much in demand, desired by many top designers who considered him the perfect embodiment of the high fashion print male. His résumé was extensive.

Ever since he was old enough to steal fashion magazines from the Walmart rack and read them secretly in bed under the covers with a flashlight, Christophe had wanted to wear expensive, form-fitting high-end clothes, including designer underwear. He had dreamed of gracing the covers of GQ and Men's Vogue and modelling for Perry Ellis, YSL and Tom Ford.

To his credit, Christophe had managed to do just that. He planned to continue for as long as he could get away with it.

Christophe had never been interested in modelling muscle tees, spandex wrestling singlets or board shorts; being asked to do the cover for Flex Magazine was nowhere near his top five list of dream assignments. He had every intention of waiting until he was at least in his mid to late thirties before willingly transitioning to fitness modelling.

Admittedly, he would gladly eat his own words if asked to do the cover of Men's Health, the one not-so-secret exception to his rule. He made a mental note to talk to his New York agency about getting it.

Needing to dry himself, Christophe moved the towel down his naked torso, rubbing the fabric over his tight abs and flat stomach. Casually, he preened and posed. It was a subtle showing off, so the other patrons could see what he had worked so hard to achieve. Christophe loved the attention he received from his body and his looks. The men always watched him with lust, jealousy or admiration.

Christophe had a firm ass and a decent-sized cock to show off; still, he wished he was as well-endowed as Phillip. Tactfully, he had looked at Phillip's package during the times the two of them had worked out together, liking what he saw.

Chuckling to himself, Christophe thought more about Denise's brother naked. *That man is brutally hot. Well, when his eyes aren't bloodshot. No—even then. That ass!*

But despite Phillip's seemingly benign nature and amiable countenance, he was Christophe's enemy—so told to him time and time again.

Phillip seemed completely harmless to Christophe, an alcoholic, certainly a buffoon at times, but not worth being someone's nemesis. He saw Phillip as a sweet, good-natured soul, lovable yet sad and lost. Someone he felt sorry for. Honestly, Christophe liked the man very much, despite his many emotional flaws.

But Christophe had consummate faith in the person who had told him that Phillip was their foe; he trusted their word completely. He did not understand why it had to be this way but had resigned himself to the fact that Phillip's destruction was inevitable. Christophe played his part in the man's inevitable downfall masterfully with only a measure of reluctance and self-reproach.

It was the least he could do; after all, his love had done so much for him over the years. And still did.

Additionally, when the opportunity presented itself, Christophe had offered to do what he did best to aid in the covert undertaking: seduction and the acquisition of anything from the seduced. His ability to separate emotions and accountability from sex was a learned trait he had mastered years earlier.

Christophe had created his own artful way of manipulating men and women to get what he wanted through the use of sexual conquest. Gender, even sexual attraction for that matter, made no difference to him; the sex was simply a task, a job that he set his mind towards accomplishing. There was rarely any true intimacy.

Christophe had years of experience as a sexual grifter; it was how he had survived on the streets of Toronto as a teen runaway. Despite its necessity, engaging in underage prostitution was not something he was proud of or ever talked about; it was a closely guarded secret.

Of course, that sordid lifestyle fortuitously led to the future life he currently thrived in, and it was a price he would gladly pay again.

Christophe was highly proficient in bed. Combined with his looks and charm, he always made anyone he set his sights on fall in love with him. Or at least in lust. Denise had never complained to anyone that she was unsatisfied.

As he put his towel down and slipped on his Dirt Squirrel boxer-briefs, Christophe checked his iPhone, hoping to see a text or a missed call; there had been no contact with his love since the previous day.

Christophe was so over keeping their relationship a secret. Once this whole sordid affair with the Cartells was over, Christophe hoped for complete, public transparency regarding their relationship, possibly even marriage. But he wasn't holding his breath.

No matter how far away they were from one another, the two of them spoke at least once a day. Christophe believed he would eventually get an explanation about everything, but he was tired of waiting, sick with anticipation and anxiety.

Miles was a nice distraction, an amusing toy to play with, but that distraction only went so far. He was excruciatingly bored with Denise; he wanted that game to be over and done.

Sadly, Christophe had no new messages. *I don't care how busy you are. Send me a fucking text!*

Providence must have heard him; Christophe's cell rang. He quickly looked at the number, hoping it was his sweetheart.

No such luck.

Ugh! Denise. Christophe was less than thrilled. A myriad of contentious thoughts swam in his head. *What does she want? Fuck, she's annoying. Will this job never end? Babe, I'd say you owe me big time for putting up with this unstable bitch if I hadn't fucking volunteered to do this. I'll keep her distracted, out of the way, I said. I want to help, I said. What was I thinking?*

"Hey, love," Christophe fraudulently gushed, his adoration for the woman feigned. "I just finished my workout. Were you looking for a devastatingly handsome date for lunch? Just let me check my calendar."

"Christophe, I need you to be serious," Denise replied, exasperated by his attempt at humour. "I have something that's going to help Phillip fight Jules. Something Mom's completely in the dark about. I'm going to use this information to destroy that bitch and put Phillip firmly back in charge! Get your ass over to my store! This is going to be awesome!"

Christophe countered Denise's last statement silently but with much vexation. *No, this is going to be a big fucking problem!*

He ached to tell Denise that not only was she a pain in his ass, she was also a terrible lay. And anything she told him was inevitably going to be used against Phillip.

"On my way. Can't wait to hear your news."

Disconnecting the call, Christophe shook his head, irritated and put out. Keeping tabs on Denise and her family had become an incredibly dull, uninteresting job, but he had made a promise, and he intended to keep it to the bitter end.

Christophe finished dressing, nodded "bro-like" at a couple of cute jocks on his way out of the changing room, and left to meet up with his fake girlfriend.

"Did she take the deal?"

Miles sat across from Jules, separated only by her imposing desk, in the very chair Amanda had recently vacated.

Though poised and ready to tell his tale of success, Miles paused before answering. *Something seems off about her.* He had noticed immediately upon entering Jules's office that his mentor was not herself, appearing painfully distracted. Distraction was not a trait he associated with her. Miles had worked alongside Jules long enough to know when something was on her mind.

He wanted to press her. He wanted to know if he could manipulate her into telling him what her problem was. Were his skills up to the challenge of luring information out of the great Jules Cartell?

After his triumph with Denise, Miles was on a high. He had to at least try, figuring he would start small with a benign concern for her health. Since she was always so centred, he would tell her that she seemed off, how that worried him, and if something was troubling her, he was there to listen. She could count on him for unflappable support. He had just helped her with Denise, no questions asked.

Miles was confident Jules would open up to him.

"Are you okay, Jules?" he asked with the most convincing, concerned puppy-dog eyes he could muster. "You seem distant, preoccupied. Is it that stomach virus that's been making its way around the office? Are you feeling unwell?"

Raising her left eyebrow, Jules scrunched up her lovely, perfectly aligned nose. Arching her back, she folded her hands together, placing them soundly on the desk.

Miles recognized these menacing cues. His gambit had failed; Jules had seen right through him. He realized that he had miscalculated her level of distraction and susceptibility. He never really stood a chance, not against her, but it was too late to backpedal.

Miles was not totally off in his assessment, though; Jules was preoccupied with things unknown to him.

While her plans for Phillip were always paramount in her head, what currently vexed Jules was her father's unavailability and elusive behaviour. She had barely heard from him since his departure from Fairporte two days ago. Also, Amanda's unexpected visit had upset her more than she thought possible.

With all that taken into account, Jules was still never anyone's dupe; distracted, sluggish, and gullible were not traits she identified with. She always recognized the use of sleight of hand and subtle manipulation as she had mastered them ages ago. Jules knew Miles was attempting to pry into her personal affairs using guile and chicanery.

"Really, Miles? It's bad enough you introduced me to important guests last night as Mrs. Cartell, but to come into my presence in my office and scry me like a gypsy's crystal ball is just too much. While I appreciate your talents, you will not hone your skills at my expense. Am I understood?"

"Yes, Ju—er, Ms. Cartell, one hundred percent. My sincerest apologies." Honestly contrite, Miles decided, though not quickly enough, on formality.

He was very aware that he had unwisely overstepped his bounds due to sheer bluster and ego. Jules was the master at manipulation, the best Miles had ever seen. He wanted to kick himself for not instantly realizing that she would easily see right through his attempt at such mind games. Good as he was, he was an amateur next to her.

Miles considered the possibility that he was now on thin ice with Jules, especially after screwing up her introduction at last night's party.

"I can't figure out what made you slip up last night, Miles," Jules sighed. "It's not like you. I've decided to forgive that incident now that you know my feelings surrounding it. I'm not going to ask you why or how. You messed up, not me, so you figure out the whys and hows and make sure it never happens again. Now, tell me what Denise said. I won't ask again."

Miles gulped, noticeably, nervously.

He needed to re-prove his importance to Jules, his usefulness. He had made enemies getting to his current position, and if Jules ever decided to demote him, he was fucked. Miles had stepped on many toes during his climb up the ladder of success. There were plenty of people who wanted him taken down a peg or two. As long as he was Jules's favourite, he was untouchable, and that could not change.

"Yes, so I brought to Denise's attention how it was beneficial for both of us to trust one another. I followed the script you wrote for me, and she bought it completely. It was quite pathetic to see the desperation in her eyes for information her mother didn't already possess. She obviously feels purposely kept out of the loop, undervalued, and routinely ignored by the rest of her family."

Jules smiled in agreement. "Denise pretends she's above them all, unblemished by her family's secrets and schemes, but I know it eats away at her. The fact that she's constantly, purposely left out of those schemes and family secrets. It kills Denise that her mother and siblings don't trust her enough to confide in her, ask her opinion or value her contribution.

"Denise acts unbothered by this, but no one buys it. She's a member of her family in name only, always on the outside of their inner circle. Excellent observations, Miles. Continue."

Miles readily complied, his sycophantic nature goading him on, eager to impress his mentor. Jules's power, especially her confidence and strategic brilliance, was a potent aphrodisiac, beguiling and inspiring.

Miles desired such power; it was addictive, an opiate. Jules was an excellent teacher, and he was a determined, quick study. Miles absorbed all Jules said and did with gleeful abandon. A covetous man by nature, Miles wanted what Jules had, even going so far as to snag himself a wealthy, blonde-haired, blue-eyed lover.

"I convinced Denise of my intentions, the reasons I'd risk betraying you, and at first, she was suspicious and skeptical of my veracity. I used the terms and ideas you suggested judiciously, and it worked. Also, finding out I'd already sold information to Stella riled her up."

"If she understands anything, Denise understands business. As I explained it, Miles, if you phrase it in a way that makes your intentions sound like a basic business stratagem, she'll see the verisimilitude of your argument."

"And she did. You were spot on, Jules." Having regained his confidence, Miles returned to familiarity. "Denise agreed that it was a sound business opportunity, admitting that she accepts self-serving and egomaniacal traits as commonplace among economic movers and shakers. Once we agreed on a price, and that wasn't easy, the cheap bitch, I told her what you wanted me to."

"Joseph taught her this verifiable truth about the ruthlessness of business," Jules added, "but she'll never acknowledge that her father helped her succeed in any way. Denise will go to her grave, saying she's a wholly self-made entrepreneur. You'll never hear me defend him or say that he wasn't a snake and a monster, but Joseph understood capitalism and commerce better than most.

"It's no great secret, really, her feelings of inadequacy. Denise the equal to Phillip in Joseph's eyes? There was never even the remote possibility that when Joseph voluntarily stepped down or died, he'd give the reins of the company to Denise over Phillip, his firstborn and only son."

Miles took advantage of Jules's need to take a breath so he could make a subtle jab at the Cartell brood. "And Sonja! It's a good thing she's so pretty. Not a lot going on upstairs."

"Sonja." Jules rolled her eyes loudly. "Everyone knows that dumb bitch couldn't run a bath. Sonja's lucky she's rich because looks fade. Beauty, Miles, is a weapon for the young. It's a sabre that dulls over time, often faster than you can sharpen it, so never think you can rely on it forever. You'll only end up looking foolish and pitiable. Remember that.

"Fillers, Botox, and plastic surgery don't cure ageing. It's good for some freshening up, but it's fooling no one. I'm not an ageist—I'm a realist. Yes, you can be beautiful at any age, but if you think you can use your looks to manipulate people in your fifties and sixties as you did in your twenties and thirties, you're delusional.

"Denise isn't moved by vanity like her sister. She understood from the get-go that to be seen, she had no choice but to go out on her own if she wanted to escape the long shadows cast by the males in her family. To not try and compete with her brother. You, of all people, Miles, should understand that. What price did Denise agree to?"

Jules was very interested in the answer. Her smile was crooked and smug.

Additionally, she took perverse pleasure in bringing up Miles's overly critical family. It was an unseemingly passive-aggressive thing to do, but Jules was still a tad irked by his earlier bravado. She could forgive herself for indulging in some bitchiness if it caged his ego and reminded him of his failings.

Jules disliked pettiness, but that did not mean she was above it.

Miles maintained his composure, even at the mention of his family. Jules had not rattled him enough to break his concentration or countenance; understandably, as his mentor, this pleased her. She had personally trained Miles to hone his imperturbability to the point of steel, and he had done so this time admirably. She was impressed with his fortitude.

"We went back and forth," Miles continued, "but Denise eventually agreed to twenty-five grand."

Jules clapped her hands together, laughed, and nodded her head spiritedly.

Miles was shocked by his mentor's behaviour. However, his instinct for self-preservation kicked in, and he kept his mouth shut, his demeanour composed, and his poker face on point.

Jules was never one to show overt joy or merriment, especially not in front of employees. Despite his elevated status and position within the company, Miles was still a subordinate. So, in response to her odd, out-of-character reaction, he simply grinned, nodding his appreciation for her jocular acceptance of his work.

"Excellent," Jules stated, barely holding back her laughter. "As I explained earlier, the cost of your information had to be high enough to show Denise you were in earnest. A monetary value Stella wouldn't blink at. If too low, it would suggest your knowledge and access to it was second-rate, and Stella Cartell never paid for second-rate.

"This is good, very entertaining. Denise is completely unsuspecting. Tell me what you told her was worth twenty-five thousand dollars. I want to make sure you said it correctly."

Miles was mildly insulted by her diminished confidence in his abilities and did not feel he deserved her subtle dig. He had followed her instructions to the letter.

"I said you planned to sabotage the Parisian deal, blaming Phillip for its failure, highlighting his drinking and lack of focus. You would reveal that he had not submitted the paperwork for trademarking the Parisian's Canadian Brand, and now several identical products were going to be released by a North American competitor, months ahead of them.

"Furthermore, you would leak this failure and his blunders to the press. A multimillion-dollar loss! He would become a laughing stock and embarrassment to Cartell Worldwide. Phillip would be strongly encouraged to step down from the board and resign of his own accord or risk a public ousting from his family's company. And Denise knows which way you and Charles would vote.

"Finally, I brought up the fact that Denise couldn't do a damn thing to prevent it, just like with Stella's ousting. She had sold her shares, leaving her without voting power, and Sonja and her mother wouldn't have enough clout to prevent Phillip's downfall."

Jules reclined in her chair, a contented expression on her face.

Miles had done his part satisfactorily, and now Jules did not have to worry about her sister-in-law getting underfoot. Denise would waste her time looking in the wrong place.

Vindictive

"Jules, I—I'm not entirely sure why we're doing this," Miles questioned hesitantly. "We won't even know for certain if the Beaubier Paris deal is a go until Monday at the earliest. So, if this is all just one giant mind game, I mean, I know Denise is a bore and a bother."

"But you want to know why I set this grandiose intrigue in motion when we both know the story won't stand up under scrutiny," Jules stated, finishing Miles's question for him.

Miles nodded.

"The contracts aren't signed," Jules continued, "and there are no patents we need to concern ourselves with yet. Denise will never find any actual proof, and the reason she won't find anything is that I don't intend on doing anything you told her I planned to do. It's all a total fabrication."

Miles enjoyed a sound con job, and playing a cruel joke on Denise was good for a laugh. This story, however, was so ridiculously complex, yet so flimsy if anyone shone a light directly on it, it seemed a waste of time, energy, and opportunity.

There had to be something more attuned to Denise's personal life they could have played with to cause her grief. Miles wanted to destroy her business, her reputation. How could this information humiliate Denise and wreak havoc on her life? When she discovered the story was untrue, she would feel stupid, gullible, but that was child's play and ultimately unsatisfying.

Miles wanted more.

Denise was in the way of his life with Christophe; he wanted her fucking destroyed. He looked to Jules for an answer.

"Okay, Miles, I'll let you in on a secret," Jules whispered with conspiratorial intent, looking around the room as if she was afraid someone might overhear her revelation. "I hope you're ready for this. It's very, very big."

Jules stopped and looked around the room again. Miles noted she appeared quite apprehensive; it whetted his appetite for this private information.

"Yes? Please, go on!" Miles was breathless with anticipation.

"I lied. I'm not telling, and you don't need to know why because it's not your concern. Don't ask again. You'll only annoy me, and that's not a good idea."

Miles was visibly shocked, taken aback, and mollified. This aggressive sarcasm was not the answer he wanted nor the answer he expected. Jules trusted him, to a degree, but Miles was not among her inner circle of confidants despite her exclusive mentoring of him. He got that now, loud and clear.

Whatever, it was fine; Miles was patient. He would graciously take her prickly personality, her pointed tone, and forceful words and play his part, small as it was, with humility and eagerness. Miles was confident that Jules would come around and eventually see his total value—his trustworthiness. He had gotten this far. He was the CTO of the damn company, and he was only thirty-one.

Miles conceded that Jules probably only trusted her father with her deepest secrets. He was deeply envious of that relationship, the closest parent/child bond he had ever seen.

His relationship with his own parents was fraught with discord, except for him being gay. They were cool with that as long as he married a doctor and had a child through surrogacy. Miles had the sense that he was a constant disappointment in their eyes.

Miles, always in the shadow of his older brother, the senior vice president of sales and marketing at the most prestigious advertising agency in Toronto, could never live up to his parents' expectations.

They had only been mildly impressed when Miles became the youngest non-family executive ever at Cartell Worldwide. His older brother, the golden child, was also the youngest executive at his company, including promotions based on nepotism. And, as his parents constantly reminded Miles, his brother had got there before him and at a younger age.

Nothing he did was ever good enough for his parents.

Miles sat up straight in his seat across from Jules. Despite her recent cacophony, she looked as poised and remarkably calm as if she had been sipping tea with the Queen of England all afternoon. *She's good. Be quiet. Listen. Learn. Don't take it personally.*

"Miles, listen, pay attention, and you'll learn much from me, but don't ever question my methods. If I wanted you to know more about my plan, you would. For now, you know what I need you to know. Patience and loyalty are what I require from you. The reward is great, never doubt that, and the time is coming when I'll get everything owed me. This company will be entirely mine soon. Now, please leave. I have things to do."

Reprimanded like a neophyte, Miles got up out of his seat to leave. "It's none of my business, I understand, and please know that I'm fully on board with whatever you need from me."

In his head, Miles silently voiced his affirmations regarding dealings with Jules. *Don't get offended; don't take it personally; perseverance rewards.* These personal precepts gave him clarity, soothing his simmering, unproductive anger.

It was anger directed towards his brilliant, uncompromising bitch of a boss and at himself for providing an opportunity for unabashed reproach. If he wanted to be as ruthless, as powerful as Jules one day, he had to be able to take the occasional smackdown and learn from it.

For the moment, Miles just wanted to get back to his office and call Christophe. He needed to hear the man's deep, hauntingly rhythmic voice tell him he wanted to fuck his brains out. He hoped Christophe was free for lunch.

"Miles, one more thing."

Swallowing his pride and irritation, Miles turned to face his mentor. "Yes, Ms. Cartell?" She was no longer Jules to him, at least for the rest of the day. He was not pushing his luck. Comporting himself, Miles regarded with some alacrity that she held the cheque Denise had given him.

"This is for you," Jules announced, handing over the cheque. "You've certainly earned it. Buy yourself something ridiculously extravagant. It's on Denise, after all!"

Jules laughed, boisterously happy; all signs of her recent displeasure and annoyance gone. She honestly enjoyed and appreciated Miles, and like a child under her protection and tutelage, she forgave his missteps. Never forgotten, never overlooked, but always forgiven because she did trust him. Just not with her plans for Phillip.

Miles felt incredibly close to Jules again. Her twisted version of parenting, of mentoring, was fine with him.

It had to be. She was never going to change.

Her legs were strong, muscular, and defined. Her black cotton skirt was crisp and businesslike from the front. From the back, the provocative slit teased erotically, showcasing those legs magnificently.

Her red pumps gave off a sex kitten, coquettish vibe. She wore them with resoluteness and authority like a dominatrix. Or the president of a Fortune 500 company. The white blouse, tucked neatly into her skirt, fit like a glove. Several buttons undone at the top exposed the beginning of a generous bosom. As she walked down the hall, her breasts bounced hypnotically, thanks to an expensive Victoria's Secret push-up bra.

At the end of her destination was a door; it opened into the foyer of one of the best suites the Château Bergé had to offer. It was five thousand dollars a night, but she knew he cared little for the cost of things. He had money to burn, and sometimes, for kicks, he did just that. She had watched him do it.

It always excited her to witness his detachment to wealth—his myriad and chaotic expressions of excess and frivolity.

She remembered with fondness the last time he had excited her with his cold, pathological immorality.

She had asked him to be ruthless, make her his toy, and use her body as he saw fit. And he had complied. She had screamed rapturously, enjoying the pleasure, the pain, and the degradation when he brought out the 9 iron and shoved it brutally inside her hot wetness.

While fucking her with his gold club, he had acted thoroughly dispassionate towards the experience. Despite his seeming disinterest, he still made her come hard.

She was so happy to have found him. He was her saviour, her lover, her patient.

Before entering the suite, she fussed with her thick, black hair. The backcombed, off her face style, was how he liked her to wear it. Thankfully, it had held in place after her travels.

Reaching into her purse, she pulled out her favourite perfume, Robert Piguet's Visa, and spritzed herself with it generously.

She knew he hated when she smelled so feminine, so pretty, and she hoped he would punish her again for annoying him. She was already moist at the thought of his strong hands around her throat, choking her as they fucked.

As hot and bothered as she was, she understood that he would want to discuss business before engaging in anything sexual.

That was why they were here, first and foremost, in Fairporte. He had important work to do: the destruction of a longtime enemy. As always, she was eager to help him, but she would be glad when this ugly business was complete, and they could return to Amsterdam, back to their games and their sadism.

Her willing part in their undertaking had begun quite some time back. Her first assignment in Fairporte, however, was just successfully completed. She could not wait to tell him it was all in motion.

Opening the door to their suite, she walked in with confidence and purpose.

Immediately, she saw him sitting at the antique French writing desk. She noted how important he looked situated behind the archaic desk in his modern Burberry suit going through papers and documents, a man possessed. He looked powerful, imposing. She was in love and totally under his spell—his thrall.

Of course, she still believed she was in control of him.

The second she closed the door, locking out the world that did not understand their love, their needs, their goals, he looked up at her, staring directly into her face with his black, dead eyes. They penetrated her to the soul with their glacial emptiness.

Occasionally—she had witnessed it—those same eyes grew big and fiery, percolating with sublime hate and rage. Dead or wrathful; those were the only two states of being she had ever experienced with him. That was how he was sexually, too, but she preferred his wrath over his detachment. She loved both sides, but one was way more fun.

"Is it done?" he asked coldly.

"Yes. She'll have the package within the hour."

"And?"

"The device is in place to let us know the instant she opens it. Your phone will start vibrating as if you're receiving a call."

"Excellent, Yasmine. Now, come here."

Yasmine obeyed and walked eagerly towards him, her heart beating faster. Perspiration built up around her hairline. She was surprised that their business had ended quickly, considering how anal-retentive he was about details, but she was not complaining.

When she reached the desk, close enough to smell his delicious skin, Yasmine whispered, "I'm yours."

"What did I tell you about wearing that perfume in my presence! You love to defy me, don't you, whore. I'll show you how I punish women who defy me."

Yasmine gasped as her white blouse was forcibly ripped off her body. She delighted in his brute strength.

He reached down and took a pair of small, decorative scissors out of the desk drawer and placed the point of the instrument flat against the quivering skin of her right breast. He pushed the sharp end down into her flesh forcefully, drawing droplets of blood. Yasmine groaned in ecstasy.

Angry that she had enjoyed his torment, he pulled the scissors out and began cutting up her bra savagely. It was soon nothing but rags and tendrils of silk stained with blood and sweat. He tore the remainder of the garment off her; this fully exposed her naked breasts to him.

Leaning in, he ran his tongue over the fleshy mounds, lapping up the remaining trickles of blood before biting down hard on a delicate, erect nipple.

Yasmine screamed, "Yes, more!"

Furiously, he turned her wanton body around, pushing her down onto the desk. Her arms flailed about before landing hard against the unforgiving wood. Her naked back, now on display, invited his carnal attention, enticing his depraved urges. He took his strong right hand and punched her viciously in the small of her back.

Yasmine coughed, initially unable to catch her breath, but then she moaned with satisfaction. Her face winced at the pain, but just as quickly, her mouth opened, and her tongue wriggled out, licking her parted red painted lips.

Moving his hand up the provocative slit in Yasmine's skirt, he aggressively pulled her black lace panties down her thighs. Then, he proceeded to force his whole fist up inside her, into her damp, vulnerable, and inviting opening. Yasmine nearly orgasmed right then and there.

"Yours, forever," she gasped, breathless and enthralled. "My William."

X

Charles looked anxiously at his Bvlgari watch for the third time since entering the taxi. Due to mechanical error, his flight from Calgary to Montréal had been late because of a delayed take-off. He feared he had arrived too late to make his meeting with Monsieur Babineaux.

When the plane finally landed at Montréal-Trudeau, Charles had quickly disembarked, grabbed his small, black Dior travel bag and took the first taxi he saw upon exiting the terminal. He had instructed his driver, an Iraqi refugee who introduced himself as Khaleel, to transport him directly to his destination as swiftly as possible.

Before Charles left Fairporte, Jules had demanded he not employ a town car or limo service during his fact-finding mission, fearing Stella could track his whereabouts through their records. Jules believed that Stella, properly galvanized, would stop at nothing to uncover her father's motive for leaving so abruptly if she deemed his sudden departure suspicious.

Not only was Charles banned from using his preferred mode of transport, but Jules had instructed him to avoid using debit and credit cards. Cash prevented an electronic paper trail.

Citing astuteness over paranoia, Jules suspected Stella was watching their movements. Both father and daughter knew that the self-styled Dowager Empress had plenty of free time on her hands since being stripped of her position at Cartell Worldwide. Stella's desire to find something useful to hurt them with was barefaced and unwavering.

Charles was confident he had taken every precaution to ensure that Stella—ever suspicious and scrutinizing—never discovered the real reason for his trip. It was a source of pride for him, remaining highly inconspicuous regarding his nationwide investigation.

Thanks to infallible planning and stealthy maneuvering, Charles believed he had successfully stayed off Stella's radar. Everyone joked that the old bitch had yet to grasp the concept of Uber.

Charles took note that Khaleel, while pleasant enough, blathered incessantly and kept twitching at random. He began to wonder if his cab driver suffered from PTSD. Charles, already on edge from his flight fiasco, wanted to tell the man to shut up, get over his discomfort with awkward silences, and stop moving about so unnecessarily. It was annoying and off-putting.

He did not say those things aloud, though. The memory of his late husband's naturally compassionate voice immediately popped into his head, offering pointed words of advice. *Don't be an asshole, Charles,* he imagined Jason saying to him in his usual caring yet no-nonsense tone.

Happy the situation brought to life the discarnate presence of his beloved Jason, Charles kept his calm. He chose to empathize with Khaleel and disregard his vexing movements and peculiarities.

To drown out his driver's chatter, Charles focused on his upcoming meeting with M. Claude Babineaux. M. Babineaux had formerly been one of Cartell Worldwide's attorneys—a managing partner, even—from the firm Joseph eventually sacked in favour of Castle Dunning and Briggs.

Retired from practicing law, M. Babineaux had completed a Ph.D. in Political Science and was now a visiting lecturer at several universities. Charles was sure that this veteran lawyer possessed the final piece of the puzzle he had been sent out into the world to solve: the secret of Phillip's first marriage.

Charles had sent Jules a brief text right before boarding the plane in Calgary. The cryptic message read: **I've conceivably found something—leverage that we can use to oust Phillip from the company.** Jules had yet to text back. Charles assumed she understood his meaning: he was not ready to discuss or reveal anything. He was comfortable with accepting her silence as shrewd perception.

Vindictive

To drown out the abrasive cacophony that relentlessly emanated from Khaleel's mouth, Charles retreated further into his surging thoughts. He journeyed back to when this undertaking—his quest to find Phillip's first wife—began. It was a brutal scene still fresh in his mind's eye, the impact on him unmistakably raw and deeply felt.

Charles's role in Phillip's downfall began only days after Joseph's funeral when Jules had left an ambiguous text message on his phone to meet her at the office.

Arriving at Cartell Worldwide's Toronto headquarters, Charles had not expected to find his daughter in Joseph's vacant office, boldly situated at the dead man's desk.

Looking around the room, Charles had instantly noticed that Joseph's presence—his larger-than-life persona—was undeniably absent. This vacated vitality had left this once imposing office sterile and wanting. The large room felt eerie and strangely atmospheric; the quiet space appeared ominous and forsaken.

None of the Gothic theatricality of emotion Charles felt—the sombreness of loss and abandonment—resonated with Jules; she appeared perfectly at ease with her surroundings. Charles noted how relaxed his daughter was in Joseph's executive swivel chair.

Caressing the expensive leather, Jules gave her father a knowing smile. She was confident in her assumption that he had spent his first few moments in her presence being thoughtful regarding his absent friend. His sentimentality was written all over his face.

As she continued looking at her father, Jules's calculated smile quickly vanished. Shaking her head, she openly judged his perspective unfavourably.

"Look at this leather monstrosity," Jules snarled. "This seat is plumped with duck feathers! Cruel and disgusting. This entire thing makes my skin crawl.

"Joseph sure loved this chair, though, didn't he, Pops? I bet the old bastard felt powerful and imposing when he sat in it, lording over his kingdom. Pompous, arrogant prick! One of the first things I'm going to do with this office when I'm in charge? Haul this out of here and set it on fire."

Jules reached out and picked up a long, slim, shiny object off the desk—an unassuming, silver letter opener engraved with the letters JC. Viciously, she stabbed the chair with it. The leather upholstery made an abrasive popping sound as the sharp blade tore into it.

Charles's mouth gaped wide in confusion; his disbelieving eyes professed surprise and distress. "Jules! Have you lost your mind? What the devil's gotten into you?"

"The devil, you say! Appropriate, but the world doesn't need made-up fiends to fear or blame when the real, human evil is so potent and three-dimensional. Do you want to talk about the evil that's gotten under my skin? I'll mention it by name, Pops. Joseph Cartell."

Charles was shocked and embarrassed by his daughter's callousness, especially in light of Joseph's recent passing and the violent circumstances surrounding his death. He reminded Jules that Joseph had always treated her like one of his children. He demanded she immediately cease speaking ill of his late friend and employer, scolding her for being so insensitive.

Raging at his daughter was something he had never done before, but Charles was angered by her egregious behaviour. He implored Jules to give a reason for her odious deportment. He wanted answers as to why she had summoned him here so mysteriously, so urgently only to rail against a man who had been their friend for years? Eventually, family.

"Are you done?" Jules asked calmly. "If so, I'll tell you why Joseph is the devil. He's a liar, a monster, and a murderer."

Picking up the folders she had kept hidden in her lap, Jules threw them all onto the desk. Their contents spilled out haphazardly in front of Charles: documents, flash drives, and photographs.

Before reaching out to investigate the documents his daughter flagrantly flung at him, Charles took a moment to gather himself.

He needed a second to process the accusatory words Jules had used to describe a man he had considered one of his best friends.

Charles was very aware Joseph had been no angel. He knew the man had done countless disreputable things in the fight against his business rivals and naysayers, keeping people under his thumb through bullying and intimidation.

That being said, by no means did Charles think of himself as irreproachable or righteous; his hands were not that clean. He had willingly helped Joseph on many occasions perform and cover up these deeds. It was the price one had to pay to stay on top of the food chain.

Neither he nor Joseph had ever crossed the line into anything more illegal than blackmail and extortion. It was just how men of their position and power did business. They could be bastards, but they were good men, family men at their core. Charles was sure it was all nonsense and misunderstanding.

They certainly had never done anything as repugnant as murder!

Feeling empowered by his convictions, Charles picked up a folder expecting to find nothing he did not already know. To his utter anguish and dismay, what he found was pure evil, chilling him to the marrow.

For the first time since the death of his husband, Charles felt like someone had just shot a bullet into his heart.

"He—he had Ambroise killed? And all those people on his boat!" Charles was barely able to spit out the words.

"Yes," Jules answered back solemnly. "I'm afraid that's just the tip of the iceberg."

There were numerous brazen photographs of dead bodies; proof of a job done, a problem solved. Charles looked over dozens of large money transfers to several accounts, all unfamiliar to him. Many for the express purpose of, according to Joseph's notation: removing threats and business obstacles.

One such account was titled "The Silver Dagger," while another, similarly colourful, was designated "The Gold Leopard."

Not everything was recent; some of the evidence dated back decades. The body count was high, and it made Charles want to vomit. He had always known Joseph kept up-to-date, comprehensive files on every move he made, that was no secret, but this was something beyond clerical. It was controlled paranoia, autocracy, and true villainy.

Recognizing the monstrous nature of what he beheld, Charles could not help but notice how masterful an undertaking it was. An entire world existed right under his nose, but not once did he ever suspect anything.

His daughter had discovered it, not him.

"Brilliant, evil," Charles whispered under his breath.

"I know, I understand," Jules consoled. Her appearance and demeanour remained stony.

"No, Jules, you don't! You don't understand! How could I have not known all this was going on? I was his lawyer, his best friend. For years, Joseph and I protected our families from our enemies—but this!"

Grabbing some of the papers, Charles lifted them into the air. Waving them around frantically, he shouted, "This is murder, Jules! Assassination! I never thought in a million years that my friend could be capable of this. I don't know the person who did these things. If Stella or Phillip ever found out I—I just—I don't know what to say."

It was unlike Charles to be tongue-tied and easily shaken, but it had all become too much for him. Reaching his breaking point, Charles gave up on words and thoughts and slumped down on the couch on the opposite side of the room, away from Jules and the damning evidence.

The vomitous feeling in the pit of his stomach returned, making its way up the back of his throat, where it thankfully stayed. Even though he felt unbelievably stupid and duped, Charles strove to remain composed.

Since the reclamation of his life—his departure from the mire of debilitating despair brought on by Jason's death—Charles had come to rely on his steadfast business association and personal friendship with Joseph. Now, in the lifespan of a single breath, all of that trust and dependency laid destroyed at his feet.

"I won't sugar-coat this for you, Pops. It's awful, yes, but it's the truth. You need to deal with it. I've already looked all of this over, but now you need to. I printed out everything I found on the thumb and flash drives. Nothing was on the server. That bastard was too paranoid that someone might hack the system and discover his dirty laundry.

"Take your time, Pops, but you need to do this. And I'm sorry, but you also need to know the truth about Stella. I never liked that vile woman."

For an hour, Charles reluctantly, yet earnestly poured over the cornucopia of secret, damning evidence. He shook his head continuously, unable to believe his trusted friend and employer had kept all this hidden from him.

Charles could not wrap his head around Joseph and Ambroise having done illegal, disreputable business together without him even knowing about it. Charles was glad Jacques's hands were clean. He liked the young man and knew Jules was friends with him.

What he discovered about Stella enraged him. What Jules had said before about knowing the truth about her made sense. It quickly became apparent to Charles that Stella had known about several of the crimes; she was even a willing participant in their design and cover-up.

The one discovery that completely blew his mind came from the last document he read.

"No! I can't believe this. Jules, you saw this?"

"Of course. I printed it out, remember."

"Right, sorry. Phillip was married before, at eighteen! And he had a child!"

"Stop!" Jules ordered. "I don't want to discuss that. Right now, we need to formulate a plan, a decisive course of action.

"First, we need to deal with Joseph and Stella's vile transgression. We can't go to the authorities with all this. It would destroy the company, ruin our reputation. Who would believe we didn't know about any of this? Plead ignorance? I wouldn't believe us."

"Vile transgressions! Are you kidding me? We can't just sit on this! It isn't right. Those people—"

"Were mostly criminals," Jules bluntly blurted out over him. "I know the innocents that got caught in the crossfire, like Jacques's mom, deserve justice—and they'll get it, I promise, but I won't throw myself on a pyre for these people.

"And neither will you! I've worked too hard to get to where I am. I've worked too hard to get you back. I won't lose everything over this.

"No, I've thought long and hard about this, Pops. The best course of action to take, to vindicate the innocent and avenge this betrayal, is to destroy Joseph's family, take his company and erase his legacy."

"Jules, what are you saying?"

"Wasn't I sufficiently clear? We're going to rip this entire empire from the Cartells and claim it as our own. We're going to start by stripping Stella of her power, removing her direct influence over the company's day-to-day operations. We'll have her evicted from her board seat, one way or another, and then we'll work on destroying Phillip."

"Jules, what does any of this have to do with Phillip? He's your husband! I know he's been jealous and petty at times, and he's obviously keeping secrets from you concerning his past, but to destroy him, end your marriage?

"There's no love lost between us for what he considers my continued interference in your relationship, which you know is only my stake in your happiness. I do believe he truly loves you. Despite his many faults, I know he's been faithful.

"Honey, I'm worried you're acting irrationally. It's not like you to lay blame where it's not warranted. The sins of the father don't always fall on the child. I know that truth first hand. You weren't to blame for my failings as a parent. Phillip isn't mean, calculating or manipulative like Joseph was—he just doesn't have it in him.

"I can't believe I'm saying this, considering how angry I am, but we need to think this through unemotionally and judiciously before we start ruining lives."

"I have thought this through," Jules stated confidently. "Phillip has to pay for what he did. And pay dearly." Jules stared at her father sternly to show him that she was resolute in her decision, her predetermined judgment.

Charles had no idea how much hurt, pain, and sadness Jules held back. She refused to cry, to show weakness.

"Jules, honey, what did Phillip do?"

Because she made every effort to appear cold and unshakable, Jules did not expect her father to understand. What she had discovered about her husband had ripped her heart to shreds. She could not tell her father what Phillip had done; she was still processing it herself.

And Jules honestly feared her father might actually lose his mind and go out and kill Phillip upon hearing the total truth. It was too risky. Jules had decided it was in her best interest to hold on to the totality of the Cartell sins until the time was right to reveal all.

"Pops, I can't tell you why Phillip is just as much a monster as his parents. Not yet. I'm barely holding in my anger about it despite how collected I appear. There are documents I can't share with you just yet, and I need you to trust that I know what's best for all of us. I've earned that trust, don't you think?"

Charles could not argue her point's veracity; it was undeniable. He owed his daughter every confidence in her abilities and intelligence. He knew she had it under control; frankly, he was all too aware he was not in the right state of mind to offer much insight into a well-thought-out plan of revenge at the moment.

"Jules, you know how much I love and trust you. You're my world. If you say it's for the best, I'll follow your lead without question. If you say Phillip must be destroyed, so be it. I'll take down the whole fucking family if you ask me to."

"I'm glad we're on the same page, Pops."

Jules made the statement without showing a shred of emotion or gratefulness for her father's complete belief in her. She decided now was the right time for her demeanour to adopt a sense of absolute coldness and detachment; it would be her armour in the coming war.

Understandably, so she did not lose her mind, Jules planned to split what she knew of Joseph's many dark, ugly secrets between her father and Jacques. She could not share Phillip's crime with her father, but she felt comfortable trusting that information to Jacques.

Equivalently, Jacques could never discover some of the things her father already knew, such as the fact that Joseph had arranged and paid for his father's murder. Jules cared for Jacques too much to burden him with that terrible knowledge.

Sharing the stress and mental weight of knowing such vile things between the two men she loved and trusted the most was the only way Jules felt she could remain in control of her plan to punish the guilty. Keeping everything to herself would eventually overwhelm her and cause her to lose focus. She recognized her own emotional limits.

"Now, Denise sold her stake in the company, so she's irrelevant, but Sonja could prove problematic. Her shares are firmly under Stella's control. Joseph's will cemented my position of power in the company, and Phillip isn't contesting. To neutralize Stella, I need to get you on the board, Pops, and her off of it. First, we should—"

Charles put his hand up in the air, cutting his daughter off mid-sentence, and waited for her to cease talking. Before Jules went too far with her machinations and schemes, Charles asked her how she came by all this evidence. And where were the incriminating files that outlined his own less-than-ethical business practices?

"There are no incriminating files that pertain to you," Jules stated plainly, winking at her father. "Well, not anymore, and we never have to discuss it."

"But Jules, I need you to understand why I did some of the things I did. You can't just—"

"I can, and I did," she interrupted, her voice unwavering and powerful. "You're no murderer, and you have nothing to atone for that you haven't already paid for in spades."

Charles knew she meant his emotional abandonment of her following Jason's death.

"I'm always on your side, Pops, as you are on mine. Understand this—it's done! As for the other part of your query? That's where it gets interesting.

"The day after Joseph's funeral, I received a package from UPS addressed to me, in care of the company, and sent by a Mr. Maurice Comstock of Livingston Graciano and Poole. They're a prominent legal firm operating out of Calgary, but we've never interacted with them.

"I don't like receiving unsolicited packages addressed to me, but it appeared unassuming. Once I had the letterhead verified and the information on the packing slip substantiated by UPS, I felt comfortable with its authenticity and opened it.

"Inside the package was a brief letter from Mr. Comstock, a keycard, and a printed résumé. After reading the letter, I realized Comstock's résumé had no relationship to the package. I appreciate someone jumping on an opportunity, even applaud their tenacity, except this time it was so obvious, so tacky. Considering the circumstances.

"But it's not about this, and by the look on your face, Pops, I'm only confusing you by referring to circumstances before I've divulged what they are.

"In the letter, Mr. Comstock stated that he'd previously been employed by the firm of Newland Babineaux Dewhurst Kahn and Associates."

Charles felt slightly on edge, even anxious at hearing the name of the firm he and Jules had convinced Joseph to terminate all ties with so he could hire their law firm. *This can't mean anything good.* "Really? That's highly suspicious."

"I know, Pops, but I decided to continue reading his letter without prejudice. If anything, the significance and purpose of the keycard needed explanation. I suspected that Comstock wanted me to know that he had this connection to us, albeit peripherally.

"And I was right. This link quickly revealed itself to be significant. Comstock had worked directly under one of the partners, and while he no longer had any ties or loyalty to his former firm, he still kept in touch with this man. On the day of the press release concerning Joseph's passing, this unnamed partner contacted Comstock. He had asked him to perform one final service.

"At the time of his former firm's split with Cartell Worldwide, Comstock was given this keycard by this partner. Why the partner had this item in the first place was not revealed in the letter, nor was the reason he did not keep it but instead gave it to an associate to safeguard.

"Once he'd agreed to mail it to me, Comstock was told the keycard's function by the partner. It's the only thing that can bypass the fingerprint identification security feature of Joseph's secondary personal safe."

Charles rose from his seat, surveying the room manically in search of something. Shaking his head, he marched over to Joseph's desk. Punching in a set of numbers on the security monitor built into the hardwood of the upper left drawer, Charles watched with conviction as it popped open.

The desk drawer was empty.

Undaunted by this apparent revelation of nothingness, Charles reached inside the drawer and pressed a button built into the top of the empty chamber. Suddenly, the large Picasso oil painting Joseph had purchased at a Sotheby's auction and outfitted in an ornate gold-leaf frame sprang forward from the wall. A hidden, high-tech safe built into the wall behind it was revealed.

"I know about this safe!" Charles snapped. "Tell me, Jules, where is this mystery second safe?"

"Pops, calm down. We both know about the safe behind the Picasso. So does Phillip, and probably Stella, too. Please, sit down and let me continue."

Frustrated and riled, Charles slammed his fist down on the desk. His hand throbbing, he looked into the stern yet understanding eyes of his daughter and instantly felt ashamed; his actions bespoke irrationality.

Shrinking from Jules's side, Charles slumped back down on the couch.

"As I was saying, Comstock was also given a passcode and told to provide me with that as well. It works in conjunction with the keycard to open the safe. He thanked me in his letter for considering his résumé, and that was that."

Charles wanted to get up off the couch and walk back over to his daughter, but he stayed where he was, idle and thoughtful.

Remaining seated in Joseph's chair, Jules did not need her father to ask her again the most obvious, important question concerning this mystery and subterfuge. She could tell he was tired of the game and wanted a direct explanation.

However, before Jules could satiate her father's curiosity, he spoke up first.

"You have a keycard and a passcode to an unknown safe. I assume this nameless lawyer and former confidant of Joseph's wanted you to open this safe and uncover these documents. Revenge? For what?

"And where is this safe? It exists, for you found all this inside of it, but I don't recall hearing you mention being told the whereabouts of it in the letter."

"Perceptive, Pops. Comstock didn't reveal the safe's location in his letter. Perhaps he doesn't know where it is. Maybe this unnamed partner doesn't trust him with that information. It's really not that important.

"No doubt, Comstock expects a reply from us concerning his résumé and interest in joining our team, and that means we have the upper hand. We'll get back to him when he becomes useful to us. I want to know who this unnamed partner is, but for now, it's not imperative.

"I knew the location of the safe the moment I looked at the passcode number. It's clever, but anyone who has watched Joseph as I have starts to see his patterns. You know what the passcode is to the safe you just opened, right? Humour me, Pops."

"Fine," Charles sighed. "It's the date of Picasso's birth followed by the date of his death. Place a capital P in front and another at the end. Voila, the drawer opens."

"Correct. Now, what do these letters and numbers mean to you? K3619409232007D."

Charles shrugged, exasperated. "I don't know. Let me think."

"No, don't guess. I can see you've had enough of this. It's the same function as the Picasso passcode but with Ken Danby. I realized the second safe was behind the Danby piece in his private washroom.

"If you push hard inwards while holding onto the oak frame, the whole thing comes off, revealing a smaller safe protected by a thumbprint identifier and security code. The keycard, when it fits into a slot, overrides the need for a thumbprint. Once you punch in the passcode, the safe can be opened."

That night, Jules had admitted to her father that she could not possibly have known opening Joseph's secret safe would have unequivocally changed both their lives forever.

Charles had had his world upended before, with his husband's death, but Joseph's years of lies and betrayal had cut deep in a different way. A way that made him feel rage and hatred, not loss and despair.

"Sir? Sir!" Khaleel shouted, interrupting Charles's thoughts, freeing him from the recesses of his memory.

"What? Are we nearly there?"

"No, sir, construction up ahead. I'll have to take a detour. It will add another twenty minutes to our journey. Sorry."

For fuck's sake, Charles silently cursed.

XI

Charles was forty minutes late for his appointment. His phone calls and the texts to M. Babineaux had all gone unanswered. Not one of his explanatory apologies for his lateness had received a single response; this had Charles quite worried.

When Khaleel pulled up in front of the university's political science building, Charles practically hopped out of the taxi. After paying the man, he quickly made his way to M. Babineaux's office. It took a minute to find the correct faculty floor, but eventually, Charles located the room.

Rapping repeatedly on the door, Charles desperately hoped the Frenchman was still there.

"Come in, Monsieur Dunning." The voice on the other side of the door was gritty yet soft-spoken.

Charles was in luck; M. Babineaux was still in his office, willing to see him.

Opening the door, Charles discovered the room looked exactly like he expected it to.

Littered with books, tomes legal and political being the bulk of the collection, the room owned a functional yet heavy-looking, old-school mahogany desk. It took up a considerable amount of space.

The professor's chair, somewhat worn, had a large, deep buttoned back that gave it a plush, comfortable bearing despite its years of use. It looked regal, after a fashion, and Charles noted it gave off a sense of stately importance to the man currently occupying it.

M. Babineaux, as he sat in his chair, showed no outward sign of annoyance or irritation. More bemusement, if anything; this surprised Charles.

"I'm terribly sorry for my lateness, M. Babineaux. There's no excuse, but if I could explain—"

"Settle down," the Frenchman interrupted. "Pas besoin de vous réprimander. *There is no need to reprimand yourself.* I am not upset. On the contrary, I am pleased to meet you. Surprised, actually, that you came at all. I expected you to abandon our meeting altogether. Sit, please."

Charles graciously sat down in a plastic and metal chair meant to accommodate a student; it was contemporary, inexpensive, and uncomfortable. He figured it was M. Babineaux's method of creating a subtle tier of importance and stature in his small office. Charles clearly understood how it applied to him. In his current position, the ball was very much in M. Babineaux's proverbial court, for without his help, Charles had nothing to take back to Jules.

"Why would you think that?" Charles questioned, genuinely shocked by M. Babineaux's statement.

"You have to ask?" A sly grin appeared on the Frenchman's face. Not sinister, but highly speculative and voraciously curious.

"I'm afraid, sir, you have me stumped as to the reason. I've travelled quite a distance to meet you. When Mr. Comstock arranged for us to have this sit down, I was very pleased you agreed without any hesitation. My daughter—"

"Yes, your daughter," M. Babineaux interrupted again, "is quite beautiful, even more intelligent, and cunning. She knows why. The reason the two of you should abandon this quest, I mean. Some things are better left in the past, dead and buried. It will lead to a dark end, M. Dunning, and much sorrow.

"Before I reveal what I know, please enlighten me as to the reason or reasons you have tracked me down after all this time. Pretend I know nothing of your intentions or why you require my help."

"With all due respect, sir, why play these games?"

M. Babineaux smiled and looked directly into the eyes of his guest. "Because I am an old man, much older than you. Because I miss the days of intrigue and control and the defeat of my competitors. Because I miss the occasions when Joseph and I would take on rival companies and defeat hostile takeover attempts.

"Basically, I miss doing the things you did for him. You see, I was you, so-to-speak, before Joseph fired my firm and replaced us—me in his esteem with you, M. Dunning."

Charles's face took on a mournful grimace. It was public knowledge that he and Jules had been instrumental in defaming M. Babineaux's law firm, poaching Cartell Worldwide from them. It had all been legal and above board. Still, many believed Phillip's infatuation with Jules played a massive part in Joseph's suspiciously quick decision to dismiss a law firm that had been with him for over a decade.

"Sir, I haven't come here to make you uncomfortable or to rub salt in the wound."

M. Babineaux shook his head. "Non! S'il vous plaît, Monsieur Dunning, arrêtez. *No! Please, Mister Dunning, stop.* I hold no grudge. On the contrary, I thank you.

"While I respected Joseph, he and I were never friends, never as close as the two of you were. I did my job, what was asked and expected of me, but I grew tired, desiring a simpler, quieter life. Yes, I had fun, but it took its toll on my health. I do not care if my former associates are bitter. I am not."

"Thank you for understanding." Charles was relieved his past ruthlessness had not destroyed any chance to get information on Phillip from this former rival, a rival he had never met before. "I appreciate your candour and rational mind. Just business, eh.

"You may not be aware, M. Babineaux, but before my husband's death, my firm was in final negotiations to become Cartell Worldwide's legal representatives. Unable to cope with the loss of Jason, I distanced myself from my work, from everyone.

"Not surprisingly, the deal fell apart without my connection to Joseph in the mix, and this is what provided your firm with the opportunity to get Cartell Worldwide. My family tragedy led to your firm's triumph."

"This web of intrigue is thick, my good man. You brought up your late husband, Jason. I wonder—has Jules mentioned anything to you about his—but I get ahead of myself. Désolé. *Sorry.* Please, tell me why you are here."

Charles's confusion grew exponentially. Why was this man talking about Jason? There was no connection to why he had come to see M. Babineaux in the first place, which was Phillip's first marriage. Charles needed to understand why his late husband and Jules were in play here. He wondered if, despite M. Babineaux's decree of indifference towards their past, he still sought revenge.

Charles was not sure if he could believe anything that came out of the old man's mouth, but for Jules's sake, he had to take that chance.

"I don't know why you'd suddenly want to talk about my late husband. I don't wish to talk about him with you. It's painful, even after all these years. Besides, what does any of this have to do with Phillip? Or with my daughter, for that matter?"

"Tell me why you are here!" M. Babineaux demanded. "I will say no more until I am sure."

Charles was exasperated. *This man speaks in riddles!*

Gone silent, M. Babineaux sat stiffly in his chair. His eyes narrowed.

Seeing that the Frenchman would no longer provide free information, Charles begrudgingly decided to talk about why Jules had sent him. It was in his best interest to play along if he wanted the old buzzard to spill what he knew.

"I'll give you the abridged version if that's acceptable. I won't leave out anything poignant."

M. Babineaux nodded. "That is acceptable."

"I see," said Stella thoughtfully. Slowly, she walked to the other side of her bedroom to look out the window. "When is it going live?"

Right before Stella was about to walk out the mansion's front door to run her daily errands, she had received a frantic-looking text from an old friend and former work colleague. The text was in bold capital letters, followed by multiple exclamation points; it was a command, not a request, to get back to him ASAP.

Stella was not someone who blindly followed commands; however, she had always been on good terms with the man, and she trusted his instincts. If he was issuing forth a plea for her attention, she understood he was in earnest and not wasting her valuable time.

Regrettably, she had not wanted her daughter's boyfriend to be the topic of such unseemly news.

"That soon? Damn. There's nothing your contact can do to suppress the story? Bury it entirely? This is just online trash, for goodness sake. They merely have to push the delete button. And if they want money, well, you know money is no object."

Stella threw money at problems to make them go away as fast and as often as she tossed around her last name to intimidate people. This time, however, it was not going to work.

"You can't be serious! That's outrageous! Who paid them that much money to publish this? How did they even get this information?"

Stella's source had few answers. A former boyfriend who worked for a popular online magazine that dealt primarily with sensationalist material had given him the inside scoop. The magazine was well known for being notoriously accurate with its facts and even more notorious for never backing down on publishing a story.

Stella had to prepare for what was to come.

And it was coming. Later that day. With pictures.

"Fine. Thank you for telling me as quickly as you did, even though it seems nothing can be done about it now. I won't pay that kind of money. I'll deal with the fallout on my end. If your inside man comes up with a name, get back to me immediately."

Stella disconnected the call, furious. In haste, she started to text Denise's cell.

Standing by the window, soundless and angry, Stella stopped pressing her finger to her phone. Eventually, she put the small object away, back into her pink Hermés vintage Birkin tote. She contorted her mouth into one of her classically wicked grins; all the same, in her estimation, her smile was prudent and charitable.

No, this will be a good lesson for Denise. Never trust anyone completely. Especially a man. She'll finally learn how to deal with betrayal. It will harden her, strengthen her. Yes, I'll let her find out on her own.

In the same amount of time it took her to select a shade of lipstick, Stella decided to let Denise suffer indignity without preparedness. She put the whole horrid affair out of her mind. Right now, she had more pressing issues of concern.

Stella strolled over to the mirror hung on the wall next to the front door. "Now then, let's go get some new shoes," she said to her reflection, checking her hair in the glass.

"As you know, M. Babineaux, I went to see your former colleague, Mr. Comstock. He had no idea what I was referring to when I asked him if he knew about Phillip's youthful indiscretion. It became apparent during our brief conversation that he knew very little, despite being the direct individual responsible for sending my daughter the keycard and passcode. Or so I thought.

"I soon discovered that he'd acted on your instruction. Comstock was just a means to an end, and all he wanted for himself was the chance to lobby my daughter for a job."

"Why are you looking for this information, M. Dunning, and not your daughter? This is about her husband. Would she not want to handle this sensitive business herself? And why now? She discovered this information some time ago, yet you track me down now."

"My daughter is very busy running a major company, M. Babineaux," Charles promptly replied, his answer sounding a bit rehearsed. "I'm used to this kind of investigative work, anyway.

You and I both did plenty of it working for Joseph. I happily took on the task for her."

M. Babineaux stared intently yet thoughtfully at his guest. Charles, in turn, waited patiently for a sign to signal if he should continue speaking or wait for a response.

Eventually, M. Babineaux broke the silence between the two of them with four simple words. "I see. Go on."

"As to why now and not sooner," Charles continued, "I can't answer that. My daughter has her reasons. This is her show, her timetable."

"Understood, and I do mean, M. Dunning, that I completely understand even if you do not fully comprehend your daughter's game."

Visibly irritated, Charles shook his head, confused. Unconvinced M. Babineaux had anything worth revealing, Charles wondered if his trip was for naught. *I'm beginning to think he may be slightly addlebrained.*

Detecting the subtle sneer across his guest's face, M. Babineaux grinned. "I am not mad or feeble-minded, M. Dunning, so please, ease yourself."

"Are you sure?" Charles asked, his tone somewhat mocking.

"Yes," M. Babineaux answered without a shred of insult in his voice. "Your daughter has not told you everything there is to know about Phillip's past. I am sure she has her reasons but know this—all was revealed in those files. She knows it all now about Phillip, but not everything I know about Genevieve Poirier and her child. Now, continue with your story concerning our mutual friend, M. Comstock."

"He's not important, is he? As I said, I believe he was merely a tool you used to get the information to Jules without you directly getting involved. Why were you so afraid to send my daughter the envelope directly?"

M. Babineaux diverted his eyes away from Charles's piercing gaze. He realized it was pointless to continue probing his guest to discover what information he and his daughter shared.

It was abundantly clear to him that Jules had not told her father what Phillip had done to their family.

Charles was not feigning ignorance of Phillip's crime for some unknowable reason; he was wholly ignorant of the trespass against him. He was only here to gather information on Phillip's first wife and child—nothing more.

M. Babineaux stirred in his chair, not knowing how best to proceed. Jules had obviously not shared with her father Phillip's crime for a significant reason known only to her. Should he reveal the full story? Jules's stratagem of revenge against Phillip appeared to be manifold, well-thought-out, and ultimately devastating. Would his interference disrupt her timetable?

Jules reminded M. Babineaux of Stella. His intimate knowledge of Joseph's wife had trained him to never underestimate that woman. He was impressed but also unnerved by Jules in the same way. Not that any of these feelings, these fears, ultimately mattered. He needed to keep his promise to himself and finally provide Genevieve with some form of justice.

He had to tell her story.

And as for what Phillip did that one night? He would let Jules reveal that to her father in her own time.

"You are correct," M. Babineaux conceded. "M. Comstock was simply the delivery system I put in place years ago. It could have been any junior associate under me, but I chose him because I knew he was especially—malléable? There is a better word in English, but it is not coming to me."

"Suggestible," Charles offered.

"Oui. *Yes.* Due to tragedies in his past, I knew I could mould and manipulate the man into becoming someone completely loyal only to me. I became a surrogate father to him.

"He never questioned me when I told him to take the keycard and keep it safe until I needed it. I knew my fellow partners would terminate his employment the minute I retired because of his unwavering loyalty to me. I arranged the move to his current firm. I kept in touch with him over the years, knowing I would eventually need him to get that keycard to your daughter."

"Again, why not just do it yourself? Not to be derisive, Sir, but you seem to have no infirmity that I can see that prevents the mailing of letters."

"Does she know you have come here to see me?"

Charles scrunched up his confused face as he uncrossed and then recrossed his legs for the third time since sitting down. "What? Yes, Jules knows I'm here. We've gone over this."

Indignant, M. Babineaux slammed his hands down on the desk and cried out, "Non!" His former calm countenance was gone, replaced by fear and anxiety.

Who or what troubled the man Charles did not know. Evidently, "Jules" was not the correct answer to his question. So who then?

"You know, sir, whom I speak of," M. Babineaux stated plainly. "She has ways of finding out everything. I saw you arrive in a taxi. Not as flashy as a limo or town car, eh? Quiet, unsuspecting. Harder to track your movements. I bet you have gone out of your way to avoid detection, non? She will fight to protect what is hers."

"Stella," Charles sighed, now understanding the cause of the Frenchman's lamentations. "I should have known. It always comes back to that interfering bitch. She's aware that you know about the secret safe and what lies inside of it. If any of its contents surface, she'll know you had a hand in it."

"Stella knows about the safe, yes, as well as some of the explosive contents within, but not all. Only I was trusted with everything. And she does not know where the safe is. Joseph refused to tell her, as did I. But she will know now that Joseph is dead, who is to blame if you use any of that information against her."

"Are you afraid of retribution? Is that it? My daughter and I have greatly lessened her influence and power. I wouldn't be too concerned."

"Then you are a fool if you think you have dulled her claws. Stella always has ways and means to strike back at her enemies.

She is a witch who can control men's hearts to do her bidding. Je étais un imbécile. *I was a fool.* She—she made me do it!"

"Who is Genevieve Poirier, M. Babineaux? What happened to her and the child? I want answers! Stella, be damned!"

The Frenchman turned from Charles's penetrating stare. Looking out the window, he noticed an abundance of dark clouds gathering. He heard voluminous drops of rain as they gained in ferocity, plummeting down from the sky. The former blue calm and quiet clarity were gone.

M. Babineaux saw the harsh, gloomy weather for what it was, and it saddened him. It was a portent, a foreshadowing of the dark things he was about to reveal.

The mood in the room had turned sombre and deadly serious for both men.

M. Babineaux quietly reflected on his many past mistakes. He gathered up all of his courage to finally reveal what Stella had him do—the truth of what happened to Phillip's first love.

"Much of this sad tale was told to me by Joseph, some of it from Stella, but there are parts that are first-hand knowledge. It all started in old Montréal, M. Dunning.

"During freshman year of university, Phillip met a beautiful girl, seventeen years of age, dark hair, pure Québecois. Her family, her lineage, went back hundreds of years. Her maternal ancestor was of the Filles du Roi—daughters of the King—and she married well. A high-ranking soldier, wealthy, but I digress. You did not come here for a history lesson.

"Genevieve Poirier's family had fallen on hard times. Her mother was a lost soul, a drug addict enslaved to heroin. Her father? Unmarried to her mother, a base criminal imprisoned for aggravated assault and arson. Certainly not a desirable pedigree for any girlfriend of the only son of Joseph and Stella Cartell.

"Worst of all, Genevieve took after her mother—a drug addict! Not heroin, but the more contemporary evil of methamphetamine. She hid her addiction well. She was a functional addict. Yes, I believe that is the term. Thanks in no small part to her natural physical beauty, she never showed any outward signs of damage from her narcotic abuse.

"From what I understand, Genevieve was a master at deflecting the concern and worry of those around her, those who suspected something was wrong whenever they noticed a change in her mood and demeanour. A flirtatious smile and a flip of her hair were usually all it took to put people at ease. She had Phillip completely enthralled and unsuspecting."

"Phillip, oblivious to his surroundings? Shocking." Charles's statement dripped with sarcasm. With more than a hint of scorn in his voice, he added, "I'm sure his drinking dulled his senses and awareness."

M. Babineaux nodded his head in agreement, picking up on the anger and bitterness in his guest's voice. "Yes, that was possibly a factor in Phillip's inability to see what was right in front of him, but I do not know when he started drinking excessively. We cannot discount that Phillip was in love with Genevieve. Love is blind, for good and for bad."

"Yes, I suppose," Charles answered, slightly chastised. His personal experience with falling for an unconventional partner came to mind. He was almost sorry he had judged Phillip so harshly. Almost.

"Anyway," M. Babineaux continued, "Stella always had Phillip on a short leash. Her eyes were—are—always on her children, near or from afar. You and I both know her network of spies is legion. Back then, it was Professors, teaching assistants, gym trainers. She even secretly arranged for Phillip's less scrupulous fraternity brothers in Alpha Delta Phi to inform on him.

"Eventually, Stella discovered Phillip's unforeseen dalliance with a local French girl beneath his breeding and social standing. A relationship that had caused noticeable damage in a significantly short amount of time."

"What do you mean? What kind of damage?"

"Phillip's once excellent grades had uncharacteristically faltered. Drinking and carousing to excess became the norm. He began to lose time while in Genevieve's presence. Forgoing family responsibilities and school duties to spend every waking moment with her. This was not the son that Stella and Joseph had raised. Phillip had always been obedient, never belligerent or any trouble, not like his fiery sisters.

"It cannot be overstated how lovely and seductive Genevieve was, M. Dunning. Sweet, arousing—a siren! She made Phillip extremely happy *and* extremely insulated from the rest of the world. This power she had over him made the young woman dangerous in Stella's eyes."

"I feel the need to ask, M. Babineaux," Charles interjected, "why do you continually refer to Miss Poirier in the past-tense? Is she deceased? Or are you simply speaking from a past-tense experience?"

"So impatient. Je vais répondre à votre question. *I will answer your question*. Yes, Genevieve is deceased, but please, I need to tell you everything now, or I will lose my resolve to do what I must after."

"Okay, fine, go on," Charles responded, not entirely sure what the old man meant. Despite the revelation, his investigative mind was still unquiet; he wanted—needed—to know more.

Feeling relieved that Phillip's first wife was dead and could not physically complicate Jules's life made Charles uncomfortable. He took no pleasure from Genevieve's death, but his daughter's happiness came before anything. Still, feeling remorseful about his easy acceptance of the woman's demise meant Charles was not totally beyond hope. He was not yet the monster Joseph had become.

Or, perhaps always was.

"As I was saying," M. Babineaux continued, "Stella had grand plans for Phillip, and they did not include some penniless French barmaid. And a drug addict! Unthinkable!

"Mother and son fought over this relationship for months, each one trying to convince the other of their righteous cause—Romantic love versus responsibility and parental reverence.

"Stella had managed to keep Phillip's situation entirely from Joseph. The rearing of the children had always been her main job, after all. That was their deal, their marital arrangement. As long as Phillip, Sonja, and Denise were where they were supposed to be—on track, I mean—then, for all intents and purposes, Joseph was not interested in his children's lives."

"That's harsh," Charles insisted. "I can't believe I'm defending that fucker, but he wasn't emotionally unavailable. It was logistics. Cartell Worldwide took up too much of his time for him to worry about the minutiae of their daily comings and goings."

"Yes, perhaps that is too harsh a thing to say. I know Joseph loved his children. He did unspeakable things to protect them—even from themselves. I know he felt confident Stella would make him aware of any significant changes and events in their lives.

"In this instance, it is safe to say that Joseph was unaware of his son's relationship with Genevieve. Well, until Stella had the unpleasant task of informing him that Phillip had, if I may be crudely blunt, knocked her up."

"That couldn't have gone over well," Charles smirked.

"Correct. Stella was furious at her son's carelessness and irresponsibility. She was also mad at herself for acting too slowly to prevent an undesirable romantic entanglement and, more abhorrent, an unplanned pregnancy. If the baby was even his. And if it was Phillip's child? Stella assumed it had been conceived as a trap to get his money.

"After admonishing herself in front of Joseph for her failure to curb the incident, Stella begged him to take action. Ever the quick thinker, Joseph conceived an insidious plan of attack. Immediately, he arranged for Stella and himself to travel to Montréal to visit Phillip and Genevieve.

"At this point, Phillip had left the Fraternity House and moved with the mother of his unborn child into a million-dollar condo paid for by his Trust Fund.

"After meeting the young woman, Joseph and Stella gave their blessing to the arrangement. It was all a ruse, of course. Joseph was confident that Phillip, blinded by love and a lifelong desire for his parents' approval, would not see through the deception.

"Eventually, Stella got Phillip out of the house, leaving Joseph alone with Genevieve. He immediately confronted her about her disreputable parents, her drug addiction, and the possible harm done to the baby due to her immoral drug use. Joseph threatened her with a paternity test. He boldly told her that if the baby was his grandchild, he would never allow a meth addict to go anywhere near it, let alone raise it.

"Brazenly, Joseph announced his cruel intentions to the young, frightened girl. He planned to publicly reveal every morsel of dirt he had on her. Every shadow would be illuminated, every dark secret revealed.

"He told Genvieve how easy it would be for him to destroy Phillip's love for her, stripping his son of his rose-coloured glasses. He would show him the parasitic creature she was—the junkie who had spent months willfully hiding this fact from him.

"Joseph rained down upon her numerous insulting names such as liar, trash, slut, drug whore. More cruel ones, I am sure, but Joseph had the decency to stop at those when recounting this tale to me. And my god, did he mean business! Genevieve was not to remain in Phillip's life another day. Joseph could be utterly terrifying when he wanted to be, eh, Charles!"

Charles nodded in agreement.

"Drug sick, her addiction nearly insuppressible," M. Babineaux quickly continued, "Genevieve eventually succumbed to Joseph's verbal battery of threats and agreed to leave. I think she must have realized that Phillip would one day see through her facade of normalcy, and what then?

"Joseph wanted her to write a letter to his son, stating in it that she did not love him and that the baby was not his. Joseph promised he would give her a substantial amount of money, both for an abortion and to start a new life. She had to go overseas to Europe, mind you, never to return to Canada.

"Genevieve agreed to the move and the letter, but she refused to hurt Phillip with further lies. She was adamant that she had been utterly faithful, totally in love with him, and that the baby growing inside of her was his. The letter had to be her truth, or she would not leave him, not like that. Her only real moment of strength and clarity was ultimately her downfall.

"Joseph, of course, had been prepared for the possibility of defiance. I never discovered how, but Joseph had obtained a syringe filled with high-grade heroin for just this scenario. Forcibly taking Genevieve by the arm, Joseph did the unthinkable and injected the drug into her pregnant body. As the narcotic took hold, she fell to the floor and sank into a stupor.

"Dazed, suggestible—thank you for that word—and ultimately receptive to Joseph's coercive influence thanks to the narcotic, Genevieve wrote the letter. He told her what to write, word for word. When he had finished being her puppetmaster, Joseph took Genevieve to his private jet and sent her to Brussels to disappear forever.

"When Phillip returned home with Stella, he found the letter waiting for him on the bed he shared with the woman he loved. Not surprisingly, he was devastated. Despite his acceptance that it was Genevieve's handwriting, Phillip refused to believe the letter's veracity. Why? Because it was true love? No, it was not that romantically simplistic. It was because M. Dunning, as you read in Joseph's files, Phillip and Genevieve had secretly wed.

"Now, we both know as lawyers, M. Dunning, that Genevieve, at seventeen, needed parental consent to marry legally in Ontario. They could have done it in Québec, with authorization from the courts, but they were worried it would take too much time. So they had gone to Ottawa to elope.

"Genevieve still had some contact with her mother, who agreed to sign a consent form, after being paid, of course. Her father had terminated his legal rights at her birth, so he was inconsequential to the matter. Phillip was over eighteen. The marriage was legally binding.

"This was a minor impediment to Joseph. He managed to have the marriage annulled quickly and quietly. He knew the right people in positions of power, and he knew their price for confidentiality. Once Genevieve's influence was removed, Joseph and Stella easily manipulated their melancholic son to get him to do what they wanted.

"After a period of sadness and self-pity, Phillip returned to his old life as if nothing had happened, even getting his drinking under control. The name Genevieve Poirier never passed through his lips again.

"All of this was in Joseph's files—the marriage certificate, the annulment papers, every accomplice, what their silence cost. Genevieve Poirier's signature was forged on that annulment agreement. Phillip, unknowingly, was a widower when he met your daughter, as I will explain."

"Hmph," Charles retorted, disappointed. "This won't help us at all."

Hours of paperwork had done little to distract Jules from her most prevailing, troubled thought. Her mind continued to race with images of her unexpected, unwanted visitor and the fear that she would be back to cause more trouble. Amanda's brief appearance in her office, not to mention their impromptu melee the night before, had done a number on Jules's nerves.

Damn that bitch! Why won't she leave me the fuck alone? Get the fuck on with your life already!

Jules strove to consciously refrain from cursing out loud, not wanting to sound boorish, uncouth or uneducated. She let go of all inhibitions inside her head where her language was as salty as a trucker's.

Worrying about what her father was up to was bad enough. The Amanda drama had nearly pushed Jules to the brink of neurosis. She was forever keeping everything together on the inside so that outwardly she displayed consummate self-confidence and resolve. She could not allow it all to unravel now. Not because of one unforeseen curveball.

Still, even though the bitch was gone, Jules was not confident that Amanda would not return at any moment to make another unorthodox social call. Amanda had promised once before to stay away forever. *Obviously, keeping her word on that meant very little to her. That woman's mental stability can't be trusted.* Jules needed to prepare herself for whatever might come.

Unlike the lawless, anarchic Amanda, Jules had logic on her side; she found strength in reason and logical thinking. She disliked chaotic variants, and so she prepared and planned for literally everything. Still, the "what ifs" always got to her. Had she planned for every possibility?

Amanda's unexpected appearance had rattled Jules's confidence and revealed that her preparedness process had flaws.

Enough of this!

Jules craved a break—a momentary respite from thinking, worrying, and questioning. Why had her father not called yet? Did he have the information she needed? Was the child alive? These were all questions that currently plagued her.

Jules was satisfied that she had finally broken Phillip enough to suit her needs, and it was now time for her to stop playing games with him and land the final blow.

However, there was still that minor setback earlier she had yet to rectify.

Jules could not have Phillip feeling good about himself for too long, and once she felt up to looking at his perfidious face, she meant to have another go at him. She had to make up for the brief, yet false, show of affection and weakness she had performed to cover up Amanda's bullshit. Jules was aware that her brief connection with Phillip earlier that day had not been brutal enough.

After making his statement at police headquarters, Phillip had immediately returned to work to see Jules. He had even entered her office uninvited to see how she was doing after her ordeal. Jules had glared at him, informed him that she was far too busy for his nonsense and told him to go back to his own office.

Jules recalled Phillip's disappointment and hurt via her return to a contemptuous state. She had expected it, desired it, but she had not anticipated the brief smile he shot her before leaving her office. An act that conveyed compassion and forgiveness for her bitchy dismissal of him. Her impromptu damsel in distress act had worked too well.

Jules understood clearly what that smile denoted; Phillip attributed her disdainful attitude towards him to post-traumatic stress and not because she hated his fucking guts.

If her exemplary performance had renewed Phillip's misplaced sense of hope that his wife's cold heart still retained a flicker of love for him, however small, well—Jules decided she was okay with that. All that meant was that she would get another chance to destroy that hope all over again. The thought of it made her breath quicken, her heart skip.

Something Jules received satisfaction from recently, without resorting to mind games, was the knowledge that Mode-Génétique Labs had successfully created the solution she had requested. A solution she had a hand in designing. At least, it was far enough along for her needs. She planned on using it in her ultimate "fuck you" to Phillip.

Now, all Jules needed was the location of her husband's child, and once she had that, everything necessary to make her plan work would be at her fingertips. She was sick of waiting for the day to come when Phillip would finally know what he had done.

All this worrying and stress had put a kink in her neck. To help both her mind and body relax, Jules had directed Nazneen to go downstairs to the Starbucks in the lobby and bring back her favourite treat: a grande, nonfat, no whip, green tea Frappuccino.

Jules loved this drink because it was icy, thick, and sweet, and it always managed to drain the tension from her body. She craved that matcha flavour—as long as it was sweetened. When that cold, green elixir ran down her throat, permeating every fibre of her body, Jules felt instantly relaxed, centred.

Looking up at the clock on her office wall, Jules realized that six minutes and four seconds had gone by already, and she was still waiting for her beverage. Annoyed, she sighed loudly, the kink in her neck tight.

Then another minute went by. Still waiting—even though the order was well known and once placed using the Starbucks app, it never took more than six minutes to make, pick up, and deliver to the office. It had been timed.

Jules drank a green tea Frappuccino twice a day. Waiting for the drink to get to her was all the irritation she allowed the process to inflict upon her, and that allowance was no more than six minutes.

"Where the fuck is my fucking green tea Frappuccino?!"

Moments later, Jules heard Nazneen's frantic bellowing down the hallway.

"I'm here! I'm coming!"

Jules's harried executive assistant sprinted into the office and placed the drink down on the desk with a look on her face that was a combination of relief and fear. Yes, her Frappuccino was here, but Nazneen knew perfectly well she had taken extra minutes. She was not at all sure how her employer was going to react.

Unfortunately for her, Jules's reaction was not positive.

"Nazneen, what is this?"

"Your drink. A grande, nonfat, no whip, green tea Frappuccino. Sorry, I was late. You see—"

Jules put her hand up to silence Nazneen's blathering attempt at an excuse. Reaching out, she picked up the drink, scrutinizing it.

"Is it now? And what colour is a grande, nonfat, no whip, green tea Frappuccino, Nazneen?"

"Um, it's green? Ms. Cartell, is there a problem?"

Jules got up out of her seat. Moving over to where Nazneen stood, she held the cold concoction extremely close to the confused woman's face.

Nazneen took a step back, startled, slightly terrified, yet she tried hard not to look so. It was widely known that Jules detested visible weakness in people. Anxious, her stomach in knots, Nazneen cleared her throat and waited for her employer to answer her.

"Light green, Nazneen," Jules stated authoritatively. "A grande, nonfat, no whip, green tea Frappuccino should be light green. This is dark green. A very dark green. A dark green colour means that the barista used measurements and ingredients that are not my specific ones. I wonder how that happened?"

Jules's tone was incredibly snarky. She was visibly pissed.

"I'm sorry," Nazneen apologized. "I'm still fairly shaken from earlier—that woman, her threats. I forgot to use the 'favourite' option in the app and put the order in manually. I—I must have messed up."

"And," Jules continued, ignoring Nazneen's contriteness, "along with a colour that signifies the wrong amount of matcha for me, it's not outside the realm of possibility that you could also have 'messed up,' as you say, the sweetness level."

Jules put her lips to the straw and gently sucked some of the dark green liquid into her mouth. Her face instantly soured, immediately conveying her ultimate opinion of the drink to Nazneen. "Just as I thought," she remarked, her top lip curled up ferociously, "hardly enough sweetener. Too heavy on the matcha."

At this point, Nazneen gave up all hope that she might come out of this unscathed.

"My instructions aren't difficult to follow. My specifications for this drink never change. I'm not speaking in tongues, and I expect my staff to also not speak in tongues. Do you know what this all means, Nazneen? Look at my face! Do you?"

"I'm—I'm not sure. No, Ms. Cartell."

"It means, Nazneen, that it tastes like shit instead of the sweetened treat I know and love. It tastes like regular green tea, just very cold. Cold, thick, basic green tea, and not at all like a dessert beverage. More like a traditional hot green tea libation you would expect to find in a teacup—just cold, like I said, instead of hot. How hard is it to order a grande, nonfat, no whip, green tea Frappuccino for me, Nazneen? Hmm?"

"Apparently, rather difficult sometimes, it seems," Nazneen quipped, attempting to diffuse the tension in the air.

"Don't be cute, Nazneen. I don't do cute. Take this away, go back downstairs, and have them make me another one—correctly this time. If I don't have a proper grande, nonfat, no whip, green tea Frappuccino in my hands in six minutes, Nazneen, heads will roll. I'm not in the mood today. Am I understood?"

"Yes, Ms. Cartell."

"Good. Leave."

"Well, there was this one other thing," Nazneen stated meekly.

Jules returned to her desk, settled into her seat, and glared at her executive assistant. Seething with discontent, she took a deep breath before speaking. "What—is—it?"

"Well, I noticed there was a parcel on my desk for you when I raced in—when I came into your office. Should I get it?"

"Fine."

Upon hearing that last exasperated word fall from her employer's lips, Nazneen dashed back to her desk, drink in hand. She put the unwanted beverage down, picked up the parcel, and brought it into Jules's office, quietly placing it on her desk. Fearing further retribution if she stayed a second longer, Nazneen walked briskly back to her station, tossed the Frappuccino in the trash, and flew to the elevator.

Blissfully alone, Jules inspected the parcel. It was larger than a shoebox, heavy, with fancy, expensive-looking wrapping.

Jules convinced herself it was a present from Jacques for cancelling their breakfast date; she hoped the package contained the black patent leather and lace Coquette shoes from Denise's boutique. She was sure she had casually mentioned to him that she adored them.

Tearing open the box, Jules discovered something horrific inside, and it was nothing Jacques would ever give her.

Her throat closing, her eyes widening in terror, Jules immediately understood what the contents of the box signified. She was beside herself with panic. He was free, and he had come for her.

William!

XII

"Pardon?"

"Forgive my acerbity, M. Babineaux, but while this story is entertaining, it doesn't help at all. Jules and I were hoping you would reveal something we could use as leverage against Phillip. Nothing you've told me is enough. It will hurt Phillip enormously to discover all of this, but I need something more than emotional torture. It's just not enough to take back to my daughter."

"I see," M. Babineaux sighed. He had been preparing for this moment for years; he had to finally unburden himself and come clean about his monstrous role in the whole ugly affair.

Dreading complete disclosure of this grim narrative, M. Babineaux knew inside his tortured soul that it was the right thing to do. He was exceedingly tired of living with the secret of what he had done. It had eaten away at him for so long that not much remained of the once potent, robust, successful man. He was now barely more than a hollow shell filled with pain, guilt, regret.

M. Babineaux had a desperate need to atone—to give what justice he could to a long-dead woman.

"Well, M. Dunning, what if I told you that one day, several years later, a drug-free and self-possessed Genevieve Poirier, with her child, very much alive, showed up on the doorstep of a certain wealthy family looking for answers and retribution."

Charles's eyes opened in surprise, his breath quickened with newly birthed excitement.

"I see I have regained your furtive attention," M. Babineaux smirked. "From this point forward, Joseph and Phillip mostly disappear from the narrative. The totality of what happened next is known only to myself and Stella.

"To preface what I did, you need to understand my motive. During my time as Joseph's right-hand man, I became quite fond of Stella and—non! No more lies! I was madly in love with her! She knew it and took full advantage of it.

"Stella and I hid our affair from Joseph quite successfully. It was a one-sided love affair, mostly sexual, but it was enough for me. To be close to her, to be her lover. She was—she is—a goddess, a vision of perfect beauty. Perhaps you cannot understand how powerful her female allure is, eh, M. Dunning?"

"I'm gay, M. Babineaux, not blind. I've always been conscious of Stella's beauty and charm. Her influence over people is uncanny. As I said, Jules and I have lessened that influence, but it took time, resources. Stella is a formidable opponent, a master manipulator. I can understand your—weakness.

"What did you do for Stella? I want to know how Miss Poirier died, but more importantly, I need to know what became of her child."

"Yes, well," M. Babineaux stuttered, perturbed at having been called weak-willed despite the truthfulness of the condemnation. "Genevieve wanted to see Phillip. She demanded her rightful place at his side as his wife and mother of their child. She demanded many things right there, in broad daylight, on the very doorstep of the Manor House. Stella rushed the woman inside to avoid a scene.

"Jackson quickly became aware of the uninvited guest, but we all know how slavishly loyal he is to Stella. He kept the other servants busy and unaware of what was transpiring around them. I always felt that sycophant was more than smitten with her. Obsessed, perhaps, like myself. He would do anything for her, anything she asked, as you will soon see.

"Stella told me Genevieve appeared clear-headed and well-spoken, but her former drug use had enacted a steep price from her. The loss of much of her memory concerning what happened to her before she arrived in Europe. Not surprisingly, she wanted answers.

"I have chronicled the entirety of what I know about the life and death of Genevieve Poirier, including full details of her conversation with Stella at the house. You and your daughter may go over all of it at your convenience. Suffice it to say that while in Brussels, Genevieve found a saviour who helped her kick her addictions. Thanks to Joseph's cruelty, she had become addicted to heroin, but she managed to overcome and survive that.

"Joseph lied to Genevieve about everything. Yes, he flew her to Brussels, but he left her there to flounder without a place to live or a cent to her name, hoping she would die from her addictions. Joseph could not kill a woman possibly pregnant with his grandchild, but her welfare once she was out of the country and out of the picture was left to chance. I know he never thought about her again once he shoved her on that plane.

"Not surprisingly, Stella was none too pleased to see her unwanted daughter-in-law again in Canada. Or alive, for that matter. She had always assumed that if the drugs did not eventually kill her, some lowlife thug or pimp would have.

"Stella was also not happy to see that the abortion had not taken place, as Joseph had promised her it had. I know he counted on the drugs—the heroin, especially—to take care of it for him in the form of a miscarriage. It did not, even though he had left her with enough of the narcotic to do the job.

"You see, Charles, Joseph miscalculated Genevieve's resolve and resiliency. Despite her tenacity, her will to live, complications arose during her pregnancy and the birth caused by her drug use.

"The boy, named Philippe, was born deaf and addicted to opioids. He had needed to be weaned off the vile substances by doctors soon after his birth. Stella told me that the child never spoke in her presence and that he suffered from facial tics. These tics I witnessed myself. But my god, there could be no denying that he looked exactly like Phillip. There was Cartell blood in him.

"Now Stella had two problems to solve and solve quickly. How to get rid of Genevieve for good and what to do with a flawed flesh and blood grandson. Stella was grateful that both Joseph and Phillip were out of the country.

"I was working downtown when Stella called me, telling me to go immediately to my houseboat anchored off Toronto Island to meet her. We often spent time alone there, away from prying eyes. She said she needed my help, my confidence, and my understanding.

"I should have known something wicked was afoot when she told me that she loved me. She had never said those words before, but it made my heart flutter. I wanted so badly to believe her. I was her slave, and I did what she asked without question. I left work and went directly to the houseboat, where I found her alongside Jackson, standing over two unconscious bodies on my deck.

"Jackson had helped her drug Genevieve and her child before placing them in the trunk of his car. For several reasons, according to Stella, all of the family's automobiles were unsuitable for transporting those comatose bodies. Too flashy, not enough trunk space or too recognizable? Who knows what she was thinking. She probably wanted to be able to pin everything on Jackson if something went wrong.

"Stella had Jackson drive her and the anesthetized bodies to the ferry and then onto the island. Once I arrived, Stella instructed Jackson to leave and never speak of what he had done to anyone. Like he would ever betray her! The sycophantic mewl!"

Charles nodded. "So, Jackson knows about Genevieve and the child. This could be useful."

"Yes, now listen! I had long stopped questioning how Joseph and Stella acquired their arsenal of narcotics, and I was never shocked anymore by their growing employment. I was happy to see that the bodies were still breathing, but breathing was not what Stella wanted them to be. She looked at me with her cold, hypnotic eyes and told me to get rid of them by any means necessary.

"She wanted them dead, sir; that was what she wanted. A child! Her grandson! These innocent lives meant nothing to her, but to Stella, they were not innocents. They were ugly problems and complications that needed to be dealt with permanently. Of course, she refused to get her hands dirty."

Charles gasped. "Stella's a vile bitch, but murdering a child! Before you go any further, M. Babineaux, there is one thing I don't get. Why you and not Jackson? He had already implicated himself in the drugging and kidnapping of two people. And, as you said, he worshipped her."

"Exactement! *Exactly!* And he would have. She did ask him, M. Dunning, but when he agreed too eagerly, Stella knew without a doubt that she had enthralled him totally. He was her puppet, and she controlled all his strings. Where was the fun in that for her? Even during this stressful time, the shrew still enjoyed playing her mind games.

"Non! She wanted to see how much—how much I loved her! How far would I go to have her? Je pleurais comme un bébé! Je ne veux pas tuer quelqu'un, je—"

"M. Babineaux, slow down!" Charles loudly interjected. "Please, in English! I can't follow you when you speak that fast and that erratically 'en français,' okay?"

"I said I cried like a baby in front of her. I did not want to kill anyone. I was no murderer, but her beauty, her voluptuous body, I wanted it all, so badly. I felt her radiance wash over me like a dark spell capturing my heart and soul. Sorcery! How could I say no? Would she abandon me if I declined? To be without her, to have her look at me with disgust, with hatred! I could not bear the thought of it.

"And who were these people in front of me, anyway? Strangers! They were nothing to me! No one would miss them, these vagabonds! I stood there, justifying my evil actions before even laying a hand on anyone. How do you say no to Stella Cartell? I have never found the answer to that question."

"No!" Charles gasped. "M. Babineaux, what did you do?"

"To my everlasting regret, I did what Stella expected me to do. I killed Genevieve. I strangled the life out of her, and I did so while crying like a pathetic, mewling toddler. So pathetic. As she laid immobile, I wrapped my hands around Genevieve's young neck and slowly crushed her windpipe.

"I—I had to watch in horror as my building pressure roused her, very unexpectedly. When she realized her plight, I squeezed harder as she struggled for breath, for freedom from my release. I looked into those orbs of hazel, dulling before my eyes, and wished for them to hurry and close so that I did not have to watch their accusatory, hateful glare.

"Within moments, my wish was granted. I held Genevieve's lifeless body in my arms."

"Jesus Christ," Charles mumbled, horrified.

"It was not completely over. The child, you see. I tell you, M. Dunning, seeing a woman murdered right before her eyes did not create even a flicker of remorse inside Stella. On the contrary, it made her resolve stronger and even brought her a sense of relief—of deep satisfaction. 'Kill the child next, hurry!' she said to me."

"You didn't!" Charles roared, rising out of his chair. His face was red with anger, his hands tightly balled into fists; he was ready to strike out at the murderer in front of him. Charles planned to release part of his anger towards the now dead Joseph onto M. Babineaux's tear-stained face.

"Arrêtez, asseyez-vous, s'il vous plaît! *Stop, sit down, please!* I did not kill the child! Philippe lives!"

Charles moved back into his chair, but his fists remained at the ready.

"I thought and planned quickly. I told Stella I could not kill a child in front of her. If she wanted it done, I had to be left alone to do the ugly task. I told her I could not bear to see her watch me do something so evil—murdering her grandson in front of her!

"I promised I would dispose of the bodies in the lake, weighing them down to prevent the tide from bringing them to shore. I said that I would go away for a few days on personal leave so no one would notice if I acted funny or odd. Not myself, you know? I was not sure that I could keep it together after—well, just after.

"Stella called me an emotional fool but bought every half-truth and outright lie I told her. I had learned a few things about manipulating her, you know, working alongside Joseph. She agreed to my plan but warned me that if I betrayed her by attempting to implicate her in any of it, she would destroy me without hesitation.

"Stella had Jackson to back up any claim she made to the authorities that it was me who had planned and committed every dirty act leading up to and including the murders. She said she would swear that I had kidnapped her. Can you believe that? The man who loved her more than anything! One minute she asks me to do the unthinkable for her out of love, and in the next breath, promises to see me go down in flames. But I loved that monster still.

"To my knowledge, Genevieve's body is still at the bottom of Lake Ontario. The exact location is in the dossier I made up for your daughter, as is the current location of Phillipe.

"I used those days away to drive the boy clear across the country, far away from Stella and Joseph. I took him to a friend of mine in northern British Columbia who owed me a big favour.

"I destroyed all of the identification I found in Genevieve's bag. The passports were fraudulent. Good quality fakes, but fake nonetheless. Not even the names on them were authentic. Still, this actually helped because it meant I could make the boy disappear much easier. My friend agreed to create a new identity for Phillipe and take care of him. I was adamant that his first name not be changed. Risky, but it felt right.

"When the boy woke up in the car on the way to BC, he cried terribly but never spoke. I told him his mama loved him but that she had to go away and he was going to a new family. He was deaf, but he seemed to read lips. I tried my best to communicate with him, to comfort him. I do not know sign language, and he never once showed that he did, either. He was very young, maybe three at that time? I have no children of my own. I did my best with him.

"After I left Phillippe, I went back to my life as if nothing had happened. I was secure in my belief that Stella believed both her recent problems were at the bottom of Lake Ontario.

"Eventually, I pulled away from Stella, my heart sick and twisted with guilt—ravaged by remorse. I could no longer stand to look at the woman I loved so much I had killed for her. This will come as no great shock to you, M. Dunning, but Stella could not have cared less. I really should have known I was just one of many secret male suitors at her disposal.

"Now you know why I said I was glad to part ways with Joseph and why I have never held any ill-will towards you or your daughter. I had to leave. Here, take this."

Hurriedly, M. Babineaux handed over a medium-sized travel portfolio.

Upon a cursory inspection, Charles realized the portfolio contained the physical representation of everything he had just been told and then some. It was everything Jules needed to oust Phillip from the company. If Phillip ever wanted to be reunited with his only child, he would have to make the ultimate deal. His family's company for the location of the son he never knew he had.

Charles felt exhilarated. He could not wait to get home and back to Jules with this vital information. However, there was one major obstacle in his path back to Fairporte: M. Babineaux, himself. The man had just confessed to killing a woman and covering it up. This revelation was unexpected, and it complicated things.

Or did it?

In his heart, Charles understood that no matter how distasteful the confession was, it could not matter to him. He had promised Jules his aid unconditionally, despite his conflicted conscience. He wanted justice for a wronged, innocent woman, but at the same time, he wanted his daughter to get what she desired, what she deserved. Revenge. For what exactly he did not yet know, but he was sure he would find out soon.

"M. Babineaux, you have no idea what you've done for my family. Still, you must understand, I cannot and will not give you solace or forgiveness for your despicable actions. You're a murderer, and don't you dare tell me you did it for love. Love, true love, would never ask someone to do such an evil thing in its name.

"I can't fathom the emptiness in your soul or the desolation in your heart. How could someone of your intelligence be so easily manipulated by a pretty face into doing something so reprehensible? You knew what you were doing was wrong, but you did it anyway. Perhaps it's a good thing I can't fully understand the depths of your immorality. I might go mad.

"You have to know it's inevitable that Stella will put the pieces together and guess your involvement in all this when we make our move against Phillip. And that will be very soon. You may be in danger from both of them—separately or together.

"Perhaps even the authorities will get involved if Phillip chooses to make the information public to punish everyone involved in Genevieve's death. I don't know all the answers or possible outcomes. I can't promise you will be kept out of whatever fallout occurs once we use this information.

"You're a smart man, M. Babineaux, with a great life, a top-notch reputation, and a long, successful, financially rewarding career. You know I have to ask this. If you've always understood the damaging ramifications of revealing what you know, why on earth did you risk it all to help my daughter?"

"I think it would be obvious," M. Babineaux softly answered as he wiped away the remainder of his tears. "I am done with the guilt and misery. Done with the emptiness and the desolation, as you so succinctly put it. I cannot bear this heavy, crushing burden any longer. I cannot breathe.

"I have punished myself by denying my heart of love. For Genevieve. For what I took from her. Did I ever think it was a fair and even trade? No, of course not, and now it is no longer enough to remain alone and ashamed. I must be penitent. I had to tell her story. Someone else had to know before I—just before. Yes, now I know I can do it.

"You have helped me tremendously, M. Dunning. You have taken my burden from me. I have kept nothing for myself. No files, nothing on my hard drive. Do with it what you will. Share it with your daughter. Or bury it. The choice, the responsibility, and the burden now belong to you.

"You are a good man, monsieur, much better than I ever was. I am not ashamed to say I am very jealous of the love you had—*have*, for your late husband. The life you lived together. I never had that kind of love. Stella saw to that! Non, I cannot blame her for what I chose to do for her. I thought that was what you did for love. Anything at all, anything you could, even if it cost you everything.

"How can I make you understand? I am not a bad person! I just did a wicked thing, but what does it matter now? I am not looking for redemption or forgiveness, just an end to it. You should leave now, M. Dunning, and do not come back. I am tired. Take what you came for and leave. Our business is concluded, and there is nothing more to say. For me, it is over."

"Fine with me," Charles asserted. He did not want to be in this murderer's presence a minute longer. Pushing his chair back, Charles grabbed the travel portfolio and stood up to leave. He wanted to go home to the people he loved.

Slumped down in his chair, M. Babineaux's body language was easy to read. He was emotionally purged and undeniably exhausted. But unburdened and free of self-recrimination? Charles did not think so, and he felt just fine letting the bastard lament alone in his dusty old office, beating himself up inside for his terrible choices and monstrous deeds.

On his way out the door, Charles stopped, halted by the sound of a hacking cough and some mumbled angry words.

"What was that? Do you have something else to say, after all?"

"Yes," M. Babineaux answered. "One final thing to say before you walk into your uncertain future, M. Dunning. You judge me swiftly, without compassion, but you will soon discover what lengths a man will go to for love. Perceived love on my part or true love in your case. Makes no difference in the end. Love is love to the heart that holds it.

"When you know all, yes, then! When you know what your daughter knows. You will understand me, then. At that moment—you will be me! I warned you about going down this dark path. Soon, Charles Dunning, you will know if you will kill in the name of love."

"Sure, whatever you say," Charles laughed as he left the room and, he hoped, M. Babineaux's life for good.

Waiting for his Uber, Charles ruminated on the sad, broken old Frenchman's final words. He knew that he could never cross that line; he was no murderer! He was not like Joseph or the men of his ilk, such as M. Babineaux and, from what he had discovered in the secret files Jules had uncovered, Ambroise Bergé.

Still, Charles was troubled that M. Babineaux appeared to know the final piece of the puzzle concerning Phillip's crime. "What is this fucking thing Phillip did in his past?" he questioned aloud.

But, as Charles told himself time and time again, Jules had her reasons for keeping him in the dark. It was almost a mantra for him.

He hoped this new information he now had in his possession was enough to hammer the final nail in Phillip's coffin. Charles hoped it was enough to ease his daughter's mind. He wanted her to share the secrets she held so close to her chest with him, her loving, always supportive, loyal father.

As the rain continued to pour down hard outside, slamming every few seconds upon the panes of glass, M. Babineaux watched thoughtfully from his office window for Charles to come into view. He wanted to make sure the man was gone before he did what he had finally summoned enough courage to do.

When the Uber eventually arrived and took his former guest away, M. Babineaux sluggishly sat back down in his chair. He reached into the left side drawer of his old mahogany desk and pulled out his gun.

"You will have no more power over me, Stella. Never again. Je souhaite que vous brûlez, sorcière, *I hope you burn, witch*," he whispered—he cursed.

M. Babineaux placed the shiny metal revolver in his mouth, aimed upwards towards his brain and pulled the trigger with confidence and purpose.

Before all his senses and movements ended forever in a quick, violent moment of thunderous noise and blood, his mind flashed on one final memory, a gruesome image. It was the face that had haunted him for years: the angry face of Genevieve Poirier. Those hate-filled, damning eyes glaring up at the stranger whose lethal grip she could not free herself from, the stranger she clearly understood was strangling her to death.

Unable to speak, paralyzed in her chair, Jules stared at the contents of the box with shock and horror. It was a clear message: a death threat! No, not a threat, she realized, but a dark promise made to her countless years ago by a demon in man's form. The box's grotesque theme was a Stygian portent.

The box contained a pair of boys' ice skates drenched in a viscous liquid the colour of blood.

Something Jules had not noticed earlier about the package when she had excitedly opened it was that it was slightly cold to the touch. Upon closer analysis, further inside the box were shards of ice laid haphazardly underneath the scarlet ichor. The pieces were broken in different ways to create various craggy shapes and sizes. *As if someone broke through the surface of an ice-covered pond. I get it, you bastard!*

Jules had just enough stamina and potency left inside of her before she had to look away to make one last, close inspection. She made out what appeared to be some writing heavily stitched into the worn leather of the skates. In a beautifully scripted style, the initials EF appeared before her eyes.

Ethan Falsworth.

Unable to look any longer, Jules shut her eyes tight. She stopped breathing, panic took over, and she began to pass out.

Instinctively, Jules brought her hands to her throat. *No, be strong! Breathe!* Her mouth opened, and she gasped her first breath in what seemed like hours but had only been seconds. Time seemed irrelevant. Nothing seemed real. Panic! She was lucid, but things were spinning fast. She was still having a hard time breathing. Her chest was tight, and she felt hot. Panic!

Jules willed her legs to move; she needed distance from the box. Several moments passed, but eventually, her limbs obeyed and pushed her, chair and all, with colossal force backward until she hit the wall. Although it was only a meter, Jules had her expanse. It was cold comfort, that small amount of distance, but it was enough to begin to clear her head.

Jules had not felt this kind of fear and anxiety since the night he had kidnapped her, the same night her dad died. Spinning her head around, she began searching. Was he here? In the building? Could he see her now? Was he close?

In answer to her harried questions and dreaded concerns, the sound of a ringtone hummed through the air. It did not come from any device she owned. The sound was muffled. Jules looked around the room frantically to find the source of the ringing. The annoying sound did not stop even after a minute had passed; it was unrelenting.

The message was clear: find and answer me.

After a tense moment, Jules's ears finally closed in on the exact location of the muted cacophony.

It was coming from inside the box.

But could Jules dare to look back inside? Could she reach in and take the device, buried in the semi-frozen, partly coagulated blood-like substance? She knew she had to. If the ringing did not stop, it was going to attract unwanted attention. *I can't let Nazneen see me like this!*

Jules shot out of her chair, much quicker than she thought she had the strength or will to do and walked back over to the box.

Peeking inside again, Jules could not see the irritating device. *Damnit! Where are you?* She wondered if William had hidden the phone inside one of the skates to protect it from moisture.

Disgusted, with a heap of trepidation, Jules forced her hand down inside one of the skates, quickly finding the very thing she had been reluctantly looking for.

Jules activated the cell, put it up to her ear, and waited. She refused to speak into it; she did not want this communication in the least. She desperately wanted all this to be a joke, sick and cruel as it was, being played on her by someone. Anyone but him! Sadly, Jules knew she was deluding herself; no one, not even Joseph, was as sadistic as William.

Eventually, a voice slithered out of the electronic device and into her ear like a deadly, poisonous viper; Jules immediately felt unbridled, paralyzing fear.

"Winter kills," William whispered. "You won't escape me this time, bitch."

Suddenly, the cell phone became very hot, and Jules's hand began to sting. Instinctively, she flung the device away from her; it landed hard on the floor, not too far from her desk.

Within seconds the phone melted into a black sludge, leaving an unpleasant smell of burnt rubber and plastic and a decent-sized hole burned into the Macassar ebony hardwood floor. At the moment, the destruction of her office floor was the least of her problems.

Jules's sapphire blue eyes welled up with tears. Letting go of her self-control, she broke down, dissolving into a sobbing mess of anguish.

The gusty air in downtown Fairporte was torrid and biting; Denise had to readjust her turquoise pashmina several times to get it out of her face. Fashion before comfort had never been such a bitch as it had been for her in the last ten minutes.

Wanting some fresh air, Denise had gone outside to wait for her date. Christophe was chronically late for most things, except when something paid for his time, and today was no exception.

"So typical," Denise sighed, indignant.

Spinning around to face her store's main window, she gave herself a good once over, making sure her make-up was still on-point and not smudged. Smoothing out her Marc Jacobs pinstriped two-piece suit, Denise checked that her hair had not become unkempt and wind-blown. She was happy with what she saw reflected in the glass. She looked good, damn good.

Too good to be waiting around for a fucking man.

In the window's reflection, a flicker of light caught Denise's eye; the gleam of an approaching car's impeccably polished silver hubcap called out to her. Continuing to observe via the window's reflective glass, Denise watched covertly as a black limousine slowly pulled up in front of her store. It proceeded to idle a meter or so away from where she stood.

Denise knew that Christophe had a penchant for expensive cars, but she did not think he would have rented a limousine to take her to lunch. Though, as she thought about it some more, the idea was not totally off the mark. *He does like his extravagances and enjoys showing off. Not to mention he owes me some damn appreciation for being tardy twice in twenty-four hours.*

Turning back around, Denise looked curiously at the unknown automobile. After getting a good look, she realized that this was no basic limo, not something Christophe could afford to purchase. Her heart went into her throat. *Holy crap! A Rolls Royce Phantom! That shit costs like four million bucks!*

Denise waited with distinct anticipation as the passenger side window rolled down. A masculine hand reached out, beckoning her to approach.

From inside his limo, William leered at Denise with a predatory gaze. He was hungry, but not for food.

His earlier interaction with Jules had gone as planned. William had felt the essence of her fear over the phone, took in its aroma, bathed in her anxiety, and it had aroused him. His limited capacity for emotion suggested to him that what he felt was contentment mixed with—desire?

William guessed that was what it was. He had gotten hard, now that he thought about it, the moment he had activated the explosive device built into the phone. The idea and the act of causing pain in others usually gave him an erection. It was amusing to him, the suffering of women, especially. *Desire, it is.*

Yasmine, currently behind the steering wheel, was William's most constant amusement.

He considered her a recreational necessity required to control and curb his fervent appetites. William's severe need, an obsession with inflicting hurt and pain upon others, was all-consuming, permeating every fibre of his being. Yasmine was useful; she helped clear his mind; she helped him plan and function in the world outside the sanitarium.

Yasmine had been instrumental in arranging William's freedom after years of imprisonment.

Her one unforgivable flaw was that she was wretchedly finite, all too human. She had limitations; her body needed time to heal. William found it maddeningly inconvenient.

As long as she was quick about it, continued to obey and amuse him, and affably aid his cause, William would keep Yasmine around. When she inevitably proved faulty and unreliable, he figured he would kill her and find someone else to do what she did for him.

Now that he was free, William no longer considered Yasmine a tactical imperative. Her unorthodox psychiatric services, while laudable, were not essential to his future. Her analytical mind still proved helpful, but William only needed, trusted, and counted on himself in the end. Everyone else? Potentially useful but utterly expendable.

William wondered if perhaps Denise might become his next Yasmine. They were all so interchangeable to him: women. Like tools or appliances, and when you broke one, you got a new one. William wished he did not need them at all, but he had those gnawing urges to satiate.

Over the intercom, William ordered Yasmine to put his right-side window all the way down so he could converse with Denise. As the pane lowered, he moved his head closer to the open space. Once Denise was in view, William smiled brightly. While his soul was black and his heart dark, his face was disarmingly sweet. He carried his family's brand of attractiveness agreeably.

Many considered the Falsworths as having a genetic predisposition towards "horse face." William's broad, masculine shoulders, wide mouth and full lips compensated for his otherwise unconventional features much better than others of his kin. He was comely yet charmingly goofy-looking; his non-traditional good looks were endearing to many.

Endearing until he inevitably opened his mouth and spewed forth a torrent of sexist comments and ugly misogynist beliefs.

William's natural cadence was robotic, and his penchant for aggressiveness often peppered his language with less than pleasing expletives. Despite his wealth and family social status, William was not a natural playboy. Interaction with others, especially the opposite sex, was next to non-existent due to being locked away for so long in psychiatric hospitals.

Yasmine had surreptitiously helped William, moulding him into what he needed to be in the world outside his former prisons. He had learned how to "act normal," constantly rehearsing what to say to people, how to manipulate his tone and sincerity, to move among them more easily.

Today, William was confident he would entice Denise to come with him and hear his proposal.

"Ms. Cartell, it's completely my pleasure to meet your acquaintance. " William's voice was intentionally warm and even, his British accent inviting. "My name is William Falsworth, and I do believe we have a mutual thorn in our sides that needs plucking out."

Denise did not immediately walk away, tell him to bugger off or appear in the slightest bit threatened by his bold appearance and overture. William knew Denise was intrigued; it was a good sign. *Keep it up, man. She'll buy it, she's a woman, after all, and they are foolish, hopeless romantics.*

Moving towards the open window, Denise furrowed her brow questionably. "Who exactly is this thorn you speak of, Mr. Falsworth?" She played it cool, but inside, she was dying.

Denise had heard the name Falsworth mentioned by both her father and Charles. She had never met one of the rich, enigmatic family members before—especially not a handsome male one. They were powerful business tycoons, internationally revered, like her family. Everyone knew they were unquestionably secretive and kept close quarters.

Denise understood how rare an opportunity this was. She planned on taking advantage of it, but she did not want to appear overly eager or too easy.

"My lovely lady, must I mention her hated name?"

Denise grinned like the Cheshire Cat. *He has to be talking about Jules.*

"Please, join me for lunch in my suite at Château Bergé, where we can talk about our little problem in private over a bottle of Romance-Conti 1975, perhaps? If that year is good enough for a lady, such as yourself, of such obvious refined breeding and taste."

Denise was not a wine connoisseur, but she figured it was an exorbitantly expensive vintage. She liked William's flattery a lot. It had been ages since Christophe had spoken with such flourish or engaged in such romantic gestures. What did she have to lose? If this man had the power and the desire to help take down Jules, she would be a fool to refuse his offer.

Once Denise agreed to accompany William, the right-side door of his limo automatically opened to allow her ingress.

Denise walked gracefully to the door, stepped off the curb, and moved lithely into the automobile. As she shifted her weight to make herself comfortable in the seat, William moved in close beside her, placing his left hand on her face. Sensually, he stroked the curvature of her bone structure.

"Perfection," William drawled seductively, gently turning Denise's face towards him. He brought his lips down to her trembling mouth and kissed her deeply.

Denise did not fight him; in fact, she eagerly moved into the kiss, her stomach in butterflies, her heart pumping, and her inner thighs burning with the fire of lust. The forcefulness of William's thrusting tongue had her squirming with delight.

Thanks to Yasmine's private instruction in the art of seducing and pleasing women, William was very conscious of what he needed to do to capture and captivate his prey. Seeing an immediate, positive reaction to his boldness gave him confidence, and he turned fully towards Denise. Moving his hand upwards to embrace the back of her neck, William pulled her in even closer.

By this point, Denise realized the futility of attempting to direct events herself. She willingly gave up control and went with the welcomed sense of anticipation for whatever delicious erotic move William planned next. Decorum, propriety and any guilt she felt for cheating on Christophe were tossed aside and forgotten. Denise gave herself over to the sexiness of the moment.

The two of them kissed in silence for several minutes until finally, as if he had read Denise's thoughts, William went further. He roughly lifted his mouth off hers and moved on to other body parts. He proceeded to lick up and down Denise's neck; concurrently, he took time to stop and nibble on her earlobes. Instinctively, she craned her head back to provide his delicious tongue more area to taste.

Not wasting a moment, William placed his left hand on Denise's thigh and not so gently squeezed it. Her breathing became laboured in response to the pressure—the sensation of strength. His brazenness confounded yet delighted her.

William moved his hand further up Denise's leg until it was on top of her crotch; then, he pressed into her pelvic area. William fastidiously unzipped her pants and undid the button. As the outer clothing came away from her body, he slid his fingers under her panties, probing deep inside her.

Denise gasped, shocked at the audacity of his moves, but she was in total agreement with them. She wanted William to touch her wherever he wanted to. Her desire for him was fathomless, insatiable.

"Yes, yes, yes," Denise moaned.

William forced his tongue back down her throat; this action stopped her cries of erotic elation from escaping into the air.

For the next few minutes, the only audible noises coming out of Denise's mouth were whimpers of deep carnal satisfaction.

William was unbelievably deft with his fingers, pleasuring his partner vigorously, making sure to expend effort, care, and loving attention. No part of Denise, nothing that might make her cum, was ignored. His digits were warm and firm, yet gentle, navigating inside his partner with the experience of Don Juan, of Casanova, of Lord Byron.

After some time had passed, William's right hand grabbed Denise's head, forcing her to look at him, and when they locked eyes, he finally made her climax. Denise came so hard she screamed; a few tears of elated release escaped, running down her cheeks.

William smiled brightly at Denise, self-satisfied but not arrogant. Yasmine had instructed him to always portray confidence after pleasing a woman but temper his boldness with graciousness and appreciation of her trust in him.

Yasmine had also taught him how to temporarily shut down his natural inclination to be smug and pompous, replacing those problematic affectations with tenderness and a smile.

William had learned how to use his whole face to emote, not just his mouth, and how to soften his eyes. Yasmine had worked with him on this falseness of appearance for weeks; William's predisposition toward inertness of emotional facial expression had been a tough piece of clay to shape.

But the effort had paid off. Denise was completely entranced. "That was amazing!" she declared. "I need to catch my—my breath. I can't believe that happened. I've never before—I mean, I've never been so—I mean! Honestly, I don't know what I mean."

"I'm glad you enjoyed it, but I'm not nearly done with you yet. We still have time before we arrive at the Château. I don't know if you've noticed, but we haven't moved away from the curb yet. And we still have so much clothing on."

William directed a very willing Denise down towards the impressive bulge in his pants.

Thanks to the limo's closed-circuit camera system, Yasmine watched the backseat performance on her small television screen with mad excitement.

Even though her desire for her lover was all-consuming—deeply obsessive and possessive—Yasmine felt no jealousy. She understood the game that was in play. Denise was merely a pawn, not the first William had enlisted. Yasmine had created psychological profiles on all their targets, instructing William on how best to entrap them. She had permitted herself to obtain pleasure from watching her lover play with his prey.

Understanding it was time to leave, Yasmine eased the limousine back into traffic, promptly heading towards their makeshift base of operations at Château Bergé.

Little did any of the limo's occupants know that they had just left a newly arrived Christophe in their dust. Oblivious to the fact that his lunch date had already ditched him, he walked brazenly into Denise's boutique unconcerned by any lateness on his part.

Jules made sure she had regained a semblance of self-control and composure before Nazneen returned. She quickly wiped away the remnants of her tears from her red face. *Breath, Jules, breath.*

"I've got it! I'm down the hall! I'm coming!" Visually out of breath, Nazneen raced into Jules's office and immediately began rambling. "I'm sorry for being late again, but I spoke to the very nice, very attractive manager. He was incredibly understanding and apologetic, not that it was their fault, and anyway, I—err, Jules, what is it? You're so pale! You look like you've seen a ghost!"

A startled Nazneen, unaccustomed to seeing Jules in such a state, subconsciously freed herself of her cold burden. She gently placed the light green beverage down on the desk, right next to the box she had brought in earlier. The box's bloody contents were exposed for the world to see.

"Holy fuck! What kind of gift is that? Forgive me, Ms. Cartell. I didn't mean to be so crass. It just startled me." Placing her gaze squarely upon her employer, Nazneen saw horror and shock in Jules's distorted visage. "Are you okay, Ms. Cartell? I, um, I brought you your drink."

"Nazneen, did the woman who was here earlier leave a number where she could be reached? Tell me she did." Jules's voice was direct yet weak.

"Yes, she did, right after apologizing to me for saying she was going to—well, you know. She told me she was staying at Château Bergé and would be there until tonight if you changed your mind and wanted to talk."

"Get her on the phone now, Nazneen!"

"Yes, Ms. Cartell. Right away."

Once Nazneen returned to her desk, it took her only a minute to get a hold of Amanda.

"I have her, Ms. Cartell. She's holding on line two when you're ready."

Jules was not ready, but she had no other options. She had always been too cowed, too paralyzed by William's all-consuming darkness to fight him. He was still the only person on Earth who had power over her, and it all stemmed from what she saw in his black, dead eyes on the day Ethan died.

Or perhaps what she did not see: a soul. William was soulless evil. Neither Joseph nor Stella had anything on William's unique brand of malevolence. No, Jules needed help, a protector, an ally against him, against his limitless capacity for vengeful cruelty and unpredictable violence; it was crucial for her survival.

She could not—would not— involve Jacques. She had never told him about William or what he had done to her. Besides, Jules knew Jacques was far too kindhearted, had too sweet a soul, and was too much of a gentleman to know how to deal with a maniac like William.

Her father had been her champion the last time, but he was not here at the moment. And if William was free from his cage without her knowing about it, then her father had failed in his promise to keep him locked away forever. But her father was not

Joseph, and Jules reckoned that there were limits to what even he could do for her against someone like William.

No, Jacques and her father were not suitable warriors for this new battle. Jules needed someone on her side now who could and would do anything to stop William, even the unthinkable. And she needed that person to do it on her behalf, willingly.

William was a monster—a sociopath. Jules understood now that she needed her own psychopath to truly comprehend how he thought and how best to fight him.

"Dammit! I need her."

Jules checked her door, making sure it was closed and locked before putting the call on speaker.

"Amanda," Jules greeted dispassionately. It sounded like she had posed a question.

Amanda took it that way as well.

"Who the fuck else would it be? I'm shocked. I'd never have guessed that blameless Jules would have made the first move. I'm flattered, though, that you took time out of your busy schedule for someone as forgettable as me." Amanda's sarcasm was on point, and her anger was still hot from before. "What do you want, Jules?"

"Please, Amanda. I need to talk to you. I need to see you."

"Are you fucking with me? I know I left my information with that useless tit you call a receptionist, but I never expected you to call. I was half crazy after seeing you, but I'm in my right mind now. Go fuck yourself, Jules! You barely wanted to acknowledge my existence earlier. Now you want to engage in conversation with me, to see me? I'm done playing games, bitch. Bye, Ju—"

"Please, Amanda," Jules frantically interrupted.

"As I said, I'm done! I'm not playing your fucking games!"

"Dammit, woman! I'm in trouble! I—I need your help."

Silence. It was deafening. Neither woman spoke for nearly a minute. Amanda heard Jules softly crying on her end of the call, and that unnerved her. This was serious; this was real; this was not a game.

"I'm coming," Amanda assured her.

XIII

"Tell me everything," Amanda demanded.

Jules could do that, but only everything she felt comfortable revealing. She planned on consciously withholding to retain an acceptable level of control and authority over her own story—her nightmare. Jules took a moment to think about just how much of her history she wanted to reveal. How much regret and suffering would need to be exposed to get Amanda to act on her behalf?

She would need to be prudent and calculated with her words, her memories, and her emotions. There must be enough poignancy, urgency, and horror within her storytelling to convince her much-needed ally that the threat level was high. Jules was sure Amanda was still in love with her and would probably do anything to gain a foothold back into her life. She was still pragmatic about her situation.

Jules knew that, in her own unstable, unpredictable way, Amanda was every bit as cunning and perceptible as she was. That was what Jules was counting on to defeat William.

However, that same keen intellect also had her worried. After their recent, unpleasant reunion, Jules was concerned Amanda would be wary and suspicious of anything she said. Acutely sensitive to feeling even the slightest bit used or played. These were unabashed facts that Jules could not deny.

So love and infatuation aside, Jules had no choice but to employ other tactics to ensure the desired outcome. Amanda would require reasonable grounds to trust her again. And that meant evidence: pain and anguish.

Damn him! It was torture, all of it. Jules did not want to remember that awful night. She never talked about it, never divulged to anyone the totality of what William had done to her. Not to her father nor the police. She had only ever disclosed fragments of the horrific truth.

Thanks to her father's brilliant legal work, those fragments, along with the kidnapping itself, had been enough for the prosecutors to lock William up. Jules had always borne the burden of what she had endured alone, but now William had made that impossible. He would not simply go away; he wanted her dead.

Even with a Sword of Damocles over her head, Jules saw no point in completely spilling her guts. Amanda did not need to know everything despite the direness of the situation—just enough to facilitate her willing cooperation.

It crossed Jules's mind to offer to pay Amanda for her time and expertise. William was just her kind of target: a misogynistic, murderous sociopath. *Who am I kidding? She'll never accept me as a client because of our troubled relationship. Personal feelings muck up business transactions. That bitch won't take my money—not a dime. I bet she'd even take my proposal as a personal insult.*

Jules tossed the option of hiring the Silver Dagger aside like so much trash. It was a better plan of attack to take advantage of the lingering torch Amanda carried for her, manipulate those emotions. *Appeal to the woman, not the assassin. I've successfully done it before, perhaps too well.*

"Stop stalling and spit it out already," Amanda ordered. "I came back here against my better judgment. Don't make me regret it."

Jules took a deep breath. Candidly, yet artfully, she unfolded her current situation.

She told Amanda everything she held in her memory and her heart about her dear, foolish Ethan. This topic was not off-limits or difficult for her to express. Eventually, Jules came to the part in Ethan's story where she had to reveal what ultimately happened to him that fateful day. How she had decidedly, yet without desire, let it happen.

Jules appealed to Amanda's sense of survival. She challenged her to try to understand her thinking at the time and not to judge her harshly. Jules recounted her childlike powerlessness in the face of crippling danger. How her logical mind, not fear or cowardice, overtook her desperate need and yearning to help her best friend.

Amanda remained silent.

Trepidatiously, Jules continued, now speaking about the misogynist, black-hearted bastard that was the adolescent William. She explained how he had been there that tragic day, arriving on the scene too late to do anything to save Ethan, who had already succumbed to the cold depths.

Jules elucidated how William's deviant nature became more anti-social and psychotic ageing into adulthood. She believed her inaction that day had transformed him further into something that looked human but was diabolically monstrous with a fathomless hatred for her.

And a burning need for vengeance.

"Later at the house, Amanda, while the Falsworths were being comforted by friends and family, I kept quiet on the couch waiting for my inevitable punishment. To my complete astonishment, however, it never came to pass. No one even remotely blamed me. Everyone, including Ethan's parents, believed it was pure luck that I wasn't dead, too.

"William shed not one tear, not one since those that had escaped his scornful eyes earlier down by the lake. He just stood there, silent and still, next to his inconsolable parents. But let me tell you—that bastard glared down at me with those dry eyes! It was a look of utter hatred and pure contempt.

"He never said one word to me or others about me. He never openly blamed me or attempted to convince the adults of my supposed complicity in Ethan's death. He just glowered menacingly at me for what seemed like an eternity until, out of nowhere, his frown disappeared. Instead of contemptuous rage, William's face became a crooked, sly smile.

"The bastard smiled at me, Amanda, but I understood right away that it was no invitation towards forgiveness. It was a false smile, one so full of menace that I felt sick to my stomach. As young as I was, I knew what it meant. My actions that day had created my first true enemy."

During Jules's tale of woe, Amanda had studied her face and cadence, noting that Jules's voice was affected and thoughtful whenever she spoke about Ethan. An obvious affection peppered her delivery, but Amanda recognized that show of tenderness all too well, having been on the receiving end of it before. She wondered how much of it was real and how much of it was tailored fabrication.

Amanda was skeptical: once bitten, twice shy.

Though suspicious by nature, Amanda observed an incontestable quality to Jules's reminisces. They exposed a measure of guilt and shame surrounding that lamentable girlhood choice; Jules had not fully divested herself of blame.

One word was written all over her face: haunted. That was the quality Jules's tone reflected. It darkened her eyes, revealing itself every time the corners of her mouth tightened when she got to the raw, emotional parts of the story.

Perhaps, Amanda considered, maybe Jules truly loved Ethan. She was not convinced.

William, on the other hand, was a different story. Whenever Jules talked about him, she spoke in a quick, almost crazed, panic-stricken manner. Fear emanated off of her; it was palpable. Her countenance oozed trepidation and alarm.

Amanda had no doubts about what she saw or how she interpreted those signs and gestures; however, she was not all that pleased with the honesty of this revelation. This frightened wimp was not the Jules she remembered, the bold woman she had trained to fight. This Jules was not the ferocious woman she had encountered earlier in the day—the one she loved despite time, circumstance, reason, and unparalleled directed hostility.

It was also not enough. No, not nearly good enough.

"And?" Amanda queried.

"Excuse me?" Jules was incredulous.

"Nope, not buying it," Amanda answered, rising out of her seat, prepared to leave. "You nearly had me, but in the end, I knew you would blow it. You're just incapable of it, aren't you? The truth, I mean. I should have known you would never be completely honest with me. Even when I explicitly told you to tell me everything, you deliver half-truths and hyperbole.

"You're so obvious in your attempts to control every fucking word and inflection that comes out of your mouth. The level of rigidity you possess is uncanny. That stick up your ass? Gargantuan. You just won't let that fucking guard down, will you? Not completely, not even when it would serve you all the better to do so. This is total bullshit."

"How dare you!"

"Shut the fuck up, Jules. It's my turn to talk. Kids are stupid and do stupid shit, and sometimes it gets them killed. It happens all the time. You were a child, for fuck's sake, and you would have just gotten yourself killed along with that stupid kid trying to save him. Get over it already!

"And call the police if you have a crazy stalker. Or find him and kick the shit out of him. You are a trained martial artist. I know—I helped train you! You know your way around a firearm. You don't need my help to deal with some crazy British asshole with unresolved grudge issues. Stop wasting my time. I'm not a damn babysitter. I'm outta here."

"No, wait, you don't understand, Amanda. Please! Stay! Okay, fine, yes, I held back. There is more to this story."

"Of course, there is! How stupid do you think I am? I know you intimately, babe! I'm not one of your puppets, one of your sycophantic employees. And I'm not your fucking father who will buy your dog and pony show at face value, do whatever you ask just because you're you. I'm not buying this frightened little girl act for a second. The Jules I knew never acted like some pussy-bitch scared of a man. Are you kidding me? So pathetic.

"Okay, I'll play Devil's Advocate. Maybe what you're telling me is true. Perhaps you honestly need my help, something only I can offer you. If this isn't all an attempt to manipulate me into doing something violent so your own hands won't get dirty, then I need you to tell me something real.

"Who the fuck is William Falsworth, and why does he seem to do the one thing that no one on this planet has ever been able to do before? Namely, turn you into a gutless, whiny bitch."

"Enough! Fuck you, Amanda! You're so brave, never been frightened of anyone or anything? Good for you! Big, strong, military brat! I haven't always been a fighter like you, taught by a crazy-ass father since you were a fucking toddler. I haven't always been able to defend myself.

"Alright, you want to know why I'm so scared of him? You want to know my truth? Fine, bitch, I'll give you some fucking truth!

"On the night of my fifteenth birthday party, the night my dad was killed, William abducted me and held me for hours, torturing me mentally and physically. He told me repeatedly that I would die horribly by his hand for what he believed I'd done to Ethan.

"William got in my head that night, Amanda, and never left. You haven't looked into his black, malevolent eyes. They steal from you what makes you feel safe, secure, whole. They rip into your soul, leaving nothing but insecurity and fear, fear of him, of what he can do to you, to everyone you love, ugly, terrible things. He can do all those things, too. He has the ways and the means.

"And now he's out! He's free!" Jules wrapped her arms around herself and shuddered. "Yes, Amanda, I'm afraid of him."

Amanda was visibly shocked by Jules's revelation. While her loss of composure was only for a brief moment, it was long enough to unsettle her. She did not like being so sensitive, so transparent; being controlled by emotion instead of controlling it went against her training. *But it's Jules, and this happened to her, not some stranger.*

Despite all her bluster and bravado, Amanda's feelings for Jules ran deep. She sat back down in her seat and stared at Jules with sympathetic eyes. This was new territory to her, feeling sorry for Jules.

"You never told me about any of this, Jules. For once, I don't know what to say to you. I'm so sorry. I wish you had felt comfortable enough to tell me this when we were together. I could have helped you. Held you, at the very least. Does your father know about this?"

"If you want the whole story, Amanda, I suggest you shut up, stop posturing, and put on your listening ears. I don't need useless sympathy. I need help in dealing with that evil bastard! If telling you everything will get me your unwavering assistance—fine, so be it. I'll tell you everything."

Jules languidly voiced her last spoken word like it was slowly sinking into quicksand. Every consonant, every vowel exaggerated. She hoped she had made her point; there would be no holding back.

"No one but me knows the complete story, Amanda. My father knows some of it, but only what I've allowed him to know. I'm his little girl, after all, and I know he could never handle the whole truth of what happened to me. I'm all he has left ever since that night.

"That damn night! My dad's death nearly destroyed my father. He's dealt with so much loss and pain. And when he finds out about Phillip! But I'm getting ahead of myself. I still believe I did the right thing—I figured it was best to keep most of it to myself. Okay, I'll start at the beginning. The day of my birthday party."

Amanda smiled compassionately, genuinely interested, and nodded in assent. "Tell me what that bastard did to you, Jules—before I kill him."

"Will you do this for me?"

William's plan sounded insane, but Denise did not know how she could refuse him. How could she decline to join forces with him now after all the things they had just done together? She had pretty much let go of her inhibitions and the sense of respectability her mother continually tried to instill in her. What happened during the limo ride had turned her inside out—in a good way.

What William proposed now was no less exciting, but it was a dangerous kind of excitement. It was the kind of stuff she had only read about in Jackie Collins and Danielle Steele novels: schemes, plot twists, and the unbridled hedonism of the rich and famous.

Again, Denise caught the wafting, pleasing scent of William's subtle yet powerful cologne. She had recognized it earlier in the limo as Tom Ford's Tobacco Vanille. The heady musk of the tonka bean, vanilla and cocoa-infused aroma ascending her nostrils was an intoxicating experience.

Denise had smelled it on a man before, but it had never had the same impact on her as it did now. William wore the cologne, not the other way around. Knowing it was at least five hundred dollars for a 250 ml bottle was not something she took lightly. Like William's showy car, it demonstrated to her that money was no object or impediment when it came to his enjoyment of lavish refinement.

While not nearly as vain and superficial as her mother and sister, Denise also liked the finer things in life. Thanks to her father's influence, she equated wealth with success and power. Despite her outward protestations of not needing a man, Denise was undeniably attracted to wealth and to the men who had it. She was a self-made woman, granted, but she had her vices, her secret desires.

Denise tried to distance herself from the old money patriarchy her father had represented. Still, she found herself drawn to men of social standing and financial power, men who subconsciously reminded her of her father. Denise had daddy issues big time. It was one of the main things she discussed at length in her regular therapy sessions.

She was aware she suffered this dichotomy between feminist idealism and sexual surrender to wealthy men. It had always been a hard-fought battle for Denise to make the right decision at the right time with the right man. With William? It had been no contest right out of the gate; he was a drug she desperately wanted to mainline.

Denise recognized that out of all her boyfriends, Christophe was the most unlike her father. He was vacuous, a little too pretty, and had no business sense. And while the sex was amazing, she never once considered what they had to be a great romance.

In the intimate space of William's limo, in the close company of a man like him, Denise felt the chemistry that was missing in her relationship with Christophe. She wanted William, and it frightened her a little bit. Her lust for this debonair stranger was undeniable.

Best of all, her beautiful, blonde, naturally flirty sister Sonja was nowhere in sight to overshadow her.

Still, Denise did not believe for a second that William would be offering her this opportunity to take down Jules if everything that happened in the limo had not happened. They had screwed multiple times and in various positions during the ride to Château Bergé; it was a very Sonja thing to do.

Denise enjoyed stepping out of her skin for once. It showed William that she was a woman of action, unafraid to experience the unknown, the unforeseen, the sensual, and tackle it all head-on. Well, that is what she hoped it showed him.

Earlier, upon reaching Château Bergé, they had gone directly up to William's suite. Walking through the main lobby, Denise had attempted to appear as demure and professional as possible. Like she had just casually met her lunch companion outside as opposed to stumbling out of his limo—where they had been fucking like rabbits the ride up—at the front entrance.

It was a good act, but she should not have worried or bothered—no one had been watching her. Truthfully, no one cared. Universally seen as the least interesting Cartell, paparazzi only photographed her if Christophe or her sister were by her side.

When Denise saw that William was in the most expensive suite at Château Bergé, she was not the least bit surprised. She expected nothing less from a Falsworth. During lunch, the two of them discussed their mutual hatred for Jules.

William kept most of his history with her close to his chest, revealing just enough to keep Denise interested. Jules had done him and his family a great wrong, resulting in the death of his brother. He was here to finally make her pay for this crime.

When Denise offered her sympathies, William smiled.

"I've always suspected Jules left a trail of destruction in her wake," Denise admitted. "I'm just shocked no one has come for payback sooner. It makes sense that it would be someone like you, someone as resourceful and powerful as an actual Falsworth! You could pose a serious threat to Jules, and now is a perfect time to act.

"My brother is defeated. Phillip could be a match for her if not for his drinking. Trying to help someone who won't see the problem is frustratingly difficult. There is also the insanity of him still being in love with that bitch.

"And the fact that Jules has the Cartell name? The power and wealth attached to it is a serious deterrent to many would-be challengers. But not to you, William. You're so confident, so determined, so handsome."

Because William's act was so perfect, executed so flawlessly, Denise had no idea what she had done with her words, large smile, and devilish wink. How could she suspect her constant fawning sickened him to his core?

William loathed insipid women—the kind of woman his mother had been. Women who needed attention from powerful men; to notice them and pay them superficial compliments. Women who needed men to make them feel good so they could forget for a time how utterly insignificant they were.

Finally, needing this encounter with Denise to end before he lost control of his performance, William broached the topic of revenge during the dessert course. And not a moment too soon, feeling his composure slipping with every passing minute. William wanted to get Denise on the path to playing her part in his grand scheme.

When Denise had asked him what his ultimate plan for Jules was, William told her he wanted Jules to have an accident that would get rid of her. Permanently. First, though, he needed Denise to get him unfettered access to Cartell Worldwide's computer system. Would she help him get payback?

Now, having thought about it for several minutes, Denise was unsure if she could commit to such an undertaking.

"What you're suggesting, William! It's—I mean! Are you serious? You're joking. You must be."

"Does my plan bother you?"

"Yes, William, committing murder fucking bothers me," Denise stated, her tone peppered with anxiety.

"I never said anything of the sort, Denise. I certainly never used that word. I said 'accident,' and accidents happen all the time. Be in the wrong place at the wrong time? Tragedy. Too bad, so sad. Fate, my dear, can be a bitch. So can karma."

"So, you fuck me, feed me, ply me with excellent wine, and then ask me to break the law. Break her? Absolutely, I'm down with that, but the rest! I don't know. I just—I—I can't go that far."

"I see," William sighed. He made sure to show Denise how disappointed he was in her answer, but inwardly he was over the moon. His ploy had worked; Denise was right where he wanted her. "I guess I was wrong about you. My fault, really, for going against the consensus."

"What's that supposed to mean?"

"Denise, I asked around Europe, in upper social circles, about the mighty Cartell family. What I heard about you, in particular, wasn't kind, but I didn't believe their slights. Idle gossip, I thought. Jealousy, for how could the daughter of the famous Joseph Cartell and his wife, the international beauty Estella, be anything but a goddess herself, a force to be reckoned with!

"Sonja was talked about very highly, but not you, Denise. I mean, when they mentioned you at all, which was practically never. When you did enter into the conversation, the consensus, as I said, wasn't flattering. I'm sure you can't help the way you are.

"Not to judge you harshly, but I see now they were all correct in their assessment of you. You're pretty, yes, sexy, sure, but that only goes so far. And put those qualities up against your beautiful sister? Not to be cruel, never, but even in appearance, you have to admit, she does look vastly more like a Cartell. Blonde hair, porcelain skin—lovely.

"I was told from the start by many close confidants that I should go to your sister for help against Jules. My friends warned me that you were just a scared child, and what I needed to fight a tigress like Jules was a lioness like Sonja. You're a kitten, I see that now, and that weakness—I mean to say, vulnerability, must be what Bennet finds so—adorable?

"That doesn't work for me. No, you don't have what it takes to help Phillip regain his freedom from the clutches of that harpy or to help me get justice for my brother.

"It's okay, Denise, not every child can inherit the best qualities of their parents. You have your talents. In business, you're an amazing—retailer, is it? That's good, really. I had fun today, but I'm afraid I'll have to ask you to leave. I need to get serious. I'll contact your sister. I'm sure you can see yourself out. An Uber will be waiting for you downstairs."

That said, William excused himself, retired to his bedroom, and closed the door.

Denise was stunned, hurt, confused. What just happened? She could not believe it. She had stood there like a moron in silence, listening to William say those things. She stared at the bedroom door waiting for him to come back out, explain himself, and apologize for the terrible things he had said to her.

After standing by herself in the middle of the room for several long, pensive minutes, Denise got the hint: William was not coming back. With what was left of her dignity, she got up and left the eerily silent suite.

Once he heard the door slam shut, William, a pernicious scowl firmly planted on his formerly expressionless face, pulled his iPhone out of his pocket. He punched in a number he had been waiting to call all day. When his call was answered, William gave one command.

"Release the story."

Ending the call, William tossed his phone on the bed. Looking at himself in the floor-length mirror, he chanted one of his many mantras back to himself through his reflective doppelganger.

"Stretch their mind 'till it snaps."

"So, Amanda," Jules began, "my parents surprised me with a Halloween Masquerade Ball for my fifteenth birthday. I already knew about it, of course. You know I hate surprises. The event was held at the Grand Tremaine, that historic hotel south of Yonge and Dundas. Everyone had to come in costume, at the very least a mask, or they weren't allowed entrance."

Jules noted her companion's not-so-subtle eye-roll.

"Yes, Amanda, I was controlling even back then. Big fucking surprise. I'm not ashamed to admit that I hired security to enforce that rule, which I'm sure has you in stitches. In my defence, there was a lot of money in the room that night, so it made sense to have them there. They ended up being ultimately useless in keeping the wrong people out.

"My father had invited Joseph. He, unfortunately, came with Sonja. Even though we went to the same school, we barely knew each other. That stuck-up bitch came dressed as Princess Diana in an exact copy of her blue-ink, velvet Victor Edelstein gown. How tacky and pretentious.

"I was properly attired for Halloween. I was Claudia from *Interview With the Vampire*. I had on the cutest wig with ringlet curls, and my dress was custom-made at Fashion Crimes. I took you there once, remember? On Queen St. West? I don't know if it's there anymore. That dress cost a small fortune, but it was worth every loonie. I wish I still had it, but William destroyed it. I'll get to that.

"My folks had done a beautiful job on the room, perfect down to the last detail, exactly how I had envisioned my Gothic ballroom. Deep purple and blood-red satin linens dripped over tables, and silver and black silk spider webs punctuated the macabre scenery. There were vampires, witches, and other tastefully horrific props everywhere—not those cheap, cartoony ones with smiley faces.

"What's up with that, anyway? Halloween should be fun but frightful, yet every year I see more and more of those stupid happy crones and smiling vampires."

"I get it. You love Halloween. Move it along."

"I'm trying to set the mood, Amanda. Paint the scenery. It's helping to build up my nerve to talk about what I really don't—oh, whatever!

"Forty minutes into my party, my dad got a phone call. One of his rich, elderly patients had taken ill and refused to go to the hospital until they'd seen and spoken to my dad. House calls didn't happen often, but with the entitled rich, I came to expect them.

"So, he needed to leave. I wasn't impressed with that decision. He begged for my forgiveness, hoped I understood and wished me a happy birthday. Dad told me how much he loved me, what a beautiful young woman I was, how proud he was of me—and—and said he'd see me in the morning. I never saw him again."

Jules's voice trailed off; tears surfaced in her eyes. She was no crier, not by any means. She believed tears were ugly and showed weakness; she readily imparted that opinion onto anyone who cried in her presence.

Talking about her father and this hated night was something Jules had never done before. It certainly was not something she had expected to do on the fly; naturally, she was unprepared for how it would affect her. She was honestly shocked by how raw the emotions surrounding her dad's death still felt. She was uncomfortable with how the pain and sorrow flowed out from deep inside her, seeking form and shape through those loathsome tears.

"I miss my dad so much. He deserves more than these ridiculous tears. He deserves justice."

Amanda was caught off guard by this sentimental segue. "What the hell are you going on about? Not to sound compassionless, but you're rambling."

"Never mind," Jules curtly replied, wiping the hated tears from her eyes. "That's for later. I said I'd tell you everything, and I meant it. I'm fine. Let's continue."

"Good, but less back story, please, and more William."

"Fine," Jules snarled. "About two hours after my dad left, my father got a phone call. I watched him answer it, and then I saw his face go pale. He ran over to Mr. Castle, the senior partner of his firm, shouted something to him, and then my father ran out of the hotel. I had no idea what was happening, aside from the undeniable fact that now both my parents had abandoned me at my own party.

"Naturally, I was livid. Growing up, I'd always understood it as a commonplace situation, my parents' work lives overshadowing our home life. But this was my birthday, the one time they shouldn't have sacrificed my happiness for their careers. That bitterness was what permeated my every thought at that moment—little did I know! Hindsight can be a real bitch.

"Several of the adults began to swarm Mr. Castle. Their voices were loud and jumbled up in a dramatic cacophony of what quickly turned into a huge commotion. All my self-entitled ass saw was a bunch of business stiffs ruining my party.

"Angry that my perfect night had been trashed by boorish adults, I stormed off to the bathroom. I screamed at every girl I found in there primping and gossiping to get the fuck out and go home—the party was over!

"What I eventually came to realize was that my childishness had created the perfect scenario for William to take advantage of. I had isolated myself from the group by hiding in the bathroom, diminishing my pool of resources by ordering everyone to leave the area. Sun Tzu would have been appalled by my tactics, my infantile stupidity, my arrogance.

"After a few minutes of solitude and self-pity, curled up sitting on a toilet, I heard the bathroom door open. Heavy footsteps fell slowly upon the floor, one after the other, but I was too much in my head to recognize that those sounds couldn't have been made by someone wearing high-heels. Or even flats, for that matter. They were plodding and heavy. Hindsight, again, but at the time, I just didn't pay attention.

"Irritated by the intrusion, I planned on taking my frustrations out on the poor, unsuspecting bitch who had dared to defy my earlier orders. As soon as I unlocked the stall, however, a massive force pushed the door inwards, knocking me violently back. I crashed into the toilet, crumpling like a rag-doll, and that damn wig fell into my face, obscuring my view.

"Before I could catch my breath or scream for help, I was grabbed, picked up, and thrown clear out of the stall into the hard vanity counter.

"Dazed, in pain, and finally separated from my wig, I felt a large hand clutch the back of my head. My entire upper torso was then whipped backward until my eyes saw the ceiling. My assailant's free hand shoved a rubber ball into my mouth. Then, a piece of industrial tape was slapped over my entire lower jaw, covering my mouth, preventing any kind of audible sound from escaping.

"The shape, the figure of what I finally, rationally accepted to be a man, and a strong one, lifted and tossed me over his shoulder. I felt him start to walk, and it was at that moment I finally blacked out from the pain and shock of the beating."

"He knew your movements, Jules," Amanda stated. "Your itinerary. Perhaps for some time. He selected that night, specifically. He'd been watching you. Waiting for the right time to abduct you. He had instruments, paraphernalia. This wasn't done in the heat of the moment: this was planned revenge. I know the difference."

"Yes," Jules agreed, "and it gets worse before it gets better. Well, better is a poor choice of words. Before getting away from him, I'll say.

"What I need to do, Amanda, before I get into what I went through that night, is make you understand how brutal and insanely evil William Falsworth truly is. What he had in store for me was calculated, I believe that, but not everything he does is so premeditated. William needs control, and I think he lives in a constant state of fear of losing that sense of control over himself, the people around him, and his environment."

Amanda shot Jules a look that spoke volumes.

"Yes, I get the absurdity of me saying that. William's needs, his deep fears and insecurities, are on a level so far beyond us so-called control freaks it's almost incomprehensible. It's much more savage and irrational.

"From what I've observed and experienced, I believe William's inherent nature is chaotic and violent. It often gets the best of him, no matter how hard he tries to reign it in so he can function in everyday society. It's something that cannot be controlled by his will alone, not for lengthy amounts of time, anyway. When this instability surfaces, it makes him angry, which in turn makes him act unpredictably. He craves the safety of predictability, of control.

"This is why he's so dangerous. In this state of discomfort, he has a complete lack of remorse for whatever maliciousness he inevitably does to make himself feel secure again. Anyone can be his victim, the target of his uncontrollable aggression! He sees enemies everywhere. It has to be why he's so anti-social. He can't control the thoughts, actions, and behaviours of others. Well, except through violence."

"He's psychotic. I get it, Jules. When people get in his way, even when they just disagree with him, he can do unspeakable things, a consequence of that perceived slight. Mental illness leading to sociopathic tendencies. Severe behavioural and impulse control issues. Got it."

"No! It's not that textbook, Amanda. You've never looked in his dead eyes and held his gaze, even for a moment. If you had, you'd understand it's something far more insidious than just a chemical imbalance and bad parenting. Something is missing inside him. He's a soulless monster. Whatever it is that makes us human aside from our flesh and blood, our DNA, that invisible human element is absent in him.

"Amanda, before William took his family's jet to Toronto to find me, he'd murdered his parents."

"Really," Amanda commented, but it was not a statement of surprise. It was cold and matter-of-fact. She expected nothing less from William considering what she had been told about him so far.

"He'd finally told his parents his version of the events leading up to Ethan's death. Well, his twisted, erroneous interpretation of those awful moments. Why did he wait so many years? Was it because he felt I was now old enough to warrant his punishment? To fully understand and comprehend what he believes I did to his brother? I probably won't ever know the real reason, but one thing I do know is that their reaction wasn't what he'd anticipated.

"I've always believed that the Falsworths must have known their only surviving son was fucked in the head. Troubled, I guess, is the proper, thoughtful, socially conscious word, but make no mistake, Amanda, he's much worse than that.

"My parents and I heard whispers about 'that mean, nasty Falsworth boy' for years after Ethan's death. How he'd done unspeakably cruel things to animals, and how he'd been violent towards his teachers and other students. The Falsworths spent a great deal of money, flexed a tremendous amount of their social and political muscle to keep him out of court, out of jail, out of the press.

"But people talk. People like the ones in my parents' social circle—shared friends. The way they spoke about that family! Concerned, hushed tones. They avoided William like the plague when in the company of the Falsworths.

"Truthfully, I think this bizarre revelation and appeal for their aid in punishing me for what I'd supposedly done was simply too much for his parents to accept. Or ignore. I'm sure the hope they had kept in their hearts for William to eventually be, or at least act normal, was destroyed that day.

"Laying on the floor of the hotel room, William told me his parents had admonished him for defiling his brother's memory. They'd rebuked his challenge to them to take up arms and join him in punishing me with the death I so richly deserved. Insane, I know, and his parents thought so too. They'd informed him, probably horrified by his crazy proclamations, that they were sending him away to a hospital for 'his own good.'

"He was a legal adult by this point, but if the Falsworths wanted him locked away, they could make it happen. William must have believed that as well, and it scared him. That's what I think must have propelled him to do what he did.

"Feeling betrayed by his own family, fearing for his freedom, I believe he panicked. William told me he attacked his father first while he slept. He beat his head in with one of his sister's resin Equestrian Award statuettes. He smashed his father's cranium over and over again until his face and skull became nothing but bone fragments and bloody pulp. His words—not mine.

"But even worse than what happened to his father was what he did to his mother. She'd been downstairs watching TV during the murder of his father, oblivious to everything. When she finally came upstairs to go to bed, he surprised her, knocked her unconscious, and then beat her nearly to death with his fists.

"While his mother was unconscious, William poured kerosene oil over her entire body and dropped her into the master bedroom fireplace, a functioning, historical fireplace. Not electric. He waited until she finally came around and was lucid enough to scream to light the match and set her ablaze.

"As the flames engulfed his mother, William held her thrashing body down with a long, metal floor lamp. He wanted to enjoy watching her flail about in the inferno, wracked with agony, shrieking, attempting in vain to escape. His last words on the matter to me were that he got aroused from breathing in his mother's char and ashes. It—excited him."

"Monstrous," Amanda whispered.

"That's something coming from someone in your line of work, but I can see you're finally getting it. I wasn't lying or being dramatic, Amanda. William is much worse than some 'British asshole with grudge issues.'"

"Yes, I see that," Amanda admitted. "Now I just wanna hurt the fucker even more before I kill him."

"Good, keep that thought. William wasn't registered at the hotel. The room he took me to obviously wasn't his. That was apparent to me even in the state I was in. That room was chosen for its proximity to my party. William needed to avoid being seen absconding with an unconscious teenager. He planned on taking me at some point that night. He might not have had a plan on how to do that and could have just been hoping for an opportune moment.

"When I came to my senses, I realized I was lying on a carpeted floor in an unfamiliar hotel room. I recognized the room design from internet pictures, so I knew we were still at the Grand Tremaine. The carpet was damp—blood-soaked. Both my hands and feet were tightly bound with twine, and the ball was still taped in my mouth.

"I didn't see or hear William in the vicinity. Working through the fear, I did my best not to panic so I could perceive my surroundings. The luggage on the floor across from me looked worn. The clothes laid out on the bed, both male and female, weren't designer by any means or fashionable for someone under sixty. There were several bottles of pills on the dresser.

"Logically—and I was clinging to logic at this point to stay sane—I extrapolated from the evidence that he'd appropriated the room from some unlucky, probably dead senior citizens. Horrifically, I soon realized how correct my deductions were.

"William eventually came out of the bathroom dragging two dead bodies behind him. Then, quite calmly, he laid their bloody remains on top of me. He chuckled as those two sanguine corpses slithered down my naked body, staining my virginal, pink flesh with their flayed putrescence. I so wanted to scream, but streaming, ugly tears was my only emotional release.

"Yes, I forgot to tell you, Amanda, that I'd been stripped naked. He'd shredded my beautiful dress into various-sized pieces, and the remains were scattered about me. Bare-ass naked, I was."

Amanda slammed her hand down on the desk and screamed, "Don't!"

"Don't what?"

"Stop it, Jules. Don't give in to sardonic humour just to push my buttons or punish me for initially mistrusting you. And you don't have to go any further. I don't need to know more. If you want to tell me everything, I'm here for you, but don't proceed further just to prove some meaningless point. You need protection, and he needs to be put down like the mad dog that he is. I'm one hundred percent in. You don't have to—"

"He didn't rape me," Jules interrupted. "Is that what you're worried about hearing?"

Amanda remained silent, visibly uncomfortable.

Jules rolled her eyes. "Please, I disgusted him. He did stick a hunting knife up inside me and told me that if I shifted even a bit during his play-by-play on how he planned to punish me, my family, he'd start moving that knife around. Slower, than faster, than slower, than faster. The blade cut me going in, and I still have a small scar. I'm surprised you never noticed it. If you did, you never said anything."

"I noticed. I spent a fair bit of time down there, you remember. I never brought it up because scars, to someone like me, in my line of work, are a common occurrence. I don't focus on them. Scars are very personal, and you don't ask about them if the bearer doesn't bring them up. It's rude and invasive. And speaking of invasiveness, was that the only intrusive thing he did to you?"

"Oh, he inflicted all manner of degradation upon my flesh, but he never stuck his pecker in me. Looking back, I guess I should be grateful for small miracles."

Amanda was perplexed by the casualness with which Jules spoke about this horrific chapter in her life. It was clear to her now why Jules had sounded so frantic earlier to procure her aid, yet she wondered how much this tragic event had damaged her.

Jules looked dramatically altered since Amanda saw her last. Her hair, always controlled and styled, looked dishevelled. Her complexion? Sallow and wane. Most noticeable was Jules's nervous behaviour; she was constantly eyeing the door as if she expected someone to break it down and barge in at any moment.

Yes, Amanda divined, *Jules is more than just rattled. She's terrified.*

And not to be discounted was the horrible scorch mark on the floor. Amanda was quite aware that it had not been there earlier, nor the lingering smell of burnt plastic mixed with potpourri and air freshener. She figured something dramatic had occurred after her departure.

Amanda decided it was time for her to start asking Jules some pertinent questions.

XIV

"How did you finally get away from him, Jules?"

"William never found my cellphone in the hidden pocket sewn into my dress. It was pure luck that he missed it when he destroyed my clothes. The police tracked its GPS. They stormed in, wrestled him to the ground, and that was that. It was all very dramatic, yet over in seconds. I never saw him again.

"My father handled it after that. It was the last powerful, able-bodied thing he did for me before he let my dad's death sink in and crush him."

Amanda stared at Jules, puzzled. "What do you mean you never saw him again? Why wasn't any of this made public? I never saw anything about a trial when I looked into your past back when we first met. Even with you being a minor, there had to have been some publicity surrounding this event. Some legal action must have been taken."

"You don't get how powerful and influential the Falsworths are, do you, Amanda? Besides, you know me! Do you think I wanted the world to know what had happened to me? So that people could forever use that knowledge against me? Judge me? Think me weak, flawed or broken? A fucking victim?!"

"Jules, come on, you were just a—"

"Don't you dare say I was just a kid!" Jules bluntly interjected. "People would have whispered about me for years. 'Did you hear about her, that poor girl? Oh, it's a sad story. Let me tell you about it!' No way. Not me! I planned on being feared, not pitied.

"I told my father that I was to be kept out of it. William murdered at least four people, including his parents, and I figured that was more than sufficient to put him away. I admitted to being abducted, but I outright refused to cooperate with the authorities on the details.

"My father, with the aid of some of my dad's hospital colleagues, had my medical records from that night destroyed. I can only guess why these people broke the law for me. With my dad dying in a car crash the same night I was abducted, they must have felt I deserved to be shielded from more pain. My dad was very well-liked, respected.

"So with my age, the missing medical records, and my own refusal to come forward, I became an unusable resource for the prosecution. Eventually, I disappeared from the narrative altogether.

"My father made a deal with Gretchen, William's sister, and their uncle, Duncan, to have William extradited. Working with Canadian and British authorities, they had William remanded to a maximum-security institution for the criminally insane to avoid conventional prison.

"Pops made arrangements with the facility to be informed if William's status changed. If there was ever a chance for his release into society, we were to be notified so we could stop it. That bastard was never supposed to get out."

"What about the murders here in Canada? Those two old people?"

"The Falsworth's paid off everyone directly involved. Or threatened them. They have a huge international influence. Judges, lawyers, the police, and even the family of those dead seniors were all bought and silenced. I don't know the how and why of it all, I just wanted him gone, and I wanted to forget. My dad had just died! I wanted to—I needed to focus on that."

"And Charles agreed to all this?"

"Yes, as long as it was understood that William was to be locked up far from us. I know my father would have killed the bastard had I not lied and said William never touched me. Come on, Amanda, this is how things get swept under the rug for the extremely rich. You should recognize the system in place for the arrogant and the well-connected. Unless it personally affects them, they don't fret over collateral damage.

"Plus, my father was barely keeping it together during that time. Once William was dealt with, he completely fell apart when he had to finally confront the reality of my dad's death."

Amanda nodded sympathetically. "We need to discover how that bastard got out, especially without you or your father knowing about it. I suggest interrogating the sister."

Stuck on the notion that William had unlawfully escaped, Jules had not considered that Gretchen might have arranged her brother's reprieve and release.

"Why would she do that? Setting William free would bring nothing but strife and chaos! His family must see that he's a monster. Why would they risk reintroducing him back into their lives? What psychiatrist in their right mind could ever be fooled into thinking he wasn't a danger to society?"

Jules planned on asking Gretchen these very questions. Soon.

"What the hell happened?" Amanda asked, pointing towards the scorch mark on the floor.

Jules showed Amanda the box; her hatred of the inflammatory thing was prodigious. She explained what the box meant, what William's not-so-subtle message was, deciphering its code for Amanda so she could fully grasp the sick mind that had created such a monstrous thing. Although she refused to touch the box's contents, Jules painstakingly connected the items to the memories and the events they corresponded with.

Amanda looked mildly concerned. "He had an incendiary device implanted inside the phone that he was able to activate from a distance."

"I have to assume," Jules casually replied.

"Wireless activation takes money and specific know-how, Jules. And you say you felt it heat up?"

Jules nodded.

"He didn't want to kill you, or he would have blown it up in your face without warning. He wanted to scare you, toy with you, and that kind of forethought takes planning. Either William's been out for some time now, or he's got several accomplices aiding him. Or both. I need some time with this. I have a friend, and this person knows everything about computers, electronics, and explosives."

"Like the explosive you used on the Bergé yacht?"

Her mouth agape, Amanda stared at Jules with a stunned expression. *How could she possibly know I was involved in that?*

"Don't look so surprised. I have all of Joseph's files, even his hidden records. Don't worry. I've protected your identity from my father. He doesn't know who the Silver Dagger is. He's never heard of Amanda Reid."

"No, I'm sure he hasn't. Not from your lips, at least."

And that was the crux of Amanda's anger; she had been made invisible and inconsequential in Jules's history.

For years, Amanda had felt retroactively erased from Jules's life. She was made a ghost without a name, and it cut deeply. It was a vast, emotional pain, a hollowing inside her, and it had never gone away or lessened with time. It had never healed through any other lover's touch.

Amanda shook her head, thinking long and hard about what she was going to say next. If she was to give everything she had to aid Jules, she needed to clear the air once and for all. Amanda needed Jules to know the truth about how she felt about her—about them. It had been a long time coming.

"Jules, I have a few things to get off my chest before I commit fully to this, and I want you to really listen to me. Don't deflect, make excuses or tell me anything but the truth. You owe me that, especially now, when you've come to me for help because you can't turn to anyone else.

"The past few times we've seen each other, spoken to one another, you've been nothing but a smug bitch. I want to talk to the woman I knew and not the sarcastic harridan you put forward for me. Don't act for me. Be real. Or even with all you've been through and all that I now know, I won't help. I'll walk out that door and leave you to deal with this bastard on your own."

Jules slumped further down in her office chair, too emotionally exhausted to counter with a witty remark or sarcastic comeback. It was time to talk about the incident at the lake. Frankly, Jules was surprised Amanda had not already figured out the reason she had dumped her so hastily and continued for years to resent her.

"Go ahead, Amanda."

"You severed ties with me with such fucking ease. The way you dropped me and threw me away was so cold and completely dismissive. I loved you, and I'd never allowed myself to love anyone before. When you left, I kept hoping you'd come back to me, and I left the door open for you for a long time. Right now, though, it feels like you're crawling back into my life because, once again, you need something from me, but not me.

"Not to be flippant, but I think maybe it's a good thing William came back into your life right now. If this morning was any indication, you desperately need some perspective and humility in your life. Your ego is so over-inflated. Frankly, you've become a real fucking bitch."

"Wow," Jules gasped, "that was harsh! Listen, I am what I am because—"

"Hey! Don't get defensive or try to rationalize your behaviour. If you do, I'll march my ass right out that door."

"I'm not rationalizing, Amanda, but yes, in my defence, I'm the type of person that, if you've hurt me, I cut you out of my life to protect myself."

"With shocking ease. For me, it was worse because it wasn't about hatred. I never felt calculated hatred toward me. What you conveyed was complete indifference—and I feel that even now. It's like I never mattered to you. At least, not enough to hate once we'd parted ways, and that's what has killed me, preventing me from moving past you. I know I've asked this before, but did I never mean anything to you?"

Jules took a moment to formulate her answer.

"You want the cold, hard truth, Amanda? It's not that you meant nothing to me, or mean nothing to me now, it's just that—dammit! Okay, yes, I use people to get what I want, what I need from them. I'll manipulate and take control. I've always been this way. When I was younger, to a lesser degree, of course, I was less cold, less calculating. I've always put myself first and made no apologies about it.

"It began with Ethan's death. It's a mean world out there. We can get swallowed up by it, consumed if we aren't prepared to fight back, conquer it, and not make bad decisions that wind up getting you killed! I want to win, to be the one in the driver's seat, but my intention is not to hurt people. I'm not a sadist like William. There are limits to what I'll do. I know when to end things before they get out of control. My control.

"And our relationship? At the time, I admired you, even cared about your well-being, but no, Amanda, I was never in love. You had something I wanted. Hell, if your brother had been available and possessed your talents, I'd have used him instead.

"The sexual intimacy between us? An act, constructed, but I never meant to hurt you with my actions. At least not to a large degree. And yes, I do hear how that sounds. I get it.

"Honestly, I figured you would tire of me, or I'd casually start to pull away. I'd conduct myself in a manner that would inevitably create a level of disinterest and boredom in you, leading to our eventual break-up. I never thought you'd fall in love with me. Not true love. You didn't seem the type, but I see I was naive to think you were incapable of it.

"Listen, even on my best days, when I really had you wrapped around my finger, there was still a certain amount of withholding on your part. I assumed that meant we, our relationship, had a shelf-life. You never let anyone get in too close, you know, including me, and I was counting on that.

"Or—or maybe I just didn't care. William hurt me, made me feel powerless, but you had power, real physical power, more than I had. I saw it firsthand. I coveted it, needed it, and I was going to get you to share that power with me by whatever means necessary.

"I went about it the wrong way, and I'm sorry. I was selfish and damaged by so many things in my past. I allowed my desire to survive and dominate to overshadow my empathy, my sense of right and wrong. Not once did I consider your feelings. You're right. It was always about me.

"In light of what you know, because I just put my utmost trust in you, can we start anew? Forgive our failings and forget the past? Fan whatever ember of friendship still exists until it ignites? You know I respect you. I've always kept your secrets. I've never betrayed your trust."

"I know," Amanda conceded. "I was never worried about that. Maybe we could—oh, I don't know! Why did you leave me so abruptly, Jules?"

"The incident at Lake Simcoe? Come on, Amanda, I would have thought by now you'd have figured that one out, especially considering what I just told you about Ethan."

"Lake Simcoe?"

"Amanda, how can you not remember? I told you I hated ice-skating. I told you I had a bad experience on a lake in my past and that I never wanted to be near frozen water again. Remember our last weekend together?"

"Oh shit," Amanda whispered.

"You blindfolded me, said you had an adventure planned, wanted me to be surprised, and I went with it. When we got to our destination, we remained outside, in the cold, but you never said why. Do you remember picking me up, carrying me like a child until you eventually set me down and tore off my blindfold? You dangled a pair of ice skates in front of my face, shouting, 'It's time to face your fear!' You took me to a fucking ice-covered lake!"

"It was never about ice-skating," Amanda quickly realized. "It was the ice, the lake. Oh, Jules, I'm so sorry!"

"You completely disregarded my feelings! What made you think you had the right to act as my therapist? I never asked you to help me get over my fucking issues! All the years of repressed guilt and shame surrounding Ethan and that damn lake came back to me at that moment, hitting me like a fucking tidal wave. My supposedly indestructible wall of reason and justification for my actions that day crumbled to dust.

"Triggered, I panicked, demanding you take me home, but you stood there, laughing, telling me how ridiculous I was acting."

"Jules, I had no idea what you'd been through!" Amanda testified in her defence. "I thought I was helping—I mean, fuck! How could I have known?"

"What does that matter? It was never your place nor your responsibility to try and help me overcome anything. I'd never crossed that line with you, never asked about the topics you didn't want to talk about. Your family, especially your brother. Not once did I ever try to act like your damn shrink or life coach. You had no right! Your mocking, dismissive attitude toward my fear and panic was eye-opening.

"That night, when I was safely at home, I realized you'd grown too close, too comfortable with me if you felt you had the right to delve into my past and take on my inner demons. I was so angry and resentful about being forced to confront things I'd buried years ago. The guilt, the shame, the what-ifs made me near suicidal that night, and you were the cause of those feelings.

"Whether your heart was in the right place or not, you forced my hand. You crossed a line of invasive behaviour that no one crosses without severe consequences."

"And you left me two days later," Amanda added, finally understanding. "I see now why you did what you did, and I don't blame you, Jules. I probably would have broken your legs if the roles had been reversed. I grossly overstepped—but I was in love. I'm not ashamed to say that."

Unsure how to respond to that declaration, Jules stared at the wall blankly.

"It's alright that you never loved me in that way," Amanda sighed. "I gave you what you needed. I guess you gave me what I needed too at the time, too. A connection in my life during those solitary days when my father and brother had both deserted me. You filled that niche.

"You also made me realize what it was I wanted to do with the rest of my life, with my skill-set, and I wouldn't be the woman I am today had you not left me and forced me to choose a definitive path. You know what? Fuck it! Ya, bitch, we're good."

"I'm glad we can salvage a friendship out of all this," Jules admitted. "An unconventional one, but a friendship nonetheless. But no hugging."

"Fuck that! C'mere!" Amanda grabbed her now definitive friend, yanked her out of her chair, and promptly gave her a bear-hug so tight it caused noticeable gasping from Jules.

Once Amanda let go, Jules stared directly into her former paramour's eyes and smiled.

Amanda grinned back, recognizing an honesty, a vulnerability, a deliberate authenticity within Jules that she had never seen before. There was a light in those beautiful eyes. There was acceptance, understanding, and compassion. Jules had brought her walls down for her, and everything ugly between them had finally been forgiven.

Reacting instinctively to an intimacy that had not shown its face in years, Amanda reached out and pulled Jules back in close. It did not matter if the intimacy was authentic or performance—it had always felt real enough to Amanda. She placed her mouth over Jules's own surprised, though not repulsed aperture, and pressed down hard.

Jules shocked Amanda by willingly reciprocating, not slapping her. The two women kissed open-mouthed; their tongues wriggled around the moist space as their chests heaved together in synchronized movements.

Amanda was the first one to pull back, breaking the sensual intimacy. "Anything?" she asked.

"Nope, nothing," Jules replied without missing a beat. "The technique was good, but no rockets went off."

"I should've grabbed your ass. Oh well, you can't blame a bitch for trying. I need to go and make a few calls. I'll get in touch as soon as I've spoken to a few of my contacts. I'll know what to do about William then, how to find him, and what his most probable course of action will be."

"How soon before he tries something again?" Jules queried. The concern in her voice, while subtle, was undeniable. "Do you think I'll be safe while you're gone? Not that I'm incapable of fighting back, but do you think he'll try something else today? Something unconventional? You know how this kind of mind works. I don't. No offence."

Amanda laughed. "Stop worrying that you're insulting me. It's my business to understand my targets. As long as you stay in populated areas, you'll be fine. He wants this to be personal, one on one. That timer on the bomb says everything. He knew you'd survive that. It wasn't even a dispersal bomb—it was contained, low level. He just wanted to scare you, let you know he was back. The phone call says as much.

"Of course, with sociopaths, there's always what I call the 'chaos factor,' so don't provide him with opportunities. Don't go to the bathroom alone, for example."

"Ha, ha," Jules responded, rolling her eyes. "Okay, I'll make security aware of—"

"Really, Jules?" Amanda sighed, cutting her friend off. "That box made its way into your fucking office! You have a deeply concerning security issue. You should check your surveillance cameras to see who brought that thing into your building. Someone here can't be trusted. Unless you hire idiots who don't follow protocol."

"It was most likely an oversight, Amanda. A mistake. William probably paid someone in the mailroom, tricked them into thinking it was a surprise gift for me or something. I screen everyone here carefully, but yes, I'll look into it further.

"That box, like you said, is merely a warning, a precursor to a larger event. Yes, I'd wager that I'm fairly safe for today, regardless if I leave here or not. He wants me to sweat it out for a bit and worry. He's petty that way."

"Okay," Amanda reluctantly agreed, "but do yourself a favour and get rid of that box and everything in it. It's a distraction. Does this building have an incinerator?"

"Oddly enough, it does," Jules smirked. "We had to install one when Mode-Génétique Labs came into the building. Some of their bio-waste is toxic and has to be immediately destroyed."

"I've read up on them. Some interesting stuff. We should talk more about practical applications for someone in my line of work. If they could manufacture products for me, it would decrease my overhead. Buying untraceable poisons on the Black Market is expensive. My imagination is flowing with ideas for further bio-weaponry."

"No way, Amanda!" Jules exclaimed, exasperated. "I'm not using my R&D company to make cost-effective poisons for you. Seriously? Are you nuts?"

"A little," Amanda winked, "but isn't that why you called me to help? I'll be in touch."

"I'm so glad you called, babe," Miles gushed as he sat up in Christophe's king-sized bed. He stretched his arms out before folding them back under his head, oozing himself comfortably back into the soft pillows. "I can't believe that bitch stood you up. Well, her loss is my gain. You were on fucking fire, babe. I won't be able to walk right for the rest of the day."

"You're fucking hilarious," Christophe replied sarcastically. While he appreciated Miles's tacky, though appropriate commendation of his sexual prowess, the whole fuck session had felt empty from beginning to end. Mechanical, really, and though he had blown his load, Christophe did not feel any less irritable or annoyed. "And don't call me 'babe.'"

Not that he had actually wanted to meet Denise for lunch, but the fact that she had stood him up bothered him tremendously. She had wasted his time, but her inconsiderate action had done something much more significant. Christophe realized with absolute certainty that his so-called relationship with Denise, her infatuation with him, her lust for him, was undeniably broken.

Christophe knew it was his fault due in no small part to the fact that he had been less than eager of late to have sex with her. He had gone down on her a few times but avoided the full-on act of fucking for several weeks. He could not get into the performance anymore. Their sham relationship had to end.

"Come on, babe," Miles cooed, "come back to bed and cuddle before I have to leave."

Christophe had not intended to spend his afternoon fucking Miles; his anger, his frustration, and his hormones had got the better of him. He really wanted to be with his actual boyfriend, not a play-toy. Miles, initially an uncomplicated amusement, had become intolerably needy. Their time together, like his relationship with Denise, had to end.

Christophe was not looking for love or a boyfriend—he already had both. Miles was no longer a fun, occasional, no strings attached hookup. He was a problematic, sentimental leech.

Cuddle! Oh, for fuck's sake. So not cool.

"Listen, Miles, we need to talk. It's time we—"

Christophe's sentence was broken, his attention diverted as soon as he heard several hard knocks on his door. They were immediately followed up by the sound of Denise's voice crying out to him.

"Christophe, are you home? I need you."

Christophe turned his attention away from the direction of his door and back to his bed. Miles, his afternoon fuck-buddy, his on-the-side piece of ass that Denise did not know about, laid about like he owned the damn place.

Unlike the horrified look on Christophe's face, Miles looked amused by Denise's unexpected appearance.

"Fuck! I'm so fucked." Despite his panic, Christophe understood this was not the time for revelations or histrionics. It was also apparent, based entirely on the gleefully mischievous look on Miles's face, the naked man in his bed was not on the same page as him.

Miles was in the mood for confrontation, itching for a fight. He hated Denise. He was jealous that she got Christophe in the light of day, in public, and he had to be content with shadows and secrecy.

Christophe had made it clear from the start to Miles that if he wanted to have fun with him, he had to agree to live with his status as a secret, occasional lover. They were not a couple; they were not boyfriends; they were not soul-mates. They fucked, and that was it. He believed Miles had always understood that, but he now realized he had given the guy far too much credit.

Too much was on the line for Christophe to fuck up now.

Denise had no idea she was being played, and Miles refused to see that their non-relationship was nothing more than a fuck-buddies situation. Christophe had to break it off with both of them, but not like this, not with angry, explosive feelings of misplaced betrayal and jealousy or a dramatic scene inside his apartment. He had nice expensive things, and he did not want two cat-fighting bitches wrecking his stuff.

"Miles, get up and get dressed!"

"Screw her," Miles smirked indignantly, tossing the covers away from his naked body. "Let her see me here." His cock was hard again.

"Oh, fuck off with that crap. Seriously, come one. Don't be a jealous little shit. Get your ass out of bed."

"Whatever. She'll go away. Just don't answer."

"There's music playing! She can fucking hear it! She knows I'm home, and even if she thinks I'm on the can or sleeping or showering, she'll keep banging on that fucking door until I answer. She didn't even buzz up! No fucking warning! One of my asshole neighbours probably recognized her and let her in. The last time Denise was emotional like this, I couldn't get rid of her. Come on, man, do this for me!"

"You're acting crazy, Chris. Get a grip."

"Fuck off, Miles, and don't call me Chris. I wouldn't be so calm if I were you. What if Jules finds out you were here and not in the office? Denise won't keep your secret. Going on a booty-call during prime work hours? Ya, that'll go over well with Jules."

Knowing Christophe was right, Miles's smirk quickly disappeared. Reluctantly, he got up out of bed, groaning, "Where do you want me to hide, *Chris*?"

Denise felt something was off about Christophe. She had come to him miserable, filled with hurt feelings looking to be assuaged, but his icy greeting at the door had instantly put her off. She felt worse than she already did. Something was causing him to act anxious and aloof around her.

Was he being spiteful because she had blown him off for lunch? Christophe was vain and had an ego, but Denise doubted he was that petty.

Something was bugging her about his apartment, too. Christophe was acting strange, but something smelled different, too, yet oddly familiar. Recently familiar. Denise could not put her finger on it.

Was she displacing? Was it William? Denise wondered whether this was some kind of bizarre post-traumatic reaction to what he had said to her.

Upon reflection, Denise did not think it had anything to do with what had transpired earlier between them. Definitely not the sex. He had been heartless and cruel at the end, but she could not help but admit the sex had been extraordinary. Despite that, it had been hard for her to hear him speak those ugly, derisive words.

Surprisingly, Denise harboured no feelings of hatred towards him for what he had said about her. What she currently hated most of all, what she was now most pissed at, was herself.

The drive back to the city had given Denise time to think, calm herself, and wipe the tears away. Somewhere inside of her, close to the surface, she recognized the truth: William was correct. What he had said about the calibre of her mettle and how others perceived her character was accurate.

Even though she pretended not to care, Denise had always known. For years she had heard the catty whispers and the mean gossip. They looked down on her, all of the elite class.
Now more than ever.

Since her father had passed, people were no longer afraid of his retribution for any disparaging words said about his youngest daughter in mixed company. And in not so hushed tones. They did not care anymore if she knew what they thought of her or heard their venomous words. What was she going to do about it now that daddy was no longer around to fight her battles?

Though some were still intimidated by Stella's potential wrath, they more than made up for their mockery of her youngest daughter by how favourably they regarded Sonja. Everybody loved the beautiful, bubbly, blonde Sonja!

No, Denise did not believe anyone was all that afraid anymore to be vocal. They were loud and proud about their dismissive attitude towards her—the brown-haired, boring Cartell girl.

William did not know her personally; he had only the opinions and viewpoints of others to go on. Denise was furious with herself that she had gone and proved those assholes right by acting like a child—the scaredy-cat who turned down his proposal. And for him to think that Sonja would not have! It killed her.

Coward. Why do I care if that bitch lives or dies? And William wasn't mean out of callousness but out of necessity. He has no reason to torment me. William came to me first, not believing those Euro-Trash pricks, and I threw his belief in me back in his face. He has a plan, a strategy, and he trusted me to help make it a reality, but like a fool, I went and turned him down.

"Hello? Anyone in there? Denise, what's wrong? It looks like you're having some weird conversation with yourself in your head." Christophe watched with uneasy curiosity as Denise's face contorted and winced. *Yep, definitely taking a face journey, mulling over something unpleasant.*

For the moment, Christophe was not panicking; Miles had finally listened to him and went and hid in the en suite bathroom where he was, thankfully, keeping his mouth shut.

"What's up, Dee? Are you here to apologize for standing me up? I have a life too, ya know. I can't be traipsing about town after you just to have you end up ditching me."

"You know," Denise began, looking longingly at Christophe, "I wear the latest fashions, the hippest styles, and still people think I'm a basic bitch. I have a brand, an upcoming fashion line, and I'm dating a famous model, for fuck's sake! I thought dating you would boost my reputation. All eyes would be on us. People would change their opinion of me, see how cool I am with Christophe Bennett on my arm.

"I've had men interested in me before, sure. Truth is, I never knew if they really desired me or just wanted my family's money and the prestige associated with my last name. Or if they just wanted to get into my dad's good graces to get a fucking job through me by getting into my pants first. I never wanted to be like Sonja."

"Stop!" Christophe shouted. He had never seen Denise so morose, and it made him very uncomfortable. And if there was one thing Christophe disliked most about dating Denise, it was her constant bitching about her sister.

"Denise, you have to stop these constant comparisons and get over this whole jealousy thing. Sonja's Sonja. You are your own person. It's not a fucking competition."

Christophe moved in close to hug Denise, but she pushed him away. She did not want a hug; she did not want to be consoled anymore. It was time to admit some cold hard facts about herself.

"Growing up, I never wanted to be silly and 'rely on pretty' like Sonja. I wanted to be intelligent and business savvy. I wanted to be like my dad, like Phillip, but I'll never be like them. I get that now. And not Phillip as he is today. The one that existed before you came into my life. He'll be back soon, to command and impress, but I wonder—what's left for me? What about me?

"The truth, Christophe, is that I was never that interested in you. You're brutally handsome, amazing in bed, very likable, and I thought that was enough for me to love you, but it's not enough.

"Even with you beside me, people still cut me up behind my back. I'm suffocating under your huge shadow, Christophe. When we go out, everyone flocks to you, pushing past me just like when I'm with Sonja or Mom. Hell, even with Jules, and she couldn't care less about being liked. She's a mean bitch, yet people fawn over her because they respect her, fear her. She's intelligent, savvy, beautiful—and blonde. I can't win.

"I came here because I thought I wanted you to console me, make me feel better. Fuck me, make me feel good, make me feel something other than this anger, this anxiety. Or maybe simply have you hold me in your strong arms and tell me that I'm beautiful, loved, but those are just empty words, empty actions. I don't love you, and you don't love me.

"I'm sorry about standing you up earlier. It doesn't matter why. I wanted to share something with you. I thought I had something to use against Jules to help Phillip—and maybe I do, but I'll probably screw that up, too. Fuck, I'm such a loser."

Standing in the middle of Christophe's living room, Denise began to cry. She held no illusions about how pathetic she looked, bawling like an infant, hands to her temples.

Christophe tried once more to comfort Denise; again, she pushed him away. She looked around the all too familiar room; as expected, nothing appeared out of the ordinary. The furniture was the same. The window treatments had not been changed. The walls, all still painted the same colour, had the same expensive artwork hanging on them. Nothing was out of the ordinary.

Nothing that is, except that lingering scent. Denise could not put her finger on why it was bugging her so much. Why did it seem so familiar? She had not smelled it before in Christophe's apartment. There were no scented candles anywhere or potpourri. She knew he hated that frou-frou stuff.

Suddenly, it came to her: Davidoff's Cool Water. That was what Denise smelled, and that was not Christophe's cologne. He was a Gautier man. If he had a new contract, he would wear that brand while doing their commercials and print ads. Denise had never heard Christophe mention working with Davidoff.

It all began to fit together.

No, it can't be him! But it makes sense now! The comment that smarmy bastard said earlier about Christophe.

At the time, Denise had been too hostile, too jealous. She had acted too rashly to see he was baiting her with his pornographic rhetoric, trying to make her jealous. But Denise got it now. He already knew the answer to his lewd question, and he was furtively throwing that knowledge back in her completely oblivious face. Parading it in front of her and silently laughing at her ignorance.

Now that she thought about it, Denise doubted it was by sheer accident that the two of them had been seated next to each other at dinner the previous night. How close they were talking to one another, how comfortable they were with each other, how familiar.

And Christophe had been acting uncharacteristically nervous and anxious around her ever since she entered his condo. Why was he keeping her in the living room, close to the exit, away from the bedrooms? It was self-preservation.

Miles.

Denise felt sick to her stomach.

That bastard's here, hiding! How could I be so blind, so stupid? It was right in front of my face the whole time, and I never saw it. I knew I wasn't crazy! Christophe's been so distant recently, pulling away from me, disinterested.

Her head spinning, Denise needed to sit down. No, she wanted to run away.

"Denise! What's going on? You look like you're going to throw up! Oh my fucking god, don't tell me you're pregnant! We've been so careful!"

Momentarily composing herself, Denise slapped Christophe hard across his beautiful, panic-stricken face.

"You would be worried about that, wouldn't you? I'm so fucking thankful we used protection every time. I had no idea you were such a whore, Christophe. Unfuckingbelievable! Well, I'm sure both of you will be happy to hear this!"

Denise took a deep breath and then screamed an uninterrupted stream of curses and condemnations. It was officially over between them.

Upon returning to silence, Denise wanted to leave the apartment in the worst way, done talking, done looking into Christophe's lying, deceitful eyes.

Denise looked around for her bag. She could not remember where she had dropped it. Her phone was inside it, and it had gone off several times in the town car on the way back to the city. It had also gone off a few times since being inside Christophe's condo. She had not answered the thing because she did not want to talk to work, hear from her mother or speak with anyone else right now.

What Denise needed was some alone time. She wanted silence and sympathy. She thought coming here to Christophe's would get her that without incident or question, but she had been so wrong.

Thanks to her cell going off again, Denise finally found her bag. Picking it up, getting a good grip on its handle, Denise swung it at Christophe, belting him hard with it. He tried to duck, but he was too slow. The bag connected with the side of his head.

"Serves you right, asshole!" Denise shouted on her way out.

XV

"Jules, are you listening to me? You seem a million miles away."

Jacques's lips were moving, his jaw animated, that was apparent to her, but Jules had only been half-listening to the words coming out of his mouth. She was trying, rather unsuccessfully, to be present. Unfortunately, she was too preoccupied with distracting thoughts to be a good, interactive conversationalist.

Jacques had called Jules to invite her to a late lunch to make up for their cancelled breakfast meeting. Needing a brief reprieve from her current predicament, Jules had readily agreed. She also desperately wanted to spend time with him. Only, she had let Jacques do most of the talking while she sat silent, distracted by her thoughts.

Oddly enough, the ugly business with William, urgent and life-threatening as it was, currently took up only a fraction of her mental acumen. What was predominantly on Jules's mind at the moment were her plans for Phillip's downfall. It was imminent, happening the very next morning.

Charles had reached out to his daughter while she was en route to the restaurant Jacques had chosen for their public tête-à-tête. He had what they needed: the physical evidence. Phillip was finally going to be taken care of, punished, and removed from the company.

Charles had intended to elucidate at length the story of Phillip's first wife and his child. Jules, however, had stopped her father before divulging too much. She did not want to know anything more than what she already did. All she needed were M. Babineaux's documents.

Ultimately, her ignorance would work in her favour. Jules had a plan to destroy Phillip emotionally, and it was wicked.

"What? Oh, yes, sorry, Jacques, I've got some things on my mind. Go on, please."

"No, I've been going on and on. I'm sorry. Please, talk to me. What's bothering you?"

Jules smiled affectionately at Jacques. Here he was, once again putting her needs and welfare before himself. He was visibly troubled by something. He had reached out to her for comfort, for guidance, and all she could be was a selfish, rude bitch to him. Too preoccupied with her issues and desires to focus on him for a few minutes. And he was apologizing to her!

Jules knew she needed to treat Jacques better.

Get in the moment, woman. "No, Jacques, we can discuss what's on my mind later. You were saying something about your Aunt Patrice?"

Jacques continued with his tale after Jules refused a second time to talk about her troubles. She gave him her opinion on his dilemma as well as some advice.

Not too long into a discussion about their complicated relationship, the sound of several loud cell phones went off, one after the other. It caught their attention, taking them out of their moment.

Jules looked around the room; the room looked back at her. She heard gasps, saw shock, surprise, and even glee in the faces of some of her fellow diners. Many of them stared intently down at their phones and then, just as sharply, looked up from them to stare directly at her, whispering conspiratorially among themselves.

"What the hell is going on?" Jules queried.

Jacques stopped a waiter and asked, "What's everyone's problem? What's going on?"

The waiter shrugged, just as stumped.

Suddenly, as if in answer to their confusion, Jules's phone went off. It was her executive assistant. She immediately took the call.

"Yes? Slow down, Nazneen! What's the issue?"

"It's everywhere, Jules, including Hello! Magazine Canada and Huffington Post. It originated from a Toronto-based online media site known for salacious articles. And, well, it doesn't appear to be idle gossip. There are pictures! A first-person account!"

"Calm down," Jules ordered. "What are you babbling about? Why should I care about this nonsense?"

Nazneen told her it was about her father.

Immediately concerned, Jules hung up on Nazneen, turned to Jacques, and yelled, "Get on your phone and look up news about my father. Anything from today." They both started searching news sites until they quickly found something that completely stunned them.

Jules's heart broke. A single word popped into her head regarding this awful moment. It was a terrible, disheartening word, and it was one she thought she would never associate with her father.

Betrayal.

"Nazneen, where's my wife? I haven't been able to reach her. She's not—um, she's not returning my texts or calls."

Phillip knew he sounded pathetic, telling his wife's executive assistant that her boss, his fucking wife, was purposely avoiding him.

He did not understand. Things had gone so well during the night after the break-in. Jules falling into his arms, of her own free will, had been unexpected, wonderful, and the first time in ages she had shown him any affection whatsoever. Phillip was starved for it.

"Sorry, Mr. Cartell, but you just missed her," Nazneen answered. "She's left for the day. She went to meet with Jacques Bergé, then returned for a moment, left instructions for everyone concerning the handling of the press, and then asked me to reschedule her late afternoon meetings."

Jacques! Dammit! I should've known. No, don't think like that. It was just a business meeting. Right, sure it was. What am I going to do?

"Mr. Cartell? Is everything alright? I'm guessing you know about—"

"Nazneen," Phillip interjected, "where is Charles right now?"

"I'm sorry, sir, but I don't have that information."

Where the fuck are you, old man? Dammit, this is going to get ugly.

Nazneen's desk phone rang. Its abrupt shrillness brought Phillip out of his head and back down to earth.

"We've been inundated with calls," Nazneen groaned. "Ms. Cartell was adamant that we are to have a 'no comment' policy until further notice. Excuse me, sir."

Phillip leaned against Nazneen's desk as a myriad of troubling thoughts swam around in his head. He had been trying to get in touch with Jules, Denise, and his mother to no avail. The press had been hounding his office for the last half hour, and Phillip had been trying to put out fires as fast as he could. *No comment! That's a first for her. Jules always has a comment about everything.*

"Jules Cartell's office. No, I'm sorry, sir, but Ms. Cartell is unavailable at the moment. Yes, I understand the urgency. Yes, I understand you're leaving tomorrow afternoon for Paris. As I explained to your associate, we've had to push back your meeting until tomorrow morning due to extenuating circumstances. Ms. Cartell is sorry for the inconvenience. Yes, I understand."

The Parisians! Phillip, unable to hear what was being said on the other end of the phone call, immediately jumped into saviour mode. He motioned for Nazneen to give him the phone. He did not want to jeopardize this potential new business deal over Charles's stupidity. *Asshole. I always knew you couldn't be trusted.*

"Sir, Phillip Cartell would like to speak with you. I can—oh, um, I see."

There was a long pause in the conversation between Nazneen and the man from Paris that Phillip did not understand. *What's the hold-up? What's he saying? Just give me the damn phone already!*

"Yes, alright, if you insist. I'll let Ms. Cartell know. Have a pleasant day."

Phillip's eyes went large with confusion and shock. "What the hell just happened? Nazneen, why didn't you pass the damn phone over to me?"

"I'm sorry, sir. I did tell him you wanted to speak with him, but he, um—he—"

"What? What's with this ridiculous hesitation? Just tell me!"

"He didn't want to speak with you."

Phillip was stunned. "What? I'm the goddamn head of this company! Why wouldn't he want to fucking speak with me?!"

Phillip was well aware that it was unprofessional to lose control and curse in front of employees. He was greatly embarrassed by this behaviour. He knew he was a better man than that, yet he still fell victim to constant bouts of anger, frustration, and improper decorum.

It all came back to his wife's contempt for him. It had mangled his self-esteem, warped his sensible nature, sapped his strength, and diminished his power. He knew he was a shell of his former self, and as much as Phillip blamed his wife for his "new normal," he had allowed it to happen.

"Yes, well, I'm afraid he didn't see it that way. He was adamant that he only wanted to talk with Ms. Cartell. He said he doesn't talk about important business matters with—ah—I mean—"

Nazneen did not know how to finish her sentence. Or if she should. She suddenly wished she had shut her mouth much sooner and taken more care with how much of her conversation she revealed. Phillip had always been kind and respectful to her; she hated having to hurt him like this. She knew Jules would have loved every uncomfortable, hurtful second of it.

"Talk to what?" Phillip angrily questioned.

"Talk to 'Ms. Cartell's subordinates.' I'm sorry, but those were his exact words."

Nazneen saw the immediate sense of dejection written all over Phillip's handsome face. He had been unable to hide his shame and embarrassment at being laid low in front of her.

"You know, Mr. Cartell, he did have a thick accent, so maybe I got it wrong. He had slipped back into French for a few words so I could have mistranslated what he said."

"No, Nazneen, I'm pretty sure you hit it right on the nose." With his tail between his legs, Phillip trudged back to his office

Closing the door behind him, Phillip sauntered over to the Jonathon Adler antiqued brass bar cart that featured prominently in the room. The deluxe bar cart displayed several high-end details like nickel and Lucite accents, two mirrored shelves, and sculpted horse head finials. It was a beauty, and it was one of the few things previously owned by his father that Phillip had transferred to his Fairporte office.

Much to his horror, and for reasons never explained to him, Jules had unceremoniously removed and destroyed many personal items from his father's former office after his death before claiming the space for herself.

That had been the first time Phillip openly fought with his wife over an inexplicably disrespectful decision she had made concerning the business without consulting him. Those items were never hers to destroy. Phillip had managed to save the cart, bringing it with him during the relocation to Fairporte, thinking it would finish off his new office nicely. It had proven comforting and been utilized nearly as often as his computer.

Phillip poured himself a stiff drink, ignored his mother's voice in his head reminding him about the dangers of drinking whiskey straight, and began to cry. Phillip had wept more in the time since his father died than he had in his entire life up to that point. He was glad no one was currently around to see him this low, including, ashamed as he was to think such a terrible thought, his dead father.

She fucking did it. She said she'd take my last name and own it, make it that no one thought she'd ever been anything but a Cartell. She's taken everything from me. My career, my reputation, my heart. Hell, my fucking sobriety. Congratulations, Jules, you broke me. All I ever wanted was your happiness. I don't know why you hate me! I just don't understand.

Phillip downed the entire glass of whiskey and then quickly poured himself another.

"What did I do?" he sobbed. "What did I do?"

In the hallway outside Christophe's condo, Denise sat on the hard, industrial carpeted floor in front of the elevator sobbing uncontrollably, feeling like a duped idiot. She wondered how many others suspected or knew about Christophe's infidelity. Was it a pattern, a history of cheating?

She did not care that it had been with a man; she would have felt equally betrayed if he had been with a woman. She had heard about Christophe's "sexual fluidity" from others, but she had never asked him about it. It was no big deal to her. What she could not deal with was that it was Miles, Jules's lackey.

Jules probably set this whole thing up to play me for a fool, to humiliate me when it finally came out. Evil bitch!

Denise had pushed the elevator's down button what seemed like ages ago, but neither of the two doors seemed to want to go past the third floor. She thought about taking the stairs but dismissed that idea. Even in her current dismal state, Denise realized the severe heels on her expensive shoes would grossly impede her trek downward.

Waiting, sobbing, and feeling sorry for herself, Denise suddenly had an unexpected moment of clarity.

Did I just break up with my boyfriend over the smell of a brand of men's cologne? I never gave him a chance to defend himself. I made all those accusations without any actual proof. I didn't even look to see if Miles was there, hiding. I don't love Christophe, but he's always been good to me. He deserves a chance to deny the charges and prove me wrong. Out of line, at the very least. Delusional at worst.

Denise wondered if she was creating fantasy and fiction in her head because of how shitty she currently felt about herself. Was she letting self-esteem issues and inane sibling envy rule her life? What if it was not about Sonja or Miles or Jules or any of those two-faced, rich assholes. What if she was her saboteur? After all, she had just cheated on Christophe hours ago with William. *I'm a damn hypocrite!*

Wiping the wetness from her face, Denise leapt up off the ground in a clumsy, unflattering manner. She ran back to Christophe's apartment with mad urgency.

Fearing she looked frazzled and a complete mess, Denise hesitated before knocking. She wanted to try and compose herself, to get her act together and control her emotions. It was time to be an adult about this. She needed to be calm, rational and hear him out—just like Christophe had been urging her to be during her ranting and raving session.

Poor Christophe. I must have looked like a crazy bitch. Go on, knock on the damn door! You got this, girl!

Denise was ready—until she heard a voice behind the door that did not belong to Christophe. It was Miles's voice, and it came loud and clear through the door and straight into her ear canals. He was there, inside Christophe's apartment, talking wildly and verbosely. Denise's stomach sank.

"He was there the whole time," she meekly whispered.

She had been right. It was all true. She could hear them both laughing, and she was sure they were laughing at her expense. Dejected, blaming herself for poor judgment once again, Denise turned away from Christophe's door and slowly walked back to the elevator.

Her phone rang again, and Denise felt she was losing her mind. Reaching into her bag, she grabbed her cellphone. *Who the hell's been calling and texting me non-stop for an hour?*

Several people had left numerous messages: Mrs. Lougheed, Phillip, a few girlfriends, and even some family friends. All of them had been desperately trying to get in touch with her. Also, there were several missed calls, texts, and email notifications from online news outlets, gossip rags, and the legitimate press. *What the hell? What's going on?* Denise had no idea. She opened the first of the texts.

There was a picture attachment: a headline. Hesitantly, Denise read it. In bold type were the words "sex scandal" and "underage prostitute." And Christophe's name. There were photos of him with another man, and the words "sexual relationship" were everywhere. It was a man she knew very well, but it was not Miles.

As Denise looked over the article, more things about Christophe's past—secret, sexual things—were brought to light. Things Denise knew nothing about that made Christophe look bad. And these things now made her look bad—worse than she already looked.

Denise, her strength and willpower sapped, dropped her arm to her side, her phone now dangling precariously from her limp fingers, and sighed loudly. She tilted her head back and looked up to the ceiling, past it, through it, towards the sky, towards wherever she hoped her father's spirit had gone.

"Everyone will think I'm stupid, Dad, a real fucking moron for not knowing, and the press will crucify me. She had to have known, that fucking bitch. She did this! She did this to hurt me, to punish me for trying to help Phillip. She's made a fool of me, Dad. Well, no more. I know what to do. It's what you would do, Dad. I know it."

Denise wanted to cry again, but she was dried up. She needed to scream, but she had no more intensity, no more reserves of moxie left.

"I'm sorry I ever judged you, Dad. You did everything to protect us from shit like this. I get it now. Jules won't get away with this. I'll show her, show them all that the daughter of Joseph Cartell is capable of anything."

Denise raised her arm to access her phone. She called the number William had deftly put into her address app during the brief break they had taken from fucking during the limo ride. Patiently, she waited for him to pick up; she was in control of her emotions now.

"Well, this is a surprise, Luv," William's deep voice stated over the phone. "I honestly didn't expect to hear from you again."

"I'm in," Denise boldly shouted into her cell. "Let's end the bitch!"

There it was in full colour, right in front of his face. It was like a car crash; Charles could not look away. It was potentially devastating to several people if he did not get under it and control the spin. The images on the rented limousine's small television screen were deeply troubling.

The inflammatory, mostly true story, was everywhere.

Charles had tried several times to contact Jules with no positive results. His iPhone showed that she had received his texts but had yet to respond. He had no idea what he planned to say to his daughter. How could he ever explain why he had kept this secret from her for years. Could he ever make her understand his all-encompassing fear of her total rejection of him?

Charles felt sick to his stomach, wondering what thoughts were going through his daughter's head. He knew there had to be feelings of betrayal. *How did they find out?*

Since his daughter was incommunicado, Charles called the number of the other individual splashed all over the screen with him.

"Hi, Babe," Charles chirped, keeping his tone even and calm. "I'm assuming you saw—okay, calm down. Yes, I'm going to find out who did this. Come on, a social-media celebrity like you will weather this just fine. These scandals inevitably work in your favour. Nothing is worse than not being talked about and all that. I'm the one that's going to have to spin this just right. My reputation and career are at stake."

"No, I'm not just worried about my career, but I have to think about the company, my law firm, and my daughter. I'm the pragmatic one in this relationship. One of us has to remain calm."

"Listen. Listen! Hon, go to the penthouse and wait for me. It's fine. You're going from an underground, private garage to your car to another underground, private garage that goes up to the penthouse! I'm nearly home. I promise to make this okay. Yes, me too. Bye."

Fuck me! If you did this to me, Stella, to hurt my daughter, I'll make you wish you'd never been born.

Several hours had passed since Amanda last spoke to Jules. In that time, she had managed to obtain valuable information concerning William.

Thanks to her father's gruelling and comprehensive curriculum, utilizing himself and a legion of instructors across the globe, Amanda possessed numerous skills and talents. Her remarkable fighting prowess was simply the showiest of her abilities. While she had vast knowledge and know-how of computers and other technologies at her fingertips, she was not the greatest at hacking computer systems and remaining undetected.

For that level of skill, she needed the best. She required the talent and resources of an individual known only by one name: Bex.

The enigmatic Bex had many facets to their business. The most pertinent to Amanda being that they acted as both her official intermediary and negotiator; Bex contracted the jobs and arranged the details, including payment, for the Silver Dagger.

Their professional relationship went back years, and during that time, Amanda had learned very little about Bex. They never dropped a feminine or masculine pronoun to refer to themselves. Their on-screen icon was a comedy and tragedy mask, revealing nothing about their physical identity. Since Bex's voice gave no hint of gender, Amanda used gender-neutral pronouns.

Bex demanded privacy and prompt payment for their services. Anyone who attempted to dig into their background found their own lives quickly destroyed. Bex used a computer like an assault rifle, digging up dirt on people and exposing their darkest, most well-kept secrets. If you picked a fight with them, you were royally fucked.

As per their arrangement, Bex kept Amanda's identity as the Silver Dagger secret from the world. It was their responsibility to weed out undesirable clients. The ones who had targets that would never pass Amanda's rigid criterion for acceptability.

Bex had unlimited contacts, and if anyone wanted to hire the Silver Dagger, they had no option but to go through them. Bex took ten percent of the negotiated fee. The price depended on the danger and difficulty of the assignment and the number of targets; however, nothing cost less than a million Euros. That was non-negotiable.

After leaving Cartell Worldwide Tower for the second time, Amanda had reached out to Bex to provide her with an explanation. How had William Falsworth managed to escape from his incarceration without making any noise? It had taken only thirty minutes for Bex to get back to her with an answer Amanda knew Jules was not going to like.

Bex had also confirmed that William was already in Fairporte, staying at Château Bergé under his real name. Amanda could not believe the bastard's brazen arrogance. He was not hiding, confident in his invincibility. Amanda got William's room number, planning on ending him before any of this revenge nonsense against Jules went any further.

Still confident that her earlier assessment was accurate, that William intended to take his time with his revenge plot, Amanda took a moment for herself to shower. Afterwards, she changed into something more befitting her new role as Jules's protector. She was not going for full-on shinobi shozoku tonight, though. In her mind, William was not the kind of enemy who warranted such preparation and precaution.

No, what Amanda wanted was something battle-ready yet inconspicuous. Something dark, sleek and modern.

She settled on a pair of skin-tight, black lycra denim pants that allowed her to move freely and kick. She selected a body-hugging, blue-black, long-sleeved top and paired it with a dark grey summer pashmina. In a pinch, the scarf was a make-shift weapon. Not that she felt she needed a weapon against William; she was a weapon.

Pulling her hair back, Amanda smoothed it out and fixed it with spray into a sleek ponytail. She finished her look with a great pair of black flat boots with a severely pointed toe.

"I'll kick him in the balls nicely with these fuckers."

The total look was solid.

"Not too bad," Amanda laughed, admiring the finished product in the mirror. "Good enough to kick the shit out of some silly British psycho-git."

Amanda had Bex tap into Château Bergé's electronic surveillance feed. On her signal, Bex was to temporarily knock out the security cameras. That would enable Amanda to get to William's suite without being recorded.

She also asked if it was possible to play around with the lights in his room. If not, that was fine, but Amanda thought it would be fun to offset him a bit. She had an idea of how to enter his suite without having to break in or cause a noticeable fuss. William would prove to be no match for her lights on, off or flickering, of that she was sure.

Once it was all over and done with, Amanda hoped Jules would feel such gratitude that she would eagerly want to rebuild their relationship. Well, friendship, anyway. Friendship; the word was odd to Amanda.

Aside from what she had with Bex, which was more or less a detached, professional relationship, Amanda had no true friends. She had lovers worldwide, but Jules had been her only real girlfriend, her only confidant.

The way their relationship had ended, so abruptly, so harshly, had crippled Amanda emotionally, hardening her further, thickening the already steel-like callous around her heart. She had promised herself never to trust like that again. Never again would she leave herself open and vulnerable to emotional pain and rejection.

Friendship was a new concept for her, but Jules was open to it. Amanda was willing to dive in headfirst, wanting to feel even a fraction of what she had with Jules before. In fact, she needed it, having lived with a cold, inflexible heart for a very long time. Too long.

Amanda looked at the time on the clock that hung above the dormant fireplace. She sent Bex the signal on her phone to begin. Almost immediately, she received a text back saying everything was in place.

"Let's have some fun."

"The solution is ready, ma'am. We're all very pleased."

The scientist, whose name Jules did not know, assured her that everything had gone according to plan and schedule; this made her very happy. Something that did not please her was the missing identification tag on the skinny, mousy-haired technician's lab coat. She planned to bring this to Dr. Akagi's attention.

Jules put rules in place for a reason, and she meant them to be followed to the letter even if her employees deemed them silly or redundant. Nothing was optional under her roof if she dictated it a necessity. The only opinion that ultimately mattered at the company was hers.

While the idea for the solution had been Jules's brainchild, Dr. Akagi, the head of the lab, was the inventor of the actual formula.

Dr. Kenji Akagi had been with Mode-Génétique Labs since its inception and was one of the biggest proponents for choosing Cartell Worldwide over Falsworth International.

Jules had nothing but the utmost respect for him, having recognized his genius immediately upon their first meeting. She readily provided him with funding giving him a wide berth to create and experiment. She eagerly supported his desire to move beyond genetics into other areas of scientific inquiry.

Dr. Akagi had a major crush on Jules, which she was well aware of. She often used this infatuation to her advantage. Currently tied up with a delicate experiment, Dr. Akagi was unavailable to converse with her about the solution's progress. Unable to wait around for him, Jules had settled for one of his assistants.

This nameless brainiac kept winking at Jules with his left eye. She suspected it was a nervous tick and not a flirtation, so she gave him the benefit of the doubt and did not reprimand him for being impertinent.

"I'm glad to hear that," Jules declared without showing a shred of actual emotion to support her elation. "I'll bring you the documents I need to be coated tonight. I need them ready by tomorrow morning. Early."

"Of course, Ms. Cartell. The new test results have been promising concerning the amount of time it takes for the solution to take full effect once exposed to oxygen. Ten seconds, fifteen at the most. Much faster than before. We understood that the time-lapse was a major issue for you."

"Yes, but that should be sufficient for my needs. Please inform Dr. Akagi that I'm very pleased and will be in touch."

"I will, ma'am. Thank you. Have a good night, er day, er afternoon."

Jules turned on her feet, rolled her eyes at the awkward man's clumsy sendoff, and left the lab. She walked down the hallway towards her private elevator.

Only she, her father and Phillip had pass-card access to this elevator. Phillip was only allowed to use it in case of an emergency. Joseph had put such a feature in place at the former headquarters in Toronto. He had restricted the access of one of the four main elevators so that it was for his exclusive use. Jules had wanted such a perk for herself in the Fairporte tower.

Unlike the other three, which had no roof access—one had to use two feet and a heartbeat on the stairs—her elevator had access to every floor, including all three parking levels. Jules always had one of her cars parked on the third garage level for when she wanted the freedom and convenience of driving herself around.

On days like today, when something unexpected and personal came up, Jules did not want the burden of conversing with her driver even though he was super loyal. She had no desire to talk about what had recently been blasted across the internet thanks to that disgusting online tabloid. Even if his intentions were well-meaning, Jules was in no mood for more conversation with anyone aside from her father or Amanda.

Once Jules got in her elevator, she pushed the button for the third parkade level. She planned to get in her blue Chevrolet corvette and drive her ass directly to her father's condo to wait for him. They were going to have words.

But something went wrong the moment she pushed the button.

The elevator went up, not down, momentarily stunning Jules; this had never happened before. The elevators were regularly serviced to prevent such mechanical screw-ups. In her high-tech building, irritatingly inconvenient situations like this were unacceptable.

"For fuck's sake!" Jules cursed, annoyed. *Fine, I'll go up, then go back down, and then someone is getting fired.*

The elevator did not arrest its upward trajectory until it was at the last possible stop: the roof. Jules rolled her eyes for what seemed like the millionth time that day. She angrily pushed the level she wanted to go to three times and waited. The doors opened. She raised her eyes and looked out the ever-widening aperture expecting to see a small, well-lit, empty landing.

What she saw instead shocked her.

A large man with dirty, dark hair, tanned, leathery skin and a nasty, cruel look upon his face stood in front of her on the landing. Jules had never seen the likes of him before.

"Ya pissed off the wrong people, bitch. Big fuckin' mistake!" the large man sneered.

Before Jules had a chance to react and implement a defensive move, the man flew into the small compartment with a swiftness uncharacteristic for someone his size. Aggressively, he pushed her back into the mirrored wall. The door automatically closed behind him, and thanks to Jules's manic button-pushing earlier, the elevator began its descent down to the third parkade level.

Grabbing Jules's upper arms, the man violently whipped her around the room several times, disorienting her. When he finished treating her like a ragdoll, he slammed her back into the mirrored wall. When her body connected with the glass this time, the force of the impact cracked it, causing a spider-web effect to spread outward from behind her head and shoulders. A searing pain shot through her back and up her neck.

Finally, Jules's instincts woke up, and her training took over. She attempted to use her right leg to knee her assailant in the groin, but the form-fitting skirt she was wearing had little give and severely limited the reach of her attack. Her move failed.

Jules's attacker laughed at her sad attempt to strike at him; in retaliation, he forced his massive, calloused hands around her neck and squeezed.

"No use strugglin', bitch. Just let it happen. Quick is better. For you, at least."

Jules could not breathe—he was killing her. She tried with all her might to separate the man's impossibly strong hands from her throat, but it was to no avail. She dug her nails into his flesh as hard as she could, but his grip remained steadfast. He was just too strong, and Jules knew he would not let go until he had crushed her windpipe.

"That's right, just let it happen. Then I can have some fun."

Jules panicked as she felt her eyes begin to close; she was blacking out.

No! I won't go down like this! Remember your damn training! It dawned on Jules that it did not matter if her attacker's appendages were more powerful than her own. *I don't have to pry his hands free. I have to make him do it for me!* She needed to find the sweet spot to direct her blows.

Clearing her mind and focusing, it came to her; Jules knew where to strike.

After throwing her arms back wide, then balling her hands into fists, Jules swung both arms forward, brutally connecting with the man's temples. Over and over, she repeated the action until the pain in his head forced him to release his grip. Jules dropped to the floor, gasping for breath, as her attacker brought his hands to his head; he was temporarily dazed and unfocused by the unexpected throbbing pain.

She had done it! She had forced him to release her, causing him pain in the process.

Jules's assailant had not considered his target, a woman, would fight back so aggressively. Even after being forewarned by his employer that she knew martial arts. Arrogant and overconfident in his size and strength, he had refused to believe a woman could ever overpower him physically.

On the floor, out of his reach, Jules thrust her right arm forward, fist still tightly clenched, and punched her attacker hard in the groin. She repeated the blow two more times until the man quickly brought his hands down to his genitals and roared in pain.

Reaching down her body, Jules pulled her tight skirt up over her thighs, freeing her legs from their inconvenient bondage.

When the elevator reached its underground destination, the doors opened. Jules picked herself off the floor and made a break for it. Unfortunately, she didn't get very far before her attacker recovered enough to act, grabbing her right leg, yanking her backward roughly. Jules barely had time to hit the ground hard before being dragged back into the elevator.

"Nah, I don't think so. You ain't gettin' away that easy. I was gonna do this quick, pretty lady, but now I'm gonna make it long and painful. And I'm gonna enjoy every bit of it."

"Not likely, you prick," Jules spat.

Ignoring the mounting discomfort from the scrapes and cuts on her bare legs, Jules twisted her body around and swung her right leg up towards her attacker. Once again, he was unprepared for her martial arts prowess and unable to prevent the ferocious kick from connecting with his jaw.

"Owwww, mutha fucka! Fine, have it your way, bitch! No more fun 'n games. I'm fuckin' done with this kung-fu bullshit."

Now the man was pissed. He pulled a gun out from under his dirty, blue denim work shirt and aimed it directly at Jules.

In the next moment, the thunderclap of a single gunshot rang out in the near-empty carport, quickly followed by the roaring echo of a blood-curdling scream.

XVI

William tossed his phone away like it was a boring novel; it landed softly next to where he sat on the sofa. "Weak-willed people are so easy to manipulate," he sneered.

Yasmine walked over and stood behind William. She began kneading and massaging his tight neck and shoulder muscles with her strong hands. "Mind games are fun, my love."

Settling back further into the soft, microfiber couch, William enjoyed both the rub down and the remainder of the Romanée-Conti 1975. He was naked and sweaty, as was Yasmine. The two of them had just finished another round of their unique brand of recreational kink.

On a massive high from the mind-fuck he had laid on Denise earlier, William had been rougher and more animalistic than usual during this last unconventional fuck-fest, leaving a nasty welt on Yasmine's left thigh. She had treated and bandaged it, but it still throbbed and hurt like a bitch. Pain shot down her leg every time she moved more than a few steps.

Yasmine loved the rush of pain and the sensations of danger and depravity. She despised the ugliness of disfigurement, however. Shallow cuts were one thing, they healed up fine, but potential deformation was the antithesis of controlled debauchery. She had taught William ages ago how to be careful with his blows and lacerations during their play.

William was acting out, certainly, but losing control? Yasmine did not believe it had gone that far. Still, she genuinely felt concerned and uneasy. She sensed something had shifted recently in their dynamic.

Yasmine partially blamed Denise's newborn intimate involvement in William's life. Yes, she knew the woman was just a pawn. Still, Yasmine worried the introduction of a new, ungoverned sexual stimulant had the potential to undo the controls she had painstakingly instilled in William.

Whether it was conjecture or an unscientific hunch did not ultimately matter to Yasmine. William's erratic behaviour was a cause for concern, requiring further observation. Sloppiness was not tolerated in her staff, her patients or her sex partners; it signified a lack of discipline. Yasmine had taken great pains to make William, if not better, functional, and backsliding was not something she would permit.

However, Yasmine was oblivious to one poignant fact: her obsessive need to be a part of William's immediate world severely limited her objectivity. In this instance, her ego had eclipsed her reasoning, scientific mind.

Yasmine refused to acknowledge the possibility that William had grown beyond her, outside her sphere of influence. She had convinced herself that she and he were equal partners in everything. She had no clue that William thought of her as just another plaything, one that was disposable and replaceable at any moment of his choosing.

To her detriment, Yasmine had forgotten the basic principle concerning William's hostility and core belief system: he irrationally hated women. And he hated them because he feared the emotional instability he associated with them.

"Enough!" William snapped, tired of being touched. He smacked Yasmine's hands away from his body, called her a vulgar name, and told her to cover herself.

Getting up, wine in hand, and without putting on any clothes, William walked over to the desk where he had set up his laptop. He sat down, pulled up several files, and then motioned for Yasmine to come over to him.

As always, she did as he instructed.

William gave Yasmine his now empty glass to hold, and she took it obediently without saying a word. She enjoyed playing subservient to him. It was part of their relationship, part of their game. Unfortunately, Yasmine had blinded herself to the fact that she was the only one still playing by the rules set in place years ago by her.

"Your personality profile on Denise was spot on, and it's made things so much more entertaining this time. I guess I shouldn't have doubted you."

Yasmine, trained to appear detached and dispassionate, held her composure, but she wanted so badly to smile. It was the first time William had ever been complimentary towards her. More than that, even: grateful.

"Thank you, William. Yes, the proper application of manipulation, intimidation, and humiliation turns even the wisest of individuals into fools. Someone like Denise never stood a chance."

Sadly, Yasmine was unaware of the irony surrounding her own words. Her infatuation with William blinded her to the truth that she was just as much a trusting fool as Denise concerning William's silver tongue. Of late, she had become little more than his errand girl—another pawn.

And she should have known better, been more vigilant, more clever; after all, Yasmine had spent years watching and studying William. Her desire for the man severely clouded her judgment.

When Yasmine first met William, he had already gone through half a dozen therapists in seven years. Her clinical work helping highly disturbed children recover from their traumas and psychosis had attracted the attention of the Falsworth family. Truthfully, she was their last hope for William; her unorthodox methods had a high success rate.

Years ago, Gretchen Falsworth had flown to Yasmine's clinic in Amsterdam for her help in treating her brother. Yasmine had never heard of the Falsworths, though several of her colleagues had warned her to tread carefully around them. Strangely, not one of her associates had recalled much of anything about William, specifically.

The Falsworth family's wealth and influence had secured the removal from public record, everything concerning William's troubled past. Their vast machinations had suppressed the truth surrounding the fire at the ancestral estate, including the related deaths of his parents. The Falsworths were masters at altering facts and changing narratives to suit their purposes.

After two meetings with Gretchen, including one with her uncle, Duncan, Yasmine concluded that the Falsworth's were a cagey, secretive, and incredibly influential clan who were all insufferably formal. She expressly instructed them to address her by her first name. Annoyingly, every one of them continuously referred to her as Dr. Kotera.

Yasmine insisted her patients and any family members in direct contact with her during the therapeutic process use her preferred method of informality. She maintained the belief that being referred to as a physician or a therapist created an immediate and highly inconvenient wall of mistrust and hierarchical power. She would always have to break through those barriers before any cooperation and healing could start.

Having just finished a taxing case, Yasmine planned on taking a break from work, stating quite firmly to the Falsworths that she could not take on new patients. Not used to being told no, Gretchen remained extremely persistent and powerfully persuasive, eventually convincing Yasmine to see her brother. It helped that Gretchen offered a sum of six figures for just one visit with William.

Yasmine flew to England, where she met up with Gretchen and Duncan; they took her immediately to the facility holding William for treatment. Yasmine learned William had been a resident at Hawthorne Hospital, a maximum-security psychiatric facility in northern England, for many years. No positive results regarding his mental and emotional rehabilitation had come about during this time.

William was still violently angry towards what he considered his unjust incarceration among madmen.

Gretchen was concerned that, without any real progress, her brother would eventually find a way to take his own life just to be free of his torment. That, or he would spend the rest of his days doped up—a living somnambulist. Gretchen was adamant that neither were acceptable outcomes for her brother.

Within the first twenty minutes of meeting William, Yasmine believed, without a doubt, that she could create emotional connectivity with this broken man. She looked deep into his eyes, searching for impressions and discarnate answers to her private, unspoken questions: *Who are you, William Falsworth? What happened to you? Are you willing to fight for your freedom, your sanity, your life?*

Incidentally, in those psychically probing moments, William was fully aware that she was there with him, this unfamiliar woman. He instantly understood she was scrutinizing him, struggling to get inside his head. It was no great challenge for him to grasp that she was searching for answers in a bold attempt to figure him out, like so many others before.

Close-mouthed, he stared right back, letting her in, unafraid of the intrusion, unafraid of what she would find. William had nothing to hide, nothing to be ashamed of. He gleefully invited her to look into his head—if she dared. People generally displayed signs of weakness and terror when they looked into his eyes, glimpsing but a fraction of his power, his presence. William assumed this curious interloper would be no different.

Except, she was different; Yasmine had no fear of him. For the first time in ages, William was genuinely surprised and intrigued.

Yasmine was fascinated by William, by his unique presence. It gave her great satisfaction seeing that even in his oppressive, unending captivity, he proved untameable. Heavily drugged, his eyes remained clear and determined. They revealed the existence of a ferocious intelligence that no amount of tranquillizers could suppress.

Yasmine guessed immediately why William's doctors continually drugged him.

They were afraid of him.

And they had all failed him.

Yasmine saw how they blamed William unequivocally for their fears and defeats; that was why they had silenced him, sentencing him to deteriorate, to disappear. Yasmine despised them all for their disrespect and refusal to understand this unique, fierce, beautiful creature. She admired William's instinct for survival in the face of insurmountable opposition.

Unlike Hawthorne's doctors, Yasmine was not afraid, uncomfortable or pessimistic. She did not share Gretchen's concern that her brother might commit suicide. She saw past the superficial slack-jawed expression brought on by the cocktail of drugs to see the supreme obstinance in William's face.

Yasmine understood this type of wilful, difficult patient; after all, working with the ones everyone else in her field deemed irreparably damaged was her specialty. She saw great power in William's eyes; it drew her to him. She saw great darkness, too, but it was seductive darkness, intriguing, addictive. To her, William was not malevolence-incarnate. He was misunderstood, all untapped potential needing order and guidance.

Yasmine believed William's mind had lost its way at some point, becoming disordered and warped. His aggressive behaviour and chaotic thought processes needed reshaping into something productive. William's intellect, his rage, his darkness required proper stimuli and channelling. They were not inherently negative things, simply directionless, and that was where she could help. Yasmine always knew what to do in these kinds of cases.

In her experience, it inevitably came back to control; William needed control, not subjugation. Yasmine wanted him disciplined, not tamed, not lessened or diminished. William needed to know how to conduct himself productively to function in society. She was confident that only she had the perspective and special training to show him the way.

Most importantly, she needed to find William's trigger. What had created this seemingly uncontrollable hostility and anger in the first place? What was driving it? Yasmine desperately wanted to know, needed to know, or all her attempts at helping him would ultimately lead nowhere.

What Yasmine did not fully grasp, however, was that William was no child; he was a fully-grown man. He had life experience, having already developed his sense of self. He had previously attempted to control and shape the world into how he felt it should be.

He was angry, absolutely, but William refused to accept what others tried to force into his head. He was not sick or crazy. He did not suffer from mental illness and behavioural problems. There was nothing wrong with him, and anyone who did not see it this way was an idiot not worth his time.

Or they were an enemy to be destroyed.

William had a goal that needed completion before he could live his life. It was about more than revenge for him; he wanted justice for his brother. It was that simple. In his mind, it was the world around him that had gone mad for not seeing how rudimentary it all was. The person responsible for his brother's death had gotten away without being punished for it.

That was unacceptable.

Yasmine believed she could modify her successful, long-practiced methods of treatment for an adult patient. Unfortunately, she had greatly underestimated William's cunning.

Diabolically clever, William had Yasmine's number from the moment their eyes first locked, completely understanding what she wanted from him. As much as Yasmine attempted to influence, instruct, and reprogram him, William never doubted he would be one step ahead of her. He knew something about himself that her educated, vainglorious, and self-admiring personality could never accept.

No one would ever, could ever, control or change him, least of all a woman.

Knowing Yasmine could get him out of his current predicament, William eagerly took advantage of the situation. He would go along with whatever she said, soak up whatever she had to teach him; eventually, the hand that fed him would get bit. He would be the one in charge; it was inevitable; William had patience.

Yasmine also overestimated William's dependency on her. She did not realize how lucid he was or how much he comprehended the world around him. Fuck the drugs—he was more powerful than them! His need for retribution on his brother's behalf forever fuelled him, stoking his inner fire.

William had a gift for recognizing the presence of opportunity, and he knew when to take advantage of it without hesitation. He was a user, always had been, and he was very good at manipulating people for his gain.

With the Falsworths' support, Yasmine quietly transferred William out of Hawthorne, out of England entirely, and over to her private psychiatric clinic in the Netherlands.

Yasmine demanded total control over William's therapeutic process. For the foreseeable future, his life was now her responsibility, and she would tolerate no interference. At least, she argued, until he was far enough along in his rehabilitation to start reconnecting with the world beyond the walls of her clinic. Yasmine stressed the importance of removing all potentially damaging outside influences.

Everyone in the immediate family agreed to the terms though Gretchen feared William would think she had abandoned him.

Yasmine's first step in William's rehabilitation was the purging of drugs from his system.

After a month, William appeared sufficiently clear-headed, his withdrawal symptoms subsided. Yasmine acknowledged this by giving him back his dignity. She presented him with a room fit for a man of his breeding.

Never believing William was suicidal or a danger to himself, Yasmine provided him with several material things for his exclusive use: expensive clothes, grooming paraphernalia, exercise equipment, music, and books. Everything was pre-approved by her, of course. Television and video games were banned. Yasmine feared they would prove over-stimulating.

Once William acclimated to his new environment, which he did quickly, Yasmine calmly, yet firmly explained to him why she had given him these things.

To be seen by society as something other than damaged goods or a violent, irrational beast, William had to remember and embrace the man he had been before losing control of himself. That started with accepting the superficial: the ego. To help William recover his sense of self, Yasmine began with what was familiar to him: wealth and privilege.

When dealing with children, Yasmine made sure to discover their "security blanket." With William, it was transparent from the beginning what that was for him. Yasmine theorized that, like every Falsworth she had met, William had an inflated sense of entitlement, liked the finer things in life, and thought himself superior to others.

Understanding this, she supplied William with the material goods to help ease his transition to her facility.

But that was just the beginning of her manipulations of William's emotions. Yasmine wanted his complete trust, to know that she was not his enemy, but as genuine as that was, he was still a project—a Gordian Knot she had to untie.

Of course, William knew damn well she saw him as an incomplete puzzle, one she felt compelled to figure out and finish.

To properly exert her influence over William, Yasmine required the correct environment; it was crucial to their success that he felt secure and safe. She needed him to comprehend his new reality. He no longer existed in an imprisoned state; no more degradation or labels or unnecessary drugs. She put a stop to his drug therapy altogether. She wanted to see his "true fires" unencumbered by meds.

William's new reality was a climate of free expression, mutual sharing of thoughts and emotions, and the absolute desire for truth and understanding. Yasmine assured William that none of it was a trap. It was a way out for him, and he was encouraged to embrace it.

Days turned into weeks that turned into months.

Yasmine conducted endless therapy sessions where she did most of the talking. In between William's self-motivated, gruelling physical work-outs and daily callisthenics, she spent countless hours diligently chipping away at his formidable exoskeleton of defensiveness and circumspection.

Confident in her belief that she set the pace, Yasmine was oblivious to the truth: William intentionally dragged his feet during their sessions. He wanted to see just how far her desire to understand and help him went before revealing his past to her, the reason for everyone's fear of him, and his all-encompassing desire to see Ethan's killer dead.

William wanted to fully comprehend where this woman was going with all of it—this "process" of hers. What did Yasmine ultimately want from him? How far was she willing to go to see him reunited with a world that did not understand him? Feared him? Who exactly was Dr. Yasmine Kotera?

William needed to understand why she cared about his welfare, if not for the money his family was paying her. Based on her appearance, demeanour, and the state-of-the-art facility she worked at, a need for money was not a prime motivating factor to treat him. Was it as banal a thing as a desire for fame? Did she desire accolades from the scientific and medical communities? What was it?

Aware of everything her brother had done, Gretchen knew what William believed to be absolute truths. She was the only member of their family who did and the only person who had visited him at Hawthorne.

As much as he could understand the very concept of affection, William loved his sister. She was the only woman on the planet he trusted. And Gretchen loved William, even knowing his penchant for misogyny and violent aggression.

Gretchen continually disregarded William's many emotional and social faults. In fact, she always did everything in her power to help him, not afraid of William like the rest of her family. She never feared becoming a target for his unpredictable animus. At least, not intentionally. She was astute enough to be on her toes around him. Wary and vigilant.

Gretchen knew William's version of the circumstances surrounding Ethan's death, and she assumed everything was a highly distorted chronicle of events. While accepting that some truth existed within the narrative, Gretchen did not fully believe her brother's account. She had never revealed her skepticism to him because she did not doubt in her mind that her brother believed his version completely.

After several conversations with William, Gretchen eventually realized that he would never stop believing it—to his detriment. She had come to accept a hard truth. Her brother would never believe Ethan's death was an unfortunate seasonal accident and not an act of premeditated murder by an eight-year-old girl.

Fearing it would backfire on her if she talked, Gretchen never spoke to any of William's doctors about Ethan or Jules, including Yasmine. William also kept hush about Jules's connection to Ethan's death. Gretchen figured if William would not talk about it, all the better, and so she allowed William to dictate the terms and time frame of his revelations. His silence worked in her favour, simplifying things.

When William told his sister that he had murdered their parents like it was no big deal, she took his admission of the crime rather well; in fact, it had not bothered her in the least. Except for the part about the fire. That annoyed her; she liked her belongings. Her parents' demise, however, was a total non-issue for her. Even learning how William had killed them and why he did it held little impact.

As the oldest sibling, Gretchen had the most experience with their parents' self-absorption and constant absenteeism. Their shitty parental behaviour had only worsened after Ethan's death. Her parents' demise inevitably proved meaningless to Gretchen.

For William's sake, the sake of the family and the company's reputation, Gretchen made sure everyone believed her parents had died tragically in an accidental fire. Her parents gone, Gretchen and Duncan, the paternal uncle who was more like a father to her, took control of Falsworth International.

But not all of William's actions during that time were so personally fortuitous for Gretchen. She had been unsuccessful in making William's murder of the two tourists and his drugging and kidnapping of Jules disappear. Mainly due to the efforts of Charles Dunning and the RCMP.

Eventually, everyone involved agreed to keep things quiet and remand William to a maximum-security psychiatric hospital in his country of origin. A conventional prison sentence, which the Falsworths did not want, and a very public, international trial, which nobody wanted, were avoided.

Gretchen unequivocally blamed Jules for William's state of instability, the one directly responsible for his mental breakdown. Anything criminal William did after Ethan's passing should be laid at her feet. If Jules had just admitted to her part in Ethan's death, even admitting to having done nothing to help him, Gretchen felt William would not have become so singularly obsessed with punishing her to the detriment of his sanity.

But thanks to everyone's complicity of silence surrounding Jules's involvement, William had the upper hand during his time with Yasmine at her clinic, at least regarding his life story. His "truth" was his power, his edge, his advantage.

Eventually, William accepted and appreciated Yasmine's authentic desire to help him. So he listened respectfully, without incident, to her unending psycho-babble. It was white noise to him, anyway. William enjoyed watching Yasmine, studying her, working the angles for his benefit.

It came to William's attention that in his presence, Yasmine always dressed very doctrinal and conservatively, her hair pulled tightly back. In sharp contrast, her catlike, slinky movements betrayed a sensuality bubbling hot just under the surface of that veneer of professional detachment.

To William, Yasmine was a woman of two minds, a woman who clamoured for control, to be taken seriously, yet simultaneously desperate to give up that control and get fucked hard. He believed every woman had the Madonna/Whore complex. He needed to deduce how far Yasmine could be pushed to explore her desires and make them manifest.

When it became clear that it was about dominance and submission with Yasmine, William deduced it was time for him to consciously metamorphose into something more intriguing than a clinical project. No matter how fascinating a patient he was to her intellectually, William saw that Yasmine desired more.

They had to move beyond the cerebral; that had become stagnant and tedious. The relationship needed to become physical—sexual.

William and Yasmine were both on the same page.

During another frustrating session, Yasmine, stymied by William's stubbornness and refusal to talk, decided to take things to the next level.

Done with the predominantly one-sided intellectual discourse, Yasmine wanted to stimulate William's base, bodily desires. She knew it was a risky move her peers would classify as inappropriate and unethical. It did not matter to her. She was desperate for a physical reaction from William.

Yasmine had chosen to wear a skirt with a provocative slit. In a bold move, she widened the expanse between her thighs, allowing the slit to extend. Then, she slowly crossed her legs in front of William, allowing him a glance at her very see-through white lace g-string.

Yasmine had moved beyond anything she had ever tried previously with a patient; after all, before William, children were her patients. It was a willing unburdening of herself morally, a refusal to be uptight. Yasmine wanted William to see her as something other than his therapist. It was a straight-up tease, an attempt to entice him, and it made Yasmine feel sexy and empowered in the process.

First and foremost, it was a test to see how much of the man was still there inside the thick casing of quiet, seething rage and supposed disinterest. Still, the part of Yasmine that was not thinking medically, the emotional and physical woman, wanted William to desire her.

Yasmine had stared too long into William's abyss, and he had enthralled her.

Astute, William saw right through the performance. Yasmine's goal was to gain access to his mind. Words alone had not motivated him to engage in pervasive dialogue. William realized Yasmine had resorted to using her body, her sexuality, to stimulate and provoke him. It was so painfully obvious he wanted to laugh.

It worked, nonetheless.

The unexpected sight of her shaved pussy, barely concealed by the sheer lace panties, brought warmth to William's crotch; it was a heat he had not felt in a long time. Yasmine was beautiful, and William was very horny. Masturbation only did so much to satiate his erotic hunger.

Aware that cameras watched him twenty-four hours a day, William often played with himself openly. He liked the idea of being watched, of Yasmine watching him, especially. He often walked around his room naked, flaunting the muscular body he spent so much time developing while trapped like an animal in his gilded cage.

William went all in. Reaching out, he put his hand on the flesh of her inside thigh. Yasmine did not recoil, her face remained stoic yet amiable, and she opened her legs wider. He worked his way up until he had his fingers under the fabric of her panties and inside her. He moved his digits around deftly, teasing, playing in the damp softness of her intimate femininity until he brought her to orgasm.

Yasmine threw her head back and sighed deeply.

William pulled his hand out of Yasmine's damp opening. His fingers wet with her juices, he forcefully grabbed her face with an intensity that both excited and intimidated her. Calling her a whore, he asked if she had liked it. She had; it drove her wild with desire for him; she wanted more of his sexual aggressiveness.

Unexpectedly, Yasmine had even felt an erotic stirring when William insulted her. That was something she realized needed further study.

Yasmine did not answer William's question, however. In time, she would tell him just how much she had liked it, but not yet. Instead, she fixed her skirt, walked over to the sink, washed her face, and walked out of his room.

William knew she would be back for more. It was just the beginning of their new game.

After this inaugural intimate moment, William completely opened up and revealed his true self to Yasmine. He felt the time had come to make her believe he needed her to understand him, help him, and make him whole.

William had always been conscious of the fact that women found him irresistible: his looks, his wealth, and his ability to ooze charm when necessary. Yasmine was no different in this regard, no matter how much professional objectivity she believed she projected. William saw it in her face every time he smiled at her, and she turned away, embarrassed for him to see how much she liked it, his attention, his flirtation.

Yasmine portrayed someone divorced from emotion, in control, but William knew better; she was undeniably hot for him. Having ensnared her just as planned, William had sex regularly with Yasmine after that, but only when he instigated it. He pushed her erotic limits in an attempt to determine her boundaries—so he could destroy them.

Though she liked rough sex, Yasmine rarely permitted herself to explore these turbulent urges, desires felt since adolescence. With William, it felt natural to her. He showed her how to escape the suffocating constraints of objective morality and accept the freedom of a sensualist's ethos. In turn, she instructed him on sexual technique, discipline, and control over chaotic emotions.

When William had finally talked about Ethan's death, Yasmine believed this pivotal revelation was the key to understanding his deep, sanity-altering rage. He simply desired justice. Yasmine knew she had finally found William's "trigger." A girl, now a woman, named Jules.

Now, in their suite at Château Bergé, currently staring at William's handsome yet emotionally sterile face, Yasmine smiled to herself. *I've done it, changed him for the better. I've broken through to the sane man buried deep inside that formerly twisted psyche, held captive for years by anger, torment, and soul-crushing misunderstanding.*

Yasmine was madly in love with William, but her desire for him had become an obsession, a pang of deep hunger threatening to consume her. She appeared indifferent to potentially losing herself in him because she believed she was in the driver's seat, the one in control. And perhaps she was once, but certainly not anymore.

"Yasmine, get this delivered to Denise immediately," William ordered. "She's on her way back to the mansion. She's expecting it. She knows what to do."

Yasmine took the USB flash memory stick from him. It looked so small and unassuming to her, but she was well aware of its powerful malevolence. Much to her discomfort, it was now up to Denise to connect it to Cartell Worldwide's computer system from the inside.

When the idea to sabotage Cartell Worldwide's infrastructure first came up, Yasmine had suggested employing a professional hacker. William had decided against using the industrial espionage experts on Gretchen's payroll. He was concerned that Jules's massive security features would prove daunting and require more time and finesse to break through from the outside than he was willing to allocate to the project.

But Falsworth International had secretly created a malicious program to destroy adversaries, and he could get his hands on that computer virus with little effort.

William originally planned on using the Cartell employee he had in his pocket to upload the virus, but he ultimately nixed that idea. He thought it would be sweeter to manipulate an actual family member into unwittingly doing his dirty work for him and then expose their stupidity.

"I'll have it sent by private courier immediately," Yasmine responded, "but I still don't see what the problem is sticking with our original plan to—"

William brought his hand around, slapping Yasmine hard across the face, preventing her from finishing her sentence. "Don't question me," he exclaimed dispassionately.

"Sorry, William. Yes, I'll take care of it at once."

Yasmine was startled but not angry with William for his unexpected violent action. She loved him, craving the roughness in his heavy touch. His slap, though delicious, was frustratingly unsatisfying. Just like it had been on other recent occasions. Yes, something had changed. Yasmine did not feel the fire in William's movements towards her, and she needed his dark energy. She wanted that passion back. She had to have it!

She could not live without it.

Everything had happened so fast Jules was still trying to make sense of it all. She needed a moment to process what had just transpired before her very eyes, what was sheer madness. *Breathe. Get it together. Get moving. That fucker was strong, and he could still be around. For that matter, so could that crazy bitch. Move.*

There was a lot of blood on the ground in front of her, but it was not her blood.

In contrast to her chaotic mind, the parking lot was eerily silent, but Jules did not trust that it was safe despite how tranquil the landscape was. Cautiously, she crept towards her car.

As Jules inched along, the dirt and grit of the concrete floor wreaked havoc on her manicure and tore at her skirt. Her clothes were stained with blood from the lacerations on her legs. The concrete had been far less forgiving on her flesh than on her attire during the melee. Her hair was crazy-looking, and parts of it stuck to her face from copious amounts of sweat.

But she was alive and moving.

Get up. You're ridiculous, and you're ruining your nails.

Even amidst such danger Jules still held a sense of humour about her situation. She used humour to keep her cool in stressful situations. She used bitchy sarcasm just as often. Sluggishly, she pulled herself up off the ground. Just a few meters from her car, Jules managed to make it to the driver's side door without further incident or damage to her person.

There was no sound of anyone else around. The bastard who had attacked her had fled the garage, screaming in pain, clutching his bleeding shoulder. He had been shot at and wounded.

But not by Jules.

"Ah, fuck."

Jules realized her purse was still in the elevator where she had dropped it during the initial attack. She just wanted to get in her car, get the hell out of there, and call Amanda. She could not go back inside to her office; too many questions would be asked about her bloody, ramshackle appearance. There was a need for both a safe space and discretion.

To Jules's utter displeasure, the entire Cartell Worldwide building seemed to be frustratingly compromised. She planned on firing her entire security team, replacing them with the same company Jacques used. Hopefully, by the end of the day.

The pain was throbbing, but Jules was supremely content with the fact that she had not taken a bullet. Most of the blood on the floor belonged to her attacker. Despite the annoying soreness, cuts, and bruises, she knew she was okay.

But she still needed her damn purse. She had to risk it.

Luckily, Jules quickly made it to the elevator and back to her car again without incident. Pushing the button on her key fob, she unlocked the car. Though it appeared her attacker had left, Jules mentally prepared for the possibility he was behind her, obfuscated in shadow, ready to pounce.

The image of Jamie Lee Curtis in *Halloween* fumbling with her keys as Michael Myers crept slowly up behind her flashed briefly in her mind. She almost laughed at the absurdity of the comparison. With no idiotic fumbling allowed, Jules proceeded with alacrity, started the engine and sped away.

Now safely out in public, driving in the direction of her condo, Jules quickly unlocked her phone and called Amanda. "Come on, come on. Pick up, bitch!" When Amanda finally answered, her strong voice was a welcome sound.

"Hey! It's not the best time for a chat, Jules, but I've got lots to tell you later. I—"

"Listen to me!" Jules brutally interrupted. "I was attacked just now at work! In my fucking private elevator and inside my fucking carport, Amanda!"

"What! Are you okay? What the hell happened? William is here in Fairporte, at Château Bergé, in the penthouse right now."

Jules was confused. "Why did he—? He hired someone?"

"I don't believe what happened has anything to do with him, Jules. William wants to get personally involved. It's pathological with him—this need to punish you himself. Torture is his thing, up close and personal, just like when you were a teenager. Trust me, I understand the type. I'm certain what happened to you isn't tied to him. Someone else is after you."

"Then this has Stella written all over it," Jules barked, infuriated. "Cheap bitch hired some ugly ass white trash thug to kill me."

"You're sure?" Amanda asked. "Are you thinking clearly?"

"Yes, I'm fucking sure!" Jules screamed into her phone. "I'm sorry. I don't mean to yell. The only people I've allowed to have access to that level besides me are my father and Phillip. This hillbilly didn't look like he knew how to use a toothbrush, let alone hack security systems or electronically override an elevator."

"I'm pretty sure Charles doesn't want you dead," Amanda joked.

"Smartass. Phillip hates me, but he also still loves me. No, he's too much of a little bitch to do anything about it. I'm telling you, it's Stella. She's desperate, and it wouldn't be difficult for her to get her hands on Phillip's code. It's not like he's much of an obstacle—I should know.

"And I'll have proof once I see the code that accessed that level today. Mind you, Stella probably interfered with the security cameras. But even if she still has someone on her payroll in the building, someone I've yet to ferret out, who blocked the feed or erased the footage, that person can't erase the passcode log. Only I have access to that."

"Then she's not concerned by that, Jules. She figures you'll be dead, and none of that will come to light. Even if your father questions the use of Phillip's code, by the time he gets around to investigating with the police, Stella will have found a way to destroy the evidence."

"Exactly, that makes the most sense. Well, that bitch just made her ultimate intent known. Stella's no longer interested in fighting me. Not legally. Not with money or words or wits. She wants me out of the picture permanently. Maybe she had help, I don't know yet, but I'll find out. That fucking fossil! I'll wring her turkey neck!"

"Calm down, Jules," Amanda cooed. "Breathe. Focus. Keeping a level head is paramount in these situations." Amanda knew Jules understood this, but because her emotions were currently highly elevated, her usual consummate control was off, unbalanced.

Amanda felt it was her responsibility, her supreme delight, to guide and aid Jules during this trying time. With both William and Stella trying to kill her, it was understandable that Jules was not all that cool and collected at present. That was what she was here for, to help Jules navigate these unfamiliar waters of uncertainty brought on by multiple murderous intentions directed solely at her.

This type of situation was nothing new to Amanda; several people had tried to kill her over the years. It was an unavoidable occupational hazard in her line of work.

"Remember, Jules, always breathe and focus. We can't allow our enemies to unravel us. Their desperation will be their downfall, and we'll take advantage of their mistakes and overconfidence. We'll deal with Stella in due course, but right now, tell me what happened. In detail. Time, locations, everything. Is your attacker dead?"

"No, as far as I know. The bastard ran away after being shot."

"You shot him?" Amanda queried. "You seem prone to gunplay of late."

"I didn't shoot him! I don't carry a gun on me. This is Fairporte, not Texas."

Jules rapidly divulged the details of her encounter, but when she got to the part where her attacker pulled a gun on her, she paused.

"And?" Amanda asked impatiently

"And right then, right before he was about to fire, a woman came out of nowhere, out from behind one of the cement pillars, with black hair and crazy fucking sunglasses. Sunglasses inside an underground parking garage!"

"She was trying to obscure her identity. You didn't recognize her?"

"No, I'd remember a woman like this. Everything she wore was expensive, designer. She was brandishing her gun, pointed dead at the guy, her arm fully outstretched and without missing a beat, she shot him. He didn't hear her coming up, even in her damn heels. The bullet went right into his shoulder and stuck. His scream was ugly, guttural. It must have hurt like a bitch. Good.

"He turned around, grasping his shoulder, completely forgetting about me, and faced her. I couldn't see his expression, so I don't know if there was any look of recognition on his part. She shot at him again, but this time she missed, and the bullet went past his head straight into the wall behind me. Then, putting her gun down at her side, she fucking smiled at him."

"No, that's not creepy," Amanda proclaimed sarcastically. "She didn't finish him off? He didn't try to fire on her or run at her?"

"Nope. He stood there, bleeding like a stuck pig, staring at her. And she stared right back. I meant to take advantage of this bizarre silent stand-off and run back to the elevator, but before I moved, the woman spoke.

"In a French accent, no less, she said to the guy, 'You are as inconspicuous as that metal monstrosity you drive. If you are the best of what 'e's been left with, then none of you are safe from me. Give 'im this message, pig—you will all pay for what was done to me!'

"Once she stopped speaking, the fucker didn't look a gift horse in the mouth and took off like a bat out of hell!"

"That's ominous," Amanda noted. "What she said, I mean. 'What was done to me.' Interesting."

"Yes, fascinating, but that bitch's issues aren't my fucking concern!"

"Think about it, Jules. She knew him. She never intended to kill him. She missed all major organs. She sent that bullet past his head on purpose. She was following him with intent, clearly, but why she decided to deal with him at your underground garage, I can only guess. Privacy? She'd been following him, but that's not important to us. How she got in is.

"Yet another weak spot to look for aside from your elevator passcode. Like I said, Jules, your security needs an overhaul."

"Thank you for that obvious deduction," Jules responded acerbically. "I'll deal with it."

"So, did she come for you next?" Amanda queried, moving on from the sore subject. Even over the phone, she could tell Jules was embarrassed to have been caught so unaware. That was not the only thing Amanda thought her old flame and student should have been embarrassed by, but she did not want to mention anything yet.

"Did she see you as a problematic witness? That said, she could have waited for him to kill you before she acted. She didn't. Technically, she saved your life, Jules. Interesting. So, what was her next move?"

"She walked over to me. I was still pretty winded from that asshole's blows."

"No excuse!" Amanda snapped. "I wasn't going to go there now, but it has to be said. You know how to deal with pain, Jules. You should have focused past it. I trained you to be prepared. You know how to deal with opponents larger than you, that have more muscle mass, and you should never have been in that position—on the fucking ground!

"You've grown sloppy and let your instincts, your muscle memory, become soft, flabby. Your responses should be instinctual. Even our sparring last night was—meh."

What! Jules almost ran her car off the road. Her anger towards Amanda's castigating words and unexpected lack of empathy towards her plight ran hot and potent, and it nearly got the best of her. She visualized Amanda's admonishing finger waving furiously in the air at her over her phone.

Pointed criticisms due to failings and mistakes took Jules back to her early training sessions with the woman. Amanda had been relentless and unforgiving in her attempt to mould Jules into a version of herself.

Thankfully, Jules managed to keep her head clear, her eyes focused dead ahead, and she remained on the road. She wanted to get to her midtown condo as fast as possible without killing herself in the process. She was almost there, and this was not the time to get in an accident. Jules took a deep breath before countering the unwanted chastisement.

But countering it with what? Anger? Curses? Resentment? She would not be fooling anyone with her self-righteous indignation, least of all herself. Amanda was completely and unequivocally correct in her observations.

Jules realized something significant. Having been so preoccupied for so long with Phillip's destruction, she absolutely had a lax attitude toward her physical training to keep her skills sharp. She had even put her sessions in Toronto with Master Hiroki on hold. What disrespectful behaviour. His time was priceless. His knowledge? Invaluable! Jules felt terrible regret and shame.

Also, she was shocked by how much she had forgotten about Amanda, about how astute and perceptive she was. *Why am I surprised? It's why I knew she could help with William. This is her life, always prepared, focused—apparently, even more than I am. Dammit, Jules, get it together.*

"You're right, Amanda. Excuses are beneath me. I should have been able to manage my opponent easily. I should have put my security under greater scrutiny. Being so assured of my invincibility is arrogance, I know, but it's just that I'm so close. So fucking close to the end of all this."

"Learn from your mistakes, Jules—if they don't get you killed first. Learn what went wrong, and then make sure it never happens again. Preparedness is key, essential. Listen, I've got to go. Finish telling me what happened. The woman?"

Jules sighed. "As I got up, the bitch walked over and slapped me! I was about to respond in kind when she stared right into my face, with those ridiculous glasses hiding her eyes, and said, 'Leave Marie Bergé alone. That bitch is mine to torture. You may 'ave Jacques, I don't give a fuck, but I'll destroy that simpering bitch.' Then she backed up, her gun pointed at me and disappeared further into the garage. I never saw her on my way out."

"Damn, you've got some crazy shit going on in your life, Jules. I'll meet you at your place later. Stay there, and don't leave for any reason. I'll be in touch. Soon."

Jules swore she detected giddiness in Amanda's voice.
What are you up to, Amanda?

XVII

William glared at the flickering lights in his suite, wondering how a place so grand, so obviously well cared for, somehow managed to have unexplained power surges. There was no storm outside, no lightning in the sky or whipping wind which might account for the odd behaviour. The annoying phenomenon had been going on for over ten minutes.

On instinct, William called out to Yasmine to ask her opinion on the matter but then quickly remembered he had sent her downstairs to arrange for the courier.

Do I have a poltergeist? Is this room haunted? How bloody quaint. Fucking hell!

Suddenly, someone knocked on the door to his suite.

William was not expecting anyone, and Yasmine had her pass-key. "Fuck off," he hollered.

"Sir, I'm sorry to disturb you," the voice behind the door chirped. "I'm Lucy from maintenance. There seems to be an issue with your room. Electric surges, I'm told. May I come in and take a look. Again, the management is very sorry for the inconvenience."

Bloody hell! A female electrician! "Hold on. I need a minute."

Butt-naked, William walked into his bedroom and threw on some workout attire. He figured he might as well go downstairs to the second-floor gym for a much-needed training session. He wished Yasmine was back; he felt she was better suited to deal with all this inconvenient triviality.

William checked himself out in the mirror; his vanity still powerfully held sway over him. He was happy with how his taught body looked in the form-fitting 2XIST navy Regimen jogger pants and matching navy Raglan bomber jacket. He pulled the jacket's zipper down a third of the way to flash some skin since his tank-top barely covered much of his waxed smooth chest.

Flexing his muscles in the mirror, William created the tight definition between his pecs that drove Yasmine wild.

Bringing his hand down to the bulge in the front of his tight pants, William squeezed his package. "A little something for the bird to drool over," he stated, self-aggrandizing. "Looking right fit."

Sauntering back into the common area, he grabbed his laptop and locked it up in the safe. He dropped his pass-key into his gym bag as he opened the door.

William knew right away that the woman in front of him was definitely not an employee of Château Bergé. He knew who she was and what she really did for a living. Visibly shocked, William had no idea that his realization showed all over his face in the form of startling apprehension and fear to the woman staring back at him.

Amanda looked directly into the face of the man she had come to kill and sneered, "Hiya, Willy-boy! You're fucked!"

Taking advantage of William's surprise and abortive movement, Amanda kicked him square in the stomach with such force that he flew backward, landing with a thud on the marble floor.

Entering the suite, Amanda calmly shut the door behind her, watching as William scrambled to his feet, desperately trying to catch his breath.

Not wasting another opportunity to inflict pain, Amanda connected her right foot hard with the left side of William's neck with a perfectly executed roundhouse kick. The heavy blow forced him back down, and he let out a ferocious cry of agony as he face-planted back onto the floor.

Amanda walked predatorily around William's bent-over form. "I could make this easy on you, but I'm not going to. You hurt someone I love. You wish to hurt that person further, kill them, even, and I can't let that happen."

Balling her right hand into a tight fist, Amanda furiously brought it down towards William's temple.

This time, however, her attack did not connect.

With remarkable speed, William brought his left arm up, thrusting the palm of his hand towards the oncoming fist, stopping the blow.

William had successfully blocked Amanda's punch. She was momentarily stunned by this unanticipated action.

How? He barely turned his head to aim. That was no self-defence move or natural athleticism. Reacting instinctively, like he knew where to place his hand to block my attack? Sensing movement? Feeling the air displaced by an advancing solid object? Anticipating direction and force with exact precision comes from years of study and training.

Then, just as Amanda had done to him a few moments earlier, William took advantage of his opponent's hesitation. He firmly wrapped his strong fingers around her fist and, with his grasp firm and unyielding, forcefully jerked his arm in a half-circle. It twisted Amanda's own captured limb so ferociously that she lost her balance and came crashing down onto the floor next to him.

Motherfucker! Amanda's thoughts were aflutter. She needed space to think, to reassess both her situation and her opponent. She realized she had made a potentially fatal mistake in underestimating William. It was a mistake she would never have made had this been a verified business contract. But this was all personal, and that had always made her careless and overconfident.

That was why she never did freebies for anyone.

But all this was not for just anyone. It was for Jules, and Jules always turned her world upside down.

Amanda needed some tactical distance to get back on her feet. She tucked her arms into her chest, squeezed her legs together tight and rigid, and rapidly rolled herself a few meters away from William. Once she was again upright, she assumed her ap kubi stance: defensive.

Placing the palms of his hands directly on the floor back behind his head, on both sides, William brought his legs up to his chest, tucked them in close, and flipped himself forward. He landed in a perfect standing position.

Amanda kept her eyes dead set on William. No one in a very long time had blocked one of her punches with such ease or knocked her off balance so smoothly. She realized that she had to rethink her plan of action and rethink it fast.

Amanda had done no prior research on her target to ready herself and prepare for a physical confrontation. William had skills; this was not going to be a walk in the park. Still, this revelation did not deter her one bit from her ultimate goal: William's death. She was the Silver Dagger. All this hoopla meant was that she would get a decent workout before dinner.

"You thought it would be that easy, Luv? Not this time—Amanda."

"So, you know my name. And you have a few moves. I'm not impressed."

"Hmph," William sneered. "I know quite a bit about you. But you and Jules? I'm assuming that's the mystery friend you mentioned earlier. I didn't know your connection. Changes nothing, mind you. She'll still die, and so will you if you get in my way. I have no quarrel with you, woman. Leave, and both of us will forget this little incident ever occurred."

Amanda laughed. "Ya, no. Not gonna happen." Glaring at her opponent, she changed her stance to one of offence, ready to strike: the wushu horse stance. "You die, I go have dinner with Jules, and we toast to your corpse."

William screwed up his eyes in anger and directed his hate-stare towards Amanda. Just as quickly as he had become enraged, he calmed himself. "Regrettable, but very well, if that is your final decision." His words were dispassionate; his tone was cold and hard.

"It is my final decision," Amanda responded, mimicking William's stalwart, British haughtiness. She was intentionally mocking.

Amanda's attempt to unsteady William with her dismissive sarcasm was a calculated tactic. To her surprise, however, he did not take the bait. Based entirely on Jules's description, Amanda had expected a rash, unstable brute. Instead, a real threat appeared before her. She now fully comprehended what she was up against: an enemy she could not easily predict.

Instead of trying to anticipate and decipher William's attack, Amanda relied on the disciplines she knew worked best for her in these close-quarters situations against a larger opponent. Moves that would take him down quickly without engaging in unnecessary sparing.

Wing Chun.

Done with both conversation and Amanda's overt derisive behaviour, William steeled himself, focusing all his attention on the coming melee. Once again, he did something Amanda did not expect; he also assumed an offensive stance. Both combatants had now chosen an aggressive position.

Amanda was familiar with his choice. She rolled her eyes. *Really, asshole? The wushu horse stance? How original.*

Thrusting herself forward, Amanda quickly closed the distance between her and William. She focused on speed and suppleness to counter his strength and aggression. Amanda suspected her agility far surpassed his, considering his solid muscle mass; William's gym attire left little to the imagination. She could use that advantage to beat him. *Push him back. Keep him on the defensive.*

Amanda punched upwards towards William's jaw. He tilted to his side to avoid her fist and then blocked the move entirely with the open palm of his left hand. It was a logical, basic maneuver. William grasped down hard on Amanda's wrist in an attempt to force her back using his superior strength; he had his footing down pat for stability.

It was a predictable move and just what Amanda was hoping he would do. She raised her left arm, bringing it up swiftly to dislodge William's hold. Her flat hand struck his wrist with tremendous force; the action disentangled their limbs. Grabbing his extricated arm, Amanda forced it down where it could be of no use. Without even needing to think about it, she swung her now freed right arm back towards William's unprotected head.

Amanda's fist was tight, firm, and determined to strike hard against flesh-covered bone. Again, William awed her. He brought his right arm up, turned it around, and blocked her punch with the back of his hand. *Bastard! He's using wing chun against me. Push him back. Surprise him.*

Thinking fast, Amanda clawed William's chest with her fingernails. He howled as she nearly broke through the skin. Then, using both arms, with all of her upper body strength, she pushed his limb viciously into his chest with as much force as she could muster.

William's legs were strong but not wholly immovable; he stumbled. His slight falter was adequate to disrupt his centre of gravity for a brief moment.

Amanda had William on the defence, and he had yet to throw a punch and strike at her with the intent to inflict damage. She let go of him and returned to an offensive stance.

William growled with anger. He enjoyed inflicting pain on women—not the other way around. He held his sore, bleeding arm and spat on the floor. "Using your fucking fingernails, just like a bitch! I expected more from the Silver Dagger."

Amanda halted her attack and let out a small gasp. William knew more than her real name. Somehow, he had discovered she was the Silver Dagger; this was unprecedented. *He knows! How? No, don't show emotion. Don't let him get into your head. Reveal nothing. Be ice. Feign ignorance.*

Ever the professional, Amanda allowed herself only a second for astonishment and alarm. "I don't know what that means, psycho," she replied coldly.

"How disappointing," William chided, still stone-like in his presentation. "You've come here to kill me but refuse me the right to address my would-be assassin properly. You can deny it all you want, but I know you, Silver Dagger. I've studied your moves and the moves of others of your ilk. My sensei's the best money can buy. So you see I—"

William's declaration was interrupted by the sound of a keycard electronically unlocking the front door of the penthouse.

Upon arriving back in Fairporte, Charles went directly to his downtown penthouse to meet up with Christophe.

Entering his home, he found the young man erratically pacing back and forth on the bamboo hardwood floor. Celine Dion's beautifully melancholic voice reverberated off the walls. Christophe always listened to "It's All Coming Back to Me Now" loudly on repeat whenever he felt depressed or anxious.

The velvet-trimmed Bergamo curtains completely drawn, Christophe explained over the din that he was terrified of helicopter newshounds taking pictures of him through the windows with a telescopic lens.

"Chris, that's being a tad paranoid, no? Nobody cares that much." All the same, Charles left the room as he found it.

The two men, having been apart for days, embraced each other energetically. They kissed deep and passionately for several moments, holding on to each other tightly until Charles reluctantly pulled away to start unpacking. Christophe turned down the music level, hit "shuffle," and finally allowed another song to play.

They talked about their current publicized situation. It was a mostly one-sided conversation, with Christophe ranting and raving about the potential fallout from the scandal and how it would affect him.

"What if my family recognizes me from those pictures? I can't let them find me! What if I lose my contracts? What if I never work again?"

Charles allowed Christophe to go off for a good long while, but eventually, he put an end to the dramatic hullabaloo. Charles knew the both of them were on borrowed time. Jules kept a suite in the same building, one floor down, and he was waiting for her to come by at any moment to confront them.

In the elevator, he had received a text from Jules saying she was at her place and planned to come up and see them shortly. The text also said she had no doubt he and Christophe were already together commiserating, and that was a scenario that worked best for her. Why? Because none of her valuable time would be wasted hunting Christophe down.

Charles was more than a little concerned that his daughter saw Christophe as prey.

Taking Christophe's hand, Charles kissed his lover gently on the lips and reassured him that it would all work out. "I'll fix it, babe. Trust me," Charles cooed, doing his best to pull the young, panic-stricken man down off the ledge.

Christophe did trust Charles completely. He trusted the older man's power and influence; it was soothing to him knowing Charles was on top of things, taking care of the situation.

Not great with confrontation, conflict or dealing with stress, Christophe was more flight than fight. Charles had both looked out for him and looked after him for years. Charles was more than Christophe's lover, his boyfriend or his partner. He was his hero.

"I know, I know," Christophe babbled, "and I'm sorry I'm being like this. I'm scared. Everything seems so fucking uncertain now, but you've never let me down, babe."

Christophe moved towards Charles, pinning him up against the wall. He began nibbling on his neck, then his ears. Charles moaned with pleasure. They started to make out again, two tongues moving furiously between two hungry mouths. Both their cocks were rock hard. "I wanna fuckin' blow you," Christophe seductively whispered into Charles's ear. "And I want you to eat my tight—"

Just then, Charles's phone pinged several times, interrupting and distracting both men from their prurient desires. Charles looked at his cell and quickly saw that Jules had sent him more messages. "She's here, Chris." He hoped he was prepared for her. He hoped they both were.

Jules followed up her texts with two loud, purposeful knocks on the front door.

Charles told Christophe to go into the bedroom and turn the TV on; he wanted to discuss things with his daughter privately first before letting her see them as a couple. With the whole "Denise thing" on top of everything else that was splashed over social media, Charles knew it was a confusing situation right out of the box.

Christophe, always intimidated by Jules, gladly ran away to hide in the master bedroom.

As he let Jules in, Charles could see that his daughter was not overly impressed with what she had seen plastered all over the internet about him. It was written all over her very annoyed face. And now, with both local and national news coverage interested in the situation, it was a public relations disaster.

Jules needed explanations and answers to some burning questions. "I can't wait to hear this," she hissed. Her face immediately went expressionless, statue-like.

Her change in demeanour did not bother Charles too much. Frankly, he had expected it. From years of being in Jules's presence, he understood that this was her most common—even preferred—facial pronouncement.

Charles was troubled by the faint traces of disappointment he saw in his daughter's stone-cold face, though. It was masterfully veiled but unmistakably clear to someone as close to her as he was. Someone who knew her as well as he did and could recognize the most subtle nuances of her behaviour. His daughter was supremely disappointed in him, in his actions, and that made him feel like total shit.

Jules informed her father that she wanted to hear about what went down in Montréal between him and M. Babineaux first. *Then* they would get into his secret, years-long "relationship-whatever" with Christophe.

Charles was not sure he was ready for that conversation. However, it came across loud and clear that any reluctance on his part to engage in complete transparency did not interest Jules one bit. She would have her pound of flesh once business was done, one way or another. Still, Charles was glad to temporarily postpone any revelations concerning his personal life, even if it meant talking about Phillip and his despicable parents.

"Okay, honey, if that's how you want to do this."

Charles told her everything. Well, not entirely everything. Jules was adamant that she did not want to hear any specific details concerning the child. As long as it was alive—that was all she cared about. Jules did not want to know the gender, the name or the whereabouts of Phillip's kid. She was utterly inflexible around this point.

Though extremely curious about what his daughter had up her sleeve, Charles respected her request. He practiced brevity when it came to the topic of Philippe—a name he never once mentioned.

Jules was genuinely upset hearing Genevieve was dead. She had not known the woman, but she felt a kinship with her. They were both casualties of cruelty. Charles informed his daughter of the litany of horrid, monstrous things done to the French woman to ensure her suffering and ultimate demise. Jules was appropriately livid, and that anger only invigorated her desire to punish the Cartells.

With calculated purpose, Jules took from her father every document, every single sheet of incriminating paper M. Babineaux had given him. She placed them in the attaché case she had brought with her and made a mental note to take it to Mode-Génétique Labs with Amanda once she had finished with her father and his boy toy.

"I'll inform Phillip that the three of us will be meeting early tomorrow morning in my office. He'll think it's about damage control over this situation with you, and I can't wait to blindside him with this instead. He should have plenty of time to acquire what we want from him and Sonja—we'll give him until the end of the workday. And I'll make sure he understands the consequences of failure."

"Tomorrow, you will have total control of the company, and the Cartells will be out," Charles grinned.

"Yes, and Phillip, that bastard, will finally get what he deserves. Now, go tell Christophe to get his ass in here. It's time I got some fucking answers."

"What's going on with the lights?" Yasmine asked as she entered the suite. "William? Is everything alright?" When her eyes finally adjusted to the erratic light show, she saw and understood what was happening. "The Silver Dagger! Here?"

Amanda was less than pleased by the fact that now two relative strangers knew her alternate working identity. Before today, to her knowledge, only three people in the world knew the direct connection between her and the enigmatic assassin known as the Silver Dagger: Bex, Jules, and her brother. *Oh no! It can't be him!*

Surveying the scene before her, Yasmine brought her hand up to her mouth in shock and horror; her stupor lasted only a fraction of a second. Yanking her cellphone out of her purse, she punched in the number for hotel security.

Amanda swiftly reached for the shuriken hidden inside her boot. The throwing-star was a last-minute decision she had made before leaving her room to give herself a weapon—just in case. Once it was in her grasp, she planned to nail Yasmine in her left eye with it.

"No," William yelled, causing Amanda to pause. "Call no one. This is a private matter. Hang up. Now!"

Yasmine did as she was told, reluctantly putting her phone back in her handbag. Before tossing the carryall aside, she removed her gun.

Amanda recognized the weapon immediately as a Steyr M9-A1 semi-automatic pistol. She had used one recently on a case and knew it handled well.

"You seem to be at a disadvantage," Yasmine sneered.

"I'm never out of options, bitch," Amanda replied, grinning ear to ear. She always portrayed an air of fearlessness and superiority in front of any opponent. Amanda's unwavering confidence usually unnerved her targets, causing them to make mistakes, tactical errors she quickly took advantage of.

Without warning, the flickering lights finally went off for good. Completely off. Near-total darkness.

Bex, you beauty! And thanks for having all the drapes closed, idiots.

Now everyone was firmly in Amanda's world, the world of the hidden assassin. This was the leverage she needed to successfully press her attack to ensure self-preservation as well as a victory against her enemy. For Amanda, this was no longer about fairness in combat or facing her opponent squarely in the eye as she came at them.

Still, Ninjutsu was not a discipline that only trained one to sneak around in shadows waiting to strike from the darkness: the unseen attack. Amanda had been rigorously trained to understand this. Ninjutsu allowed her to exploit her target's fear and uncertainty and use that leverage against them in either one-on-one or group combat. It was as much cerebral as it was physical.

Adaptation and improvisation were elements Amanda had mastered over the years. As her target's defensive abilities ranged, so did the locales she fought in; also, the unforeseen factor occasionally reared its head to make matters more complicated. And interesting. Her rashness, her unpreparedness today, proved to her that even she could make the same stupid mistake others had often made regarding her.

The surprise of sudden darkness had no disabling consequences for Amanda, as she suspected it did for her opponents.

Amanda wanted the gun out of play first; moreover, she was physically closer to Yasmine's position. Timing, speed, and distance were crucial factors in disarming a weapon.

Thanks to her almost eidetic-like memory, a long-practiced skill learned from unnervingly patient Spanish monks, Amanda had a perfect recall of the layout of the room. That, and the positions of her opponents.

With the grace of a prima ballerina, Amanda leapt onto the soft couch without making a sound. She was invisible and close enough to her prey to strike with deadly accuracy.

When Amanda landed atop the sofa, her feet sunk slightly into the luxuriously supple cushions, but it did not impede her balance or alignment. She was in position, barely a meter away from where Yasmine stood, ready to attack.

Amanda, eyes accustomed to seeing in the dark, trained to make out shapes and contours in the absence of almost all light, deciphered that the erratically moving outline in front of her was Yasmine's arm. Amanda deduced that the woman was furiously trying to aim the gun in multiple pointless directions, searching for her target.

Like a viper about to strike, Amanda locked her arms in place. She had chosen the physical location of her blow.

"Where is she?" Yasmine shouted.

Amanda answered her with a fast, severe blunt face punch.

Yasmine, unable to comprehend the crippling wallop that came out of nowhere, dropped the gun as she brought her hands up to her throbbing face and cried out in pain. She screamed for William, but no response came from him.

After successfully disarming her target, Amanda immediately followed up her hook punch attack with a debilitating blow to the woman's soft, exposed throat. This move was meant to push her back, unbalance her, and it did that and more. Yasmine crumpled to the ground, gasping for breath, unable to comprehend or combat the unrelenting, aggressive force that assailed her.

For the moment, Amanda was done with this target. Yasmine, unarmed and physically damaged, was no longer an immediate threat. Now it was time to finish William.

Amanda found it odd that he had done nothing to aid his partner. Much more disconcerting, William had remained unnervingly quiet during the brief attack. Too quiet. Uncomfortably quiet. *No, he's nothing. Adapt. Listen. Be silent. Be invisible. Find him. End him.*

Amanda moved stealthily throughout the room. As she hunted for William, she successfully avoided the furniture and the other potential obstacles previously memorized that might be in her path. Until she bumped into an urn, causing it to fall over and shatter.

And then she nearly fell into a potted plant.

Those things were not where they should have been. Not according to Amanda's memory, and her memory was steel, unfailing.

He intentionally moved these items to unbalance me, so I'll give my position away. How did he know to do this to impede me? And to do it so silently! Who taught him? Who taught him about me?

And then she remembered what William had said earlier. Her worst-case scenario had been brought before her. She had to accept it; she had been betrayed by her own blood. *That vindictive piece of shit!*

Unfortunately, Amanda had picked the wrong time to stop and ponder the truth surrounding William's training, her familial betrayal, and the necessary future confrontation with her brother.

Unlike his opponent, William was unencumbered by distressing thoughts and emotions.

Clear-headed, he took full advantage of both his manipulation of the room's objects and Amanda's sudden immobility. He struck out at her like a cobra. His evenness, his dispassionate countenance, and his inability to become distracted by emotion were his sword and shield.

If the lights were on and Amanda could read William's frighteningly stoic and confident physiognomy, she might have readjusted her opinion that he was no threat to her.

Amanda's moves were instinctual and her keen senses, unhindered by her preoccupied mind, heard and felt the subtle change in the air-conditioned atmosphere around her. It was nearly undetectable—nearly, but as the shadowy shape of William's thrusting fist came towards the side of her face, Amanda sensed its arrival.

And just in time to move out of its way.

Amanda now fully realized William could also move in the shadows. Unlike her, according to his proclamation, he did not possess the same number of years of training she did. Sure, he was good at manoeuvring in the dark, but she was its master. She had no doubt that her ability to perceive spatial impressions far exceeded his.

Done playing around, Amanda grabbed William's arm while it was still in the air in front of her and pulled him in close.

With the Ninjutsu technique Taki-ori, she took his wrist, locked it in place, and then bent it to cause torrents of pain. Bringing her left leg up, Amanda kicked into his abdomen three times with her knee, knocking the wind out of him, temporarily preventing him from defending himself. Keeping the Take-ori on William's wrist, she clamped down hard on his elbow, locked his arm against his torso, and forced him to the ground.

Now in a position to break William's arm, Amanda applied the correct amount of pressure needed and waited to hear the snap of his bones.

Suddenly, someone began pounding hard on the main door of the suite.

"Mr. Falsworth, this is hotel security. We've been notified of a disturbance coming from your suite, possibly of a violent nature. May we come in? Sir? We are authorized to enter your suite. Sir? Okay, we're coming in."

No, not now, dammit! Amanda had no choice; she had to retreat. The opportunity to take out William had passed.

Amanda pushed William back down to the floor, hard, and ran to the balcony doors. There was no way she could get out the way she came in without having to fight her way past hotel security.

So, Amanda resigned herself to the only other option: the terrace. She planned to jump down to the next level, break into the suite below and escape out their entrance where she could then quickly make it back to her room.

It was a dangerous, outrageous plan but necessary.

Regrettably, Amanda had lost the advantage of anonymity. She realized she would have to grab her things and leave Château Bergé fast. If William talked, they would know where to find her. She had used her real name when checking in so Jules could contact her if she desired to. A foolish, reckless decision.

Amanda hoped William also did not want the added attention, himself, and would keep his mouth shut about the exact details of what transpired. She decided she would wait and find that out far away from him, back in town at her secondary base of operations. She always had a backup plan.

William could not see what Amanda was up to, but he knew she was attempting to escape. *Fine, let her go. I have the upper hand. She's aware that I know her identity and can expose her should I choose to. Another time, Silver Dagger.*

Amanda unlocked the glass doors and went out onto the terrace. Whipping off her scarf, she wrapped it around one of the bronze gargoyles for stability. Hopping over the side of the balcony, she skilfully scaled down the wall.

Once safely on the terrace below, Amanda attempted to snap her scarf back, but it would not budge. She decided to leave it. Time was not on her side, and she could not waste the seconds she did have to retrieve a scarf, even if it was Hermés.

Amanda was thankful the occupants of the suite below were absent when she broke in.

This isn't over, Falsworth!

"I'm waiting."

"Well, Jules, you see, ah," Charles began hesitantly. Christophe sat on the couch, too afraid to speak or make eye contact with Jules. "Chris and I are a couple. We—well, we—oh man, this is hard."

"Stop," Jules groaned loudly. "It can't begin like this. I got it. The two of you are together—and *that* I'll get to in a minute. How did you two meet? When? If those pictures tell the truth, Pops, then you lied to me about meeting him a few years ago on a golf course. I want the details. And don't lie to me— ever again! And I can't wait to hear how Denise fits into this."

Charles was afraid to tell Jules that the news footage—well, that some of the news footage was true. The pictures showing him and the stuff about Christophe being a teen prostitute were facts. But how could he tell her his total truth? That he had done those things grieving the loss of his beloved husband. And pulling away from her, his only child, at the same time. Charles did not have the words.

"Just tell me the truth," Jules responded as if reading his mind. "Start by telling me when you two met. Was it—was it after dad died?" Jules suddenly felt sick to her stomach.

"Of course!" Charles shot back, pained by the look of overt disappointment on his daughter's face. "I would never have betrayed Jason! I loved your dad. I still do, always! A love so profound his death nearly destroyed me. You know that! I wanted to die. Even my love for you, my beautiful daughter, couldn't console me. And for that, I'll always feel ashamed.

"It was after you decided to emancipate yourself, Jules—which I should never have agreed to, in hindsight. I should have stepped up and been your father, but I was so broken. I'm so sorry."

"I've forgiven you for that already," Jules answered dispassionately. "Move forward."

"Damn, that's my ball-busting daughter there, Chris." Charles chuckled. He was a very proud papa, even when she bossed him around.

"Okay, during that time, when you weren't living at home, Jules, I used to walk the streets a lot. To lose myself, I guess. I wasn't going into the office anymore, or doing much of anything, really, but I'd leave the house, drive to Yonge and Bloor, park the car, and walk the downtown core for hours. Just walk, let the wind hit me, and think about Jason.

"One day, I was aimlessly walking around Gerard St., near Church, when this goth approached me."

"I was Emo," Christophe corrected.

Charles rolled his eyes. "Sorry, this *Emo* approached me and asked if I was looking for company."

"So, that part is correct," Jules interjected, turning towards Christophe. "You were a prostitute. That alternative-looking douche in those photos is you."

"I wasn't a douche, I was cool, but yes, only it's not like what you think. Let your father finish first before you judge me—judge us."

"Jules, please," Charles pleaded, "let me explain. As I was saying, Christophe was Chris back then. I know he hates being called Chris, but that's who he was when we met. This cute guy dressed in combat boots, PVC pants and a My Bloody Valentine t-shirt. He had black and purple hair, eyeliner, the prettiest smile. No tattoos or piercings that I could see."

"Tats aren't my thing," Christophe asserted.

"Like I fucking care," Jules sneered.

"Sooo," Charles went on, nervously, "right away, I could tell he was good-looking. Though he was hiding his looks behind all this makeup, dyed hair, and alternative stuff."

"There's nothing wrong with guys wearing makeup," Christophe exclaimed. "I looked cool."

"I know, Chris, that's not what I'm saying. It was a mask for you, back then, more than an enhancement or just self-expression. You know what I mean. We've talked about this. Let me continue.

"I wasn't sure how to respond, but something told me not to tell him to bugger off. Loneliness? Boredom? Maybe I was looking for a distraction. No feelings. No strings attached. Yes, I know how that sounds—cold and callous. But he was a rent-boy, after all, a sex-worker, and I doubted this was his first time at it gauging by how comfortable he was approaching me.

"I figured he also didn't want anything more personal from me than my money. It was a business transaction he had instigated by approaching me—he wasn't asking me out on a date. So I thought, well, what else did I plan on doing that day. Well, except I—"

Charles paused. He had almost let something slip, but he decided to continue keeping that dark secret to himself for the time being.

"Anyway," Charles continued, "I took Chris back to the house, and we, ah, we—"

"You fucked," Jules stated, finishing his sentence for him. "Don't get all prudish now just because I'm your daughter," Jules sighed, shaking her head.

"Fine then, yes, I fucked his brains out. Not in my bed, though. Not where Jason and I slept, made love, I couldn't—ever! But yes, we fucked. I took all my anger, my sadness, my frustration, and my bitterness out on him. I channelled all that darkness and negative energy that had built up inside of me, and I put it into the sex. It went on for hours, and it was beyond fucking amazing. I felt alive after feeling empty for so long.

"And no, I didn't care how old he was. I never asked, but I'm not going to lie—I knew he probably wasn't eighteen. I don't make excuses for it. I know how it sounds, for fuck's sake, but I didn't care at that moment, and I don't care now. That beautiful Emo saved my god damn life. I—I—"

"What is it? What aren't you saying? Why do you keep pausing?" Jules knew her father was holding something important back.

"Jules, I—boy, this is hard to say, but I know I have to come clean. You need to understand. Honey, I planned on taking my life that day. There was a gun in my car, and I was just building up the courage to do it. It was going to happen. I couldn't live any longer with that huge hole inside of me. I was so tired of feeling empty and sad all the time, day in and day out. I was incomplete without your dad.

"Jason and I were together since my second semester of University. We fit perfectly, yet we were total opposites. He was my everything, and he'd been taken from me. All that was left of me was a husk, barely half a man. I couldn't stand being without him anymore. And you deserved better, Jules. A better version of me. A better father.

"But if I'm speaking my full truth here, I have to admit I wasn't thinking about you at all. I just wanted peace. If I couldn't be with Jason, I just wanted it all to stop. I didn't care about what it would do to the people I'd leave behind, including you. And I have to live with that. If Chris hadn't come up to me that day, at that moment and talked to me, I wouldn't be here right now to live with my regrets, my shame."

Jules's mouth dropped. She was shocked. No, horrified.

"I—I had no idea it had reached that point for you. I knew you were sad, depressed, of course, but if I had known it was that bad, I would never have left you. Suicide! I never thought—! I'm sorry, Pops. I forced myself to live with my pain, pushing it down so far that I became so cold, numb. I was so concerned with my life, my future." *Like usual. Just like with Ethan, you self-absorbed bitch.* "I'm so sorry."

Jules walked over to her father and wrapped her arms around him. Charles reciprocated, and they both started to cry.

Remaining seated, Christophe stared in awe at the father-daughter fusion hugging and crying. If anyone had been looking at him, they would have seen how uncomfortable he was in the presence of such raw, unfettered emotion. Christophe had not known the full extent of Charles's trauma regarding the death of his husband or how instrumental he had been in that pivotal, life-and-death moment. It was a lot for him to absorb.

"Chuck, you never told me you planned on killing yourself the day we met! Fuck me! That is some heavy shit. I guess—yay for me? Good job?"

Charles hated being called Chuck by anyone apart from Christophe, and even then, it still had a grating effect. Christophe figured if Charles used the hated "Chris" abbreviation, even with the best intentions, well, boohoo.

"All I was looking for that day was a rich guy to spend his cash on my sweet ass," Christophe commented sarcastically but truthfully. "And I could have picked anyone, but I chose your dad, Jules, because there was a look in his eyes. Lost. Sad. I was drawn to him. I recognized it, that sense of inner dysphoria because I understand that feeling, that deep sadness, that sense of confusion.

"Plus, and any street hustler will tell you this, melancholy makes for an easy target, and an easy target means fast money. You were a good prospective punter."

"A what?" Jules cried out, pulling away from her father. She took a moment to wipe the moisture from her eyes. She made sure not to get any of her makeup on the expensive, delicate fabric of her silk blouse in the process of quickly removing all evidence of her temporary, emotional weakness. "I know I'm going to regret asking this, but what the hell is a punter?"

"A john, a client, a customer," Christophe explained. "Someone who pays for sex. The guy who took me in and showed me the ropes when I was new to the streets of Toronto was from the UK, and that's the word he liked to use. His name was Colin, but who the fuck knows if that was his real name or not because he went by different ones all the time.

"He's the prick who took those fucking pics. That fucker sold me out! It had to have been him. He was the only person I told about you, Chuck. He must have followed me one day and taken pics of us together for his own kink. No fucking loyalty! Dirty cocksucker!"

Charles went over to the couch, sat down next to Christophe, and looked into his angry, red face. Smiling warmly, Charles put his arm around Christophe and squeezed tight. "I said I'd take care of it, Chris. Calm down. I'll find this Colin guy, trust me, and I'll take care of him too. Don't worry, Hon, I can spin anything."

"So, Pops, did you start to see *Chris* regularly after that?"

Charles took note of the affected way his daughter said Christophe's abbreviated name: aggressively, suspiciously, and disapprovingly.

"Yes, I did, and you don't have to be so dismissive towards him. As I said, he's the reason I'm still here. Oh! Right." His voice trailed off.

"Oh, right," Jules caustically mimicked.

Charles sighed loudly. The sensitive, apologetic, thoughtful girl he had been hugging just moments earlier was gone. She had morphed back into the judgmental, accusatory, and disappointed daughter she had been when she first entered his suite. And that was the one he desperately did not want to face.

She has every right to be pissed off at you. A couple of hugs isn't going to change that. You just informed her that she hadn't been enough to stop you from planning to kill yourself. And you revealed that it was a teenage male prostitute who saved you. Tell her, explain everything, or you'll lose her, man! Say something!

"Jules, honey, please let me finish," Charles begged. "Allow me the time I need to fully make you understand it all—our story, our history. I hate seeing that look of outrage and disappointment on your face. Like I've betrayed our bond. It's killing me, but I know I deserve your anger. Please, will you give me the time and the latitude to fully explain everything?"

Jules sighed heavily. "Okay, I won't say another word until you're done talking. Well, I'll try anyway. I'll also try to hold off all judgments regarding *this one* until then, too." She crooked her neck in Christophe's direction. She hoped the disdain in her voice, in the affected way she had said those two words, was unmistakable.

Not knowing how long it was going to take, Jules eased herself into the pride and joy of her father's living room. A Napoleon III 19th century armchair in distressed blue velvet with white braiding and buttons, low bankrolled arms, and tufted detail. Despite the era in which it was made, one that often favoured pageantry over practicality, the plump, velvet-cushioned seat was as inviting and cozy as it looked.

The chair was not her style at all, but Jules knew her father shared Stella's fascination with antiques and not her love of clean, sleek lines and modernity.

Jules wanted to be in a comfortable, seated position to hear the rest of her father's story, yes, but it was not just about that. She also chose the chair because it was a better option than the alternative: sitting on the couch next to Christophe. That was not going to happen.

Crossing her legs, Jules settled in for the long haul.

A master at faking charm and sincerity, William quickly convinced the over-excited security team that it had all been a great misunderstanding.

He explained how the electrical issue had startled both him and his companion, causing them both to panic when the lights went off. William apologized profusely for the noise. He asked to have the room billed for the damage caused in their rampage across the suite, such as the urn, trying to find a light source, like the now opened terrace doors.

After the security team left, William instructed Yasmine to keep her mouth shut. "I'll deal with Ms. Reid in my own time, on my terms. Now that I know she's connected to Jules, and in my way, I'll add her to my list."

It was an organic creature, William's list of enemies to be dealt with, capable of growing and expanding. And it would never be finished. Never be completed. There were always new obstacles, new adversaries, and old wounds to take care of.

If William took anything positive away from this violent experience, it was that he had not felt so alive in a very long time. Even when he realized Amanda was about to break his arm, his dick had hardened. William knew she was a lesbian, but that did not matter to him. If he decided he wanted a piece of her, he would take it, violently, if necessary. He hoped it would be.

He understood now, seeing her up close in action, just how good a fighter the Silver Dagger was, how deadly, and he wanted another crack at her. Next time, however, he would manipulate the scenario so that he had the advantage.

"Yasmine!" William called out.

"Yes, my love," she answered from the bathroom.

"Go outside, untie that scarf from the gargoyle, put it on around your neck, take off all of your other clothes and come back to me—on all fours."

XVIII

Charles sighed as his daughter opted to sit as far away from Christophe as possible without leaving the room entirely. It added another level of frostiness to everything.

No, he would not let it rattle him. It was fine for now; Jules could despise Christophe all she wanted. Charles was sure that, eventually, she would come around and see what a wonderful man Christophe was, acknowledging and appreciating all that he had done for them.

At the moment, however, he would be satisfied with just finding a way to remove the irascible grimace off his daughter's face.

"Alright, I'm listening," Jules announced.

"Thanks, honey. It means so much. After that one instance together, it didn't happen again for some time. Chris and I didn't talk much that first night. It was pretty much just, ah, business. He'd given me his phone number, saying I should call or text if I wanted to hook up again. He warned me he wouldn't be easy to contact without that number. He was a street hustler. He didn't have a professional profile on escort websites.

"I held on to that number for months, too afraid, too uncomfortable with any new intimacy to commit to seeing a hooker a second time. I hate using these labels, Chris. Whore, hooker, prostitute. I don't want you to feel demeaned."

Christophe shrugged. "Just say sex worker, but I don't really care. They're just words. I'm fine with whatever descriptor you choose, babe."

Charles winked at him, and it lit up Christophe's face.

It had the opposite effect on Jules, however.

"If you say it, I believe it," Charles beamed, ignoring his daughter's blatant eye roll. "Eventually, my desolation and my libido overwhelmed my fear of new intimacy, and I called him. Chris and I started seeing each other, and I became a repeat client of his. I called, picked him up, and we always went back to my place where it was clean, safe, and private."

"Right, so private. Not according to those fucking photos."

"Come on, Chris, let it go," Charles barked, his tone commanding but loving. "It's over and done. Anyway, Jules, I found that the more I was around Chris, the less bleak I felt about everything. At first, it was all business, no strings, but the more time I spent with him, well, dammit, he just made me feel better. And not just with his body.

"It's hard to put my emotions at that time into words. We started having great conversations about life, about all kinds of things, after the sex was over. He lingered around, we cuddled, and I wanted him to stay. I liked his company.

"After a while, even before we had sex, we'd sit, drink, and talk for hours. I saw Chris's insatiable thirst to learn about the world, to be more than what he was. His enthusiasm for the future was exciting. To be in his presence, to be aware of his energy, his joy of discovering new things—it was intoxicating. Even when he took his youth and passion for granted, as young people often do, thinking time is irrelevant, and they're all immortal. It was still charming.

"He did what he did to survive, Jules. Not because he loved fucking a variety of not always attractive or hygienic strangers. Risking his health and life doing what he did was something he was keenly aware of, and he always practiced safe sex."

"Oh, always, I'm sure," Jules retorted condescendingly. She gave a withering look towards Christophe, and he immediately shrank from her daunting gaze. It was hard for Jules not to be judgmental, sassy or sometimes just downright mean and bitchy. In her mind, she honestly believed she was trying.

"Really, Jules?"

"Sorry, Pops, it just slipped out," she stated with a devilish grin.

"Fine, *we* always used condoms," Charles corrected himself. "Honestly, that's not the point here."

"No, I did always use them," Christophe affirmed. "Well, after the first few months of being on the streets, anyway. Colin and a few others, mostly druggies, often barebacked, and some of them got HIV or other shit. I didn't want that for myself, so when I got tested at the free clinic, and all my results came back negative, I wrapped it up every time after."

Jules was not convinced, but she dropped the matter, telling her father to continue.

"Chris listened to me, Jules, and appreciated my advice. He took what I told him about my experiences and applied them to his own life. He had dreams and aspirations. It was like talking to you, even though I'm sure you're loath at this point to see similarities between the two of you. He had ambition. I'm telling you I saw nothing but genuineness, gratitude, and even fondness in him, fondness towards me, a customer. And someone much older than him.

"Sure, maybe you want to think he was just fond of my money and the luxuries I possessed, but I'm telling you I knew better. He had a fondness for what we were doing together outside of the bedroom. He had a brand of maturity that, well, surviving alone on the streets as a teenager can give you, I guess.

"You should understand that kind of unexpected maturity in someone so young, Jules. It was admirable, intoxicating. He was something I'd never before experienced. And it has never been a father/son feeling I have with him. I've never seen him at the age that he is. He has an old soul, you could say. Chris's lively spirit brought my wilted one back to life like I was absorbing his very essence, but not as a parasite. More like shared healing? It's hard to put into words.

"And he was so different from Jason. I think—I think that ultimately created the connection. Had Chris reminded me of your dad, I wouldn't have been able to see anything in his face except Jason staring back at me. A constant, haunting reminder that he was gone, dead, and that this was all just a delightful, sexually gratifying illusion. An unsustainable suspension of my misery. But what's between us is genuine, beyond just sex.

"What I need you to understand most of all, Jules, is that my revitalization thanks to Chris's involvement is not a reflection on you. It never was. It has nothing to do with my love for you or your love for me. I never expected you to help me face and deal with your dad's passing.

"Especially not after what happened with Wi—ah, with *him*. I'd never have put that kind of pressure on you or that kind of heavy responsibility on your teenage shoulders. It was my job to take care of you, protect you, especially then, more than ever, when Jason wasn't there anymore. And I ultimately failed at that.

"Once I dealt with *him*, I had nothing left. Nothing to make sure you were emotionally well and dealing."

Jules gave her father the stink eye. "Stop!" she demanded.

It was just one word, but Jules had broadcast it with bold intensity, hoping her father understood what she wanted without having to say it out loud. Stop talking about William.

Charles got the message loud and clear.

"Don't worry, honey, Chris doesn't know who or what I'm talking about, and he won't pry into our personal history. He respects our shared secrets and the need for them, even if he doesn't understand our reasoning or our motives. You can trust him."

"Perhaps. And perhaps not."

"Chris is trustworthy, Jules! Oh, anyway, where was I? With Jason's parents dead, his brother in Japan, and my parents being the assholes that they are, I needed outside help and support for you.

"Thankfully, I had the sapience to ask Gregson to watch over you when I couldn't successfully be present in your life. He promised me right on the spot, without even having to think about it, that he'd watch out for you. He said I didn't even have to ask as he was already doing it. Gregson loved you like a daughter, Jules. He was the best, and we both know he kept his word and then some.

"You amaze me, sweetheart. You could have survived and still flourished if both your dad and I had died that night. You're so strong. I don't know where you get all that strength. Rubbed off from your dad and me, sure, but you were born with it. A born survivor. A born leader.

"I knew I had no right to take your hard sought independence away from you. You were doing so well on your own, and I didn't want to—fuck!"

"Didn't want to—?" Jules prodded.

"Yes, I have to say it. Coming back into your life at that point, with your intensive school schedule, responsibilities, and social life, would have been an intrusion, especially with Chris in tow. How could I have explained having an eighteen-year-old boyfriend to you, Jules? You believed I was basically a somnambulant, inconsolable shut-in. It was just so complicated, so messy."

"You should have tried!" Jules insisted. "As you stated, I was very mature for my age. You never gave me the chance to understand, to process your so-called messiness."

"You're right, honey. It does sound like I'm making excuses to justify my choices. I selfishly wanted more time for myself to figure out my place and purpose in the world, a reason for living outside of being a husband, a father or a partner at my firm. Being your father means everything to me, Jules, but at that time in my life, as much as you mean to me, well, at the time, I wasn't sure it was enough.

"What I'm trying to say is, I felt like I'd totally failed you and that you were probably better off without me. Jason was always so much stronger than me emotionally. So much better.

"Don't shake your head, Jules. We both know he was practically a fucking saint. Opposites attract, and all that. I know, I know. I wasn't thinking clearly. I was feeling sorry for myself. I know that's why you ultimately left. You hate people feeling sorry for themselves.

"And Chris was outside of us, you and me, my other life. Something similar to what I had with your dad, but its own entirely new entity, just the same. I needed that now that I had lost my role, my identity as Jason's husband. It was something that was all mine. Chris took me out of myself because he was never a part of what made me so broken in the first place.

"Do you understand, sweetheart? Am I making any sense? Or am I making it worse?"

"Yes, I see," Jules answered in a monotone voice. "No, you're not making it worse. I've never held you to an impossible standard of perfection, you or dad. I've always had my share of disappointments, sure, like when you both would choose work over me, but I survived. I knew you both loved me. I came to understand the level of responsibility you had to others."

Charles exhaled appreciatively. He was relieved to know that, fundamentally, Jules understood what he was trying to get across. Still, he was saddened to hear her claim that she had been disappointed by her parents several times over the years.

"We never *chose* our work over you, honey. I hate that you've thought that for so long. We had our adult responsibilities, as you said. Like every parent, you often have to make grown-up sacrifices that inevitably disappoint your kids to make things work and to acquire financial security and such. You were always number one to us. Always!

"Your dad loved you more than the world, Jules, and I love you more than anything. I need you to know that. Sorry, Chris, but well, you know."

Christophe smiled, nodding his head. "It's true, Jules. Your father's always been more concerned with you hating him for thinking he'd replaced your dad with me if you found out about us than with me resenting him for being kept on the down-low. I'm fine with it, really. I'm okay with second place."

"More like a distant third," Jules sneered. Even if she came to accept that what her father had with Christophe was genuine, and that was a big if, it would never be as powerful as the intimacy and connection between her parents. *True love never dies.*

"Very funny," Christophe scoffed.

"*Anyway*," Charles continued, "I realized over time that I'd become smitten with Chris. It was an affection that differed from my feelings for your dad, Jules. Not as strong, nothing could ever be what I felt—*feel*, for your dad, the love of my life, but profound nonetheless. I needed to know if Chris felt the same way about me. The same level, the same depth of emotion.

"I asked him to give up his hooking and let me take care of him, but not as a parent figure. I told Chris I saw him as a man, not a boy, and I wanted him to be mine. He was now eighteen, halfway to nineteen, a man, and I wanted him to start his adult life off right. I told him that while he couldn't move in with me, as I wasn't ready for that, I wanted to buy him a place to get him away from the rat-hole he called home.

"My only other requirement besides separate residences was that I wanted him to commit to me. I wanted him to be my boyfriend. It sounds so corny, saying it out loud, but I wanted him all to myself. Chris, tell Jules what you were thinking at the time. I don't want to overstep or say the wrong thing. Not about this."

Christophe looked openly concerned. He was very intimidated by Jules; in fact, he had always been terrified of getting on her shit list. Christophe dealt with some of the biggest divas in the fashion industry; compared to Jules, who chewed up and spat out anyone who crossed her, they were a cool ocean breeze. Being up close in her world as Denise's boyfriend had given him a front-row seat to the way she eviscerated Phillip daily.

Yes, Christophe felt very intimidated; both he and Charles were walking on eggshells here.

In turn, Jules very much *looked* intimidating, staring Christophe down with her questioning, doubting, distrustful eyes. To say that Jules was dubious of Christophe's motivations was an understatement. That said, she believed in her father's ability to judge a person's character, so she told Christophe she would hear him out.

"Jules, I was totally in love with your father, head over heels in love, almost from the start. I mean, come on! Chuck's intelligent, worldly, sophisticated, and hot as fuck. Now and back then.

"His sadness, his vulnerability? All of it just made him all the more adorable. And the whole age thing was never an issue for me. Sure, your father had money, Jules, and that was a nice bonus, but I had lots of wealthy customers. None of them ever got through my defences the way Chuck did. I kept my true feelings for him close to my chest. It's just what you did in my situation.

"You see, the street kids, the ones who traded sex for money, they were always telling me not to get involved or too nosy. Never ask too many questions or give too many answers. Never reveal my truth or fall in love. Emotions are like treasure, so bury them sort of thing. You don't want them used against you. A pessimistic, sad way of thinking, ya, but a reality.

"Emotions can get you killed in sex work. You get involved, start messing up a client's personal life? They don't want their spouses to find out, or their bosses or their friends. They want an out-of-the-ordinary sexual experience, but an uncomplicated one. You need boundaries. I knew that if I complicated things by trying to make a place for myself in their real-life, I could end up floating face down in Lake Ontario with my head bashed in."

Jules and Charles exchanged knowing looks. They were both aware that Genevieve's final resting place was Lake Ontario because she had become a complication in someone's life.

Christophe, not noticing the slight conspiratorial connection between father and daughter, continued with his story.

"You think some punter who you believe is a terrific guy, treats you like you're special, won't turn on you in a heartbeat? Think again. Closeted men can be dangerous. They're scared, insecure, often ashamed of their authentic sexuality despite whatever bravado or macho veneer they showcase outwardly. If they weren't, they wouldn't live a lie. Sad, but that's our fucked up, repressive society.

"Some guys will do anything to keep their secrets, like beat the hell out of you and leave you bleeding to death in a motel because you said you're in love with them. Or even more stupid— you asked them to leave their spouse for you!

"And maybe they do love you back, but you can't leave the shadows, become the real thing. They can't deal with that severe of a life change. How will people view them, judge them? It's too problematic. It's easier to get rid of you than live authentically.

"Remember, you're just a whore, not a person to them, so they can fuck you or fuck you up and not feel bad about it. Not feel anything at all. You can always be replaced and eventually forgotten.

"So ya, I was nervous about telling Chuck I loved him. I knew he was no closet case, but I also knew he was a little messed up in the head. I wasn't blind or unaware of his issues. He was still dealing with Jason's death, I knew that, but he was a very different man from when we'd first met. I wanted to trust him, but I'd learned not to trust anyone but myself.

"I felt so fucking stuck. I resigned myself to keep doing what I'd always done—stay handy, friendly, interested, but emotionally unavailable. It was the smart thing to do. At least, I was phenomenal at pretending.

"When Chuck revealed his feelings for me, I could have died from happiness. He wanted to change his life to accommodate me, to make a place for me! That was all I needed to hear. Fuck the living arrangement obstacle—that I could work with. He'd promised me more than anything I ever thought I deserved or would ever get. Even if my brain was screaming at me to be cautious, my heart wanted what it wanted."

Christophe pointed at Charles and smiled. Charles blew him a kiss.

Jules rolled her eyes again and sighed loudly. *Not yet. Don't say anything. Soon. Keep it together. Anger is energy. Use it. Focus.*

Charles understood his daughter's annoyance and empathized with her hurt feelings. That didn't mean her constant use of antagonistic, passive-aggressive eye-rolls was not doing his head in. *Jason, my love, if you're listening, give me the strength to deal with our beautiful, intelligent, and oh-so fucking obstinate daughter.*

"So," Charles resumed, taking over from Christophe, "I set him up in an amazing loft downtown on Queen St., near the waterfront. After that, we wasted no time in creating the man the world would come to know as Christophe Bennett."

"Ya, it was time for a change," Christophe laughed ebulliently.

He still had not picked up on any of Jules's pointed, passive-aggressiveness towards him. He honestly thought she was just a bitch by default, and annoyed haughtiness was just how she treated everyone.

"I wanted a new beginning, an updated look, but most of all, I needed a name change. I couldn't use my real one, and I didn't want to, anyway. I've never told anyone except Chuck what my full name is. I have family issues, concerns for my safety, and I don't want them knowing where I am, what I look like. That's my personal shit. Chuck knows all about it, but I'm not getting into any of that with you, Jules, no offence."

Jules smirked. She was part curious, part annoyed, and quite pleased that Christophe had developed a little more backbone regarding confronting her verbally. She respected strength, even from those she did not like, but she would destroy them in an instant if they attempted to use that strength against her.

"Christophe, I couldn't care less about your narcissism, your convoluted history or fucked up family drama. I promised my father attentiveness, not interest, and that only goes so far. Continue, but your tale of transformation better be brief. If I wanted to learn about the trials and tribulations of underage prostitutes, I'd watch the fucking Documentary Chanel. At least then I'd have a bowl of buttered popcorn to sustain me through the tedious parts."

"Oh, Jules, for Pete's sake!" Charles cried out.

"Fine," Christophe grumbled. "I'd run away at a very young age. I changed my look immediately into an Emo boy to disguise myself, in case people came looking for me, distributed pics of me as a kid to the cops. At eighteen, I was pretty sure they wouldn't know what I looked like anymore. But even as an adult, I couldn't risk them recognizing me and complicating my life.

"Over the whole Emo-thing, I went back to my natural look, with some improvements. I got my hair done professionally and got my teeth fixed. I've always known that I was good-looking, but I got the small bump on the bridge of my nose removed anyway. Chuck bought me amazing designer clothes. He was right when he said earlier that I was hiding my looks behind my Emo-boy persona. It was an intentional disguise, although I liked the aesthetic."

Jules coughed loudly and waved her hands around manically, creating an unnatural but necessary break in Christophe's verbose recount of his life makeover. She did not want to hear about it anymore. Jules was over patiently waiting for the answers to all her questions.

She wanted to know how her father could be in a long-term, intimate relationship without ever telling her. Why was he still hiding it after so many years? Jules understood it had nothing to do with Denise; her relationship with Christophe was not that old. What possible reason could her father have that explained why he was still with a man who was now also Denise's very public boyfriend? It made no damn sense to her.

Jules did not want to accept that the only other viable possibility was that it had always been about her. She feared the ugly truth: her father was so afraid of her reaction to a new love in his life that he made himself live a relationship in secret for fear she would reject him. What did that say about how he saw her? Or about the kind of power she had over him?

What? Did he think she believed he was a celibate monk? Jules had always assumed he had lovers, even though she hated the thought of her father being with anyone but her dad. She never pried or inserted herself into his private life outside of their relationship as father/daughter and business partners. Charles never brought anything personal up in conversation, himself.

And now Jules understood why. She had always thought she was doing the right thing by respecting her father's privacy; after all, she never felt the need to tell him about what Jacques meant to her. But did he think so little of her? That she was that inflexible? Jules felt insulted.

Despite their closeness, their bond, Jules and her father were not exactly friends, not in any conventional sense of the word; they did not hang out like buddies. Charles was Jules's mentor and main confidant when she needed one. He was more than her father, for sure, but Charles was not her BFF.

Jacques was the closest thing Jules had to a best friend. What spare time she had she tried to spend with him. Unfortunately, Jules was also in love with him—and he had a wife, so that very much complicated their friendship. Surprisingly, she now had Amanda back in her life to add to her stable of friends; it was a small stable.

"Stop, no more!" Jules barked. "Honestly, this vapid editorializing! Christophe, I don't care about your fucking makeover or your family drama. I can guess the rest. Despite this secret that my father has somehow successfully kept from me for years, I know him, and I know what he's capable of. You wanted to become a professional model, have a new life. Let's see now—hmmm."

"Jules!" Charles suspected his daughter was about to let Christophe have it, and he feared he was incapable of preventing it. Giving Jules a stern look, he walked over to stand next to Christophe, who remained seated on the couch, frozen in place. Charles felt the need to at least attempt to curtail her oncoming hostile, condescending verbal attack. At least, he hoped it was only verbal.

"He's a big boy, Pops. He can take it. All the cards on the table now, and all that, eh?"

"Hit me with your best shot, Jules," Christophe invited.

His words were mostly bluster and bravura, for Christophe was not sure he could take it. He was no fool. Jules was a formidable opponent. He had seen her sling mud like no one else and read a bitch to filth—and tears—in under a minute. He recalled Denise telling him that just last night, Jules had brought Marie Bergé to tears. Upset her so much she left the party and never came back.

But Christophe was not about to let Jules make him look like a little bitch in front of his guy. He was not ashamed of his relationship with Charles, and even if he was more than a tad afraid of Jules, he was not going to back down.

"As I was saying, *Chris*, you're good-looking, I'll give you that. A little generic for my taste, mind you, but I guess I get what the fuss is all about. You're tall, fit, poised. Whatever." Jules mimed a mocking yawn.

"I bet you liked playing dress-up with your sister's dolls, mixing and matching their polyester skirts with a variety of tops and shoes. You voraciously read the Vogue and Cosmo magazines that your white trash mommy stole from the local Walmart. All in secret, of course, because everybody wanted you to play football, bully fat kids, and not be a sissy.

"Eventually, you ran away to the big city with dreams of being the next, oh, I don't know, Boyd Holbrook? My father called in a few favours and created a brand new legal, public persona for you. A no plot holes history that would stand up under any scrutiny. My father is very good at what he does, and I'm sure he was behind the contract you got with your first modelling agency. The rest, as they say, is history. See, Pops, I didn't attack him."

"Not by your usual standards, no, but you were certainly trying to demean him."

"True. Pops, tell me why you kept this relationship a secret, especially from me? I get that, at first, you had your reasons, reasons you believed had merit. I'll even allow for a few more years, say if you wanted to wait until I finished school, but make me understand your choices beyond that!

"When I came back to you, after law school, now an adult, you acted like I had to pull teeth to get you to react to me. But you were already better! You played me, lied to me, wasted my time, so ya, I feel a little sore about it."

"Because I thought you'd hate me!" Charles bellowed. "For thinking I'd forgotten your dad, which I didn't! I never could! But I thought you'd think I was trying to replace him. That's it. It's that simple, and I hear how stupid it sounds now. The longer it went on, the longer I hid it, the less I wanted to rock the boat. Fear is a horrible thing.

"Chris wanted me to tell you, tell everyone. I don't give two shits what anyone else thinks, so I have no problem telling the world, but I couldn't risk losing you if you didn't see it my way. How could I risk it?"

"I could never hate you, Pops," Jules vigorously stated. "I can't believe you'd ever think that. Even at your worst, even when I chose to leave, I never hated you. I didn't feel like I was abandoning you at the time, just giving us both space to deal or not to, in your case, with dad's death. Today, I've learned just how badly it affected you, and that's my sin to atone for. I never hated you for abandoning me emotionally.

"Did it disappoint me? Yes, especially your self-pity, but I was still a teenager, emancipated or not—a kid! I was selfish, like a teenager is supposed to be. I was mature for my age, sure, and I made a bad situation work for me, but I never looked down on you. I believed you'd snap out of it eventually, with or without me. I adapted. It's what I do. Did you think you'd live this way forever? That I'd never find out?"

"Honestly, I tried not to think about it," Charles shamefully admitted. "It was working, after all, and when I did think about it, I kinda prided myself on how good I was at crafting the whole thing. Ego, eh?

"Chris's notoriety as a sexually fluid Lothario helped take the pressure off him to own a committed relationship—until Denise, but that isn't real. No one ever questioned me, the long-suffering widower, about my love life, including you."

Jules looked Christophe up and down. "Sexually fluid, huh?"

Christophe was the one rolling his eyes now. "Yes, I've had sex with men and women, but my core sexuality, if I must define it for you, is gay. Publically, I'm gender non-bias because it enhances my international appeal, creates mystery. Fantasy is my business. Sex, to me, is a commodity, a skill, a way to get things in life, to have power over people.

"In my past, I've fucked women, like Denise, if I needed something from them, but there's no real attraction, no desire. It's mechanical, and I'm a damn fine mechanic. I have to rely on my face, my body, and my sensuality. It's what I know. I'm not as educated or as clever as people like you and your father."

"Big news, tear out the front page," Jules sarcastically quipped.

"I get the *Golden Girls* reference, bitch," Christophe retorted, annoyed. "I may not have the kind of intellect or quick-wit you have, but I've learned how to influence people and get what I want through sex. I learned a lot from being a whore. We all use what talents we possess to the best of our abilities, often just to survive in this world. Your father accepts me for who I am, all that I am, and vice-versa."

"I do, babe, but don't call my daughter a bitch. And Jules? Please don't disparage Chris's intelligence."

"Right, Pops, my bad, because he knows how to use big words like dysphoria and cocksucker and understands the purpose and power of an adjective. Like in the sentence, 'That fucking dysphoric cocksucker!' Your boyfriend is the next David Suzuki, obviously."

"Jules, you're acting rude and being unnecessarily mean. It's an ugly look on you. Chris hasn't done anything to you. I know you're hurting and mad, but take it out on me, not him."

"How chivalric!" Jules roared. "This is a love story for the ages. The high-powered attorney lost to despair, and the teenage prostitute with a mysterious past who restores the broken man's faith in love. Somebody call Lifetime because the script is writing itself. Paul Gross can play you, Pops, and there has to be an actor on one of those *Degrassi High* shows interested in stretching their range—among other things—to play Christophe.

"You know, Pops, I'm convinced dad is looking down from the after-wherever approvingly with bated breath for the inevitable Christmas-movie sequel."

The sarcasm dripped acerbically off Jules's tongue. There was no way she could bring herself to see Christophe as worthy of her father's affections. She could not understand how her father could love any man who was not her dad—insurmountable physical separation be damned! *This whole thing is ridiculous!*

"I like to think he is," Charles quietly stated. "Approving. Your dad was the nice one between the three of us, sweetie. He saw the good in people, their value, outside of what they did for a living or how much money they had. He saw hearts and deeds and gave everyone the benefit of the doubt. He was loath to judge, to be mistrustful or suspicious. We need to be a little more like him."

Jules glared at her father with hurt in her eyes.

"You say you're trying to understand me. Can't you do the same for Chris? Give him a chance, Jules. Please."

"First, I'm not a snob, and I resent the insinuation that I am! Second, you know better than anyone why I am the way I am. I don't trust anyone but myself and you."

Jules trusted Jacques, too, but she deliberately kept him out of the conversation.

"Yes, Pops, I still trust you, even after this secret, this betrayal of trust—because that's what it is, a betrayal. You've spent years hiding this and lying to my face. It's just because someone outed you two that we're here now doing this."

"Honey, I said I—"

But Jules cut her father off before he could get another word out. "And you!" she said accusingly, once more turning her attention back to Christophe. "You expect me to run into your arms and welcome you into my family? You're Denise's boyfriend! Explain that one to me first, you vapid, morally questionable, passed-around fuck-boy!"

"Morally questionable!" Christophe cried out, deeply offended.

That had done it. That was the straw that broke the camel's back. Christophe was pissed off, fed up with Jules's judgmental, verbally abusive behaviour towards him. He did not particularly like the nasty names she had called him, but her questioning his moral fibre stung. Stiffening his resolve, Christophe prepared to launch into a tirade of the most abusive language he could quickly think up on the spot to haul back at her.

However, Charles was faster on the draw and spoke first.

The older, more even-tempered man was afraid the discussion had finally reached a breaking point. Things were about to be said in anger that neither one of the two younger people could ever take back or apologize enough for later. Charles had experience with burned bridges and harboured life-long resentments, and he would not recommend them to anyone.

He spoke up for Christophe on his behalf, whether he wanted him to do it or not.

Charles elucidated the facts concerning the relationship between Christophe and Denise in a series of clear, concise, articulate, and expletive free sentences. He made sure Jules understood that Denise had been nothing more than a reconnaissance mission and how she meant nothing to Christophe. And, with his complete knowledge and approval, Christophe had been doing it all for her.

Charles wanted to tell Jules how much of an ungrateful cow she was being, but she was still his daughter, so he kept that opinion to himself.

"I never asked for his interference," Jules asserted. "I never asked you to seek outside assistance. And if Denise or Stella had discovered his true motives? Christophe could have ruined everything! What were you thinking? And what, I'm supposed to be grateful?"

Charles stifled an involuntary chuckle. *Grateful? Funny that you should use that word. Boy, do I know my daughter.*

"Yes, Jules, you should be. I didn't ask him to get involved either, but sometimes the people who love us want to help entirely of their own accord. I told Chris just enough without getting into the nitty-gritty. He relayed things to me, like what the Cartells said in private when we weren't around. He kept tabs on them. Tomorrow he'll end things with Denise."

"Trust me, it's over," Christophe stated. "She kicked me in the nuts this afternoon."

"There, you see, Jules, it all worked out. No harm, no foul."

"Except for Christophe's nuts," Jules sneered.

"Both of you are acting like children fighting over nothing," Charles stated emphatically. "Fighting over me? There's enough of me for you both. Chris never once asked me to suppress my love for or disregard my memories of your dad to be with him, Jules, and I never would! He wanted to be an active part of your life. I was the problem. Chris is an amazing man, honey, and much more than the public persona you've only known."

"So, you trust him, Pops? The two of you are committed to one another?"

Jules had a reason for asking this. It was finally time to reveal what she had discovered months ago about Christophe, something she believed her father was unaware of. Jules did not want to hurt him with this information, but she had to put all her cards on the table, clear out all the skeletons from the closet.

"Completely," Charles stated emphatically.

"Interesting. So, Christophe, the whole Denise thing is *apparently* just a performance my father turns a blind eye to? I see. Would you also care to explain why you're currently fucking my company's CTO?"

Christophe's face went white as a ghost.

"Yes, it's a 'gotcha' moment. I make it a practice to know as much as possible about those in my employ. Those I've placed in positions of power, at least. And Miles Chen isn't just my CTO, Christophe. He's my protégé. I have a vested interest in his loyalty, decision-making ability, and his potential for creating problems for me."

"Jules, it's fine," Charles asserted.

"No, it most certainly is not!" she objected loudly.

Charles took Christophe's hand, held it tight, and looked into the young man's eyes lovingly, with no judgment. "Chris doesn't owe you an explanation for that, Jules. It's none of your business."

"What! Are you kidding me, Pops? Suddenly something is off-limits? Have you lost your damn mind?!"

"No, it's okay, Chuck," Christophe voiced gently. "We said we'd tell her everything. She doesn't have to understand or approve. It's not essential to building a relationship with me, and she'd probably find out anyway. She's remarkably good at keeping tabs on people! Especially now that she has—what was that term? Right, a *vested interest* in protecting you from being hurt by me.

"Something we glossed over earlier, Jules, is my response to your father's requests of me. I did agree to both—with a stipulation to one. I stopped hooking, but I choose not to practice sexual monogamy."

"Oh no," Jules moaned. "Pops, please don't tell me you two have an open relationship."

"No, we don't have an open relationship," Charles quickly answered. "At least not emotionally."

"That's what an open relationship is, for fuck's sake! Both parties screw outside of the relationship or the marriage or the *so-called* commitment. Eventually, someone always gets hurt. It's not sustainable or respectful. I need a fucking drink."

"What Chuck is trying to say is that I'm committed to him and only him. Emotionally, your father has my heart exclusively. I'm in love with only him, but I have a strong sex drive and like to fuck hot guys. It's not a reflection on my attraction or my commitment to your father. I don't see these guys I hook up with as anything more than human sex toys. Miles is recreational, nothing more."

Jules snickered loudly. "That's not dehumanizing at all," she criticized.

"That's not my intent!" Christophe barked back. "It's just not emotionally connective. I'm always very open and upfront that I can't commit emotionally to any of them. Or have any desire to. They don't need to know why, and if they don't like it or start to get too attached, I break away immediately. I don't owe anyone justifications for my feelings. I'm on PrEP."

"These things are always messy," Jules voiced. "Pops, how can you be with someone who can shunt you out of his thoughts to get his dick wet with some random? Place you on a shelf in the back of his mind until you're no longer a distraction? How is that cherishing or respecting my father's love, Christophe? Are you really okay with this, Pops?"

Christophe remained silent, his face red, unsure if he felt angry at being judged harshly—or ashamed for a possible truth brought out in the open.

Charles shrugged. "I can't be with your dad, Jules, and I don't want anyone but Chris romantically or sexually. I choose not to stand in the way of his choices as long as it's not drugs or anything illegal. He's always accepted me even with the baggage I brought into this relationship, the secrets, the proclamations of necessary confidentiality and concealment. He loves me without question, without judgment. How can I not accept him for who he is?"

"Well then, I guess we've said all that's needed to be said," Jules huffed, "and we'll have to agree to disagree on this. People shouldn't invite trouble into their relationship. You say your behaviour isn't a negative reflection regarding your feelings towards my father, Christophe? I think it is, but you guys do what you want. This thing with Miles ends today, though. It's too close to home for my comfort level."

"Fine," Christophe agreed. "I'm not here to make trouble for your dad, Jules. Or you."

"We'll see. I'm keeping my eye on you. It's painfully obvious my father trusts you, and Jacques, whose opinion I value highly, seems to like you, so that's something, I guess."

"I'll take it," Christophe grinned. "It's a start."

Jules cocked her eye at him. "Yes, a start," she said flatly. Picking up the attaché case with the prized documents inside, she left her father's home.

"Wow," Charles snickered, "that went better than I thought it would!"

"It did?" Christophe asked incredulously, thankful they were finally alone again.

"Absolutely! I was certain she was going to punch you in the face at some point before she left."

XIX

Nazneen checked the time on her phone as she strolled around the roof, taking in the new additions to Jules's botanical menagerie.

Created exclusively for use by Jules and all of her top executives, Cartell Tower's urban rooftop garden was breathtaking. It was a convenient, private retreat from both the muggy, summertime city streets and the enclosed, air-conditioned interior of the concrete building.

Jules took pride in letting people know that she had skillfully designed the area herself. She had discovered and then controlled the perfect balance of placidity between the rushing winds and the humid stillness that hung in the air.

The various water features frequently emitted sprays of mist that cooled and soothed. The greenery ranged in size and shape and aided in controlling the breeze on a windy day from ruining the tranquil scene with the occasional cyclonic intrusion.

From groundcovers to shrubs, every plant and tree that went into the design, including Kousa dogwoods, Dwarf Hinoki cypresses, daylilies, and climbing hydrangea, had been selected by Jules.

However, Jules did not create the garden solely to appreciate the beauty and zen-like quality it provided; she was a practical woman and liked the science behind it. She was all about reducing the overall heat absorption of the building, which would then reduce energy consumption. Jules appreciated a pretty face as much as the next person; still, she required substance and value behind any comely veneer.

During the planning stage, Phillip had suggested adding lavender to the mix. Faking enthusiasm, Jules had heartily agreed, letting him think she valued and respected his opinions. At the last minute, however, she deviously swapped it out with Japanese Wisteria, providing her with another opportunity to disappoint and annoy her husband.

As she walked among the fragrant blooms and pleasant greenery, Nazneen reminisced about the many things Jules had done to humiliate and belittle others. In Phillip's case, downright degrading them. Among those many memories? The time Phillip had nearly cried when Jules mocked and ridiculed him during the inaugural tour of the urban garden for publicly questioning her about the omission of his lavender.

As sunset fast approached, Nazneen marvelled at how the golds and violets gradually took over the sky from the receding light blue and grey hues. Though she had come up to the roof garden for a specific reason that had nothing to do with botanical appreciation, she craved the solitude it provided. It was a place to think, find solace, direction; sadly, the pretty vista and tranquillity of the space did little to alleviate her anxiety.

Wracked with guilt for what she had done, Nazneen's mind was awash with dark thoughts, shame, and the fear of exposure. She felt conflicted. Nazneen did not hate Jules; it was never as simple as that. She certainly did not like her, but she had never wanted to see her physically injured. That was not what she had signed on for.

Everything was meant as a game, to annoy Jules, to mess with her head, get a little payback, petty or not, but things had taken a turn for the sinister. The level of betrayal being asked of her now was something Nazneen could not justify. This was no longer a game of harmless revenge against an uncompromising, impossible-to-please employer. It had to stop; at least, her involvement did.

Jules paid Nazneen well, a wage far higher than any other executive assistant at Cartell Worldwide. Nazneen appreciated the salary, but she still regarded Jules as a horror to work for, a boss who demanded perfection without fail. Though occasionally praised for her excellent work ethic, Nazneen felt Jules's commendations lacked heartfelt emotion. The expectation was that everyone should be going above and beyond in their duties at all times anyway.

Nazneen had worked for Cartell Worldwide for nearly two years, Jules's only executive assistant to last beyond the three-month probationary period. To say Jules was difficult, hard to work for was the understatement of the century; Nazneen's work/life balance was out of whack.

It was one thing to understand intellectually, that Jules only demanded what she gave of herself, and Nazneen got that, but emotionally she was defeated. She had grown more bitter over time, realizing that nothing she did would ever be good enough for Jules.

That bitterness had eventually got the better of Nazneen.

He had gotten the better of her, too.

"Hello, Luv."

At the sound of his voice, Nazneen turned around to greet the very man that had sent her down this dark, dishonest path. She had been expecting him. He stood behind her, smiling seductively. Nazneen was unsurprised that he had made it up to the private retreat without difficulty; she had willingly given him her access codes some time ago.

Nazneen was not a top executive, but she had some privileges, such as access to the roof garden. As Jules's executive assistant, she was the only exception to the rule.

Nazneen had always thought it was a kindness bestowed upon her for excellent work until she one day overheard Jules tell the real reason to Miles. The preferential treatment was so Nazneen could bring Jules a green tea Frappuccino directly when she was up on the roof, taking a rare moment to relax. It had nothing to do with rewarding good work.

Everything was always about Jules's convenience.

Nazneen's bitterness and growing resentment towards Jules had made her vulnerable to manipulation. It was that vulnerability that he had taken advantage of with his intellect, charisma, and, especially, his body.

When first approached by him six months back, in a bar just a block from Cartell Tower, Nazneen had been instantly taken in by his looks and charm. She had just finished another frustrating workday in a series of seemingly unending frustrating workdays. Somehow, like magic, he had managed to not only pick up on the origin of her shitty mood but knew exactly how to take her completely out of it.

He was unlike any man who had tried to hit on her before, saying all the right things to make Nazneen feel better, feel special. It was seduction without sleaziness or arrogance or cheap pick-up lines. His approach was masterful.

After an hour of flirtatious conversation, which included a thoughtful discussion of her Parsi heritage, they had gone back to her apartment to share a lot more than a bottle of whiskey.

When he later revealed that their meet-up was not by chance, Nazneen was anything but hurt. She had not felt used or betrayed but instead felt a conspiratorial bond in that moment of revelation. She felt completely understood. Of course, he knew the right way to approach her and gain her interest. Of course, he got her frustrations. He knew what it meant to have Jules affect one's life.

Nazneen had listened to his pitch with a great deal of interest. His sweet words, his charm, and his powerful, magnetic presence had hypnotized her into giving him exactly what he wanted from her: information and access.

It was supposed to have been a short-term thing. Just some pranks, a game. But their partnership turned into weeks of espionage and information gathering, finally culminating in the explosive event in Jules's office.

Nazneen was abhorred by what she had done. What was in the package she had delivered to Jules on his behalf was nothing short of a reckless, dangerous stunt. It was way over the top and not the harmless mental mind-fuck Nazneen had expected. These games had to stop. Nazneen planned on putting an end to it.

She had called him to meet. The rooftop garden was his suggestion because of its level of privacy and infrequent use after work hours.

Meeting at the tower put her in a risky situation again. Nazneen would have to distract the guards in the security room, get them out, and get herself in to erase the camera footage of him, including his entering and leaving the building.

Nazneen had expressed her fear and concern to him about meeting at Cartell Tower. If she was not supremely careful and lucky, her involvement could be exposed. She would definitely get fired and possibly charged with criminal mischief. She did not know all the things Jules might do to her, and she was not interested in finding out.

When he could not have sounded more indifferent to her plight over the phone, Nazneen realized once again how big a mistake getting involved with him was.

She was unbelievably thankful both Jules and Phillip had left for the day, preoccupied with Charles's drama.

Nazneen did find something odd, though. Denise had shown up quite unexpectedly, disappearing into Phillip's office for a short time. But Nazneen had minded her own business. It was in her best interest never to question a Cartell about their comings and goings.

Now, all the Cartells were gone, and Nazneen was alone up on the roof. Alone with him.

"Mr. Falsworth."

"So it's Mr. Falsworth, now, Nazneen? Well, I can work with that. It'll sound just as good as William when you're screaming it aloud as I'm fucking you over that bench there."

"No! No more of that! I'm out, and you need to leave me alone. You've taken it too far this time. There was a fucking bomb in that box! A bomb! That's terrorist-level shit. Are you insane?"

"I have to say this is a surprise and a tad disappointing. I thought I was clear, Miss Balakrishna, when I said that the stipulation of you playing this game with me is that I make the rules. There is no out unless I say so."

"I don't give a flying fuck what you say!" Nazneen roared. "And screw any threats of exposure. I'll make sure Jules and the authorities know everything I did was under duress, under threat of violence to me, my family. I can lie very convincingly, as you've discovered. Jules will believe me over you in a heartbeat. From what I gleaned from her expression and response to receiving that package, she knows just how crazy you are!

"I'm out. Just accept it and stop whatever else you've got planned. It's over. I'll be changing all my codes and passwords the moment you leave this building."

William moved closer to Nazneen, doing so in a way that appeared wholly casual and non-threatening. He asked her to reconsider her decision, promising her that he had meant no harm. It was just a game to him, nothing more, and he apologized for going too far with the theatrics. It was all deception, all guile. William lied through his teeth, claiming it was just a childish prank that had crossed a line due to his technological ignorance.

Gradually, he inched closer and closer toward Nazneen.

"It doesn't matter. Stop playing these games, and leave Jules alone. I'm warning you! I regret ever letting you into my life. Damn you and your British charm for manipulating me, for getting me to do any of this!"

"You didn't seem so manipulated when you willingly spread for me, your legs in the air, Luv."

"Fine, yes. I guess I have only myself to blame for being so gullible, so weak."

"So that's it then, you're done with me, with all this?" William asked, now barely a meter away from Nazneen.

"Yes! Go away and leave me alone!" Nazneen turned away from William.

That particular dismissive act infuriated him.

"Don't turn away from me, you fucking bitch! Not like she did to my brother! Not to me!"

With lightning speed, William turned Nazneen back around and viciously punched her in the stomach. Instinctively, she bent forward, clutched her gut, and wailed in response to the unexpected pain.

But William was not done. He hauled off and knocked her down to the ground. This second punch was so severe William was convinced part of Nazneen's skull cracked against his bare knuckles. He smiled at the thought of it.

Rendered nearly incapacitated from the two powerful blows but still conscious, Nazneen meekly called out for help, but her words were slurred and incoherent. Her plea for salvation was ultimately pointless; no one was around except the two of them.

Grabbing Nazneen by both arms, William dragged her over to the East facing side of the building.

Her arms immobilized, Nazneen tried kicking herself free. Unfortunately, her legs flailed about uselessly. All her disorganized, feeble attempt at escape did was cause her to lose one of her moderately priced shoes. It flew off her foot, landing in the Koi pond.

"No bitch tells me what to do," William muttered under his breath. "I make the rules! Me!"

When he reached his desired location, William lifted Nazneen, raising her small, listless body high above his head. When he was sure he could make it past the metal guard rail, he threw her over the side of the building with extreme force.

As Nazneen plummeted downward, torrents of air beat against her already battered body. As she reached ever closer to the ground, the intense slapping of wind in her face eventually roused her to the point where she understood her dire situation. Nazneen tried to scream but was unable to utter even a yelp, too terrified of the fatal inevitability of her doomed future.

Nazneen's body landed with a bloody splat on the black and grey asphalt of the narrow alleyway that separated the Cartell building from the large but significantly less impressive one next to it.

William immediately called Yasmine and explained that their inside person at Cartell Worldwide was no longer available for exploitation.

"No, not Denise. Our original pawn. Poor, unfortunate Miss Balakrishna took a long trip from which she won't be returning. I guess I let my temper and impetuousness get the better of me. No matter, I got what I wanted from her."

William placed Nazneen's purse at the base of the wall she had been thrown from. Next, he walked over to the pond, fished her single shoe out of the water, brought it to the ledge, and placed it strategically on its side, near the handbag.

Yasmine was still yammering in his ear.

"Yes, I disabled the damn security feed. Stop mothering me! It's bloody annoying. Thanks to that pathetic cow, Denise, I was never here. It's the tallest building in the city, and Jules made sure no one, not unless they were in a helicopter, could photograph or video this platform. It's dark enough now, anyway, and I've created some theatre here to infer a story. It's fine. If not? I don't give a toss.

"Frankly, I'm getting bored and impatient. I'm moving up our timetable. We have control of the building, and it's time to finish what I started years ago. I want that bitch and her father dead. Charles is back in town. Tomorrow, yes, before the Silver Dagger complicates things further."

William stood up on the ledge, balanced himself, and peered over the side of the building. Squinting, he focused with laser-like intensity to see what he could of the corpse below. He marvelled at the kaleidoscope of colours and textures the mangled body had created all over the urban canvas.

Unable to see his work in the kind of detail he would have preferred due to his severe vantage point, William still considered it a thing of beauty.

"You really ought to see the view from here, Yasmine. It's bloody fabulous."

The moon hung heavy in the sky over Jules and Phillip's mansion.

Tired, Jackson planned on retiring to his bedroom in the basement as soon as he finished the one task he had left to do. Taking the last of the cutlery out of the dishwasher, he placed it carefully back inside the heavy mahogany wood, velvet-lined flatware case. He gave each piece considerable care and reverence. It was Stella's designer flatware, after all.

Jackson placed the case back into its assigned drawer in the large, rather oppressive-looking antique French china cabinet. It was made from figured French walnut and had been carefully refinished by a master woodworker. This piece was yet another of Stella's interloping antique monstrosities.

Denise and Stella were the only family members who supped at the house that evening, both women arriving home at a late hour. No one had called or texted Jackson to say they were running late or not dining at home. The chef, refusing to work overtime, had left Jackson to prepare dinner himself.

It was not unheard of for entire meals to occasionally wind up in the trash wholly uneaten. Jackson hated the waste but was used to the erratic, unappreciative behaviour of the Cartells.

After serving the meal, Jackson had remained in the background, spying, listening in on the conversation between mother and daughter. Having seen the news footage concerning Charles and Christophe, he was dying to know more.

Throughout the entire awkward dinner, Stella had appeared entirely unfazed by the scandalous revelations. She had openly admonished her daughter for her complete lack of awareness and ridiculous naivety.

Immediately after dessert, both women had eagerly separated from one another, withdrawing to their separate quarters.

When Phillip finally arrived home, Jackson had kept out of his way but watched as the man staggered through the front doorway, tripped over his own feet, and fell on his ass. Eventually managing to pick himself up, Phillip shuffled down the hallway towards the front living room, planted himself clumsily on one of the sofas, and quickly passed out.

Even from his hidden position, Jackson had smelled the reek of alcohol radiating off Phillip's skin and clothing.

Just that morning, the front living room was the site of disarray and chaos. Now the whole area had been cleaned up, repaired, and returned to its original state as if nothing had happened.

Satisfied that his chores were complete, Jackson began the trek to his room. At the sound of shattering glass, he paused, terrified that the perpetrators of the break-in had returned. Jackson's paralyzing fear quickly morphed into blatant annoyance when he heard Phillip's foul-mouthed whining.

"Of course, now he's awake when I want to go to bed," Jackson whispered to himself, irritated. "Wrecking the place in one of his drunken bouts."

Cautiously, Jackson walked back through the kitchen and down the main hallway. He eventually found himself in the front room where Phillip had previously been unconscious on the sofa but was now quite animated. The broken remains of several wine glasses littered the wood floor.

Another wine glass was thrown at the wall, a measure from where Jackson stood. This time, Phillip aimed at a large, framed art piece, and as the high-quality crystal slammed against the UV coated glass, it shattered loudly into dozens of shards that crashed to the floor.

"Sir, are you alright? Is there anything I can do?" *Aside from getting cut to ribbons by flying glass, you drunken idiot!*

"Wha?" Phillip turned towards the direction of Jackson's voice. As he did, he lost his balance, falling back onto the sofa.

Jackson noticed the near-empty bottle of Jackson-Triggs Delaine Cabernet Merlot in Phillip's left hand. He grasped it like it was the last bottle of water in the middle of the Sahara. Jackson also noted the empty bottle of Shiraz on the floor.

"Sir, let me help you to bed." Jackson attempted to lift Phillip off the sofa and get him on his feet. "Lean on me, sir. Let's put the bottle down. Please, sir, work with me here." Phillip was completely unhelpful; he was nothing but dead weight. "Sir, you're too heavy. You're dragging us both down!"

"Let go of him, Jackson. Let him fall."

Like a thief in the night, Stella appeared from the shadows. Again, she crisply instructed Jackson to disentangle himself from Phillip's lumbering body.

Jackson did as Stella ordered.

"Let him sleep it off here, on the floor. Just go to bed, Jackson. I'll deal with my son in the morning."

XX

The picture Jules held in her hand was a copy of the one stuck up in the corner of her large bedroom mirror. She had placed this copy in a small, thin black metal frame with white linen matting and kept it on the left side of her work desk.

As she continued holding the photograph close to her face, Jules did not feel the usual sense of loss and sadness. Staring down lovingly at the big, toothy smile on her dad's face, an almost imperceptible grin emerged across her own in response to the memory. She felt proud of herself, having done what was necessary to avenge him, and it was almost over.

Hurt and loss were not the only feelings this image produced, just the most prevalent ones. There was love, of course, and the photo also gave Jules courage and fortitude.

The photo was a reminder of why she forced herself to endure countless nights lying next to her husband. The image stimulated her hatred, evoked the importance of her mission, and gave her the strength needed to channel her rage into overcoming her disgust of Phillip. Every time Jules felt sickened by his skin, smell, his heat so close to her, she endured.

Had endured. Jules was done with that, finally.

On the night she discovered Phillip's crime, Jules had vowed to make him suffer for what he had done to her family. She wanted his punishment to be full of torment and stretched out over time. Jules wanted—no, *needed* him to die inside, day after day until the time came to plunge the metaphorical dagger straight into his heart.

Phillip deserved emotional torture, and Jules had to be the one to enact it, no one else. He had to want her, love her every hour of every day, and continuously be rebuked by her.

And she had kept true to her word, becoming forbidden fruit to him. To Jules's delight, it had driven Phillip, a hopeless romantic, steadfast to fidelity, nearly insane.

It was deliberate emotional and psychological warfare. Phillip's every kind, loving word, spoken aloud or whispered into Jules's ear? Treated like a poisoned arrow, deftly deflected by her with pugnaciousness and contempt. Every gentle, probing, and lustful touch? Rejected outright with hostile disgust.

Well, except for the previous night's embrace, but that did not count. That had been a calculated move, a feint made necessary by Amanda's unexpected intrusion. It was not a moment of actual emotional weakness on her part. And Jules had already rectified that situation.

From the beginning, Jules needed Phillip to continue desiring her despite her outward bullying behaviour and dismissive attitude towards him. Her plan to make him suffer over an extended period might not have worked otherwise.

Despite her loathing of him, Jules occasionally teased Phillip, riled him up, drew him in with her looks and sensuality. Just enough to give him hope that she might come back to him, that she would finally return his undying love.

Taking control of the company legally, not just in spirit, had been more about punishing Joseph and Stella than hurting Phillip. Jules wanted him to lose much more than money, power, and prestige. Death was too good for him. Framing him for something terrible he had not done only to watch him rot the rest of his days in prison was also too good for him. Jules wanted Phillip to lose something more—more than his freedom or his very life.

Jules wanted Phillip to suffer in the same way her family had suffered. A loss for a loss, and it had to be significant.

Recently, Jules realized she could not break Phillip any further doing her usual shtick. He had become almost numb to her vitriolic behaviour, especially with his excessive self-medicating with alcohol. That conclusion had been the impetus for finally getting the information from Mr. Comstock she had been sitting on for ages.

The time had come to strike the final, devastating blow against Phillip and his family.

The sun's rays burst through the large bedroom window, signalling that morning had come; in fact, sunrise had been several hours earlier. A cascade of illumination swarmed the bed with abandon. The drawn curtains had remained open and unfurled since the maid serviced the room the previous day.

The teeming warmth embraced Phillip's body, comforting and soothing it with its inviting heat. The intense brightness attacking his closed eyes, however, roused him from his slumber. Groaning, Phillip immediately brought his hand up to his aching forehead; he was brutally hungover.

"Jules? Jules, we have to get up. That meeting we—oh my head!" Phillip reached across the bed, his eyes still adjusting to the morning light, and felt for his wife. Sadly, all he encountered were sheets. "Jules?"

Silence.

No water was running in the ensuite bathroom from either the shower or the faucet that would have informed him his wife was in there, simply unable to hear him. Or just plain ignoring him, which would have been more her style.

Phillip shook his head vigorously back and forth in an attempt to pull himself together and get his faculties aligned. He quickly realized he was still fully dressed in the previous day's clothes, now booze-soaked and pungent. However, he did not remember coming home, making it up the stairs or getting into his bed.

"Geez, that light!" Phillip closed the curtains and allowed the darkness to ease his suffering. His headache demanded pills. He remembered that there were some in a bathroom drawer.

But what else could he recall? Phillip tried hard to think, tried to focus past the dull ache in his head, and although his memories were still a bit murky, he was able to recollect a few things.

He remembered a text from his wife had come to him at some point in the evening. He was sure he was at a bar when he had received it. The text mentioned an important, must attend, no questions asked meeting in the morning in Jules's office. She would explain everything to him then.

Drunk at the time, Phillip did not have the awareness to think much about it. Now he assumed the meeting was most likely about the mess Charles had brought down on them and the subsequent damage control needed in the wake of it.

But why was Jules not in bed with him? *What time is it anyway? Maybe she's already up and downstairs. Or left for work without me, most likely.*

Looking more carefully at the side of the bed where Jules slept, Phillip saw that it was barely disturbed. Only his side looked slept in; in actuality, it was a total disaster and in desperate need of cleaning. There were traces of dried vomit on his pillow and on the floor. It became very apparent to Phillip that his wife had not slept in their bed last night at all. And by the looks of things, he did not blame her.

But was that the reason he was alone?

Phillip was very aware that his wife had been spending a considerable amount of time in recent weeks sleeping at the downtown condo, away from him. *She doesn't want to be near me because I disgust her. I can't go on like this. I have to talk to Jules, make her understand. Make her — I don't know. Tell her how I feel. Tell her I'll change, make everything like it was!*

Phillip picked up his phone and checked the time; he was beyond late.

Pulling himself out of bed, Phillip undressed quickly, the smell of his spoiled clothes ripe and offensive. He sluggishly made his way into the bathroom, downed some pills, and stepped in the shower to remove the ugly remnants of the previous day off him.

After he felt appropriately clean, Phillip got out of the shower, shaved, and hastily performed his daily skin regimen. As he moisturized his face, he stared deeply into the mirror, like he did every morning, hoping to discover something new about himself, something hopeful and regenerative.

Overlooking the bags under his eyes, Phillip saw the same specimen of physical perfection he always did. As always, he knew it was just a pretty shell covering a broken man. The only actual rejuvenation going on in his life seemed to be his taught, flawless skin. It was depressing, but he was still thankful for his beauty.

Phillip picked out a navy Gucci suit, a white Calvin Klein shirt, and a pink silk tie.

A comic book geek, Phillip put on the DC Comics Nightwing socks he had purchased online. They were highly unconventional, but he loved his crazy socks. It was a trend Denise had said many professional men were glomming onto to reclaim a sense of rebellion in a buttoned-up, corporate world. Phillip was fine with jumping on that particular bandwagon.

He popped on a pair of dark brown Kenneth Cole lace-up shoes to finish his look.

Before spritzing himself with a nearly empty bottle of Eternity, Phillip realized he had yet to style his hair. "Shit, where did I put my hair wax?" Once he found the product, he styled his blond locks and briskly left the room.

He practically leapt down the stairs to see if Jules was still somewhere in the house, but he did not make it far before he heard a disembodied voice barking orders at him. A voice that was all too familiar but did not belong to his wife.

"Phillip, come in here now, please."

His mom was courteous in her request, but Phillip knew it was insincere. It was an order; any good manners and graciousness on his mother's part was nothing but ingrained decorum. Sighing, Phillip did as his mother commanded, making his way to the dining room where Stella sat alone at the table, reading a magazine between bites of peach slices.

Phillip did not want to discuss anything to do with Charles, the company or his wife. He just wanted his mother to stay out of his business and let him handle everything. She did not need to concern herself with his problems.

"Now's not a good time, Mom. I have to get to the office, and I'm already late. Did Jules already leave?"

Stella ignored her son and his question.

"Jackson, get me some dry toast. I'm not interested in this buttery slop on the table. First, pour me a glass of orange juice. Is this freshly squeezed? It better be freshly squeezed."

"Yes, ma'am," Jackson assured her. "I squeezed it myself this morning."

"Fine. Now hurry up with my toast. Phillip, sit down here next to me. I have something to say to you."

Phillip rolled his eyes, sighed heavily, and took a seat.

"Don't sigh and roll your eyes at me. It's disrespectful, and I raised you never to disrespect me. I've come to expect that sort of behaviour from Denise, but not from you, Phillip! I will not tolerate it from you."

"Sorry. Mom, where's Jules? Did you see her leave?"

Stella smiled like she had a secret she could not wait to tell.

"Well, darling, Jackson informed me this morning that your wife didn't come home last night. Interesting. Did you have a nice restful, restorative sleep?"

Phillip recognized the obvious sarcasm embedded in the question and knew it was a trap. Remaining silent, he looked out the window, ashamed. Phillip figured that his mother had seen him last night drunk, possibly belligerent. What could he say? What did she want him to say? On top of all that, Jules had not come home, had not slept in their bed next to him. Again.

"Nothing to say? I don't blame you. I love you to death, Phillip, but I'm over this asinine behaviour of yours. You destroyed multiple pieces of crystal glassware last night and a picture. Thankfully, it was one of Jules's tasteless art pieces, but the crystal goblets were mine!

"You need to get this ugly drinking issue under control. It's inexcusable, and your father would never have stood for it. I will no longer stand for it. You are your father's legacy. Am I making myself clear?"

"I'm sorry, Mom. I'm sorry I've disappointed you. So sorry."

Phillip teared up, putting his hands to his face to hide his shame. He knew how he looked, a grown man crying like a baby over broken glassware, but it was so much more than that for him.

"Mom, I think my marriage is falling apart."

Stella laughed in Phillip's face. It was a belly laugh, deep and raucous; it was a highly insensitive, totally inappropriate response to a heartfelt statement. Stella was oblivious to Phillip's genuine pain because she had a heart of stone regarding anything Jules related, including her son's complicated feelings for the woman.

"What an absurd statement. My dear, sweet boy—it already fell! Get up to speed. The sooner we get that bitch out of our lives, the better."

"Thanks, Mom. Thanks for the support."

Stella put down her magazine and looked at her son squarely in the face. Her focus was now one hundred percent on him.

"Phillip, you need to hear this. I won't be doing you any favours if I lie to you or hide what I know to be true. I've tried before to have this conversation, but you've always brushed me off. Well, not this time, buddy.

"Son, Jules never loved you, and the quicker you realize that, the better! Look at you! That woman has practically taken over our company, reducing you, the rightful heir, to nothing more than a perpetually drunk figurehead. Handsome though you are, Jules has completely neutered you.

"That woman is nothing but a conniving, manipulative tramp! Absolutely no good for you! You deserve happiness, Phillip, but you'll never get it as long as you're under her boot heel. And that's where you've been for far too long."

Red-faced and too angry to remain in his mother's unsympathetic company, Phillip wiped away the remainder of his tears and got up to leave.

"Don't you dare get up and walk away from me! Sit your ass back down! We're going to talk about this since you were the one who brought it up in the first place. Put on your listening ears and focus. Whether you like or agree with what I have to say or not, you're going to hear me out. Every word, because I know I'm right. Mother always is."

Phillip sat back down.

"I've always supported you, Phillip, and I'll continue to. Remember, I was there for you during all that unfortunate unpleasantness with Genevieve, as was your father, but I'll never enable you or pretend for you.

"It's no secret that I wasn't a fan of your hasty marriage to Jules. She used her ample feminine charms to ensorcell you and your father. She's only ever been interested in our company. Charles's friendship with your father was authentic, I know that, but there isn't an authentic bone in that skinny bitch's body."

"That's not true," Phillip shot back. "She did love me! Does! Oh, I don't know. I hope she does, but I know she did! It was real. She was happy. We were happy until—until dad died. I don't know what happened after that. Something changed in her."

"Are you blind? Your father was an obstacle, impeding her future success. Even with her ego, as ballsy and conniving as she is, she knew better than to take your father head-on. I doubt even Charles would have supported that move. She's not stupid, I'll give her that, but she was planning, plotting, biding her time.

"She was fake and phony from the start, Phillip. Get it through your head! I wouldn't be surprised if she killed your father, herself, or hired someone to do it! I've always had my suspicions."

Phillip raged against the accusatory, damning words his mother directed towards his absent wife. He slammed his fists repeatedly down on the table, glaring at her for the first time in his life with open menace and resentment.

"How dare you say such a thing!" he bellowed. "How dare you accuse my wife of something so heinous! Dad most likely took his own life. He seemed depressed at the time. I don't know why he did what he did. So violently. That horrible explosion. I—I don't want to talk about that. And she had nothing to do with it! That's just crazy! I never knew you to be so hateful, Mom. So cruel. You're acting just like—"

Phillip's eyes went wide, and he paused. It had been an instinctual thought; still, he could not believe what he was about to say. He had fallen right into his mother's trap. He had taken the bait even when he knew better, even when he had prepared himself ahead of time for her cleverness and subtle manipulations. She still got him.

"Cat got your tongue, dear? Allow me to finish that sentence. You were about to say, 'Just like Jules,' correct? I was acting hateful and cruel, just like your wife. Do you get it now?

"And as for your father taking his own life—what rubbish! You should be ashamed of yourself for suggesting such a thing. Someone did something to him! We never found his body, did we? No! Pieces of skin, tissue, and blood, yes, but not him! He wouldn't have done that to himself. Someone wanted him dead—and it was probably her!"

"No, you don't understand. I can't believe that. I can't believe anything even remotely so disgusting or evil. I can't! Don't you understand?"

"No, Phillip, I don't understand."

"I still love her! I love her!"

Stella could not believe her ears. Phillip had said the one thing she did not want to hear and absolutely could not accept. All the same, once she gave herself a moment to allow her son's lamentable words to wash over her, she found herself oddly unsurprised by them. Stella had long suspected that even with all the horrible things Jules had said and done to him, Phillip would never divorce her over any of it.

Phillip's statement was irrefutable proof of what Stella had always feared; his heart was too big, too easily manipulated. His softness often worked in her favour, but it just as often worked against her.

Stella understood her dilemma all too well. Phillip, easily misled by love, or what he believed was love, would always be limited in his ability to make rational, necessary, logical choices in life. Stella wanted him to make the correct choices, especially regarding the difference between the right and wrong kinds of people and relationships.

It had all happened before with Genevieve.

Phillip had been struck dumb and rendered helpless by Jules, like a child, but he was still her child, and Stella would never abandon him.

This was why she had finally opted to have Jules killed. Just like with Phillip's first marital mistake, Stella had taken things to the extreme to free her son from the weighted chains of romantic idiocy. She feared Phillip would always lead with his heart and his penis instead of his common sense and intellect. Lead with foolish emotions until it was too late to see the awful truth of what he had done—the terrible consequences of his actions.

And then it always became her problem. But Stella was very good at fixing problems.

"You get all that from your father," she said aloud, even though she knew Phillip had no idea what she was talking about.

"Mom, I have to go."

Stella watched her disgruntled son get up, grab his jacket, and depart for the office. Though she remained silent, her thoughts were loud and clear. *That woman will be your downfall. Which is why I'm finishing this. That bitch is as good as dead.*

"Jules, I've been notified that Phillip is in the elevator, on his way up," Charles announced excitedly, waving his cellphone in the air. "Jules?"

Walking over to his daughter, Charles put his hand on her shoulder, squeezing gently. He knew the photo she had in her hand, the one she had been obsessing over all morning, and understood what it meant to her. Charles opted not to acknowledge or react to it; it was Jules's private moment. He respected the deep emotional connection his daughter had to his late husband.

Charles was aware that when his husband was alive, Jules favoured him. Jason had routinely indulged Jules, openly relishing his role as the "fun parent." In contrast, Charles had been the disciplinarian, the doting yet authoritarian parent, the practical stick-in-the-mud who put his foot down and said *no* the most.

Why Jules was gazing at that specific image all morning, Charles was not sure. He hoped it was because it brought her comfort looking at it and not due to feelings of resentment towards him and the awkward revelation of his relationship with Christophe. Charles missed his husband terribly, just as much as his daughter did, longed for him every day, but he was afraid Jules no longer believed that.

"Honey, are you okay? Are you ready for this? We can postpone. It doesn't have to be today."

Gently putting the framed image back on her desk, Jules turned around and answered her father. Charles stood almost on top of her now, looking, in her opinion, unnecessarily concerned.

"I'm fine, Pops, and this is happening now. And where the hell is Nazneen? It's past nine! I had to get my own damn Frappuccino this morning!"

"No, you didn't, liar!" Amanda barked from the couch. "I went downstairs and got it for you! It's not nice to fib to your father. No phone call or text from her calling in sick or saying she'd be late?"

Having made it clear to Jules the previous night that she was not leaving her side until they had dealt with William, Amanda had come into the office with Jules.

After hastily removing herself and all traces of her presence from Château Bergé and relocating downtown, Amanda had gone directly over to Jules's condo. She had spent the night in one of the guestrooms.

They were friends once more, but Jules had reiterated one final time to make things abundantly clear to Amanda that they were not "friends with benefits." As the evening progressed, the two women had indulged in several glasses of Pinot Grigio, strategized, and compared notes.

Jules admitted to her information gathering failures. She described her multiple attempts to contact Gretchen and Duncan Falsworth to discover what they knew about William's release as "futile endeavours." Gretchen's people refused to speak to her outright; Duncan's assistant, while more courteous, was just as frustratingly unhelpful.

Jules believed their unwillingness to take her phone calls strongly suggested that they were both aware William was a free man. A free man who was out to get her *and* had access to a considerable amount of money.

Amanda confirmed Jules's assumptions.

Without disclosing the name of her source, Amanda revealed everything Bex had discovered about William, starting with how he had gained access to his previously frozen accounts. She was certain William was on his own in this plot against Jules, with the lone exception of Dr. Kotera. No wire transfers from Gretchen or any other Falsworth into any of William's accounts had occurred.

Amanda also divulged why no one at Hawthorne had alerted Charles to William's transfer to the Amsterdam facility. Gretchen had paid them all off with an amount far more than Charles's yearly stipend to the hospital to keep him abreast of things. Every time Charles had contacted them for updates, everyone had lied through their teeth.

Aware of the Falsworth family's bribing and bullying tactics, Jules was not the least bit shocked. As for Hawthorne, Jules planned on severely punishing those involved in the plot to undermine her father's arrangement.

Amanda recounted her confrontation with William; she included in the narration everything Bex had discovered about Dr. Kotera.

Jules was less interested in William's psychiatrist than she was in his fighting abilities. She dismissed Dr. Kotera outright as someone deranged who needed to have their license revoked. Jules figured the woman was just another pawn of the Falsworths who had gone native from being around William too long. He had gotten into her head, warping it.

Jules wanted to know when and how William learned advanced martial arts and the creation and use of computerized explosives.

After a few moments of strained silence, Amanda reluctantly admitted that, based on William's loose tongue, her brother had been hired at some point to train him. He had betrayed her by revealing who she was, her working persona, and her everyday appearance.

At that point, Jules pointedly asked Amanda if her brother was the Gold Leopard, the assassin for hire so colourfully designated in Joseph's files. Amanda confirmed he was. She had not seen or spoken to him in years, and he had taken the comic book-like alias after learning she had begun using one.

Amanda had said little else about her brother that night, even declining Jules's request for his legal name. His physical description and age had also been off-limits. Amanda had refused to go into any further detail outside of what Jules already knew.

"No, Amanda, I haven't heard a peep from her," Jules stated frankly. "This just might be Ms. Balakrishna's last day."

"That's interesting," Amanda had her suspicions about who was responsible for the security breaches, and someone like Jules's executive assistant had access and opportunity. "We need to look into this further. Nothing is coincidental, Jules."

With a great deal of suspicion, Charles watched the easy, playful interaction between his daughter and Amanda, a woman he had met for the first time just an hour earlier. Jules had told her father that Amanda was an old friend of hers from University who was aware of everything and here to help.

Charles accepted the vague explanation at face value like he accepted everything to do with his daughter, but his mind was not at ease. He was so tired of mysteries and secrets,

Suddenly, the door to Jules's office opened.

"Nice of you to finally join us," Jules acerbically stated as Phillip walked into the room looking sheepish.

"Sorry, Jules, I didn't mean to be late. I forgot to set our—my alarm." It saddened him terribly that there was little to no sharing of anything anymore in their relationship.

Jules rolled her eyes. Despite his professional appearance, Phillip had not applied enough concealer to successfully cover the dark circles under his eyes. They were not all that bloodshot, but Jules guessed that had more to do with eye drops than with him not being hungover, which he so obviously was.

"Please, I doubt in the state you were in you, you even set the damn thing. By the way, Mr. Jules Cartell, I spoke briefly with M. Petit last night. He casually mentioned that he refused your offer to speak with him. That had to hurt, but I'm sure you soothed your poor, battered male ego with a nice bottle of Jack. Alright, let's begin."

Phillip was used to Jules's insults and mocking comments at his expense, and so her nasty words only stung a little. Well, perhaps more than a little. He was surprised she had held back on the contempt and ribbing as much as she did.

Still, Jules's bitchiness was not what was making his blood boil. What was pissing Phillip off was the prominent look on Charles's face.

Smugness.

Phillip wanted to be professional and in control of this meeting. He had thought about it a lot in the car on the way over. He wanted to be able to deal with the issue of Charles's indiscretions made public calmly for the company's sake. But his father-in-law's crooked, shit-eating grin was too much for him to bear. It triggered him, and it took all of Phillip's restraint not to lunge fists first at Charles.

"Let's begin? Fuck that! First off, Chuck, we have a big problem, here, you and I! What I want to do is drag you into the alley and beat the living shit out of you for what you and that cheating slut did to Denise. And I'm not sure yet that I won't do just that. What is it with Christophe, huh? Model by day? A fucking prostitute by night? Is that it? And you're a—well, I don't want to say what you are. Screwing a damn teenager!"

"You son of a bitch!" Jules screamed back. "Don't speak to my father that way!"

Enraged, Jules motioned menacingly towards her husband, but Amanda snapped her fingers, put her hand up, and shook her head.

"Get control, Jules," Amanda boldly stated. "Don't give in to anger. It's weak and beneath you. Emotions betray logical action. Don't feed his fire. He's just baiting your father with his size. Basic intimidation tactics, and it's so pedestrian, so obvious. He wants it to get physical. He thinks his best method to communicate his position of power is through masculine brutality. Deep down, he believes he can't compete and win any other way."

Much to Phillip's relief, Jules halted her angry, hostile forward motion and regained her composure.

Staring into her father's eyes, Jules looked for some direction, some understanding, some clarity of purpose. If she had ignored what Phillip implied about her father, that was nothing short of a betrayal. Jules hoped her father interpreted her heated reaction as full support and total condemnation of Phillip's despicable, invalid insinuation.

Turning back to Phillip, Jules sneered, "He was the legal age of consent, you ignorant prick."

"Don't, Jules, he's nothing," Charles stated. "Don't explain. We don't owe him a damn thing. Let him vent. You and I know the truth. I have nothing to be ashamed of. Phillip is just overcompensating, anyway. Displacing. He won't come for you, not physically, but he'd gladly take out his frustration and aggression on me. It's not rocket science. Ms. Reid is quite correct."

Charles became momentarily silent; just the same, he smiled warmly at Jules to let her know he had not fallen apart. He knew he could never explain well enough the love he felt for her, especially his feeling of pride in that moment of instinctive familial protection. Jules's rush to his defence was recognized and very much appreciated, but he did not want her to throw down with Phillip over him.

"He doesn't care about who I fuck," Charles continued, cutting Phillip off just as he was about to speak up for himself. "He doesn't give a shit about Chris, either.

"Phillip is using Denise as an excuse to act like a big man and come for me. He and I both know why he wants to take a swing at me. Don't we, Phil? And it's not because of Denise's hurt feelings over a guy she only ever saw as arm candy to showcase how cool she was to the paparazzi and glitterati. She's embarrassed now, but she'll be over it by New York Fashion Week.

"You're no big brother protector, Phil. You're just a dumb jock dipshit who's afraid he's been neutered beyond hope by his mother and his wife and thinks this might be his one last chance to prove he's still a man. He's baiting us, Jules, honey, looking for a fight."

Phillip turned away for a moment from Charles and Jules and looked directly at Amanda. He smiled awkwardly, somewhat suspiciously, and gave her a quick once over. Phillip noted that this mystery woman looked remarkably similar to Jules, right down to the creme-coloured designer suit and meticulously styled blonde hair.

Politely apologizing to Amanda for his language and his anger, Phillip introduced himself in an authoritative, confident manner he hoped presented himself in a better light. With his arm outstretched, Phillip boldly approached her.

Amanda snickered, remained seated with her arms crossed, and refused to shake hands with Phillip. She did not verbally communicate this refusal; her body language and pernicious sneer spoke volumes. And, like he had done to her just moments earlier, Amanda gave Phillip the once over, making sure he got just how unimpressed she was with what she saw. Her visual attention was vaguely threatening.

"Christ, you people! Birds of a feather, eh? This isn't over between you and me, old man. Not by a long shot. One day, Chuck, you'll get what's coming to you! Jules, what the hell is going on? And who is this rude woman? Does she have something to do with this cloud of shit now hanging over us? Is she some

PR barracuda you hired to spin this whole thing into something we can survive?"

"Boy, you really are an overly dramatic douche," Amanda laughed. "PR barracuda? Wow. Jules, was he this much of a tool when you first met him?"

Phillip's face went red again, but this time it was partially from anger and partially from exasperation. *This nasty bitch is a clone of my wife.*

Jules ignored Amanda, keeping her focus on Phillip.

"We aren't here to discuss my father's situation, Phillip. I'm already on top of it. If you thought that was why I'd arranged this meeting, you're wrong. We are all here for a very different reason. Now, shut your goddamn mouth. I'll tell you when you can speak and when you can be of use.

"You're going to sign over the entirety of your interest in the company to me. You're going to willingly relinquish your legal claim to our jointly owned shares so that they will be in my name only.

"I'm also going to need you to get your hands on Sonja's shares and have them transferred into my name, too. Today. And make sure she doesn't become a problem. Trust me, it's in your best interest if this all goes smoothly and time is not on your side.

"Finally, you're going to render our prenup null and void. My father has prepared all the necessary paperwork. It just involves your signature in a few places. Am I making myself understood? I'm talking slowly enough for him, right everyone?"

Phillip's face instinctively expressed a look of pure, unadulterated shock. His stomach twisted into knots as he looked around the room at the three stone-cold, inscrutable faces staring directly back at him.

"What? You're fucking insane, Jules! That's not even remotely funny!"

"No, I'm completely sane and deadly serious," Jules replied calmly. "So is my father. Ms. Reid, on the other hand? Not so sane, so I suggest you don't piss her off. As I was saying, you're going to relinquish full control of this company to me. End of story. I'll get you a pen."

Phillip laughed hysterically. "You've lost your goddamn mind. Or this is some sick, twisted joke. Another one at my expense! I don't know who you are, Ms. Reid, or what your purpose here is, but I know my wife and her father are just trying to fuck with me again.

"To think I told my mother this morning that I still loved you, Jules. Even after the horrible shit that you've put me through—still put me through! What the fuck was I thinking? Fuck all of you!"

Turning his back on the people he viewed without question as enemies, Phillip proceeded towards the door. Before he managed to open it, Jules uttered something devastating that compelled him to stop dead in his tracks.

"If you ever want to know what happened to your first wife and the child she bore you, Phillip, you will turn around and march your ass right back here."

The air in the room went still, and all sound died; you could have heard a pin drop on a carpeted floor—it was that eerily silent.

Phillip felt his heart skip a beat or two at the mention of his first wife. But a child? That was unexpected. And ridiculous. *What is she talking about? How does she even know about Genevieve? And what child?* There had not been any time to think about starting a family with Genevieve. They had only been married a hot minute before she left him, and Phillip never spoke of her.

"What did you just say, Jules?" Phillip demanded, his tone pointed, angry.

"You heard me. If you ever want to know what happened to Genevieve and your child, you will surrender this company to me so I can remove all traces of the Cartell stink from it. That's the deal, asshole, your past for my future.

"I'll give you the truth. I'll reveal every despicable thing your parents did to keep you from the woman you married and the child you never got the chance to raise, to love. All in exchange for your family's complete removal from this company. There is no room here for negotiation, Phillip."

Jules walked over to her desk, instructing Phillip to join her. He did, still somewhat dazed and confused, but he obeyed like a good subordinate.

Charles took a seat next to Amanda on the faux leather couch, knowing Jules would call on him when needed. He still had no idea what Amanda's role was, but he remained impartial, trusting that his daughter knew what she was doing.

Once Phillip was at her desk, mute and pliant, just like she wanted, Jules explained what the various manila envelopes neatly stacked one on top of the other contained. Disoriented, Phillip meekly took the pen Jules offered; his hand trembled as he held the writing tool between his fingers.

"This isn't happening," he whispered.

"Yes, Phillip, it is," Jules smirked.

"No, none of this is real."

"It's all quite real, you mumbling idiot. Shut up and pay attention!"

The first file Jules showed Phillip contained the legal documents he needed to sign to nullify their prenuptial agreement. Jules had already signed it in preparation for this moment.

"I never cared about it, you know," Phillip admitted as he signed the document. "I never wanted it. I never asked for one."

"Oh, I know. It was Stella's idea, but you never stood up to her. I'm just as much at fault. I signed it too, knowing what it meant, but I was foolishly in love and thought it didn't matter. Well, it looks like I was right, after all. It didn't ultimately matter."

Jules allowed a few stray giggles to escape. It was girlish, and she hated silliness in grown women; this one time, however, she allowed herself to indulge in some involuntary mirth. It was all coming together. She felt unbelievably satisfied watching Phillip crumble before her very eyes.

"Once we start divorce proceedings, your hag of a mother won't be able to influence you to enact those little clauses she put in there to fuck with me. She didn't want me to get what I deserve, and that would have proven quite problematic for me. Problematic, Phillip, not insurmountable.

"Still, I'm not interested in a legal battle even knowing I'd win in the end. This makes things so much easier, no? Nothing to say? Well, on to the next one, then."

"This manila envelope contains the papers for share transfers. Phillip, do you know why your dad made sure both of us inherited his shares equally? The real reason he wanted my name on them, next to yours?"

With little energy, Phillip shrugged. "No. I just always assumed he thought we made a good team. And we did, once."

Jules snickered loudly. "How pathetically sentimental."

"Mom thinks you were sleeping with dad before and after we were married," Phillip bluntly stated, on the verge of tears. "She came to me a few weeks after the funeral, convinced you had blackmailed him into putting you in his will. I told her she was crazy. If you blackmailed him, why loop me in at all? Why not just cut me out completely? She thinks you killed him or hired someone to do it, to get him out of the way."

Charles was unable to stifle a laugh. The idea that his daughter had something to do with Joseph's unforeseen demise was preposterous. "Stella's accusations are just absurd soap opera delusions. Nothing but the rantings of a bitter, defeated woman."

Jules agreed. "Ludicrous, yes, but I have to admit it's entertaining to hear. I hope that old crone's spent years torturing herself with thoughts of my young, luscious body getting it on with her husband. Perhaps even in their bed, in that tacky, over-decorated house in Rosedale. I hope that old bitch suffers daily!"

"You're a terrible person," Phillip declared, tears now streaming down his face.

"Sometimes," Jules agreed, "but only when I have to be. No, Phillip, I didn't kill your father, nor did I sleep with him. Yuck.

"Back to your father's will. Joseph knew you were, oh, let's say—limited, and I was not. He doubted you, Phillip. You started strong, but your father saw the signs as time went on. He wrote it all down, his every thought, his every fear that you weren't good enough to replace him. To take the helm one day, so to speak. But he knew I was.

"Still, you were his son, a blood Cartell, unlike me, as you've generously pointed out before, and you had to maintain a position of power and influence in the company. He hoped that by rewarding me with joint leadership, I'd eventually raise you to my level of excellence.

"Sadly, you've only fallen further down. Your pathetic, childlike tears suggest as much. You can't handle the pressure. You fold over and over again, and then you wait for someone else to fix your mistakes. You're such a disappointment. It's no wonder Genevieve left you. Or did she leave you of her own free will? Aren't you just dying to know?"

Phillip took a deep inhalation of breath, stopped crying, and wiped away the remnants of moisture left on his face. The results of deep sobbing still marked his tan flesh but how dishevelled he looked was the last thing on his mind. Phillip stared deeply into the cold, shark-like eyes of his wife and demanded to know what happened to Genevieve.

"No," Jules declared.

"Tell me! Tell me what you know about her, you demented bitch!"

Amanda watched as Phillip puffed up his chest aggressively, but she did not move closer to Jules.

Not liking the aggressive posturing of his son-in-law, Charles got up off the sofa and walked briskly over to where Jules and Phillip huddled about the desk. He put himself between his daughter and her huge, angry husband.

"This third folder contains the documents you need to get Sonja's shares in the company transferred out of her name and put into Jules's," Charles explained. "Once she signs them—today—get them immediately back to us. Our patience is limited."

"Get it done and get it done fast," Jules sneered. "I don't care how you do it. For your sake, Phillip, Sonja better not be a problem or Genevieve and your son, or daughter, or was it, twins? Well, in any case, you won't ever find him, her, or them. Lost to you forever, and it will be all your fault because you couldn't get your vapid little twit of a sister to do what I wanted.

"And make sure Stella is kept in the dark about all this, or I won't give you anything. Not one sheet of information. Not a date, not an address, not even a recent photo to show you whether or not Genevieve still has a needle stuck in her arm."

Jules instantly regretted that last part the moment it slipped out of her mouth. Genevieve had never been her enemy, but Jules hated Phillip so much she wanted to hurt him any way that she could. Jules had taught herself to use any weakness an enemy had against them. Only, it had not felt right using Genevieve's drug use as a weapon against Phillip.

Especially considering Joseph had been responsible for the woman's heroin addiction.

"You're lying," Phillip howled. "She was never a heroin addict. Or whatever drug uses needles. All these lies! This sick game! My mother was right about you all along. I'm a fool, a dupe, okay, but I'm not stupid enough to give away my company. I won't sign any of these, you sick bitch. Fuck the prenup. You can divorce me if you want, I don't care, but I will never screw over my family. I'm not relinquishing shit! I'm not afraid of you, Jules."

"You should be, Phillip, but that's neither here nor there at the moment."

Jules was genuinely surprised by Phillip's sudden fortitude, but she was prepared for it just the same. She pulled a flash drive out of the right pocket of her white, fitted Donna Karen blazer and held it up before him.

"This little trinket contains all the information my father and I have collected on Genevieve and her offspring. With help from your father's secret files. Lots of files you and your mother didn't know existed. But someone knew, and after Joseph blew himself up, this source came to me and told me where to look for them. Oh, Phillip, you've no idea the depravity I found secreted away inside those files."

Jules tossed him a few pages from out of the mysterious, and as of yet unexplained, fourth and final folder. "This is just a taste of what I have on Genevieve and your offspring. What does it say? What does it show you about your parent's involvement in Genevieve's disappearance? Take a good, hard look. Do you still want to protect them? Still want to be a part of that legacy?"

Jules did not want to let the cat out of the bag too soon by telling Phillip his first wife was dead. She wanted him to read what was on the paper and despair over it.

"No, this isn't true! My father would never have done that to her, treating her like garbage. You made this up! How could you be so evil? What did I ever do to you to make you hate me like this? To do these horrible things to me?"

Jules wanted to scream directly into Phillip's red, tear-stained face, telling him exactly what he had done to deserve her teeming hatred but now was not the right time. Soon, though, later today, when the company was free of the Cartell contagion and solidly under her control. She could not wait to go back to being Jules Dunning-Bainbridge and rename and reorganize the company.

"It's all real. Every word is the truth, and I'll even tell you that you have only one child. See, I'm not so terrible.

"Now, let's talk about legacy. You speak about family pride, Phillip, about love? Now you know. Monsters. That is your pedigree. Your father was scum, and your mother is no better. She wanted to kill your baby, both before and after it was born, and when you finally read the whole story, you'll see the fetid, rotten stock you come from. That is your legacy!

"And you, Phillip? You're just as bad. No, you're worse! The worst kind of monster. You're the kind that destroys lives and doesn't even know they've done it! You're a selfish, entitled, alcoholic piece of shit!"

"Shut up, shut up!" Phillip screamed, covering his ears. He could not take any more of Jules's verbal and psychological abuse. Not knowing the truth of what happened to Genevieve was too much for Phillip to bear. Was she dead or hiding from his family? He thought about the years of fatherhood denied him. Did he have a son or a daughter? He needed answers!

Phillip had no clue where all Jules's anger and resentment came from, its origins. He had done nothing but be a good husband to her since their wedding day. *She's baiting me, taunting me out of spite. She's just evil. That's it. Plain, pure evil, and she's played me for a fool since the first day we met.*

Suddenly, Phillip wanted that flash drive more than anything else in the entire world. A hot, invigorating fire erupted in his gut, transforming him from a once dormant, sedentary mound of dirt into a powerful and volatile volcano. Not for a second longer would he be victimized by his wife's unending manipulations.

Acting on some subconscious driving force, Phillip moved to take the flash drive from Jules. He attacked Charles first, grabbing the older man by his significantly less muscular arms; with Herculean force, Phillip flung him into a wall.

Charles, unable to react quickly enough to prevent the assault, landed hard against the painted surface and slumped down onto the floor, stunned outright.

With a crazed, desperate look in his eyes, Phillip rushed Jules.

Before he could get to her, however, Amanda was on top of him with cheetah-like speed. Her powerful leg connected with his abdomen, and as the breath left Phillip, Amanda moved in close, uncomfortably close.

Her body entwined with Phillip's, Amanda swiftly reached behind her back, went under her suit jacket and brought forth a blade. She placed the formerly hidden weapon at Phillip's throat, pressing in far enough to hurt but not draw blood. She knew the precise amount of pressure needed to break the skin, but they were not there yet.

"Try something like that again, and I'll be serving you your nuts for lunch. Clear?"

"Crystal," Phillip gasped.

As Amanda disentangled herself from Phillip, she gut-punched him hard for good measure. "Handsome but stupid. You fuck with Jules, you fuck with me, and you don't wanna fuck with me, remember that. I'm pretty sure I felt some stirring down there. Strong women get you hard, eh?"

"Crazy bitch," Phillip wheezed.

Amanda shrugged. She could not deny it—she was a tad loony. "Present," she joked.

"Thank you, Amanda. I think he finally understands his place."

Jules's expression of gratitude was genuine. She was glad she did not have to sully herself by touching her husband, even if it was to knock him the fuck out to defend herself. She would have enjoyed hitting him, but after her recent scuffle in the garage, she was perfectly okay to sit this one out as she was still quite sore.

It had taken a significant amount of make-up to cover the bruises around her neck. Jules did not want to risk smudging or removing any of it because of another physical altercation.

Her gold Burberry silk neck scarf aided in obfuscating her injuries, and it looked amazing on her. She wished her accessorizing had come from a purely fashion-conscious choice rather than trying to hide the by-product of an attempt on her life.

Jules hurried over to her father. Helping him up, she asked if he was hurt. Charles replied that he was fine, just winded.

Gasping for air, himself, his breathing uneven, his stomach sore, Phillip sobbed and admitted defeat. He promised he would do whatever they wanted as long as they promised to give him the information. He begged for it.

"Once I have Sonja's shares, it's a done deal. I'll hand everything over to you, myself. You have my word on it, Phillip.

"I'm thankful Denise went and dumped her Cartell stock a while back without any collusion or deceit needed. Knowing this day would come, I had Jacques quietly buy up all of it for me, every last share. He used a few dummy corporations to keep you ignorant of his involvement. I have to remember to pay him back for his very willing aid. Sometimes, it's nice to have friends, isn't it?"

"I hate you," Phillip whispered, glaring at his wife, his face filled with contempt.

"Yes, I can see how I'd be easy to hate," Jules conceded. "But you, Phillip? You were so fucking easy to break."

XXI

The rustic punched metal wall clock showed it was five minutes away from three in the afternoon. Jules was hypnotized by the timepiece and its black metallic hands. They methodically moved time along, but to her, it felt as though all temporal movement had stopped. She understood it was only an illusion, a trick of the mind, a matter of perception, but it felt real.

Jules was too focused on the plodding, systematic movements of the clockworks. She wanted time to hurry up, but in wishing for it to happen, she had become lost in the moment, stuck between seconds. Time was cruel, and it was toying with her.

All Jules could think about was Phillip's recent text, confirming he had what she wanted and was on his way back. This knowledge was what made time appear fathomless and still: the endless, monotonous waiting for her revenge to be claimed.

Despite her outward show of restraint and control, Jules's emotions raged inside her. Relief and excitement, of course, that all her planning and plotting had worked, but also apprehension because something she had put off doing for so long now had to happen. As much as she wished she could spare her father this pain, the truth had to come out.

How would he react? What would he do? These had always been her worries. There were so many variables. Jules realized that even with all her preparation, she could not control everything, could not protect everyone from the fallout of this final revelation.

Jules was glad to have Amanda nearby for support; her self-appointed bodyguard had refused to leave her side. She missed Jacques, but his comforting presence would complicate things for her emotionally. She needed a clear head. Shaking off her worries, Jules pulled herself away from the mesmerizing effects of the clock to look over at her guest.

Amanda sat on the sofa, in the same spot she had been in for hours. She believed her unexpected involvement had spooked William and that the most probable result was him moving up his timetable. Would he try to take Jules out or perform another one of his sick, twisted mind fucks? Whatever he had planned, Amanda would be there to stop him.

From her desk, Jules watched Amanda work furiously on her laptop.

"Jules, you won't like this," Amanda stated, looking up from her computer. "I was able to hack into that online tabloid's computer system. Their security is a joke. I found out who sold them the story about your father. Well, they didn't pay for the story, exactly."

"Stop talking in riddles and get to the point."

"Someone emailed the story to them with an attachment—the photos. This party paid them, and I mean paid! A million bucks to make sure it ran yesterday. I also found a few emails and documented calls from a guy on Stella's behalf trying to get them to pull it, but she didn't offer nearly enough."

"Odd that she gave up so easily. Stella's not usually such a cheap bitch with Joseph's money."

"I've taken the entire site off-line and deleted all the images I could find," Amanda confirmed, proud of herself. "This won't get rid of everything in the long run. It's the Internet, and those pics are out there."

"Appear weak when you are strong and strong when you are weak."

"Quoting Sun Tzu, eh? Appropriate. I understand what you mean."

"It is what it is, Amanda. No one is running and hiding from this. It's all about the spin. Even if this could hurt us, at least in the short term, my father and I will appear united and unconcerned, business as usual.

"M. Petit, the Frenchman whose company I threw that party for? He tried to break our deal, concerned for his reputation should he do business with a corporation currently under a scandal. I politely told him that if he reneged on our deal, I would take it personally and do whatever it took to bankrupt them. Threatening him like that is such a Joseph thing to do. They won't remain friendly or cooperative with us under duress."

"Then why do it?" Amanda questioned. "Their company is worth only a fraction of yours. Why bother?"

"Because I can. And because it's the principle, dammit! I don't like people disparaging my father. Let's be real here. Nothing he did in those pictures is all that scandalous compared to any celebrity sex tape. No one knows the actual story yet. Only the demented ramblings of some coked-out street whore who took some blurry pics of an intimate moment between two people. I'll tell the story I want people to know."

Amanda nodded. "Oh, I have no doubt, sister."

"I'd ask for the name of the party that went after my father, but from the amount paid, I can guess. I'm sure the real intent was to mess with me through my father. Embarrass me, compromise my company's integrity, sully the reputation of Castle Dunning and Briggs, etcetera. There's a money trail leading directly back to William, correct?

"Bingo!" Amanda shouted. "A direct transfer from one of his overseas accounts. I can't dig deeper without alerting them to a cyberattack. The banks William keeps his money with are all heavily fortified against that. Gretchen was smart to move her brother's accounts, once unfrozen, to these institutions. Do you want to re-freeze anything or transfer all his money to you or a charity? I've done it before. I have someone."

"No, you've done enough. I do appreciate it, Amanda, really, but the last thing I need right now is to become an active enemy of his entire family. I know they all think he's as crazy and delusional as we do, but they don't comprehend how dangerous he is.

"Even Gretchen, no matter what misplaced guilt she feels for locking him away, must realize he's undeniably unstable. If she helped that doctor get him declared sane, she did so out of a misguided sense of sibling love and loyalty. No one, including her, thinks he's better, let alone cured.

"It's unwise to attack their money. All the Falsworths use the same banks, and even if we only go after William's money, they'll still see it as an assault on the family. They're that paranoid. I've avoided them my entire adult life. No, we'll deal with William another way, as we agreed, and keep his family out of it. Just like we're keeping my father out of it."

"Whatever you want, Jules," Amanda agreed. "Why all these distractions, though? Throw you off your game? Scare you? From what you've told me about William, it seems hugely out of character for him to engage in all this foreplay. He's single-minded. He comes for you and kills you. This extra stuff takes planning and deviousness, so it has to be Dr. Kotera—or his sister. You may have to accept the fact that she's in on this."

Jules thought about it for a moment.

"No, Gretchen's too smart for this kind of exposure. I can't see her risking her family name over me. I bet she thought she could control William once he was free, but he's gone rogue. She may have underestimated the good doctor's abilities. That, or her allegiance. But you're right, these games scream manipulation, and I'm sure it's Dr. Kotera. What is her agenda? Like William, she knows who you are."

"And that bitch pulled a gun on me!" Amanda sneered. "Don't worry, I'll deal with her."

Jules knew what that pointed statement most likely meant, but she could not concern herself with it. While she had every intention of going after the online publication and Hawthorne, Jules had not given much thought to Dr. Kotera. *Perhaps it's best if I leave her to Amanda.*

"Email me everything you have on William. And as far as that cyber-rag, whatever it's called, I'll deal with those scumbags later."

"*We* will deal with them," Amanda corrected.

Jules smiled. She truly appreciated having Amanda's unique expertise helping her. The bitch had her back, and it looked to be an ongoing thing.

At the sound of her phone buzzing, Jules looked down to read a new text. It was from lobby security. Phillip had entered the building. "Phillip's back."

"I guess that's my cue to cut out," Amanda declared. "I want to check in with your security again. Remember, if you need me, holler."

Earlier, Jules had asked Amanda to leave the room once Phillip returned with the signed documents. When her father discovered the truth, she did not want him to process everything in front of a stranger.

"Thanks, but I'm pretty sure I can handle Phillip," Jules replied somewhat sarcastically.

"I wasn't referring to that fucker. I meant your father. Are you prepared for what he might do? He'll want to kill him. Attack him, at the very least. Are you completely sure this is the right move, Jules? Do you know what you're doing?"

"I do, Amanda. At least, I hope I do."

Amanda waited by the elevators, watching for one of the doors to open. When one finally did, she ambushed the sole departing occupant, assaulting him with a contemptuous sneer. She wanted to kick the shit out of Phillip as he walked on into the hallway, but she respected her promise to Jules to keep her hands off him.

"She's expecting you, and you better not disappoint her, fucker, if you know what's good for you."

Phillip sneered back but refused to acknowledge Amanda any further. A folder in hand, and with a severely pissed-off look frozen on his face, he quickly turned from his antagonist, marching angrily towards his wife's office.

Amanda grinned knowingly, recognizing the truth behind Phillip's irascible responses. It was an anger born of defeat and actually directed at oneself. It was acceptance, no matter how distasteful, of being conquered. It was a realization of and hatred towards one's weaknesses.

Amanda had personal experience with feelings of deep bitterness and confusion; the acerbic look on Phillip's face resonated with her. Her own conflicted feelings for Jules had made her a victim of that same kind of inescapable self-hatred in times past. Amanda's continued, percipient grin suggested a kinship with Phillip, but it was a relationship devoid of empathy.

"That's the price you pay, asshole," she hollered down the hall. "You never get out whole and unscathed. Not with her. Suffer!"

Despite the distance now between them, Amanda heard Phillip call her a bitch under his breath. She could not have cared less about his name-calling. Phillip's shattered pride was not her priority, no matter how entertaining it was. She was here because of William.

Practically deserted, the main executive-level had only one receptionist currently at the front desk near the elevators. Miles was still around, per Jules's request, and the security detail remained at the ready. The rest of the employees on this floor had been told to leave, no explanation was given. Jules expected compliance; she got it.

The truth was, she did not want a grand audience in case her father totally lost it on Phillip after the final revelation.

Amanda turned towards the receptionist and flashed her a brief, flirty smile.

The woman was slim with big tits—Amanda's type—but it was the overall package that had piqued her interest. Straight auburn hair, blunt-cut bangs, a pair of pink two-toned Prada eyeglasses, a cream, tight-fitting blouse, and a charcoal-grey pencil skirt. Amanda could not see what shoes she had on because of the desk, but she fantasized that they were red pumps. *This bitch is working some sexy librarian realness.*

The receptionist returned Amanda's obvious flirtation with a curt half-smile, almost a sneer but slightly friendlier, and then quickly turned back to her computer screen.

Amanda had been shut down cold. She snickered, slightly amused by the outright rejection. *Okay then.* She proceeded down the east hallway to check on Miles and make sure that he was occupied and out of the way.

Despite his senior executive position, Miles had been ordered by Jules to remain behind and act as her assistant in Nazneen's inconvenient absence.

When Amanda got to Miles's office and saw through the glass partitions that he was on the phone, safely preoccupied with work, she left him to his own devices.

Turning the corner, Amanda made her way down to the security station, intending to scrutinize for the third time that day the building's security protocols. She wanted to make sure the guards were monitoring everything, prepared for anything, and following her instructions to the letter. Jules had given Amanda carte blanche to dictate and enact anything she so desired concerning their safety.

Amanda had been prepared for the security team to consider her an unnecessary, interfering nuisance. Initially, the guards had been taken aback by her bossy attitude. Amanda's unexpected involvement intimated to the men that Jules no longer had faith in their ability to be an autonomous, capable agency, ensuring the safety of everyone within the building.

And they were correct. Jules felt the recent gross lapse in the building's security was unacceptable. It was not about disrespect; it was about disappointment and lack of trust.

At first, the prideful men had perceived Amanda as an unnecessary babysitter. Her military experience and considerable knowledge of firearms and surveillance equipment soon earned their respect. They acted professionally, keeping their word choices respectful.

The security room was not huge by any means, but it was big enough to adequately house several burly guards. Amanda wanted to check in again, making sure they were vigilantly watching for any sign of William and Dr. Kotera. Every member of the security team had been briefed on Jules's enemies.

There were more security guards on the ground floor level. Amanda had visited them twice already since getting Jules her first Starbucks drink. She doubted William could get past the ground floor check-in points, but she was taking no chances. Anything out of the ordinary or suspicious was to be immediately looked into and reported back to her.

Amanda was thankful for her paranoid perseverance when she got to the end of the hallway and realized the door to the security office was ajar. That was not a good sign. The security door was electronically controlled and designed to close automatically if left open by human forgetfulness.

Her senses alert, Amanda glanced at the control panel where one had to punch in a code and use a key card to get in; the light that signified it was working was off. *Someone has cut the power, but the lights are still on out here. This is a system hack!*

Amanda positioned herself on the right side of the door and took out the blade she had used earlier on Phillip. Jules had forbidden her from bringing a gun into the building. Ever prepared, Amanda had hidden several bladed weapons on her person strapped to her body. All were easily retrievable. She wished she had been this prepared during her first encounter with William.

Moving closer to the aperture, Amanda peeked inside the security office. She was able to quickly determine one major thing: there was no movement inside the room. No one was standing up, either. Thanks to the light emanating from the hallway, she made out shapes that appeared to be bodies. All were immobile.

Amanda kicked open the door. To avoid a surprise bullet or three, she immediately dropped to the floor. Channelling her Capoeira training, she contorted her body into a strike position. Her blade was ready to jab, slice, or fly.

On the off chance that she had somehow missed something, she trusted that her brutal assault on the door had been enough to startle them, buying her time to counter any move made against her. She doubted anyone lying in wait for her would expect an attack from the ground outside a doorway.

However, nothing immediately happened.

Cautiously, Amanda stood up. Now that the hallway light fully shone through into the room, she quickly scrutinized her surroundings. Two security guards were slumped over a desk, while another was on the floor in a corner. Dead. All three had their heads bashed in by some unknown hard, blunt object. Blood was everywhere.

"Damn," she sighed. "The bastard's here."

"Take them," Phillip barked, throwing the folder of signed papers at Jules. "I hope you choke on them."

Jules winked at him mockingly, laughing, "I bet you do." She was elated. All the required legal documents she needed to take total control of the company were signed, dated, notarized, and safely in her possession. All parties involved had done their part; everyone willing, under duress or deceived.

Charles looked everything over with a fine-tooth comb. Once he was completely satisfied that Phillip had not attempted any deceitful manoeuvring, he excused himself and headed to Jules's private bathroom. Once inside and behind a closed door, he intended to place the documents inside the secret safe.

Phillip did not notice Charles leave with the signed documents. His need to build on the morsel of information he had looked at earlier had become an all-consuming obsession. His eyes focused squarely on Jules and the one remaining folder on her desk.

"Not that I care how you did it," Jules stated, "but I'm glad you got Sonja to sign everything so quickly, so efficiently. She didn't ask to read what she was signing? No request to have a lawyer present? Just did it without question, eh? I guess it's a good thing she trusts you implicitly, Phillip. You sure got her fooled. Such a good brother. What an unbelievably stupid bitch she is falling for your act."

"You're the only bitch I see," Phillip growled. "Betraying Sonja was one of the hardest things I've ever had to do! She believes I'm borrowing her shares to use them against you. You don't know how much I wish that were true.

"All this for money, Jules? For power? You have all of that! I don't understand any of this. Control over the company? You pretty much have that, too. Why do this? You could have just left me! You're despicable. You—you're a stranger to me! Who are you?"

Jules laughed at the question.

"I'm the woman who took this company, alright, but not just away from you, your sisters, and your horrible mother. I took it away from that dead bastard father of yours, too. You call me despicable, but your family is the real evil. Your father and mother are monsters, and now not one of their children has any claim to this company. Try to buy in again, and I'll know and stomp you to dust. I've destroyed Joseph's legacy of evil. That's what I wanted, Phillip.

"I'll be changing the name, of course. How does Dunning-Bainbridge Worldwide sound? I think it has a nice ring to it. Yes, this is a good day. And I'm not done yet."

"Just shut up! Give me that damn folder already! I did what you asked! You promised. Give it to me!"

"Of course. A deal's a deal. I said I'd hand it over to you myself, and I keep my word."

Jules picked the folder in question up off her desk, but it was not the same folder she had shown Phillip previously. This one looked the same as the previous one, the documents were the same, but it was shrink-wrapped. Also, the USB flash drive, the very one that backed up the documentation, was nowhere to be seen.

Phillip yanked the package out of Jules's grasp. He looked curiously at it, confused by the odd, unnecessary use of shrink-wrapping. Phillip assumed it was just another mean-spirited game played on him by his demented wife to prolong his torture before learning the truth. Frantic to discover what he could about his child and the fate of his first wife, Phillip savagely tore the plastic covering away.

And that is when Jules's ultimate, final act of revenge sprung to life.

The folder, and every piece of paper inside of it, became inexplicably damp. Then, everything began to dissolve.

Horrified, Phillip tried with all his might to hold onto the liquifying papers to keep them whole and intact, but it was a hopeless cause. Everything oozed through his fingers onto the floor, creating an acrid stench. Eventually, nothing remained, not even soggy pulp. It was all gone.

Shaking violently, Phillip turned his perplexed, hateful gaze towards his wife.

"What? How? I don't understand. What have you done, you crazy, fucking bitch?!"

"I'm not crazy, Phillip," Jules plainly stated, a wicked smile on her face. "I'm vindictive as hell, but not crazy."

Exiting the bathroom just as the papers began to dissolve in Phillip's hands, Charles had watched the entire spectacle in awe and bewilderment.

The expression on his daughter's face sent a shiver down Charles's spine. He hated seeing her look so sinister, so wickedly gleeful in response to another person's shock and pain, even if that person was Phillip. He did not want her to become like her enemies in the process of punishing them. He was greatly unnerved and concerned.

"Jules, honey, what are you doing?"

"You see, Pops, I've been working closely with Mode-Génétique Labs on something. They were already moving beyond genetics into other areas, and I just happened to have a great idea for them. A solution that completely dissolves certain types of biological matter at an accelerated rate when coated in it and oxygenated."

"So, you're a fucking scientist now!" Phillip hollered, red-faced, his neck veins bulging.

Jules walked over to where her husband stood and slapped him hard across the face.

Phillip took several steps back, stumbled, and fell onto the sofa. Completely shocked, he rubbed his throbbing cheek. For the first time in his life, he was afraid of his wife.

"Don't interrupt again! As I was saying, once the solution is generously applied, there's a time delay before it activates, dissolving the material. Getting that under control was the tricky part, but I needed that time delay. I had to get every piece of paper in that folder coated. Paper is one of the things the solution works on. If the coated object is immediately sealed air-tight, the disintegration process is arrested.

"Here's the best part! According to the testing done so far, the solution never seems to degrade or lose potency. Once exposed to oxygen again, the chemicals instantly activate, destroying anything coated lightning fast. It turns the organics into a harmless, inert gas as it dissolves. It will have many positive applications for the environment and waste removal once perfected and tested vigorously. At the moment, I just need it working at baseline efficiency."

"But why, Jules?" Charles queried, feeling deep concern for his daughter's state of mind. "You got what you wanted. It's all yours! You promised to give him the information. What harm is there in letting him know what happened?"

"She's a lying, deceitful, power-mad viper," Phillip angrily testified, near tears again.

"Sticks and stones and all that, but never call me a liar. I kept my word, Phillip. You had everything in your hands. It's not my fault you couldn't read it fast enough.

"You see, Phillip, you took something important from me. You took something I loved deeply. In return, I now take something equally as important from you. How does it feel to be tortured by such a loss?"

"What the hell are you talking about?!" Phillip screamed. "I never took anything from you! You've taken everything from me! My company, my confidence, my self-worth. You've trashed my reputation, maligned my character, crippled me emotionally. You targeted my family, forcing me to betray them. You poisoned the memory of my father and ruined my relationship with my mother! Everyone thinks I'm an idiot and a loser.

"And now you've stolen my child from me, stolen my chance to know them and be with them! How could you do this, Jules? What did I ever do to make you hate me this much? To make me suffer like this?"

"What have you done? I'll tell you, you selfish, alcoholic bastard! It was you! You killed him! You killed my dad!"

Phillip's eyes went wide with complete surprise and confusion. It was a deranged statement and an ugly accusation. One he never in a million years expected to hear. His mouth hung agape, contorted in disbelief and disgust.

"That's insane! That's a completely insane thing to say to me. My god, what's wrong with you? You've completely lost your damn mind! Charles, are you listening to this? Dislike me all you want, but can you abide by this nonsense? You know this isn't right! This is just too much! She's gone too far!"

Charles hated to agree with anything Phillip said, but he certainly could not disagree. Moving within reach of Jules, he gently took her by the arm and spun her around towards him. "He's right, Jules. This has gone too far. How could you bring your dad into all this? What a ridiculous, mean-spirited thing to say! Stop this. It's finished."

"It's not finished! I'm sorry it has to be this way, Pops, but it's time for the truth. The whole truth. You need to know, and that bastard needs to know what he did!"

"Jules, I'm begging you, please don't do this," Charles pleaded. "It was a terrible accident. Phillip had nothing to do with it. Don't lose yourself now by making things up to try and hurt him further. You're only hurting yourself—and me."

"I understand, Pops," Jules sympathized. "You're confused, but I know what I'm talking about. Everything we know about Dad's death is a lie. That thing I wouldn't tell you about before? This is it. All of it was in Joseph's files, written down in explicit detail. This is what changed my attitude toward Phillip forever.

"It wasn't a poor decision made by a tired truck driver that ended dad's life! It's all been a huge lie masterminded by evil people to protect one of their own at our expense. It's going to hurt you, Pops, but I have to tell you the truth about what really happened that awful night."

Jules turned towards Phillip and glared menacingly at him. "I'm going to tell you both!"

XXII

Amanda noticed something immediately; someone had deactivated the security monitors. *He doesn't want anything recorded. The bastard believes he's walking away from this. How did he get up here? How did he get the jump on these men?*

Determined to get to Jules, Amanda turned to leave the room but found her exit blocked by William. Standing directly outside the door, he was dressed in head-to-toe combat gear. Tight-fitting, dark navy cargo pants, a tactical grey compression t-shirt, and black military combat boots.

In both hands, William held what Amanda initially thought were polypropylene police batons; a more detailed look revealed them to be Southeast Asian rattan. Darkly stained, almost black.

"Escrima sticks," he announced pompously. "I see you examining them. Do they look familiar? They're a tad bloody, but I think you can still make out the leopard emblem. A gift from your brother."

The mention of her brother infuriated Amanda. Once again, the realization that he had degraded himself to train one as unworthy as William for no better reason than financial gain enraged her.

"Those twats didn't know what hit 'em," William chuckled. "I'm well trained in the art of Arnis, bitch. Or Kali, if you prefer. I knew you'd be here."

"Yes, it's time we finished this," Amanda coldly replied, and then she removed her jacket. As she did this, she forsook the blade she held by deftly wrapping it up in the discarded garment.

"The last time we met, I wasn't truly who you thought I was. That person was too antagonistic, too verbose with her prey, allowing false expectations and ego to blind her. This time is very different. Today, William Falsworth, you truly face death. Today, you face the Silver Dagger."

With that said, Amanda—Silver Dagger—shut her mouth, turned her lips into a tight, thin line, and opened her eyes wide, hawk-like. She was now the assassin: cold, determined, and unafraid. Reaching around her back, Silver Dagger expeditiously freed two ebon blades from their holders. The deadly sharp karambits were twins in appearance; their design was entirely modern, not as severely hooked as they traditionally were.

"Nice, but that's not a very practical outfit to fight in. A little on the supermodel side, no? I don't see it offering much protection, Luv."

"Appearances can be deceiving. This fabric moves with me like a second skin. I don't need armour. You're nothing to me."

"And you've put yourself in front of my prey. Your mistake." William backed up, beckoning his opponent to follow him into the hallway. "Shall we?"

Silver Dagger nodded. She understood William's statement was an invitation rather than a question; it was his acceptance of the inevitability of battle. This fight was to begin civilly, with respect. She was amazed William had any respect for a woman, but then again, she was no ordinary woman.

With determination and focus, Silver Dagger walked into the openness of the wide hallway. Not that she needed space to kill him. *Maybe it's not about respect at all. Perhaps he's just too scared to fight me in close quarters. He needs the space, especially to use those sticks effectively. Amateur.*

Facing her opponent, Silver Dagger noted that her back was to the South, towards the direction of the elevators and Jules's office. William's arrogance and self-confidence spoke volumes. What was to stop her from racing down the corridor to alert Jules to his presence? Nothing. *He's not worried about having to chase me. He wants this fight. So, you desire combat over a gun. Do you have something to prove, fool?*

Perhaps, but more to the point, she certainly did.

To her knowledge, Silver Dagger had never before fought anyone trained by the Gold Leopard. She desperately wanted to trounce William, devastatingly, and have that fact get back to her brother. She knew it was prideful, but William encompassed everything she hated about her brother's arrogance and cruelty.

It was the worst kind of sibling rivalry, created and encouraged by their father. It had gone on for years until death finally silenced daddy dearest's antagonistic tongue. At that point, each sibling had vowed to stay out of the other's way.

However, an opportunity now presented itself. One Silver Dagger was not about to turn down. She could take out her grudges against the Gold Leopard peripherally by beating the crap out of one of his acolytes. She was a master Kali martial artist, and if William wanted to play it that way, so be it. She would show him who was truly better in the discipline.

William moved menacingly around his end of the hallway, his psychotic gaze fixed squarely on his opponent, a haughty look cemented on his face. With the sinewy strength in his arms, he made his weapons dance fluidly yet aggressively. The hardwood sticks made a rhythmic whipping sound as they cut through the air.

Silver Dagger was thoroughly unimpressed with William's Hong Kong cinema theatrics. She was not fucking around; this was deadly serious to her.

Crouching low, her knees bent but not locked, Silver Dagger waited pensively to strike. William had height, and so it made sense to her to formulate an attack from a lowered position, using her shorter stature to her advantage. His weapons had greater reach, and so she intended to make his arms work hard if he wanted those sticks to connect with any part of her body.

Which she was confident they would not.

Silver Dagger brought her left arm back, bent at the elbow, preparing to use the blade in that hand to swing out and upwards for an attack on William's abdomen or kidney. She also considered going for his armpit if it became open and exploitable. As she had learned long ago, a solid shot to an armpit could be surprisingly devastating.

In contrast to her left arm, Silver Dagger kept her right arm high, closer to her head for defence, but bent and flexible enough for an offensive facial attack. Her specific targets were William's eye-sockets.

Ordinarily, she would not hesitate to attack, but Silver Dagger held her position. She wanted to see what William would do once he stopped dancing around and posturing. The beginning stance determined one's ability to move, defend or attack, and if done incorrectly, it prohibited instant movement.

Silver Dagger expected William to completely extend his arms out, lock his elbows in place and cross his sticks out in front of his lower body. That would leave his head and neck wide open. He would have to first uncross his arms before being able to strike out or defend himself. Highly inefficient. *Are you going to pose for me, asshole? The effective fighter strikes in one count, not two. Come on, Willy, be predictably stupid.*

Aware of his opponent's preparedness and readiness to begin, William finished flitting about in a taunting manner to assume his chosen fighting position: the Forward Stance. Generally used for an offensive attack, this position was also preferential when the fighter wanted to quickly bridge the distance between himself and his opponent, especially during weapon-based combat.

William brought his left foot forward, about two steps in front of the right one, and bent his front knee, placing a considerable portion of his weight on that leg. He kept his rear leg straight with just a slight bend for flexibility and quick manoeuvrability. Both legs were shoulder-width apart to maintain a strong balance.

Raising one stick to defend his head and upper torso, William lowered the other to defend against attacks to his most vulnerable body parts. His arms were bent, positioned correctly.

Silver Dagger smirked at her opponent's anything but stupid choice. Pressing her attack, she launched herself forward, jutting her right arm out, the karambit deftly gripped in her hand. She aimed to slice across William's face, thinking to blind him with either a torrent of blood or the destruction of an eyeball or two.

Alert, William moved nimbly to intercept the blade. The karambit's razor-sharp metal bit into an escrima stick; however, the wood was incredibly dense, making the bite shallow. William promptly knocked the blade out and pushed his attacker back.

Thrusting his right arm forward, William hoped to connect his baton with his opponent's bent elbow. He wanted to bash the bone as hard as he could.

And he played right into Silver Dagger's hand. She had counted on him doing something aggressive and reactionary. Instinctually, she pressed her advantage, now that William's right side was open and vulnerable, and went straight for his right kidney.

Avoiding his oncoming weapon with grace and ease, Silver Dagger swiftly spun away from the predictable attack. Swinging her arm around, she brought one of her blades crashing into William's right side. The weapon easily penetrated his compression shirt and went into the flesh up to the hilt.

William grunted, refusing to cry out in pain.

Having seen the potentially fatal blow coming, William had shifted his weight just enough to change the position of his body. He avoided having his kidney or any other major organ in that area pierced. His side hurt like a bitch, though.

As Silver Dagger pulled her blade out of William's body, the wound began to bleed.

Quickly deciding that it was an injury he could ultimately recover from, William ignored the pain and blood and got back into the fight.

Each combatant used their knowledge of Arnis, its teachings and methods, against the other without restraint.

Both opponents understood that the focus of combat was about defending against and reacting to specific angles of attack. It was not just defending against blows to various body parts or particular strikes with certain weapons. William and Silver Dagger were each adept at recognizing the angles of their opponent's onslaught of aggression: stance, positioning, balance, and point of attack.

Each party jabbed and kicked, slashed and parried, attacked and defended; however, no one landed another wounding blow.

Realizing both of them were astutely predicting and defending against the other's moves, Silver Dagger decided to get creative to gain an advantage. Showcasing incredible agility and balance, she ran up the wall to avoid another of William's expected roundhouse kicks to her head. As she came back down to the ground, she brought her fist down hard on his unprotected jaw, his escrima sticks too low to the ground to protect him.

William staggered slightly, but his momentary uncertainty bought Silver Dagger enough time to strike out and slash at her opponent's hands. The cuts were not deep, but they stung enough that William dropped one of his weapons.

When the stick hit the floor, Silver Dagger kicked it down the hallway. Then, she performed a roundhouse kick of her own that viciously connected with William's chin. He stumbled backward but caught himself before falling to the ground.

"Cunt!" he cursed, spitting blood onto the floor.

Silver Dagger snickered, amused by her opponent's anger and frustration. *Yes, get angry, lose focus, make mistakes.* She understood why he was pissed off, and it was not just from the pain.

William was losing; they both knew it; he could not defeat her. She was just too quick, too relentless. Frustrated, William had gone almost entirely on the defensive, and that was a death sentence when fighting a killer as well trained as the Silver Dagger. It was all too horrifically apparent now to William that she would soon break through his defences and strike a fatal blow.

Propelled by an all-consuming desire to humiliate and then kill William, Silver Dagger continued to attack as a warrior born. William defended himself as best he could, but eventually, one of her kicks landed square in his gut. Not only did it knock the wind out of him, but it forced him down to the ground.

His breathing was uneven, his abdomen throbbed, and the still seeping wound had stained his shirt terribly. William was a bloody, tired, sweaty mess. The last remaining escrima stick fell softly out of his hand and onto the floor where it stayed, motionless and ineffectual.

"You had to know it would end this way, Falsworth. I'll tell Jules you cried at the end, pleading with me to spare your worthless life. She'll like hearing that."

Before Silver Dagger could move forward, her blades poised to rip William apart, the front desk receptionist appeared from around the corner. Looking at the startling scene, she put her hand to her mouth and gasped loudly.

"Oh, for fuck's sake!" Silver Dagger spat out. "Could you have worse timing, bitch?"

Oddly calm, William remained stationary on the floor. "Looks like we have an audience, Luv."

The receptionist promptly began rummaging around in her oversized handbag.

"Don't call the police," Silver Dagger ordered. "Run to Jules's office, and tell her what you've seen. Don't bother screaming for security. They're toast, trust me. Just do as I say. Go get your boss and Mr. Dunning! Got it?"

"Oh—okay, I'll do that," the woman stammered, but her hand remained inside her bag, fishing for something.

Unconcerned by the panicked woman's fidgeting, Silver Dagger turned away from her, focusing her piercing gaze back on William. "Ignore her. Now, where were we? Right. Me fucking you up. Permanently."

"You sure about that?" William challenged.

Silver Dagger was about to counter William's bullshit bravado, considering his current predicament, with a sassy comeback. Unfortunately, something stopped her from successfully pursuing that endeavour.

An extraordinary amount of pain suddenly shot through her entire body, like someone was beating her with a dozen baseball bats, repeatedly slamming them against her over and over. Her muscles contracted and spasmed as if she had suddenly developed a Charley horse in nearly every part of her body. The agony was unrelenting.

With her central nervous system betraying her, Silver Dagger tried to control her balance and comprehend what was happening to her body. Her eyes bulged, and multiple skeletal muscles started cramping and seizing up terribly. Though her vision was now compromised, unfocused, she was able to make out the blurred shape of what she believed to be an X26 taser gun in the hands of the receptionist.

"You—stupid—bitch!" Silver Dagger painfully spat out.

Eventually, under the electrifying assault, Silver Dagger collapsed. Riddled with unexpected pain but still semi-conscious, she tried valiantly to fight back against the paralyzing effects of the attack, but it was no use. She watched, helplessly, as the receptionist walked over to her, bent down, and revealed something surprising.

"Should have looked a little harder at the details instead of focusing on my tits," Yasmine declared, taking off her glasses. She pointed at the lace front application of her wig.

"Stop yapping and go get my weapons!" William commanded.

"Are you okay, my love?" Yasmine queried, deeply concerned. "No, you're injured!"

Ignoring her, William picked himself up off the floor and turned towards his incapacitated enemy. "What you're feeling, Silver Dagger, is the effects of 50 000 volts at 26 watts on the human body. Nice, huh? Always good to have a backup plan.

"I hate to admit it, but I can't beat you in a fair fight. I hoped I could, but I'm not as arrogant as you may think. You call it toxic masculinity, but it's just my truth—I'm superior to almost everyone else. You're just one of those blasted, bloody exceptions. At least at combat, anyway. Yasmine, my weapons! Now! Pick up the karambits, too."

While Yasmine ardently collected the weapons, William prowled around his captive.

"Don't worry, Amanda, or whatever you call yourself, I won't kill you. Out of respect for my Sensei, your brother, I'm going to tie you up and lock you away in the security room with the other dead weight. Pun intended. I know you'll eventually free yourself once the effects of the taser start to wear off, but I'll be long gone by then after I've killed that bitch. Good luck with finding me."

William ordered Yasmine to get the first aid kit from the security office and tend to his wound. After she successfully stopped the bleeding and bandaged everything up, she reached into her purse, grabbed a gun, and handed it over to him.

"Yasmine, return to Château Bergé and wait for me. I want to do the rest of this in private. Make sure everything is ready. I want to leave immediately upon returning. Gretchen has a jet waiting for us at Toronto Pearson International. Have you been recording what's been going on in there?"

"Yes," Yasmine assured. "It's still recording."

"Good. Now go!"

Yasmine tried to kiss William goodbye, but he pushed her away. "Enough! Go and do something useful. You're doing my fucking head in."

Viciously rebuked, Yasmine walked towards the elevators with a heavy heart. Still, she believed things would return to normal once they were back in Amsterdam, his obsession with Jules a thing of the past.

Once alone with Amanda, William dragged her into the security station and tied her up using a rope he had stashed away earlier in the room. He tossed the karambits into the trash can as an open insult to the Silver Dagger, and then he placed his escrima sticks at her bound feet.

"A reminder of your defeat today. Damn, Amanda, you look fine tied up like that."

Bending down, William licked up the side of Amanda's face. To him, she was no longer the unbeatable assassin; she was just another piece of ass. "If only we had more time. Now, if you'll excuse me, I have something to listen to before I pay a visit to Mr. Chen."

Though paralyzed, Amanda's mind had already begun to clear. One powerful thought floated around inside her head as she looked dead into William's gloating face, his wet, thick saliva now stuck to her cheek.

Oh, bitch! You're gonna pay for that!

"Phillip was at my party, though only briefly," Jules calmly began. "Drunk, belligerent, and looking for his father. It was around the time dad left to see that patient, Pops. A little before it, actually."

"I was not!" Phillip screamed. "I didn't even know you back then! My sister was, ya, and my dad, but not me. I was drunk that night, sure. I even fell down the stairs at home from my stupidity. Aside from a quick trip to the emergency room with a nasty cut and a terrible headache, I never left the house that weekend. I told you this!"

"What you recall! What a fucking joke! I have the hotel security footage from that night. That's why we couldn't get any video of William from hotel security, Pops. Somehow, Joseph had managed to get his hands on it before the police procured it."

"Who the fuck is William?" Phillip asked, frustrated. "What are you talking about? Let me see this footage!"

Jules quickly realized her original plan to verbally recount the events of that night to both her father and her husband was not going to work. Phillip was erratic, questioning her constantly, and she knew he would not stop interrupting her despite her earlier warning. Her father, on the other hand, was beginning to shut down and close himself off to the truth, refusing to listen, refusing to participate.

I guess it's option B, then. Jules ordered Phillip to get up off the sofa and sit in her chair.

He was sick of being bossed around by his wife, but Phillip obeyed, nonetheless. Mumbling angrily to himself, he shot her a nasty look as he made his way to her chair.

Next, Jules politely instructed her father to sit down on the newly vacated sofa. He also did what she asked, but with no fuss or furor.

Without wasting any more time, Jules activated the giant TV built into one of the bookshelves; with the press of a button, the previously mentioned security footage appeared on the screen.

"Watch, Phillip. Seeing as you want more proof than just my word, you'll want to look these over too."

Jules opened up one of her desk drawers, pulled out another manila folder, and threw it on the desk. Grabbing Phillip roughly by the chin, she forcefully directed his head back and forth from the screen to the papers in front of him. He put up no resistance.

"You'll see that your father was quite thorough in his account of what transpired that night. Take your time going over everything, Phillip. I want to enjoy watching you die inside as your reality crumbles to dust."

Releasing her grip on her husband's chin, Jules went and sat down next to her father. She grabbed his hands with her own and held them tight. She saw nothing but pain and turmoil in her father's eyes, the same emotions that had crippled him years ago.

"Pops, I need you to listen to me. I need you to hear me out, all of it to the very end. Can you do that for me?"

"Yes," Charles replied meekly, turning his head away, unable to look any longer into his child's face.

Undeterred by her father's trepidation, Jules reopened an old, barely healed wound.

"What Joseph and Phillip were arguing about that night is irrelevant to all this. Phillip was making a spectacle of himself, so Joseph ordered him to go home. He knew Phillip was drunk, could smell the alcohol on his breath, but he never told him to grab a cab or get someone else to drive him. He allowed his highly intoxicated son to get behind the wheel of a car in an erratic, emotionally charged state.

"Phillip and Dad were going to the same part of town, down the same stretch of road, but it was Phillip who was speeding and driving like a madman. Eventually, he caught up to Dad. Pops, he was the one who crashed into the back of Dad's car, forcing him off the road and straight into that tree.

"The cop who was first on the scene happened to be on Joseph's payroll. What luck for the fucking Cartells! He didn't immediately call it in, request an ambulance, or do anything other than making sure Phillip was okay. He chose to get the ball rolling on a quick cover-up to protect the son of his secret, wealthy boss. He was one of many dirty cops who looked the other way and made things disappear for Joseph.

"That cop and other crooked officers diverted traffic away from the scene, and once that was in place, Joseph was promptly informed about what had happened. With Sonja in tow, Joseph got to the scene from the hotel in record time."

"But O'Malley, the truck driver!" Charles shouted. "He admitted to it!"

"That lying sack of shit didn't come on the scene until just after Joseph did," Jules angrily revealed, "somehow avoiding all the detours. Remember, Pops, O'Malley only admitted to not seeing Dad's car in his blind spot until it was too late to stop his truck from forcing him off the road. 'It was too dark,' he'd said! Utter horseshit, but no one doubted him because there was no alcohol or drugs in his system.

"Pops, Joseph bought O'Malley's compliance and participation. The minute details don't matter. What's crucial for you to understand and accept is that Joseph convinced that scumbag to take the blame. On top of his truck payments, O'Malley had gambling debts, big ones. Joseph promised to take care of all of his financial woes plus a bonus million-dollar payout.

"O'Malley saw an opportunity, he took it, and he got away scot-free with money in his pockets for just one big lie. Until three months later, after all the dust settled, when Joseph had him killed. Another unfortunate vehicular accident. Joseph hated loose ends. The potential for blackmail, you see."

Still seated on the sofa, Jules turned her head and stared daggers at her emotional wreck of a husband. She knew he was listening to her even though his watery eyes continued to gaze down at the damning documents in front of him.

"Phillip's BMW was still functional enough to drive," Jules stated, turning back to her father. "Joseph had to get it and Phillip away from the scene. He had Sonja drive Phillip to the hospital in his car. That lying bitch is just as guilty, just as complicit. Sonja concocted that phony story about Phillip falling down the stairs at home, taking it upon herself to drive his unconscious ass to the ER. Apparently, she forgot 911 existed.

"Lies, Pops, all of it! Phillip was in that state because he'd been in a drunk driving collision where he'd killed the driver of the other car! My dad! Your husband! Phillip is responsible for his death, and the entire Cartell family, except for Denise, knew about it and willingly covered it up!"

"My Jason," Charles whispered, tears welling up in his eyes.

Jules grabbed hold of her emotionally devastated father and hugged him tightly. "I know, Pops. I'm here."

"But he was my friend, Jules! He knew my husband. How could Joseph do that to me? He knew the entire time we worked together, hung out together, that his son had killed my Jason. He knew the entire time! I was fooled by him again. How could I have been so fucking blind?"

Out of the corner of her eye, Jules spied Phillip at her desk. He had become white as a sheet; his eyes were red and puffy. Phillip was still reacting negatively to the security footage put on a repetitive loop, the damning files, and Jules's damning words. As he held the papers in his hand, practically crushing them, he continuously protested against what he had just learned about himself.

Jules heard Phillip lament, saying over and over again that none of it was true, but she understood that her husband, by the look in his eyes, did believe it was true. And that newfound knowledge was destroying him; Jules delighted in his torment.

Disengaging from the hug, leaving her father to process his emotions and collect his thoughts, Jules got up and stormed over to where Phillip sat, paralyzed by his waking nightmare.

"You did this, so fucking accept it!" she screamed. "You killed my dad, Jason Bainbridge. That was his name. He had a husband, a daughter, a life! You took all that away from him because you're a selfish, careless, narcissistic drunk who got behind the wheel of a car and believed he was invincible! You thought the rules of society didn't apply to you. *You* took him from us!

"It sickens me knowing your father played me, that he was aware of what you did and still facilitated the two of us getting together. Only a monster would do something so vile! Putting the two of us together was a sick, obscene joke. Me, falling in love with the man I should have been hating as the murderer of my dad.

"Maybe Joseph, in his twisted reasoning, thought that his only son and the Cartell heir was such a great fucking catch he owed it to my father to give you to me. Like it was some fair trade for killing my dad! Like it made things secretly even between our families, alleviating any guilt he may have felt.

"Fuck that! You're nothing like my dad, not even close to being his equal, and to make things square between us, well, that will never happen!"

"But—but, you stayed with him, Jules," Charles muttered. "Why? How could you, knowing what Phillip had done?"

"I had to take into account our plans for the company, Pops. It was about timing, in part, but it was so much more than that. It wasn't enough for me to hurt Phillip just once by revealing his crime. He had to be punished, broken a piece at a time. Day after day, week after week, month after month, I made that personal sacrifice until there was almost nothing left of him to destroy.

"Robbing you of both Genevieve and your child is cold comfort for what you've done, Phillip, but it does help reduce some of the hurt. But there can be no forgiveness for you. Never!"

Jules hauled off and punched Phillip in the face. And then she hit him again. She needed to let out the rage that had bottled up inside her before she exploded and did something even worse than indulge in a few punches.

"Do it, do it," Phillip whimpered, granting her permission. "I'm so sorry, so sorry."

Phillip's acceptance and encouragement of the pummelling only served to enrage Jules further.

"Don't you fucking dare! You don't get to play the martyr! You don't get to apologize and think I'll buy it! You don't get to tell me it's okay to hurt you."

"I get it now," Charles murmured, looking up at Jules from the sofa. Anxious, he repeatedly rubbed his hands together.

Jules momentarily paused. Despite fists still tightly clenched and aimed to continue their assault, she turned around and looked quizzically at her father. She was concerned; there was an odd look in his eyes that unnerved her.

"Pops? Are you okay? How are you doing with all this?" Her questions sounded scripted and ridiculous to her. *How the fuck do you think he's doing! You've had ages to process all this!*

Through tears, Charles looked into his daughter's face and explained his enigmatic comment. His voice was surprisingly calm despite the rage that teemed within him. Curiously, the unmitigated grief Charles felt from reliving Jason's death provided him with a sense of clarity and composure in this terrible moment.

"Something Babineaux said to me when I criticized him for being weak, succumbing to the charms and affections of Stella. For doing an unspeakable act in the name of love. He warned me against mocking him. He said I would know one day if I would kill in the name of love. Once I knew everything.

"That bastard knew, Jules! That's why he kept probing me for your reason for doing all this. Why now? Why not before? Why go down this path at all? He must have believed you were finally looking for a way to punish Phillip for what he did to Jason. Because he knew, and he wanted to know if I was aware of it. But I didn't know, not then, but now I—"

"Forget about him, Pops," Jules interjected before her father could go on any further about something that made no difference anymore.

"Phillip, you must remember Claude Babineaux. Your dad's former right-hand man? It's thanks to him we got what we needed to finish you. He knew so much, but I wouldn't get your hopes up that he'll tell you anything. And you can't blame me for that.

'It's all over the news. Babineaux was found dead in his office this morning. It appears he shot himself in the head. I wonder why he would do something like that? I guess some people won't wait for others to punish them. Perhaps you should kill yourself, Phillip, and save my father the trouble of compromising his principles. No, you're much too cowardly to do something that honourable."

"Please, stop," Phillip whimpered.

"But I'm on a roll," Jules sarcastically declared, "and my news gets better! I purposely never read anything in those files concerning your child. I also destroyed the only flash drive that contained the truth you so desperately desire. All the hard copies are gone. No laptops, no computers, and no magic genie lamps anywhere hold a single shred of info. Nothing in the Cloud, either.

"And with Babineaux dead, my father is the only one who knows who your child is and where they are—or even if they're still alive. Seeing as you killed his husband, though, I doubt he'll tell you anything."

"I think I'm gonna be sick," Phillip announced.

"Of course, you are," Jules scoffed.

Without warning, the door to Jules's office flew open, and Denise practically launched herself into the room. Fire in her eyes, she scanned the area looking for her brother. It took her only a few seconds to locate a brooding, bleeding, fat-lipped Phillip sitting zombie-like in Jules's chair.

"Get away from him, you bitch!" Denise shrieked. "Phillip, don't tell them anything! My god, your nose is bleeding. Phillip, speak to me! He's fucking catatonic! What did you do to him?"

"You've got to be kidding me!" Jules exclaimed, rolling her eyes. "Who the fuck are you supposed to be? The Calvary? How the hell did you get through that door? It's supposed to be locked."

"A new friend told me you were up to something, Jules, and that I should get over here quickly. I hate you for what you did to me!" Denise instinctively turned her attention towards Charles. "And I hate you too, pig! You and Christophe can go fuck yourselves!"

Charles did not react to the harsh words fired at him, let alone Denise's unwelcome, unexpected presence.

"Right now, I'm more concerned about my brother. Don't think you can push Phillip out of his own company now that I know what I know! He'll be ready for you!"

Jules's response to Denise's not-so-subtle hint of some forthcoming revelation of supposed damning information was to show total ambivalence towards it. That, followed by a huge smirk.

"I'm guessing you're referring to that completely untrue story I had Miles feed you yesterday. I was hoping it would play out a little longer, mostly for my amusement, but one must adapt to changes and bumps in the road. Miles is very appreciative of the money, by the way. How kind of you to enable his shoe addiction."

"Fake?" Turning towards her brother, her face red, Denise stammered, "Phillip, I—I—"

"I—I—I!" Jules loudly parodied, cutting Denise off. "Oh, for fuck's sake, girl, give it a rest. I can't believe I'm going to ask this because I so don't care, but who is this new friend that knows my business?"

Before Denise could answer, a voice came from the hallway, chiming in on her behalf.

"That would be me."

With a casual gait, William entered Jules's office. He had Miles in a vice-like grip by the neck. With his free hand, he held a gun, pointed at his hostage's right temple.

If the strained, horrified looks on the faces of everyone in Jules's office revealed anything, it was that the room was now in a mercurial state of panic, disbelief, and terror. It was a veritable storm of mixed emotions.

William's stone-like face revealed nothing except confidence and belief that he was in total control of this situation. He had the gun, after all.

Almost no one moved a muscle; fear and shock appeared to afflict nearly everyone with mass paralysis. Denise, however, managed to turn towards her brother, looking for support; unfortunately, he remained frozen in place, his eyes firmly fixed on William.

The silence and inaction were deafening until Phillip finally stood up and hollered for security.

"Sorry, mate, no one's coming."

XXIII

"Please, don't kill me," Miles begged.

"What the hell's going on here? Will Falsworth? I haven't seen you in years! What the hell are you doing, man?"

"Ask your wife, Phil," William sneered. He remembered Phillip hated hearing his name shortened, and he intentionally did so to piss him off.

"Amanda!" Jules screamed out the doorway, desperately trying to alert her friend and protector to the present danger. The familiar feelings of powerlessness and fear instinctively returned. She hated this uncontrollable reaction whenever she thought about William; not surprisingly, having him physically in front of her after so many years was overwhelming.

"Don't bother with all that nonsense, Luv. She's quite unavailable."

"What did you do to her?" Jules demanded, barely holding on. She felt like her fifteen-year-old self again. *Don't lose it. Don't let him see weakness, or he'll use it against you.*

Charles, overcome with anger and hatred at the unexpected sight of the man that once kidnapped his daughter, jumped off the sofa. Without thinking, he lurched aggressively toward William, screeching, "You sick bastard, I'll—"

"You'll do nothing," William loudly interjected, preventing Charles from finishing his threat. Holding fast to Miles, who remained limp in the unwanted, strangling grip, William quickly moved the gun away from his hostage's head and pointed it towards Jules.

"Stay back, old man," William threatened, "or your precious daughter gets a few new holes in her. Not life-threatening ones, but still quite painful. I need her alive a wee bit longer, but I'm flexible on the state of her condition. Jules, get your father under control, or I promise you'll see his bloody corpse on the floor imminently. Both of you back the fuck up!"

Jules motioned to her father with her arm to move backward, away from William. "Do what he says."

Thinking only of his daughter's safety, a still enraged Charles moved back towards the sofa.

Jerking his gun in a downward movement, William not so subtly motioned to Phillip to sit his ass back down in the chair.

Begrudgingly, Phillip obeyed the silent command. His head was spinning, the knowledge of his role in the death of Jason Bainbridge crushing him. Still, he was sensible enough to recognize the immediate danger to himself and everyone around him.

No matter how much Phillip wanted to act, it was not the right time to try and disarm William. Yes, he was bigger and stronger than his old schoolmate, but he did not have an advantageous position to rush him. That was the plan when the opportunity presented itself. Phillip just had to get out from behind the desk fast enough to take action.

Unlike her brother, Denise was confused, unable to process the scenario in front of her. This display of aggression was not what William had led her to believe was his intended plan for Jules. This scenario in front of her in no way fell under the parameters of an ingenious murder scheme done cleanly, quietly.

No, this was very much the opposite of that.

Denise hated Miles for what he had done, wanting him to pay for humiliating her, but she did not want him to die over it! He was a lying, thoughtless, self-serving manwhore, just like Christophe, but death should not be the payment for those crimes. Denise was not that bitter and angry!

Denise believed Jules was the mastermind, the puppetmaster, behind every vile thing done to her family in recent years; she alone deserved the worst punishment.

Despite her honest desire to help her brother and stop Jules's tyranny, Denise was deeply concerned that she had screwed up big this time. She now realized she had made a horrible mistake in trusting William. It was another shitty judgment call concerning the men in her life. Men who always seemed able to manipulate her feelings and blind her to the truth about them.

"William, I don't understand," Denise stammered. "This isn't how it's supposed to go down!" *Are you batshit crazy?*

"Shut up, slag, you've done your part! Everyone shut the fuck up and stay put! I think you will all find what I'm about to say fascinating. I heard most of your sad, pathetic tale, Jules, and I have to say I rather enjoyed it. Quite the show. Brilliant! Good enough for the Royal National Theatre. The problem is, it's not exactly the truth.

"Don't get me wrong, I thoroughly relished every painful revelation, especially knowing the suffering it brought you. Still, I feel it's my duty, my responsibility even, to enlighten you all as to what actually happened that night. One of the few things I learned in therapy that wasn't total bollocks was this—own your truth."

"What are you talking about?" Jules demanded. "What truth?"

"Seeing that look of fear on your face, Jules, is getting me so fucking hard right now. Seeing you in pain is bloody exciting, just like last time. Yasmine says it's a characteristic, a physical manifestation, that is, of my psychosexual control issue when dealing with the female gender. And you, Jules? You're the quintessential object of my apparent condition. My ultimate trigger, so I've been told.

"But I think it's much simpler than all that head-shrinking rubbish. I want you dead. I need you dead. I can't allow you to exist in a world where my brother doesn't, knowing you're the one who fucking killed him! Why's that so bloody difficult to understand? The desire to make sure you paid with your undeserved life is what kept me going all those years I was locked up in that nuthouse. Death is the least you deserve for murdering Ethan!

"Yasmine made me see that you had to suffer, but I'm done with all that now. Revealing your father's lies, humiliating him was deeply satisfying. His betrayal of your trust was just like your betrayal of my brother's trust. I know it had to have messed you up good, but I realized last night I'd lost the plot. All these complicated games of intrigue got me off track. You need to die, murderer."

"I didn't murder Ethan," Jules calmly stated.

"Lying bitch!" William hissed.

"I'm not lying, and you know this! Ethan's death was an absolute tragedy, but it wasn't my fault. He walked onto that lake without me, miscalculating how thick the ice was, and fell through. There wasn't anything I could have done to save him."

"Lies!"

"Listen to me, William, you're sick. Dr. Kotera is using you, manipulating you. She's confusing you by using your pain and anguish over Ethan's death for her twisted games. You need help. Please, let me get you that help."

Jules tried hard to bottle up her fear and hatred for the man in front of her to approach the dire situation in a calm, clinical manner. An appearance of fortitude and bravery was a must. She was pretty sure it was a pointless endeavour despite all her bravado and projected confidence. Jules did not want to exacerbate the situation by further antagonizing William with threats, insults, and condemnations. He had the gun.

And he still had not answered her question about Amanda.

William's unpredictable nature was Jules's greatest threat and a huge obstacle to overcome in this precarious, dangerous moment. She understood the need to confront a rational man. She had to gain control over the situation, buy time, and get answers to her questions.

Most importantly, she needed to get her father and Miles out of this whole thing in one piece. Denise and Phillip could fend for themselves.

Though rationality was not something she truly believed was possible with William, Jules did not know what else to try. There was no other previously formulated plan concerning him, just the one with Amanda dealing with him.

Jules never thought she would have to see William. Not to engage him in conversation, a battle of wits or anything on a person-to-person level. She fully expected Amanda to have killed him long before he ever got a chance to get near her.

"Did you just try to rationalize with me, you manipulative bitch?" William spat on the ground in front of Jules. "My brain's been poked and prodded by Europe's best. I've spent years battling wits with countless shrinks, and you think you can use psychobabble on me? That's your attack? Bloody pathetic. Reid was much more—predictably entertaining."

"What the hell does that mean? Where is she?" Jules was unable to mask the desperation and worry in her voice.

"Don't be so daft! Read between the lines. She was predictably physical in her attack and not so annoyingly chatty. Enough already! This isn't about her."

William stopped talking, pressed his lips together, and contorted his mouth into a tight line. Squinting, he looked at Jules with hard, hateful, dark eyes. It was akin to a psychic attack meant to menace and unsettle her.

William's darkness was an infection, and as much as she fought against it, Jules felt his essence penetrate her. She believed her mental and emotional defences, once sturdy and protective, were now being systematically destroyed by his seemingly insurmountable evil.

Despite being very familiar with his monstrous behaviour, expecting and preparing for it, William's soulless inhumanity still managed to knock Jules sideways. Waves of nausea coursed through her body at the thought that he had probably killed the security guards and Amanda.

Slowly moving his head side to side, William gazed around the room, peering into the faces of his hostages. Except for Miles, who was completely unaware of how lucky he was not to have to take in the unsettling gaze. William's ever-changing look, his shifts in mood and temperament, going from righteous anger to snarky, foul-mouthed mockery and back again to his standard cold, dispassionate countenance, was undeniably off-putting.

After a moment of awkward silence, Jules whispered, "She is to me." It was a delayed response to what William had said about Amanda's importance. *No! Don't play into his deceptions. She's hurt, unable to get to me, but not dead. She's the Silver Dagger! He's trying to manipulate you, don't let him. Play along until you can take control of the situation. Keep him talking.*

"How did you get into the building and past my security?" Jules asked. "And how did you supposedly hear what we've been talking about in this closed-off room?"

"You have both Denise and the late Miss Balakrishna to thank for all that."

"What do you mean, William? What did you do? Where is Nazneen?"

"Phillip, I'm so sorry," Denise sputtered.

"Shut up, Denise!" Jules ordered. "Where is Nazneen, William?"

"Nazneen, Nazneen, Nazneen! What happened to Nazneen?" William laughed maniacally. "She was my eyes and ears inside your company for months, collecting information about you, your father, Phil and others, and passing it all on to me. She was also kind enough to provide me with all her passwords and a copy of her keycard.

"Nazneen and I had many deep conversations about you, Jules, over a drink—or in bed. Emotionally battered by you, she was eager to help me in my cause. I didn't have to wear her down much at all. You took care of most of that for me.

"You seem surprised, Jules, that she betrayed your trust. Really? Yes, I've been in Fairporte for months, and I've been in and out of your building numerous times. Overworked, unappreciated, and emotionally abused, Nazneen was only too eager to manipulate your security protocols for me.

"She was so paranoid you would find out about her, and I used that fear to my advantage. I got her to think fucking your head of security to gain his trust and get access to the control room was her bloody idea. Like all women, using her body to get shit by screwing with a guy's head. Thanks to her actions, I was a ghost you never saw, never realized was around. So much betrayal, Jules, and all of it right under your nose.

"Nazneen was responsible for getting my gift to you yesterday. My little reminder of your crime! She did that for me, and you fired some poor, innocent bloke in the mailroom for it.

"In all the time I was banging that bird, the one thing I couldn't convince her to do was get me access to your office, to put a listening device in there. I wanted to hear your vicious, poisonous tongue for myself. But no, that level of invasion was taking it beyond the scope of spycraft she was comfortable with. Bollocks to that, considering the shit she did for me! Things my sister will use to her advantage soon enough.

"Honestly, all she had to bloody well do was lift the damn passcode from you or your father. Well, it seems Miss Balakrishna's dislike for you, Jules, had limits, after all. Because of her fear of you, perhaps? Maybe her secret admiration of you? Who the bloody hell knows! I never undervalue myself, but this time my charm and my cock only got me so far.

"Last night, that bitch tried to cancel our arrangement, telling me she was done with it all—done with me! No one dictates terms to me, so I fucking cancelled her!"

"You killed Nazneen," Jules affirmed.

"Yes, you daft cow! I threw the useless twat off this building's roof last night. A lovely garden you have up there. Now, I didn't give a toss about her, but I made it look like she jumped. It felt like the right thing to do.

"When I got back to Château Bergé, I took time to ponder that decision, concluding that it must have been my subconscious working on my behalf. Once again, some of that psychiatric rubbish penetrated this ol' noggin here. My subconscious saw what I couldn't see with my actual eyes—at that moment, I mean. Suicide over suspected murder was a more fitting end, more proper."

"Why is that?" Phillip asked aggressively.

"Because, Phil, people should think death is preferable to working for a manky bint like Jules. That being in her rotted presence day after day is like slowly being eaten alive. Like living with flesh-eating Ebola. Everyone should know what she is. A disease! She infects people. People should know what lengths a person would go to escape her affliction, to rid themselves of that infection. The infection of you, Jules, the destroyer of lives!"

Jules shuddered, realizing that William considered her as much of a disease, infectious and destructive, as she believed he was. She could not stand to hear it. The idea of being anything like William, of anyone thinking she was anything like him, disgusted her.

"None of you will be alive to contradict this narrative, anyway," William added.

"And Denise's part in all this?" Jules finally asked the question on everyone's mind, especially Phillip's.

"Yes, Denise!" William shouted. His excitement over finally revealing her involvement was unrestrained. He rubbed his hands together like an overly dramatic villain from an old penny-dreadful. "She was more than happy to help me out with whatever I asked of her, and what I wanted from her was access. Cartell's firewalls are too strong to hack externally."

"Damn right, they are," Charles growled.

"Don't look so chuffed! I haven't got to the good part. As I said, Nazneen wouldn't give me access to any of your offices. I had to change tactics, alter my plan. I thought, 'Who's the weakest link in the top executive chain?' That would be you, Phil.

"I considered approaching you directly, mate, but I thought I might as well get some extra fun in before my endgame. A good shag with a Cartell sister was a pleasant thought. Sorry, Phil, you're a nice-looking bloke, but not my type. Since Sonja wasn't around, Denise, the black sheep of the Cartells, was my way in.

"Using your many insecurities against you, Denise, including your sibling rivalry with Sonja, was fucking child's play. Revealing how everyone was in on the joke, but you—you being the joke, of course—was my favourite part. I had that online rag release the story as soon as you left my suite yesterday. Tricking you was like taking candy from a baby. Fucking you was pedestrian, at best, but I bet Sonja's fucking wild in the sack!"

Jules and Charles both turned at the same time and glared daggers at Denise.

Phillip hung his head down; he felt immense pity for his sister and guilt that he had not been a better brother to her, a better protector.

Denise looked like a deer in the headlights: petrified and shocked. She also felt utterly humiliated and deeply ashamed.

"I'm not going to get too detailed about it," William declared. "Suffice it to say that the program Denise uploaded onto Phil's computer last night on my behalf—but of her own free will! I can't stress that enough! She was one hundred percent on board with whatever was necessary to destroy you, Jules.

"What she uploaded is what Gretchen colourfully calls the Espionage Virus. An ace piece of Falsworth designed malware. Gretchen would kill me if she knew I was blabbing about it. As I said, I won't be getting too technical, and it's not like any of you are going to get the chance to blab."

William chuckled and increased his grip around Miles's throat, causing his hysterical hostage to beg again for his life. Snickering, William put the gun back to Miles's temple. "Quit sniffling, or I'll blow your brains out."

Miles closed his eyes, hushed himself, and returned to his former statue-like state.

"Once uploaded," William continued, aiming his gun back at Jules, "the malware gives its controller a backdoor into the network. Total access to every computerized system linked to the mainframe from any external source the controller chooses.

"Every access code in Cartell Worldwide's system is mine. I got into this building last night and today because I control the security cameras, the electronic locks, the elevators, everything. The things my sister will learn as she goes through all your files, your programs, your entire network. Raping your company of its secrets, destroying or reprogramming anything and everything.

"And before I forget. That little thing I said about knowing what you were talking about in this room? How I alerted Denise to what you were up to today? The malware upload also includes listening and recording capabilities. Again, thanks, Denise."

While her father kept the focus of his angry, judgmental eyes on Denise, Jules turned her baleful gaze back to William. As much as she wanted to slap the shit out of her sister-in-law for the trouble she had caused, Jules understood that Denise was ultimately just a pawn. William used her because she was gullible and weak. Not blameless by any means, but not worth the focus of her current ire.

And as much as she hated to admit it, Jules had to give William credit for weaponizing Denise's foolishness to such effect. He had both outmanoeuvred and out-thought her on this; she never saw it coming.

"No," Phillip whimpered, turning around in his chair to face his sister. "Denise, what have you done?"

"I swear, I didn't realize what I was doing, Phillip," Denise protested, her face beet red, her eyes watery, and her nose a runny mess. "You have to believe me! He manipulated me! I was so upset over Christophe, and I thought William—I—I just wanted to get Jules out of our lives!

"I thought I was getting him access to Jules's private computer. He said I could do it through yours! He—he said he had new technology—and—and I believed him. He said it was just about her! I didn't know! I wasn't thinking! I'm so sorry!"

"Will you shut the fuck up already, you whiny bitch!" William bellowed. "You wanted her dead as much as I did! You're not innocent! You went for my plan just as quickly as you opened your legs for me. You wanted it so bad, you lying whore!"

William moved his gun off Jules and aimed it at Denise.

Instinctively, Phillip moved to protect his sister. Extricating himself from Jules's office chair, he positioned himself between Denise and the gun.

"Such bravery, mate," William laughed. "I could easily shoot through you, fucker. No, not yet. You have to be alive to hear my final revelation. Everyone shut the fuck up! I'm trying mighty hard here not to kill everyone now and be on my merry fuckin' way. Your face, Jules! Looking at your smug face drives me mad! Every time I look at it, I want to smash it into a bloody pulp. Smash your fucking face in. Smash it—"

William's voice trailed off. His whole body began to shake, and his breathing became heavy, laboured; he was losing control.

Jules was all too familiar with the deranged look on William's face. She understood that if she did not refocus him immediately, they would all pay the price for his violent instability.

"Why is my account wrong, William? Don't you want me to know? Don't you want me to feel pain before killing me? Don't you want me to suffer as Ethan did when he slipped into the icy water, and I did nothing to help him? I thought you said I deserved that suffering?"

Jules did her best to pull William back from the edge of total insanity with her carefully chosen words. If she could re-channel his hatred for her back into his rational desire to tell her his secrets, it could shift the balance in her favour. William could not be outright controlled, but directed, influenced, that was possible. Dr. Kotera had managed to do it. *Where are you, anyway, Kotera? Did Amanda get to you? Amanda, please be okay.*

Suddenly, as if Karma, Fate, Fortune or all three heard Jules's private thoughts and decided to throw her a bone, William grimaced and lurched forward. It was a brief movement, a mere flicker of pain registering on his face. Jules noticed something she had not observed earlier. Something that now offered her added hope for survival.

William's bloody shirt was torn on the left side, almost imperceptibly so, and bandaging was visible through the tearing upon closer inspection. He had been in a fight; that was obvious to Jules. William was hurt, and his momentary lack of focus had allowed his injury to force him to wince in pain.

Now Jules had something to exploit. She suspected the person who had stabbed William was Amanda. *They fought! It's bandaged, so I bet the cut is deep. Good on you, girl, but I wish you'd gutted him.*

"Yes, yes," William wheezed and huffed. "You have to know, have to suffer."

Everyone in the room was on edge yet alert, anxiously waiting for their captor to regain his control and composure.

William shook his head a few times, clearing away the cobwebs and chaos from his mind.

Taking a deep breath, he manoeuvred Miles about half a meter out in front of him. Then, once suitably positioned, William brutally smacked the back of the man's skull with the gun. As a result of the severe blow, Miles promptly fell to the floor, rolled in front of Jules's desk, and immediately lost consciousness.

"That's better," William sighed, his breathing once again even and relaxed. "I can move my arms around freely. The gun, too."

"You're hurt, William," Jules stated, hoping to throw him off his game. "You need medical attention."

"It's nothing, a scratch," William growled. "Like you give a shit about my well-being. That bitch got a few good shots in, I expected as much considering who she is, but I'll be fine. And I'll blow your fucking kneecaps off if you try to insult my intelligence again with another attempt to manipulate me. Now, as I was about to say—oh, where should I start? Yes, I know.

"Your birthday, I was there at the hotel that night, hiding in plain sight, a mask over my face, watching you, Jules. It wasn't a great plan I had, but some aspects of it had forethought. I was playing it by ear for the most part.

"It's funny, but I used to be so big on planning everything out to the last detail. Until you killed Ethan, and after that, something changed. I started to react so much more to things instead of planning out what to do. You did something to me that day, witch. A curse? More like a slow infection. You're a disease, contagious.

"But this part isn't about you. It's about your dad, the dead one. I watched Phil crash the party and flag down his father. The two of them had themselves a right argy-bargy. During the argument, I saw Bainbridge leave the hotel. Moments later, Joseph told his belligerent, drunken git of a son to stop making a scene and go home. That's when I had a devil of an idea!

"By separating himself from the crowd, your dad had gone and made himself an easy target, much like you eventually did, Jules, by going into that bathroom. Phil, you left right after Bainbridge did, so I followed. Your car was parked on the street, which was perfect because no valet meant no waiting. I kept my mask on, so Bainbridge wouldn't recognize me. He was still waiting for the valet to bring his car around. It was all so perfect.

"Phil and I were never great mates, but we knew each other socially. We had both gone to the same private school in Switzerland. The same one both our dads had gone to when they were our age. I was a year ahead."

The acute realization of having been duped by his former schoolmate made Phillip wince, and he cursed himself for not listening to his old friends. Everyone had warned him about William, saying he was a damaged head-case. "The guys were right about you all along," Phillip confessed.

"And just what were those wankers so right about?"

"They warned me about you, Will, said you were unpredictable, untrustworthy, and had a real mean streak. Told me to avoid you at all costs, but as usual, I was too damn ready to give someone the benefit of the doubt. I refused to see those guys as anything more than teenage bullies and you, their misunderstood victim.

"You always seemed so sad to me, Will. So lost. Always alone. I never saw you being mean or hurtful to anyone or anything. You were always cool with me. I felt sorry for you because you had no friends on campus. We didn't hang, but I stood up for you. I never saw the terrible things they all claimed you did, but now I have irrefutable proof. They were right. You're unstable! A fucking maniac!"

Phillip hated himself for being so stupid and gullible. Again, someone had manipulated him into seeing a picture, a personality, a so-called truth that was contrived and entirely fabricated for the selfish benefit of another. "Boy, what a fool I was."

"And still are ya wanker," William chided. "A bloody fool to trust and marry that bitch! Phil, you're so bloody daft. I used you back then, and I'm completely unapologetic about it. You were the most popular, the most athletic. Everyone liked and respected you, but even great Achilles had a weak spot. You're too bloody soft on the inside. Always were the biggest sap I'd ever met. The gentle giant and all that tripe!

"Everyone hated me back then. None of those fucks ever bothered to try and understand me, befriend me, but I quickly realized I didn't want them to. Screw 'em. Still, they sure as shit liked to pick on me. Until you came along, mate. Playing you was so easy it was criminal, just like your simple sister.

"Oh, I knew you were sticking up for me, intimidating those wankers on my behalf, warning them not to touch me. That's what I wanted. It's why I acted the way I did around you—to get you on my side! I was fine to fight them, but why should I get hurt if I didn't have to. Bollocks to that! Not when you could just as easily run interference for me. Did I ever say thanks? No? Well, don't look for it now."

William winked at Phillip and produced a sinister, mocking smile. He followed it up with a brief chuckle.

"Can we get back to that night in Toronto?" Jules impatiently asked.

"Of course," William responded, anxious to get to the meat of his tale. "When I approached Phil, I tried ever so nicely at first to convince his drunk ass to let me drive him home because I was so concerned and all that shit about his safety. After all, I was an old schoolmate just looking out for his bro."

The level of sarcasm in Wiliam's voice was high, and everyone in the room picked up on it. The fact that he could not have cared less about Phillip or the well-being of anyone on the road potentially at risk from his drunk driving was obvious. Phillip had been a pawn, a means to an end, and nothing more.

"You were irritatingly friendly, Phil," William continued, "and infuriatingly uncooperative! Even though I didn't have any beef with you, I had to be an asshole and get mean. There wasn't time for subtle persuasion. Bainbridge was getting into his car, and I had to follow him if my ingenious plan was going to work. I couldn't lose him—I didn't know where he was going!

"When you turned your back on me to get into your car, Phil, I conked you over the bloody head, and as you started to collapse, I pushed your drunk ass over into the passenger side. I got in the driver's seat and took off in your sweet ride, following Bainbridge."

"Goddammit! His name is Jason, you evil prick! Jason!"

Charles seethed with open hostility, despising how William kept dehumanizing his deceased husband by referring to him by his last name only. The way William spoke it so contemptuously like it was the name of a venereal disease drove Charles mad with hatred.

"I don't give a toss what his fucking name was," William snarled. "Shut it, old man, I'm at the best part.

Charles kept silent, but he wanted nothing more than to get the gun away from William and shoot him in the head, right between his hard, dead eyes. "It didn't take long before the right circumstances made themselves known. It was the darkness. Bainbridge, having taken that exit off the highway going down that back road short-cut. The total lack of motorists. The trees. I waited until just the right moment to run your father off the road, Jules, as hard as I could. I pushed his car into that tree so bloody forcefully, praying his neck would snap on impact."

"You're lying!" Jules shrieked. "I read Joseph's account. It was Phillip! You're trying to torture me, but I won't play your sick game. Don't listen to him, Pops!"

"Still so bloody sure of everything! The airbag? Malfunctioned? Sure as shit did, but the seat belt wasn't dodgy one bit! That sucker worked just fine. Damn it all, but if your old man wasn't still alive after I hit him! Of all the rotten luck, the seat belt saved the bastard, but I couldn't have that.

"I got out of the car and walked over to him. He was all cut up, half-conscious. I not so gently grabbed him by the back of his head and turned him towards me. I held on to him fast while I undid his seat belt and let it fall away.

"Is that a look of comprehension I see on your face, Jules? Now you know what caused those contusions to the back of his head.

The police and coroner reports didn't mention them, but I suspect you've seen the original reports. The ones Joseph Cartell made disappear? I bet those reports mentioned bruising, some odd finger-like compression marks on the back of Bainbridge's neck and head. Well, that was my hand, my strong fingers pressing down on his flesh!"

William silenced himself to give Jules a minute to let it all sink in.

Even though she was sickened by the poison spewing forth from William's mouth, Jules believed every vile word. She had read the original, undoctored reports. The paperwork was in those secret files. Jules doubted that Joseph had even bothered to read anything before having his version of the events of that night produced and set to record to protect Phillip.

The originals completely supported William's narrative. Jules had dismissed the bruises as nothing more than the result of her dad's head whipping back into the seat a few times. Now, listening to William's confession, Jules felt she had no choice but to believe him.

"Aaand," William bellowed, gleefully carrying on, "gripping the back of that motherfucker's head hard—as hard as I could—I smashed his face into the steering wheel over and over and over!"

"Stop!" Charles screamed in anguish, in hate. It was too much for him to stomach: the sinister revelation, the ugliness, the horror, the look of pure joy on the face of his husband's murderer as he described the killing. "You bastard! I'll fucking kill you!"

Incensed, Charles furiously charged at William like a raging bull.

Jules, terrified, concerned for her father's safety, screamed for him to stop, but the situation had moved beyond her control. With split-second thinking, she decided she had no choice but to act.

William, unruffled and steely, turned his gun on Charles and fired; the bullet exploded out of the barrel.

While Denise and Phillip cried out in panic and horror, Jules managed to push herself and her father out of the direct line of fire. Her reaction time was uncanny.

Unfortunately, it was not enough for the bullet to miss both of them completely, and it more than grazed the side of Charles's head. He was not dead, as William had intended, but he was far from unhurt. The wound was nasty, blood spurting out of the cranial gash with abandon.

Charles needed medical attention fast.

William laughed heartily, taking great pleasure and satisfaction from the panic and anguish his actions had wrought. "Stupid old fuck."

While Denise remained immobile, screaming her head off, Jules and Phillip rushed to Charles's side. His body convulsed, and garbled, incoherent words erupted from his quivering mouth. Jules emphatically told her father not to talk, for she was there with him and would fix everything.

It wasn't a total lie; she had her doubts about the level of help she could affect, but she refused to let her father die without trying something, anything. She had to appear strong for him.

Instinctually, Jules's training took over, and she went into triage mode. Rapidly removing her linen jacket, she threw it at Phillip and ordered him to tear off the sleeves and rip them into strips. He obeyed without question. Jules took those strips of fabric and bandaged her father's head with them, attempting to arrest the bleeding.

Thankfully, her quick thinking and action had bought her father some needed life-saving time. Jules understood it was a temporary stop-gap at best. She had to get him to a hospital.

William looked upon the scene in front of him with much amusement.

"My story's nearly done. I don't care if you stay on the floor frantically engaging in pointless activity while I talk. Whatever."

Once again, William's volcanic elation had promptly morphed back into cold indifference. His wicked gleefulness, his ghastly grin, had disappeared completely.

Without thinking of the potential danger to himself, Phillip moved to put himself between Jules, her injured father, and

William. His need to protect people, like when he had become a human shield earlier for his sister, was an all-consuming drive.

Jules was stunned that Phillip had voluntarily, without any hesitation, leapt to her father's side to aid her. And now, he stood bold in her defence. Jules was sure her husband had every intention of taking a bullet for her if necessary, and that was a difficult thing for her to accept.

This was not the man who had said he hated her mere hours ago. A man whose hatred Jules expected, even desired, but now everything had changed. Phillip had not killed her father. She had been punishing and torturing the wrong person. Her husband! A man she had loved! Even after all her misplaced cruelty, Phillip still wanted to help and protect her. It was just too much for Jules to think about now.

Putting all thoughts of her complicated relationship with her husband to the side, Jules remained focused on finding a way to subdue William quickly. Time was running out for her father.

Denise was a total wreck. Now that her brother was no longer in front of her, protecting her, she moved as far back as she could until she hit the wall directly behind the desk. She wanted as much distance from William as possible, even knowing that there was truly nowhere in the room where anyone would be safe from his murderous aggression.

"What have I done?" Denise whimpered, her face awash with guilt-ridden tears.

No one heard Denise's self-accusatory lamenting over the surprise return of William's unrelenting, maniacal chuckling. His dispassionate solemnity had vanished. He began to tell the remainder of his story with gusto.

"After Bainbridge finally croaked, I went back to Phil's car and moved him into the driver's seat. That was my plan all along. I wanted to fuck with your life, mate. See what would happen when you got blamed for everything. I like to fuck with people. After all, my brother had his life taken from him, an innocent, so fuck off to the rest of you!

"I should have known Joseph Cartell would never let something like that happen to his pride and joy. Even being a total drunken sot, you were still his legacy, mate. He took care of things nice and tidy, the prick.

"When I found out that Phil had escaped my plan, I was pissed. Still, it all worked out in the end. You eventually discovered what Phil had done, Jules. Well, what I wanted everyone to think he'd done, and you so brilliantly went to work destroying him. When I found out that you'd married him, I thought fate was taking the piss! How twisted is that? You can't make this shit up.

"Now, some poor bloke had the misfortune of driving by after I set the scene and unwisely decided to stop and help. Well, I helped myself to his car after I killed him and shoved his body in the trunk. Here I thought I'd have to wrangle a cab to get back to the hotel as fast as I could. Stupid git. Never help anybody! Don't know that basic thing you deserve what you get!"

"You're sick and demented!" Phillip roared.

"I'm not sick! It's justice! You're just too thick to see it."

While Phillip and William continued to scream at each other, Jules stayed low to the ground near her father, silent yet attentive. Phillip's bravery, which Jules appreciated but felt bordered on stupidity, considering how antagonistic he was towards a psychopath with a gun, was something she could take advantage of.

Assessing the situation in front of her, Jules determined the time was right to disarm William. With the gun out of play, Jules believed she could take him in hand-to-hand combat. Amanda had said he was well trained, but then so was she. *I can do this. I have to.*

Jules had leverage against William. He was injured; she was not. Jules planned on exploiting William's wound, believing enough pain would force him to drop the gun. She was going to cause him much pain.

Prepared to act, Jules took stock of her husband's current usefulness. As long as he stood in front of her, Phillip's size provided cover and obscured her from William's full sight.

Jules edged closer, ever so slowly, towards her enemy. She calculated all the angles: the current position of the gun, William's outstretched arm, and Phillip's physical placement in the room. *Yes, this will work. Distract that scumbag a few seconds longer, Phillip. I only need a moment. Don't fail me—as I failed you.*

Jules's worry was unfounded. Bold and undeterred, Phillip kept his dauntless stance against their insane captor. His gallantry, his concern for the safety of others over himself, bought Jules the time she needed to strike.

From her crouched position, Jules shot up fast and furious, like a coiled viper, grabbing William's wrist and latching on tight. To get the gun pointed away from a human target, she tried to force William's arm back at the elbow. Lamentably, even using both her arms, Jules was unable to disarm him. His strength was unrelenting.

Seeing that she needed to get William off-balance to gain an advantage, Jules went for his bloody wound. Keeping a firm hold on his wrist with her right hand, she balled her left hand into a fist and punched him hard on his injured side.

William winced but barely moved at all.

Without wasting another second, Jules went for the wound again, but this second attack was more brutal than the first. Instead of blunt force, Jules tore at the rip in William's shirt, enlarging it, revealing the dressing. Tearing the bandage off, fully exposing the wound, she clawed at the wet, fleshy opening like a lion eviscerating its prey.

This time, William's reaction to her assault was far more profound. He wailed in pain, bent forward, stumbled, even—but the gun remained in his hand. Jules was infuriated; she increased the viciousness of her attack.

Phillip stood immobilized by the sight of his wife in action. He knew she had martial arts training, but he had never seen her actually fight before. He was in awe, but more than that, he was greatly surprised by how much the whole thing excited him. Jules's aggression, ferocity, and determination were things to behold—when they were not negatively directed at him.

Phillip remembered his attraction to those qualities in his wife. Her boldness and her fearlessness. Her firm, shapely leg, currently bent upward, furiously battering William's abdomen. Yes, he liked all of it a lot.

Suddenly, Phillip realized it was not the best time to sit back, admiring his wife's display of strength and talent. He promptly snapped out of his erotically charged reverie; he wanted to get in at least one good punch before Jules inevitably subdued William.

So, with tremendous force, Phillip hurtled his entire body forward with two main objectives in mind: get the gun and knock the fucker out.

Though knee-deep in his struggle with Jules, William had some awareness of his surroundings. He saw Phillip barrelling towards him, but due to Jules's vice-like grip on his wrist, he could not direct and fire his gun at the oncoming mass to protect himself. William was not arrogant enough to think he could overcome Phillip's strength while contending with Jules's fighting skills, so he decided to cheat. Sort of.

When Phillip was almost on top of him, William kicked out his leg and nailed his would-be attacker right in the nuts.

Doubling over in pain, Phillip's hands instinctively dropped down to cup his package, leaving his upper body wide open, unprotected.

Taking advantage of that vulnerability, William kicked Phillip hard in the head, sending him flying backward, causing him to land on the floor with a tremendous thud.

"The bigger they are, the harder they fall," William snickered.

Phillip had the wind completely knocked out of him, his head and groin throbbing in pain. He was out of play, temporarily neutralized.

Unfazed by Phillip's unsuccessful attempt to help her, Jules's attention remained focused on her attack. William would not give in and go down, and she was tired of fighting with him to get him to drop the gun. In a desperate attempt to bring him to the ground, Jules kicked his legs out from under him while simultaneously pushing her fingers further into his now much bloodier wound.

"Hurts, doesn't it, fucker!"

William scowled. It did hurt; in fact, the pain was staggering.

Almost immediately after Jules's verbal taunt, the physical agony he suffered became too much for him to bear. William's arm spasmed erratically, his fingers clenched, and the gun went off. Not once, but twice. He cursed Jules's name before dropping the weapon to the ground.

A blood-curdling scream rang out seconds after the second shot, but Jules blocked the irritating noise from her mind. She had no time to be distracted by the return of Denise's panic and hysteria. *Ignore her. Ignore everything. You have to keep focused.*

Now that William's only visible weapon was out of play, Jules understood this was her best chance to take him out.

Releasing her grip on his wrist, at the same time retracting her other hand from the bloody wound, Jules whipped her body around to face her enemy. When she was in position, balanced and centred, and her adrenaline pumping, she repeatedly punched William in his stomach and face fast and hard.

Eventually, in too much pain to efficiently defend himself, let alone go on the offensive, William succumbed to the beating and lost his footing, crumpling to the floor.

Jumping on top of him, Jules grabbed William's flailing arms, forcing them to the sides. Using her legs, she pinned him down, wrapped her ankles and feet around his thighs, and pushed into his groin to prevent him from throwing her off. William tried to kick, but all he managed to do was wiggle and jerk about like a fish out of water, his arms and legs rendered useless.

Intending to crush his windpipe, Jules forcefully put her forearm against his throat. *Push down, do it. Just fucking kill him!*

William's eyes were huge and wild, crazed. He was furious at being laid low, defeated. He spat out insult after insult and cursed Jules's name again. He had devolved into a beast, frothing at the mouth, biting.

"You're nothing but a rabid dog. Rabid dogs get put down."

Jules began applying tremendous pressure to William's throat. She wanted to kill him, but as she commenced her willing descent into murder, something bothered her tremendously about what she was doing. Jules did not believe it was her conscience; she felt absolutely no pity for William or remorse about wanting him dead. Still, something nagged at her.

As she watched William struggle, desperately gasping for air, his face red with fury and indignation, Jules started to second guess her actions.

Along with a weird pang of discomfort in the pit of her stomach, Jules suddenly felt that what she was doing was inherently wrong. Killing William was somehow—wrong. No, not killing him. She knew he deserved to die; it was *her* killing him that was wrong.

Somewhere deep inside of her, Jules felt her dad's presence. His voice echoed inside her head, begging her not to do this. His voice, the one she remembered being cheerful and upbeat, was sad and distressed because—because he did not want this for her! Jules instinctively felt that of all the terrible things she had done over the years, this would be the one unforgivable sin.

This is nuts! This creep is deranged, a murderer, a kidnapper, a sexual torturer! How can I feel this way? Dammit, dad, is this dishonouring your memory? Why am I feeling this way? Are you here with me, dad?

It became all too clear to Jules. If she killed William with her own two hands, she would become him. She would become the horrible, life-taking thing he claimed she was already, that murderous, unforgiving disease. She would be no better, no different than those other monsters she reviled: Stella, Joseph, and Ambroise Bergé.

The image of her and her dad from her favourite photograph flooded Jules's mind, drowning her in indecision and shame.

"No, I won't become you," Jules declared softly, staring into William's grimacing face. "No matter how much I hate you, I won't dishonour the memory of my dad by doing anything you would do. No matter how much you deserve it, and you do deserve to die, but not in his name." *I'm sorry, dad. I miss you so much.*

Jules slowly lifted her arm off William's throat. Reaching over him, she picked the gun up off the ground. Once she had it pointed directly in William's face, she extricated herself from his body.

"Get up, scum," Jules ordered. "Slowly. Good. Move your ass over by the door, but keep your beady eyes on me. You're going to pay for your crimes, William, but I won't stoop to your level. You won't take that part of my dad from me. His light."

"What a fucking joke," William growled, backing up towards the door. He rubbed his throat and then spat on the ground again. "I knew you didn't have it in you. You're weak, like all women. Stupid, sentimental, useless. You got lucky with my brother, I guess, but you're no killer."

"Maybe she's not, but I sure am fucker!"

Jules watched in astonishment as William's entire body jerked. A look of confusion, of bewilderment, came over his face. His eyes turned glassy, unfocused. Twitching a few times, he murmured something inaudible and then chuckled like an idiot. As blood pooled in his eyes and escaped from his lips in rivulets, he completely lost his balance and fell forward.

Sprawled across the office floor, William gave up his last breath.

Peering down at the dead body, Jules marvelled at the two ornamented objects sticking out of the back of the head.

When William was forced back at gunpoint by Jules towards the open doorway, Amanda had snuck up behind him. Never one to second guess herself, hesitate or feel anything resembling indecisiveness, Amanda had plunged her two karambits deep into William's skull.

"Asshole! Where's the other one? Believes she can zap me and walk away scot-free! Guess again, bitch. Sorry about this, Jules. I messed up earlier. It shouldn't have gone down like this."

Jules ran over to Amanda and hugged her. Amanda hugged back, though she was more than a little surprised by the intensity of the gesture.

"Lady, I'm just glad you're not hurt," Jules shouted. "My father's been shot and needs an ambulance! I've got to call 911!"

Turning away from Amanda, Jules put the gun down, grabbed her purse and moved quickly to where her father was. Crouching down next to him, she took out her phone and called for an ambulance.

As Jules frantically barked orders at the 911 operator, Amanda walked over to William's dead body. She pulled her blades out of his skull. After wiping the blood and tissue off her weapons, Amanda placed them back in the holding straps sewn into her cotton-Lycra blend top. Then she went over to the gun and picked it up off the floor.

Right as Jules finished her call, Amanda put two bullets into William's skull.

"Amanda!" Jules screeched as she fiddled with her father's soaked-through bandages.

"What? I waited for you to hang up." Amanda took a good hard look around the room, assessing the situation. "Jules, things have become too complicated to throw the body in your incinerator and pretend like that bastard was never here. Someone has to be held accountable for all this, and William is it!

"So, the cops and my weapons? It will be too much of a hassle for you to try and explain the existence and purpose of such exotic blades. Not that I'd leave them behind. Sentimental reasons. The gunshots have nicely obliterated their punctures.

"It's up to you, Jules, to explain how you shot that pig from behind. It shouldn't be too hard. You have the training, and you're a crack shot. The police will assume you managed to wrestle the gun away from William. Get creative and sell the story. I was never here. Make sure you fire the gun yourself before the cops get here in case they want to test you for residue.

"And Jules, your dad's going to be fine. I've seen worse head trauma, and those people made it through okay. Listen, I've gotta go. That Miles dude is out of it, but make sure that idiot husband of yours understands it has to play out this way."

"I will!" Jules assured her friend. "Phillip isn't what I told you he was. He didn't do it! Oh, never mind, I'll explain it all later. Thank you, Amanda, for everything. I'll make sure Phillip and Denise cooperate. They won't be a problem."

"Denise? Why would you—oh, shit! Jules, I assumed you already knew."

"Knew what? What are you talking about?"

Amanda told Jules to turn around and look towards the back wall.

Phillip, recovered from William's cheap shot, sat on the floor, softly crying amid a pool of blood. His muffled tears were for him alone. His was an inconsolable pain, much worse than what he had felt when his father passed.

Denise, his favourite sibling, was dead, killed by one of William's stray bullets.

Heartbroken, cradling his little sister's lifeless body gently in his arms, Phillip silently cursed the name Falsworth. But cursing them was not enough. Not for him.

Slowly, Phillip raised his head, and through wet eyes, looked deep into the face of his wife, finally understanding what she must have felt all this time. The kind of anguish that could motivate someone to do what Jules had done to him, to his family.

And now he wanted to go down that dark path. Denise's murderer was dead, but Phillip wanted revenge on the corrupt people that had helped him.

"They have to pay, Jules," Phillip stated, his face contorted with rage and hate. "Teach me how to do it, how to make them all pay."

Made in the USA
Monee, IL
29 November 2021